Waking Up Gilligan

A Novel by J.R. MacLean

For Marina, and for all seekers, particularly those with a sense of humour. Namaste.

"Enlightenment, don't know what it is..."

Van Morrison

Episodes

Prologue

The enlightenment of the Divine Bhagwan occurred, as enlightenments often do, under the most extraordinarily ordinary circumstances. Of course he was not yet the Divine Bhagwan, but a brilliant young professor named Akshat Bharadwaj Chandrashekhar, Sanskrit names which mean *invulnerable lucky bird who holds the moon in his hair knot.* He grew up on the banks of the Mutha River at the western edge of the Deccan Plateau. There, the mists of the morning cling to the great *ghats* like the innocent aura of a child soon to be burned away by the merciless sun of experience.

The enlightenment was presaged some ten years by an itinerant astrologer, a man named Arjun Qavi (*Peacock Poet*), who read twelve year-old Akshat's chart and saw the benign influence of many lifetimes of arduous meditation, including stints as extremely high ranking monks for the belly-laughing Bodhidarma as well as Rinzai, the Zen stick-wielding Master of insight. The child had paid his karmic dues. Thus, as a precocious and supremely loveable pre-teen, he teetered on the cusp of eternal radiance. The signs were so favorable, the disposition of the planets so benign, that the great event's occurrence was not a question of if, but when.

The astrologer went on to say, however, that though the enlightenment would be brilliant and supremely juicy, there was a flaw in Akshat's chart: a worrisome retrograde in Saturn which over-ventilated Jupiter's ascendant. A flaw which, were it magnified by the child being spoiled, might

5

well cause him to become the most lazy and irresponsible Godhead-realized soul to ever grace the skin and air of this benighted Earth. The year of the reading was 1941. Well beneath the rickety, lantern-lit table where Akshat's father and the peacock poet sat, on the opposite side of the world, the morning sky over Pearl Harbor was being darkened by Japanese aircraft even as the ovens were fired up in Auswitch. The word 'benighted' applied as thoroughly as ever before or since. Akshat's father vowed that though Akshat was the only child of a beautiful mother from a wealthy family (she had married for love, well below her appropriate caste), paternal duties would not be shirked and the boy would learn the habits and value of a good day's work.

Akshat's father worked for the British Raj, delivering cigarettes, whiskey and other crucial supplies to the garrisons manning the forts strung along the frontier formed by the Sayadri Hills. Young Akshat would often accompany him on the shorter runs, riding beside him in the cab of the old truck which would grind and groan up and down the steepest slopes in low gear while the child leaned out the window and drank in the fragrances of the roadside blooms. It was, alas, the very year of the reading that Akshat's father, on a longer run by himself, caught by an early monsoon rain, had a transmission gear slip at the wrong moment. His vehicle slithered down the bank of the road into a great chasm. His neck was broken as he hurtled through the windshield. Only one sigh escaped his lips as, half submerged, he died in the muddy waters of an overflowing creek bed. Thus it was that young Akshat was left in the care of his mother, whose great beauty was matched only by the generous indulgences she showered on her son as he continued to grow.

Her father, who had amassed a great fortune selling tea to the British, had, as every intelligent being should, devoted the latter years of his life to the study and practice of yoga and meditation. He had tutored his grandson in the practices as best he could while constantly being astounded at how effor-

6

tlessly young Akshat mastered the most difficult *asanas* and *pranayama* techniques. Blessed with great physical beauty (albeit of a rather petite stature), a precocious aura of serenity, and prodigious mimetic and intellectual powers, the boy was, at the age of twenty one, gifted by his grandfather with one of the only thirty-seven Rolls Royce Silver Clouds extant in India in 1949. Two years later, after he had become the youngest professor of philosophy in the history of the great university at Spoona, India, Akshat was turning the key in the vehicle's ignition just as the first monsoon rains of that year came crashing down.

Nothing happened.

The engine was still.

In that moment, instead of trying the key again, as anyone else would, Akshat Bharadawaj Chandrashekar realized a full and perfect enlightenment. He became the Rolls Royce; he became the turbid sky piled high with thunderheads, the pelting rain and the foliage that thrashed in the wind behind the Philosophy Building. Interior space and exterior space melted into one, he felt and knew the Godhead in all things, including every quantum particle of his physical body. He was consumed, buoyed, and exalted by the silent bliss out of which all things arise.

It is said (and written — as were many things, though not the astrologer's prediction which was known only to Akshat's father — in the great tome *The Sound of One Teabag Steeping)* that the Divine Bhagwan (as he later came to be called by his sannyasins, or disciples) remained in that Rolls Royce for many hours, letting the enormous ordinariness of what had happened sink in. Despite his achievement, the culmination of many lifetimes of meditation, the vehicle remained in stillness when, at a point later in the evening, he turned the key again. So it was that Cheerstha, the proud owner of the only tow truck in Spoona at that time, summoned at six o'clock and appearing on the scene a mere three hours later, became his first sannyasin and lifelong mechanic.

But this is not Cheerstha's story, nor is it that of the Divine Bhagwan though he is certainly a key figure. It is a story that occurs many years later, in 1982 and 1983 in Ronald Reagan's America. It came to pass that besides Cheerstha, over the years as many as a hundred other Indians recognized the achievement of Akshat Bharadawaj and became his disciples. There may have been more in another age, but India, emerging as a nation from the dominance of the British Raj, was in the nineteen fifties and sixties far more interested in material than spiritual gains. Enlightenment was out. Cars and toasters were in. It was only in the sixties and seventies when more and more Westerners, inspired by Kerouac, Ginsburg, Leary and Watts began hitting the 'Dharma trail' to India that the Divine Bhagwan's career as a guru really began to take off. Young people who'd had their fill of cars and toasters, of the war in Vietnam, Kent State, the military industrial complex, who'd heard and seen and sensed that God and conventional religions were indeed dead moved from West to East in a steady stream, seeking to fill a spiritual vacuum with the essential wisdom of a living enlightened Master. So successful was the Divine Bhagwan in attracting such disciples that his ashram in Spoona overflowed. When the Master went into a period of prolonged personal silence, a decision was made by certain unscrupulous power-mad disciples to build a new commune in the wealthy West, on an enormous Ranch purchased in the Oregon high desert. Thus the clean, clear waters of enlightenment flowed to a country where a spiritual thirster is born every minute.

It is in that commune that our story begins; the story of what happens to a young Canadian named John Price and renamed Satyam Gilligan by the Divine Bhagwan. John Price Jr. is an ordinary fellow, though more intelligent, sensitive, repressed, horny, adventurous and unhappy than most. He has become a disciple (sannyasin) of the Divine Bhagwan through the mail and fortuitously avoided the heat and diseases of India by timing his disciplehood to coincide with the Master's coming to America. He did not avoid, however, the so-called 'sitcom stage' in the Divine Bhagwan's naming of his sannyasins. This was a product of the Master's love affair with Western TV shows and movies, a love enabled by the new VCR and video cassette technology that his disciples happily provided him with. Gilligan's journey from Toronto's Cabbagetown to Oregon was via California. He is with a somewhat older woman named Bala. Both are about to meet the Master for the first time.

1. The Assassin

"How old was she? Fourteen?" Bala is pissed off.

"Eighteen. She said she was eighteen." Gilligan's tone is casual.

"And when did she say that? Before or after she stuck her tongue down your throat?"

"During, actually. I nearly barfed. Foolish child. Very friendly though."

"You're not funny."

No, I'm not. Swami Satyam Gilligan, formerly known as Mr. John Price Jr., is genuinely rueful. *Why am I sticking it to her like this?*

Ma Prem Bala, formerly known as Chicita Barrett-Conqueso, a statuesque, gap-toothed Californian who resembles a sun-baked, fleshed out Lauren Hutton, has doffed her travelling sweats and is about to don a crimson cotton shift. Her hair falls over her face as she turns away from Gilligan and moves to the far end of their newly assigned tent. The contours of her naked back are highlighted by the early afternoon sun penetrating the fabric stretched above her head. It is very warm. And they have to get going. Gilligan senses it is 'comfort her' time. He settles his hands on the brown silk of her shoulders.

"Look, I'm sorry. We picked her up; she got in the van, sat beside me. You were up front. She got friendly in the extreme and — "

"I know what happened! I was sitting right in front of you!" Bala shakes off his hands and pulls the frock over her head.

"Hey in there? Be cool. It's time for drive-by." The female voice floats in from the dusty main street of their particular 'suburb' of tents erected for the Master's Day festival. Its tones are those of the 'loving reminder': reassuring and therapeutic.

"Hey out there," Gilligan singsongs back. "We're cool. We're just in here minding our own fucking business!"

"I'm afraid there's no such thing, Swami." A tendril of hostility creeps into the therapeutic sweetness. "You are in a commune now. Remember why you are here."

Sandaled footfalls recede along with murmured conversations and laughter. Scores of other new arrivals are heading towards the roadway where the Master will drive by.

"She's right, Gilligan. We're here to be with the Divine Bhagwan. This is it. Let's go."

Gilligan puts his hands on her shoulders again, gives them a little squeeze through the red cotton of her dress. "We've still got a few minutes."

He crosses to his side of the tent, kneels in front of his backpack. Their van, loaded with sannyasins from Los Angeles, had driven through the night. After arrival and processing at Mahaclaptrap, the commune's welcome centre, it had been a hot walk to their tent in the high desert heat. He could use a fresh t-shirt.

"She's a busybody, a bloody therapist, no doubt." Gilligan attempts to deflect attention from his own transgressions to the bodiless voice beyond their tent walls.

"She was trying to help. You're being a dick. Again." The last word is a lash.

"Nothing would have happened with that Vavaloma chick if you hadn't gone up front to sit beside Yoyorod, speaking of dicks. No wonder the Master gave him that name. It means he's a total Yoyo, with a rod."

"We were in bucket seats! I was nowhere near him! I think this is it for us, Swami." Bala's voice is sad. She is hugging herself as she slips her feet into her Birkenstocks.

Gilligan feels her sadness. He is sensitive and empathetic to the extent that he often mistakes the feelings of others for his own. His own distinctive spark is lost deep inside, smoldering under layers of defensiveness. Like a neglected child, it constantly struggles to be heard. He reflects back on the riotous van ride. Marijuana brownies, lovingly baked back at Stonedharm, the very loosely run Divine Bhagwan centre in Los Angeles, became something of a food staple as they all had to be eaten before arrival at the communal Ranch in Northeast Oregon.

That sannyasin chick hitchhiker — Vavaloma — was kind of young, eighteen or whatever. Seven years younger than me, but then I'm seven years younger than Bala. Now it looks like I'm losing her. For what? Smooching with a teenager? And Bala has been great-

He recalls the last time they had sex, on Bala's big bed in her room behind the great stairs of Stonedharm. She had done a shoulder-stand afterwards, her brown feet with their orange toenail polish against the faded wallpaper above the headboard. *Odd habit. She's done that a few times...* Something from behind his guilt and the THC embroidering his bloodstream flashes into his mind, bits of experience that suddenly add up.

"You're using me," he blurts. "You're fucking using me to get pregnant."

"Using you?" She turns to face him and pulls her hair back from her face. Her eyes are moist. "You said you loved me."

"I did, and I do. You're incredibly far out. But those shoulder stands you've been doing? Telling me your birth control method was vasectomy? You are trying to get pregnant! No wonder you don't want to stay here as a summer worker like I do!"

"Gilligan, wake up! I'm thirty two years old. My biological clock is ringing off the hook! And I really am into you." She comes and puts her arms around him, her head on his chest, evidently now ready to be comforted. "I mean, I haven't noticed you suffering."

His voice is gentler. "The problem is I'm only twenty-five and I am an uptight dick. I'm not ready to be a father. Not with you."

"That's OK." She begins stroking his temples, ears and ponytail. "Aside from one or two personality flaws, which likely aren't genetic, you're perfect breeding stock. Once it happens, you'll be off the hook. I promise. And don't you think you've loosened up quite a bit being with me?"

She kisses him. He responds, kissing her back. She is right. Despite, the rather Canadian frigidity that plagued him through his young manhood, sexual chemistry was a non-issue over the entire month they've been together.

"The Master's coming, drive-by, we've got to go." He pushes the top of her dress down and begins kissing her breasts. They are warm under his lips with a thin, salty sheen of perspiration. Her hands twist his ears, urging him on.

"Come on," she whispers. "A quickie for the road. I'll skip the shoulder stand."

They are quick, quick like young rabbits. After an exhilarating minute or two, Gilligan lifts the flap and peers down the main street of their tent city. It is as empty as showdown time in High Noon. A small tumbleweed skitters by. Beyond the tents, across a sagebrush-dotted field, rises a steep road bank, its top densely picketed with red clad disciples lined up to greet the Master as he drives by.

"Bala! For fuck's sake. You said you'd skip the shoulder stand! Come on! He's coming!"

They scramble from the tent and run. They have only a few hundred yards to cover, but beyond the graded bank, where the road curves and rises to meet a cowboy-movie sky, appears the first sign of the Master's cavalcade.

"Gilligan! The water truck!"

Bala, her long hair streaming, points to the chrome stacks glinting on the distant snake of the road. Windshield, grill and wheels appear as the stainless steel tanker truck, which dampens the road ahead of the Master, trundles over a hump. It is reaching the sweeping curve that is the runners' objective. Gilligan hears dim shrieks of appreciation as cool droplets spray overheated legs and feet. Well up the undulating road, which is lined on the driver's side by a crimson border of sannyasins, bright headlights wink into view, shimmering double in the moist heat. Satyam Gilligan John Price Jr. feels Him. The One he has come to see.

He lengthens his stride; his lungs start to burn. *Damned smoking. I've really got to quit.*

He and Bala scramble up the pebbled bank. Created mere weeks earlier, it is smooth and free of weeds. They reach the crimson line after the tanker with its dangling sprinkler has passed. There is an earthy smell of moisture on dust. The Divine Bhagwan is notoriously allergic, so moistening the unpaved road with pure spring water is essential. A head with beautiful long blond hair turns with a quick smile of amusement.

"You're just in time folks," says the bright-eyed young man whose happiness circuits are clearly nearing bliss-overload status.

Gilligan and Bala quickly find a spot behind two college-age girls. The road exhales warm vapors. The rumble of the tanker recedes to their left as it executes a stately right turn that will take the Master's cavalcade through the massive commune's town centre, then past the airport and onto the road to Heiferville. The chitchat, sporadic singing, gossip, giggles and laughter from those lining the road quiet as the headlights approach. There are gasps and feminine squeals of anticipatory delight. The girls in front of Gilligan and Bala sway, their hands clasped together.

The lead car is a showroom condition white Ford Bronco, with gold trim. The driver is huge, a hulking figure with a fierce-looking black beard. The steering wheel is a toy smothered under his hands. Imposing as he is, the vehicle is dominated by the woman riding shotgun on the running board to his left. She is petite, with an athletic but feminine build. Her jet-black hair is cropped short. Her right arm, slung over the rearview mirror holds in its perfectly manicured fingers the oblong black box of a Motorola field radio. Its stubby rubberized antenna quivers as if in delighted readiness to do her bidding. Her eyes, hidden behind wrap-around mirrored sunglasses, scrutinize the members of the line as she mutters into the Motorola.

She is Ma Anand Deela, personal secretary to the Divine Bhagwan, Chairperson and President of Bhagwan Communes International, Bhagwan International Enterprises and Bhagwan International University, where she holds doctorate degrees in Philosophy, Business Administration, Media Studies, Transcendent Psychology, Meditative Insight Therapy and several other disciplines yet to be created. She has been acclaimed by the Bhagwan Insight Institute (which she also chairs) as an *Acharya,* or teacher, a mere rung below actual Master on the spiritual ladder. But all her powers flow from the first title: as personal secretary to the Divine Bhagwan, she is the only being to whom he has spoken in more than a year of public and personal silence. Like Moses, it is she who must deliver, and even interpret, the Master's wishes for his throngs of devotees. It is she, for purposes of her own, who has brought the Divine Bhagwan to America.

She is stylishly attired in a hip-hugging designer skirt cinched smartly at the waist by a burgundy leather ammo belt. Its silver bullets, polished daily by a privileged Swami, glint in the sunlight. Slung in a holster is an Uzi semiautomatic pistol. The reflective silver of her sunglasses nicely complements the twinkling slugs on her waist. The ensemble is topped by a burgundy Peace Force cap tilted just so on her haughtily held head. There is something coiled and feral in her demeanor, as if at any moment she could pounce from her perch and put a bullet or three through someone's brain.

Gilligan's 'friendly' all-Canadian smile creeps insipidly across his face. He is a Toronto lad of mildly mixed race, cereal-fed in serial suburbias. He has long dark hair pulled back in a pony tail, a prominent nose, and large, Bambi-brown eyes. If he is noticed by danger, bland good will is his default posture.

"So that's Deela," says Bala. Like Gilligan, she was a mail-order disciple and is seeing the Master and the Ranch big shots for the first time. They share a disdain for authority.

"Yeah, she looks like a cross between Clint Eastwood and Patty Hearst."

"I *must* get some bullets like those," whispers Bala.

Laughter leaps to Gilligan's lips but the Master's vehicle is nigh. It is a refinished, bulletproof Rolls Royce said to have been formerly owned by Idi Amin. It approaches noiselessly, except for the quiet grinding of Michelins on gravel. The famous hood ornament, the *Spirit of Ecstasy*, resembling a caped Catwoman preparing to dive, is another item sparkling silver in the sunlight. The vehicle, belying its thuggish history, has been painted pool-bottom blue with a sparkling disco finish.

The white-bearded visage of the Master barely peeks over the steering wheel. His diminutiveness is enhanced by the capaciousness of the cowboy hat perched atop his head like the shell of a walnut over an acorn. He is wearing a magnificent embroidered robe of the same deep blue as the hat. His right hand rests atop the steering wheel. His left moves in a slow, rhythmical, backhanded wave of benediction to the passing disciples, like a leaf-laden bough in a summer evening's breeze, indiscriminately showering benedictions. His lustrous brown eyes scan those of his sannyasins, allowing them a fleeting glimpse into eternity. Gilligan's mind roils as the Rolls, and his turn to meet the Master's gaze, approaches.

Will I be zapped, transformed, mercilessly exposed? Should I be feeling more? Maybe a friendly wink is in order.

Women gasp; there's a muffled sob or two. Hands folded in namastes, overwhelmed disciples sag into each other as he passes. Tears squeeze or gush from scores of closed lids, then fall to become one with the dust retardant on the road. The Rolls is just ten yards away. A preternatural silence falls. Gilligan is spellbound by the hand's metronomic wave; the limpid eyes sweeping over the line. His turn is coming. He realizes that he is wringing his hands, which are supposed to be folded in a gentle namaste.

Relax you fool. Accept the bliss!

He meets the eyes of his Master. They look vaguely puzzled, almost frowning. There is a commotion just ahead. A voice is shrieking.

"You ain't no god! You ain't no god!"

A slender figure in black pants, black T-shirt and a New York Yankees baseball cap steps forward from the line, almost into the vehicle's path! His garb stark against the red backdrop of the devotees' clothing, he jabs the air as he shouts the words over and over in a kind of frenzy, as if he were leading a cheer at a football game.

"You ain't no god! You ain't no god! You ain't no god!"

The sannyasins nearby, in various stages of oblivious bliss-filled rush, mouth words like 'Wow, you really should stay in line'. The man squats down, withdraws from his pant leg a long hunting knife.

"Hey, that guy's got a knife!" Gilligan lunges forward, impeded by the two young women still swaying in some other world. The man advances quickly, arm upraised, towards the Rolls.

17

"Prepare to bleed, Mr. God!"

He launches himself at the vehicle. Ludicrously, he tries to stab the Master through the closed window. Several swamis, led by the fellow with the long blond hair, and including Satyam Gilligan, jump on the assassin's back and wrestle him to the ground. The knifepoint slides down the thick glass and wedges itself into the fissure at its base. There it sticks as the Master continues at the same ceremonial pace, his backhanded wave undisturbed. His gold Rolex Oyster, one of, it is said, many hundreds gifted to him by wealthy sannyasins, appears first on one side and then the other of the white bone and bark-textured handle of the weapon. Beside him, Ma Nivea, his beautiful companion of (it is said) many lifetimes, is gesticulating, frantically urging him to drive faster as she speaks rapidly into a Motorola.

Swami Gilligan is not too preoccupied to notice the milky smoothness of her skin, the delicacy of the hand gripping the Motorola. He throws a quick namaste to the rear of the Rolls as it moves on by him at unchanged speed. He is now part of a swelling red knot, which sucks in members of the line like a black hole. Dust, dislodged from beneath the patina of moisture on the unpaved road, hovers over them like a diaphanous mushroom cap.

The would-be assassin's thrashings subside. He is held face down, his baseball cap upturned beside his head. His hair is short and greasy black. Though he is a young man of about Gilligan's age, the crown of his head is balding. His body is so slight it could easily belong to a twelve year-old boy. A German swami (male disciple) is loudly lecturing, spluttering into the fellow's ear a stream of incomprehensible invective. A burly ma (female disciple) with close-cropped hennaed hair begins to berate her countryman for not berating the assassin properly.

"In English you stupid. He cannot understand you!"

Nivea's Motorola-ing has its effect. Deela's Bronco, forty yards ahead, roars into a skidding U-turn. It fishtails wildly, forcing some of the crimson faithful off the road and down the stony bank. Deela, gripping a strut of the side mirror, draws her Uzi as the Bronco skids to a stop inches from the mob tightening around the prone assassin. She jumps from the running board and fires a staccato burst of warning shots into the blue Oregon skies.

"Everybody freeze!" she screams. "Step back from the body."

"Hang on there a second! I ain't dead." The protest comes from the assassin.

"No." Deela's voice is pitched like fine china. "Not yet."

A bright red Peace Force Jimmy, which typically follows the Master's car at some distance, roars up to the scene. Four peace officers disembark. These are samurai sannyasins, specially trained in eastern martial arts. Two carry curved swords. It is said that these samurai are capable of preternatural feats such as deflecting bullets with their swords or cleaving a man in two at the waist with one swipe. It is not said how such feats are verified.

Deela kneels and nestles the business end of her gun barrel into the hollow at the base of the fellow's head. The crowd recoils, including the German, whose lecture ended abruptly with the discharge of Deela's gun. She looks up at the arriving samurai.

"Put away those stupid swords!" she screams. "Follow Bhagwan! No one is protecting him!"

Indeed, the unattended Rolls Royce is now gracefully making the turn towards Hemlock Grove and the centre of Bhagwanville. The four quickly jump back into their Jimmy, accidentally slicing off a headrest in the process. They take off after the Rolls and assume the lead car position.

"Lamborghini," Deela says to the huge Italian Swami who is her driver, "cover this guy. If he moves, fill him full of lead."

"Fill him fulla lead?" says the Swami doubtfully, moving towards the Bronco to get a blanket. His huge size and bristly black facial hair give him an intimidating appearance, which is belied by very soft brown eyes. The German Swami mutters to him, under his breath:

"Vith your gun. Cover him vith your gun!"

Lamborghini begins to perspire profusely as he draws his weapon. He grips his pistol in two hands with all the comfort of a housewife holding a rattlesnake. The crowd moves back a little farther. Someone near the rear slides down the pebbly slope with a startled cry.

"Stay there, shithead," barks Deela, giving the fellow's neck a sharp jab for emphasis. She whips her Motorola to her lips. "Deela to Hemlock Grove. Deela to Hemlock Grove. Over"

"Roger Dayla. Chloe here." Unmistakably Australian, Chloe is the powerful CEO of Bhagwan Communes International.

"Chloe. Code Red. Repeat, Code Red. I've caught the redneck runt just west of town. I want a video crew and the 'Totally Positive Times' here now... Yes I want the helicopter... I know it is supposed to shower down the rose petals as the Master drives through town. Radio Lionheart to dump the petals quickly and then pick up Lurchamo and his camera. Take a news release... Our Master was not harmed. Repeat. Not harmed. A divine force turned the assassin's blade. Over."

"Roger Dayla. Chloe out."

Deela re-holsters her Motorola and presses her gun barrel tightly into the middle of the assassin's premature bald spot. This is the *Sahasra*, the most sacred of the seven bodily chakras, the point from which the thousand petaled lotus of the fully enlightened consciousness unfolds.

"No, no, dear sweet Jesus, save me sweet Jesus, save me please."

Deela squats there for a long time, as the assassin mutters prayerfully.

She is watching the Rolls Royce, as are the others, who are re-forming the drive-by line. The helicopter has appeared and is streaming a crimson flow of rose petals from its side, like holy blood baptizing the faithful below. They carpet the main street of Bhagwanville, a 'town' which consists mostly of construction sites and trailers. The Master is forced to turn on his windshield wipers, so thick is the scented deluge. Lamborghini holsters his pistol with a big sigh of relief. The Rolls makes a left turn at the Ranch's restaurant, where festive patio umbrellas peek between the trunks of poplars. The vehicle disappears behind Mahaclaptrap, the welcome centre of the commune, a renovated ranch outbuilding used by the former owners (the no-good McStonehead brothers) for fertilizer storage.

This initiates the Fallachami ritual, in which every sannyasin falls in the direction of the Master's exit while shouting 'Yahoo!' as loudly and joyously as possible. The Master has designed the ritual to prepare his people for the day he leaves his body. The moment a Master leaves a disciple's presence is a small death, and death, like birth, is a peak experience which should be celebrated. The Fallachami's visual consequence is an impressive domino effect as the red-clad figures topple to the ground down the contours of the road, arms stretched towards the Master. The resounding 'Yahoos!' echo from the nearby hills in a fading grumble akin to the guttural mantras of monks within a temple's dome.

Gilligan averts his eyes from the Deela/assassin drama for a few moments to enjoy the toppling wave. It reminds him of the synchronized dives of bathing-capped swimmers in the old Esther Williams movies. All fall except Deela. "Yahoo!" tears from his throat as he topples partly on Bala, partly on one of the college girls. A wave of bliss washes over him like warm Pacific surf.

A few minutes later, the video crew and the Totally Positive Times arrive to document the capture of the assassin.

"OK," says Deela, her gun still to the fellow's head. "Are we ready to roll?" She tips her officer's cap to a slightly more rakish angle.

"Ready!" shouts the camera operator who is perched in a cherry-picker's basket at the end of a Lull's extendable boom.

"Today—" Deela talks to the camera as she clips the mike's power pack next to the silver bullets, "July 6, 1982, on Master's Day, the holiest day of our year, this man dared to desecrate the First Annual Universal Celebration and attack a present day Jesus— an Enlightened One whose commune here in Oregon is making the desert bloom. But for every Jesus there is a Judas, and here, on his belly, lies the snake. His knife" —she holds the blade high for the camera, giving it a moment to zoom in— "his knife, inches from the Divine Bhagwan's throat, was thwarted by divine grace."

The thud-thud of the Ranch's helicopter resounds as it swings from behind a hill. The cameraman, who is slender and very pale, straddles its open doorway. A breeze ruffles the forehead strands of Deela's glossy hair. She holsters her gun and stands up.

"I want to let the Divine Bhagwan's ten million disciples worldwide know that he is safe. Our Master is OK. In fact-" She bends off-camera and whispers into the assassin's rather waxy ear: "What's your name?"

"Dillard." The gun barrel's removal from his crown chakra is yet to convince Dillard it is safe to raise his head.

"Dillard here has just told us that being so close to the Divine Bhagwan has touched him incredibly deeply and he's considering taking sannyas and meditating during his time in jail!"

This elicits a cheer from the sannyasins within earshot. The knot of people around the prone, slug-like figure has regrouped into a throng that threatens to overflow the banks of the road. Deela motions the camera closer.

"And I say this to Ronald Reagan: your redneck CIA spies will not kill this planet's only enlightened being. I would scratch their eyes out rather than allow harm to come to one hair of my Master's beard! Listen America, the world needs the serenity, the bliss offered by the Enlightened One. If you don't believe me, come to the Ranch and see for yourselves. There are still a few days left in our First Annual Universal Celebration and we offer a wide range of courses at our International Meditation University. If all government leaders would just come here and do dynamic meditations every day, the world would be transformed!" She motions with her free hand for the camera to draw back and up. As it does, she shouts:

"OK, people lets hear it! Yes, Divine Bhagwan, yes."

Deela's invocation, like a rock dropped into a still pond, swiftly ripples through the throng: "Yes yes, Bhagwan, oh yes yes yes"— an early sannyasin hit with easy to remember lyrics— is sung with gusto. Bongos, guitars, tambourines and other instruments, always a part of the drive-by celebration, begin to play. The crowd puts their arms around their neighbors' shoulders and sways with the beat. All hearts sing their praise to the blue Oregon sky, and to the cameras, one perched atop the lull boom's maximum extension, the other in the helicopter hovering overhead.

Satyam Gilligan, with one arm around Bala and the other around one of the college girls, sways ecstatically. He is awash in feelings of excitement and a religious sense that he is a crucial part of history. What happens here means something, matters deeply to him and is the hope for a very sick world. Here in the Master's commune, if he is fortunate enough to be accepted as a summer worker, he will surely be awakened and find his destiny

2. Hemlock Grove

The original ranch house for the former Big Snake Ranch is now, though renovations are ongoing, a trendy vegetarian restaurant featuring succulent fake-chicken brie burgers. A huge deck has been added at the front. Its umbrellas, framed by the trunks of tall, rustling poplars, can be seen from almost anywhere on the main street of Bhagwanville. Tucked out of view on a gentle hill well behind the restaurant is Hemlock Grove, an L-shaped amalgamation of trailer homes. Named by the Master to honor the courage of Socrates (a fellow enlightened being), these serve as Deela's domicile and the headquarters of Bhagwan Communes International.

The north side of the L is Chloe's office, the central power node for the commune's daily workings. A shingle hung above the aluminum door proclaims OFFICE in silver lettering. It creaks ominously as Gilligan, an hour after the assassination attempt, climbs the three wooden steps and enters. The office is long and narrow with orange hexagon-patterned linoleum on the floor. Centered near the back wall is a burl-grained walnut desk. Behind it is a chunky, robust woman of florid complexion. Her features have a wolf-like cast, in contrast to her hair which is in tight curls like blond lamb's wool. Lined up across from the desk, which nearly spans the room's width, are three straight-backed wooden chairs. Covering the wall behind Chloe is a huge poster of the Master. Dressed in white, his white beard flowing, he is namastaying his way from his white Learjet onto the airport tarmac. Beside him, radiant and smiling, is smooth-skinned Nivea. The forty point caption reads: THE DIVINE BHAGWAN COMES TO AMERICA.

Chloe, in her loud Australian-accented tones, is interrogating a ma who sits in the middle of the three chairs:

"So why do you want to leave the ranch?"

"Well," begins the ma, of whom Gilligan can see only long black hair and the edge of a very light-skinned profile, "I just don't think I can take it anymore." Her voice is quavering.

"Can't take what anymore?" Chloe leans forward, folds her hands and transfixes the woman with her bead-like, icy blue eyes. The ends of her fingers twitch like the feelers of a praying mantis.

"It's just that I was told I'd be in a trailer within a week and now its been four weeks and I'm still paying a hundred dollars a day to stay in a tent and its really cold at night and they can't even get me an extra blanket. Then Swami Krishna John Wayne and I had something really beautiful and now he's seeing a German ma. I love the Divine Bhagwan, but I want to go home and eat in restaurants again!" The epilogue to this speech is a few sobs which she bravely tries to master.

Chloe has not changed position. Her fingertips go still. "So, you got dumped. What a shayme." The woman's sobs renew. She starts fishing in her purse for a Kleenex. "We're not in the outback here," continues Chloe. "Our Zorro the Meditator restaurant is open."

"Yes, I know. I helped urethane the floor three days ago. I've still got a headache." She presses two fingers to the bridge of her nose and leans her head back in the chair. A haze of perspiration on her forehead glistens like streetlight on snow.

26

"What do you want?" Chloe's eyes flash up at Satyam Gilligan.

"Oh, yeah. Hi. How are you doing?" His greeting is ignored. "I'm here to see about staying at the ranch. Ma Slipsma suggested I talk to you."

Slipsma, his former girlfriend (her name was Daphne then), went to the Master's ashram in Spoona, India nine months earlier, in the fall of 1981. As one of the top guns in Tydass, the Ranch's cleaning department, she is now Gilligan's friend in high places.

Chloe subjects him to a long, piercing look.

"Wait." She stiffens an arm in the universal halt gesture. "So—" Chloe returns her attention to the ma who has somewhat regained her composure, "how many days did you pay for?"

"To the end of July. I would like to have my money back please."

"It's not refundable I'm afraid. It's been spent on doing your Master's work, work that you don't seem to be cut out for!" Chloe whips a form from the top drawer of her desk, and takes a pen from its holder—the rumble seat of a ceramic 1930's roadster driven by an impressively rendered likeness of the Master. She clicks the ballpoint.

"Now, you can go or you can stay. What will it be?"

The ma looks at Chloe. There is a long silence.

"Well?" demands Chloe.

"You can't just take my money like that." Her voice is a low, incredulous murmur. She draws herself up into a more erect posture. "I have some rights you know."

"Rawts! Rawts! Don't talk to me about rawts! Do you love Bhagwan or not?"

"Of course I do!" She is beginning to cry again. She lowers her head, stares dully at the trailer's ochre tiles; her hand goes to her mouth.

"Well! Are you surrendered to him or not?" Chloe stands up and shouts: truculent and bullying. "You committed to six weeks and six weeks is how long you should stay!"

"OK. OK. OK. Never mind—just let me go home."

"No problem. I need forty dollars for the transportation and sixty for one night at our new Rancho Hotel in beautiful downtown Portland. Your bus leaves from Mahaclaptrap at six. You'd better get packing."

Wordless, her shoulders slumped, the woman rummages in her purse. She withdraws a plastic rectangle.

"Do you take MasterCard?"

"Of course."

Hugging her purse to her chest the ma steps past Gilligan with a quick, wounded glance. He feels a brief urge to hug her, but there is too much at stake to risk being spontaneous now. The opening and closing of the door admits a brief blaze of sunlight and a waft of warm air.

He is now alone with the dreaded Chloe and the hum of the air conditioner. She rolls her eyes for a moment in the direction of the vanquished ma, the left corner of her mouth turns upwards in a dismissive scowl. She shakes her lambswool hair, settles back in her chair, and slowly toes the desk drawer shut.

"So, you want to stay do you?"

Gilligan nods. He remains standing.

"Do you have any money?"

He shakes his head.

"What do you have to offer us then?"

"I'm a Canadian with construction experience. I'm a— well, I know how to lay bricks, just an apprentice really but I bet you don't have too many bricklayers here."

"No. And we don't have too many bricks either!" She picks up the phone.

28

"Slowma? I've got a Canadian here says he knows how to lay bricks. Can you use him? Yes. I know we don't... Rawt. Maybe stones? The ceremonial Yahoo! Waterfall? Rawt. Rawt then." She hangs up, leans back in her chair and thoughtfully bites a thumbnail while staring at Gilligan with eyes like smooth blue stones.

I'm being probed; this woman, so close to D.B., no doubt is looking into my soul, checking my aura. His feet, fearing the impending freight of rejection, incline subtly towards the door.

She chomps through the nail and spits it into a metal Bhagwan-imaged wastebasket next to her desk. It makes a surprising clang.

"Okay," she says finally. "You'll need to speak to Slowma over at Bang Pas Zoo. Can you remember that?"

"Slowma. Bang Pas Zoo. Right on!" says Gilligan, filling with elation. "Thank-you Chloe, thank-you so much!"

The phone warbles like a cheerful cricket. He moves towards her. She snatches up the receiver, uses it like a cross to ward him off.

"Don't even think of hugging me! Yes. There is a Swami here. Yes, skinny. No, he's a Canadian. Rawt. Rawt." She hangs up.

"Seems you were a bit of a hero at the assassination. Could be some cake coming your way." She winks at him. "Wait for Dayla in her trailer. Through that door." She motions to the wall behind her.

"What door?"

"Rawt." She gets to her feet and reaches down to the base of the Bhagwan Comes to America poster. Like a gigantic window shade, it rolls up to reveal a shiny, solid metal door. "Through here. And don't tell anyone about this!"

He resists the urge to salute, or bow. *Just arrived and already privy to esoteric secrets. Unbelievable!* He swings the door open and steps through.

Chloe draws the giant photo back into place. She sits at her desk and withdraws a huge wad of money from a lower drawer. She begins counting and sorting it, wrapping it into tight packets suitable for transport. These are some of the proceeds from the influx of sannyasins and other visitors for the First Universal Celebration. The activity reminds her of working for her dear old dad. He flew a small chartered plane all through the outback and Indonesia. After his fatal crash in South Queensland three years ago, searchers found a suitcase full of similar currency packets amidst the wreckage, along with quantities of cocaine welded into a secret compartment beneath the floor of the aircraft.

The loss of her father launched Chloe on her spiritual journey. It began in Europe when she met Lucifia at the Hamburg Bhagwan Disco, and culminated in the ashram at Spoona where she met Deela and the Divine Bhagwan.

Gilligan pushes through a black curtain into a large house trailer. It is at least double the width and twice the length of Chloe's. The space is decidedly uncluttered. At the far end is a counter fronting a kitchen. To its right is a dining area, but there is no table. Faded blue vertical blinds barely contain the bright desert sunshine beyond the patio doors.

Behind the kitchen counter a very tall, thin Ma with close-cropped hair and granny glasses is dipping a butter knife into a ceramic bowl. She gathers a glob of icing and smoothes it over a large circular cake. The icing and the cake are very dark chocolate brown.

The centrepiece of the living area is a huge round coffee table surrounded by low slung, black leather sectional furniture. Laminated within the dark glass of the tabletop is a detailed aerial photograph of the entire Ranch. It has neatly lettered labels which indicate the various landmarks: AIRPORT, TRUCK FARM, VAN GOGH BRIDGE, POPE PAUL SEWAGE LAGOON and an arrow pointing to Hemlock Grove with the words (REMEMBER WHY) YOU ARE HERE. Covering a third or so of the topography at the approximate size and thickness of a small refrigerator door is a copy of *The Sound of One Teabag Steeping*, the heavily illustrated story of the Master's life. The table is supported by a wide black base that might have been sectioned from a massive barrel.

"Hi. I'm Satyam Gilligan."

The Ma behind the counter is plain looking, of indeterminate age. Gilligan's interest ends with her plainness, but she is paying no attention to him whatsoever. "I'm here to see Deela." This is said with a note of importance. It's not every day there is an attempt on the Master's life. There can't have been more than half a dozen all told. The details he can contribute are doubtless crucial. He clears his throat loudly. *Is this beanpole a little deaf?*

"Wait," says the ma, not glancing up. Her focus on the cake is laser-like.

Gilligan continues his stroll through the trailer. Fronting the kitchen counter, on the wall to Gilligan's left is an access door, identical to the one through which he entered Chloe's office. On the same wall, opposite the round map table, is a large picture window. Between it and the entry hangs a collage of photos. Most of them feature the Master and Deela: Deela helping him into a Rolls Royce; Deela preceding him off the Learjet; Deela kneeling at his feet with her eyes closed; Deela on the Tom Snyder show holding up his picture. There are newspaper articles and headlines about the Divine Bhagwan and/or Deela: *Guru Attacks Pope; Sex Guru Invades America; Guru's Secretary Denounces Reagan; Secretary Announces Seduction of America*.

The window affords a particularly beautiful view of the Ranch. It's towards late afternoon now and the lower angle of the sun brings out the textures in the sage-speckled hills. Rock outcroppings hunch among the hills like staunch fortresses glistening with rust. Little Snake Creek winds into the distance from left to right, roughly paralleled by the Path-less Path Highway. There is a lovely trestle bridge called the Van Gogh, about a kilometer away. There, a spur of the road crosses the creek and leads through a heavily armed security checkpoint and the Gateless Gates. Beyond these, nestled be-tween two softly rounded hills, lies the Master's house, which he, in his inimitably mischievous way, has dubbed Shangri Ohlala.

"Satyam Gilligan," he repeats. "I saw the assassination attempt this afternoon."

She continues icing the cake.

Fine. Deela's not here. I'm expected to wait. I'll wait. I'm surrendered, I'm in the flow. But what to do? No TV. No reading material… I'll meditate! Here in the very heart— the political heart anyway— of the Buddhafield. What a day I'm having! Seeing the Master for the very first time, the assassination attempt, acceptance as a worker in the commune, now summoned to head office. Here, I will sit and hone my awareness, plumb the profound depths and scale the heightened vibes of this very special place.

He chooses a spot on the far side of the dining area, beside the vertically-blinded patio door. He peeks between the blinds. No deck, just a drop of six feet to the sun-drenched soil. The door to Chloe's office swings shut. *She must be taking another meeting.* The muffled sounds of hammering and the roar of one of the old school buses that are the primary means of transportation at the Ranch pulling away in the front of the restaurant reach him through the glass panes. It is pleasantly cool, despite the intense sunshine. From overhead comes the drowsy hum of air conditioners.

Should I settle into the lotus position, show how adept I am? No. Too painful. Besides, I've never been able to hold even the half lotus for more than a few seconds. Buddhafield or no Buddha-field, I doubt I can do it now.

He eases his butt to the floor, uses the paneled wall, cool and faintly redolent of lemon scented cleaner, to support his back. He breathes deeply.

It's good to be accepted as a summer worker in the greatest socio-spiritual experiment the world has ever seen. Here we will create the New Man, a man who is not ruled by the petty, grasping ego-mind. A man who lives authentically and in the moment. After my nauseatingly comfortable bourgeois upbringing, this is more like it. Meaning. Importance. And chicks. So many chicks. He closes his eyes, turns his attention inwards, lets out a self-satisfied sigh. *Now which method to use? Vipassana? Humming? The Secret of the Golden Flower? Or should we just do the Lounging meditation, where you hang out with as much awareness as possible? The Master has taught so many.* He is still trying to decide, choosing one method and then another, as he drifts off to sleep.

He dreams he is in a tranquility tank, floating in embryonic bliss in salty, softly oiled water. But something has gone wrong. Sharks are in the tank with him. He feels a scaly fin scrape his cheek. Instead of new age music, he is hearing the hovering, circling sharks. They are talking about him.

"Well, well. What have we here?"

"He was there at the attempt on the Master. You said you wanted to see him."

"Yes, I thought we might play him as a hero to the media. But turns out he's Canadian; it won't work. Hey, Swami, Swami! Wake up! Come on buddy, wake up!"

Deela is shaking his shoulder. Gilligan's cheek is against the warm fabric of the vertical blinds. He comes to with a start; Chloe and Deela hover over him. Their faces seem tinged with repugnance, as if they'd just found someone else's shit in their toilet. Embarrassed, Gilligan scrambles to his feet. He pulls one of the vertical blinds down in the process. It folds itself in two across his hand.

"Oh Christ, I'm sorry," he stammers. "I'll pay for it."

"Never mind Swami," laughs Deela. "But remember you're here to wake up, not fall asleep!"

A group of people gathered around the map table laugh. "Now have a piece of cake before you dismantle my entire house." More laughter. 'Cake with Deela' is considered to be something of an honor at the Ranch, awarded on sannyas birthdays or for meritorious service to the commune.

"Patipatacake, put this back up will you?" She hands the blind to the dour beanpole girl.

Satyam Gilligan stands for a moment rubbing his eyes. He's a little disconcerted. The shadows have lengthened in the scene beyond the picture window.

"Here Swami," says Patipaticake, who has deftly snapped the blind back into place, "you sit beside Deela. You can be a guest member of the Innermost Circle." Her grip is painfully strong on his arm.

He settles onto a cushion alongside the couch on which are sitting Deela, Chloe, and another ma named Lucifia. She is a gangly, dark-eyed German, good looking in a borderline-fiendish Natasha and Boris way. She is in charge of the commune's health clinic, named Hippocrises by the Master. Gilligan doesn't know it, but these three are the unholy trinity of the 'Bitches' that rule the Ranch.

Deela takes a quick bite of the chocolate cake. She is still wearing her gun and silver bullets.

"Listen up everyone!"

Her voice is a velvet hammer. Its cadences are a singsong, with undertones of playful irony. She has the gift of seeming to be letting her listeners in on a joke which only they are special enough to appreciate.

"Welcome to this emergency meeting of the Innermost Circle. The national media will be here in a few hours. The Portland guys sooner." She pauses, takes a breath, surveys the ring of solemnly attentive faces around the table.

"Our Master has been attacked! A vicious, unprovoked, premeditated knife assault perpetrated on our holiest day during the holiest of our holy rituals— the afternoon drive-by. The world needs to see, to know, that we will not tolerate any more attempts by the prejudiced right wing anti-freedom anti-love redneck goofballs who want to crucify our modern Jesus. We intend to expose our enemy in the bright spotlight of public opinion. We've got to let the world know who they are, let the world see what kind of cancerous, putrid slime would dare to harm our Master! Lurchamo, how's the video coming?"

A British fellow, cadaverous in aspect, with very pale white skin which contrasts starkly with his black eyebrows and hair, answers.

"The video should be ready for distribution in about an hour." His voice is hollow, as sepulchral as his appearance.

"Good. I want to see it before we send it to the networks. Now where's our assassin?"

"Bring him in, Lamborghini!" shouts Chloe.

Sergio Lamborghini (he of the reluctant trigger fingers) and another large Peace Force officer emerge from Chloe's office flanking the handcuffed assassin who looks wispy and insubstantial.

"Sergio, how many peace officers have you got assigned to this guy?"

"Four."

"I want a dozen officers around him when the media gets here. I want him to look like the most dangerous assassin since Sirhan Sirhan. You related to Sirhan, punk?"

The fellow shakes his head.

"Who sent you? Hoover? Reagan? The CIA? The so-called Million Friends of God's Country? Who?"

No answer.

Deela brings a little teasing charm in her voice.

"Don't worry, we're not going to eat you. You haven't been abducted by aliens!" There is a burst of laughter at this. Everyone laughs at anything even mildly funny that Deela says. "Now come on, Dillard, that's your name isn't it? You did this to impress someone, didn't you? To make a name for yourself?"

"No! I got that already. My Daddy's famous."

There is something venomous in his voice that seems to galvanize Deela. She vaults the map table and stands directly in front of him.

"Your Daddy's famous?" Flirting. Threatening. They are very nearly the same height, though his posture is hunched: a cringing worm before Deela's bright-eyed robin. Her voice turns flat.

"So, Dillard, what's your last name?"

"Just Dillard will be fine Ma'am." He smirks at her.

"Just Dillard. Would you like a piece of cake, Just Dillard? It's chocolaty and delicious..."

Dillard licks his lips. It is evident he is hungry.

"Is it Duncan Hines?"

"No, it's conjured from scratch by our own Patipaticake. Try some. It's not poison."

His eyes, as dark as Deela's, dart from face to face.

"Look, see, I'm eating it. Yum yum. I'm not dying. Oooh, Dillard... this is just delicious. Take it now before I gobble it all up." She holds it under Dillard's nose. "Un-cuff him, Sergio. Let him eat the cake."

Dillard reaches out a hand, licks his lips, swallows. Stops.

"What's the matter?"

He looks down at the carpet, whispers, "I want a clean fork."

"Ohhh. Does our widdle assassin want a queen fork? Patipaticake, bwing us a queen fork. Quickly. Diwward wants one! Thank-you."

As she turns back to Dillard with the instantly proffered second fork, the cake falls from her plate to the floor.

"Oh my, sloppy me. Dillard, would you be a dear and pick that up?"

As he instinctively reaches down, she grabs a fistful of his hair, kicks his feet out behind him and pushes him, shrieking in pain, face first into the cake. She drops her knees onto his shoulders, releases a fearsome shriek and, straddling the back of his head, raises the two forks like a bullfighter's picadors and plunges them deeply into each of Dillard's fat-deprived buttocks. Dillard screams along with Gilligan, Lamborghini, and everyone else around the table except Chloe and Lucifia who exchange knowing grins. Deela steps back, hands high over her head, jogging, ecstatic. The forks quiver, buried the full length of their short, dessert-style tines.

Dillard squalls fearsomely, rocking his buttocks from side to side. His bony hand reaches back but wavers short of touching the unwelcome new appendages. There are sheens of blood the size of silver dollars on his pants at the points of entry. The ends of the handles move towards each other as Dillard clenches, as if they are trying to kiss in silvery unison. Gilligan's guts are seized up. His mouthful of cake is a soggy, un-chewed gag.

"Oh my," says Deela. "What an unfortunate accident. I must have slipped. Silly me."

"Yeah," chuckles Chloe, "what a shayme."

Deela again squats over Dillard.

"Now," she says in the even, calm tones of the lecturing parent, "we are at a very special fork in the road. I'm going to ask you again. What is your name?"

"Dark," he says miserably. "Dillard Dark."

"Dillard Dark. Dillard Dark?" The excitement in her voice grows. "You wouldn't be related to Alvin Dark now would you? Our ultra wealthy neighbor from across the river? The shoe guy?"

There is a long pause.

Deela's voice is a gleeful singsong. "Dillaaard...you're holding out on me..." She straddles him, her weight on his shoulders, facing his rear. "I just got the strongest urge to play bulldozer. Look! Here are my control handles!"

She grips the forks, burbles engine noises, spreads the nuzzling handles, then moves and twists them like an exuberant child. Dillard squalls, screams, and capitulates.

"Ahhhowww! He's my father. My father. I'm a mistake the great Alvin Dark made a long time ago. But I'm the only son he's got!" He is sobbing. "Please don't hurt me any more."

"Now Dillard. No one wants to hurt you—but sometimes growth is a painful process. To see you opening up like this is really beautiful." She stands up and paces, backdropped by the vista beyond the huge window. She taps the crook of her fist to her chin, thinking. "Dillard has suffered enough," she announces after a few seconds. "We need to help him to find his true self, to build on the insights that he has had here today. Chloe, it's time to bring Ma Angelica into Dillard's life. See if we can get him to relax and open up even more."

"Rawt boss." Chloe exits to her office.

Lucifia appears with a first aid kit. She has the two peace officers carry Dillard, still face down, the shiny handles of the forks dangling, through the kitchen and into a bedroom beyond.

The curtain on the doorway from Chloe's office puffs open. Sergio Lamborghini enters with the sexiest chick John Price/Satyam Gilligan has ever seen—Ma Angelica. With long honey colored hair, she is wearing a thin red cotton skirt and a maroon T-shirt that has a picture of the Master and the words Yes Bhagwan Yes stenciled on it. The shirt is fetchingly small. It clings to her full but astonishingly pert breasts which levitate its front hem to reveal a generous half moon of suntanned midriff punctuated by a stunningly piquant 'innie' navel that Gilligan instantly wants to penetrate with any and every protruding portion of his body. She is Little Annie Fanny in the flesh, a Vargas girl come alive, the Playmate of the millennium. Her nipples jut into the T-shirt's fabric, stretching it taut between them in a shallow, sexy suspension bridge.

"Ah Angelica. I've got a little mission of mercy for you," says Deela. "Please help out Lucifia in the bedroom. We've got a guest in some distress."

Angelica briefly glances at Gilligan as she passes. Her doll-like grey eyes are as empty as her body is full. Deela speaks to him sharply.

"You aren't here."

His heart sinks. *She has seen through him, his lack of presence, his habitual distractedness. A mere glance and she can tell he is unworthy.* "I'm not," he confesses. "But I am trying to work on it."

There are some titters from the assembled sycophants.

"I mean that you haven't been here. You know nothing. You've seen nothing. I don't think the world is ready to understand some of our more spontaneous little moments. And say nothing about the assassination attempt to anyone in the media. I thought we might use you as a kind of hero, but we can't draw attention to any foreigners being here." She nudges Gilligan with the tip of her cowboy-booted foot. "Now you'd better get out of here before you have to forget anything more. Through Chloe's office. Chop chop!"

Gilligan is spellbound to the point of feeling an entitled reluctance to depart. He's also twisted up inside, his fascination bundled with repugnance with what he's just witnessed. *That poor Dillard guy.* Yet he's heard of therapy groups back in Spoona where limbs were broken. *The Divine Bhagwan has always said enlightenment is a perilous path, one meant only for the courageous.* He backs towards the stainless steel door, wanting absolution, or at least to be acknowledged as he leaves. Deela seats herself at the map table for a whispered conference.

"People, the assassination issue is peanuts. I have huge news from the Master which could really make the shit hit the fan—" Deela glances up, notices Gilligan dawdling. Her eyes, very nearly black, are compelling, with beautifully formed eyebrows. "Sergio, would you make sure Swami Canada there finds his way out?"

"Now come on Swami, you gotta go. I'm gonna get in trouble." Lamboghini tightens a burly arm around Gilligan's shoulders and ushers him through the curtain. The tightly fitted door hisses, then clicks shut behind them.

3. Bang Pas Zoo

Bang Pas Zoo, the construction department of the commune, has its office in a trailer on Bhagwanville's Middle Way, the town's main drag, as named by the Master. Swami Satyam Gilligan walks from Hemlock Grove, past the old ranch house, now known as the Zorro the Meditator restaurant. It is a sister to one already established in Heiferville, a 'real' small town beyond the edge of the Ranch's twenty-eight square mile domain. It, much to the consternation of local residents, has been largely bought up by the commune or by wealthy sannyasins who wish to be near the Divine Bhagwan but outside Deela's direct authority.

The 'tourists', those who have come for the First Annual Universal Celebration, are out in force, drinking beer and sipping cappuccinos on the white-tabled patio. Sitters have a fine shaded vantage point from which to observe the street activity beyond the slender trunks of the poplars whose leaves rustle seductively above. They are here to celebrate their Master, to meditate and Rolf and encounter, to massage and be massaged. They are students, stockbrokers, lawyers, housewives, divorcees, drifters, businessmen, wild women, artists, therapists and more therapists. It is early July 1982 and the fallout from the sixties and seventies- the drugs, the death of religion, Kent State, skyrocketing divorce rates, and the disastrous war in Vietnam- have conspired to produce a surfeit of screwed-up people, ushering in a golden age of gurus.

On the street in front of Mahaclaptrap, where vans of new arrivals and the school buses which are public transportation at the Ranch disgorge, two young women scream in unison, then sprint into a mutual vertical tackle, screaming: "Chanti! Chanti! Chanti! Ingrid! Ingrid! Ingrid!" They topple to the ground in a tangle. What a joy to see each other again!

41

What's the latest? What groups have you done? We met at Alchemendra's didn't we? Weren't you at Ojai? Eek, eek, scream, scream, laugh, laugh and tomorrow I'll hate you for screwing my boyfriend.

The men are much more dignified and cool. "Hey Swami, how are you doing?" Maybe a quick hug, a smiling handshake. "What was your name again? Right, Prem Kobasa. I knew it was Prem something. He names all the fags Prem." Laughter. "It's better than being an Anand, man. Bunch of wankers."

"You still with, oh man what was her name? The redhead?"

"Anand Premdoor. No man, that's over. She's with an Australian Swami in the Peace Force. You know, man in uniform. Big gun. It all kind of sucked in the end."

"Right. Well. You go with the flow, man. Catch you later."

Swami Satyam Gilligan maneuvers through these swirling currents of human energy. He is intent on reaching Bang Pas Zoo trailer, and so becoming part of the Master's great work. A guard dog is patrolling a row of offloaded luggage, sniffing for drugs or weapons. Any such found will be confiscated and secured by the commune's hierarchy. Farther west, a Bang Pas Zoo crew is working on the foundation for the new mall.

Across the street from that project is the trailer Gilligan seeks. Inside, bearded architects are sliding T-squares and triangles on angled work surfaces. A thin, sprightly ma named Arcana greets Gilligan and delivers him to Slowma's desk. The head of construction at the Ranch is a large, plump woman, with very kind bovine eyes.

"So you've come to worship with us," she says.

"Worship?"

"Yes. Here at the Ranch, our labors are not simply work, they are worship, an offering out of gratitude and love for the tremendous gift that the Divine Bhagwan is giving us."

"You're kidding me? Since when?"

"Two days ago." says Arcana. "We've had problems with the authorities, particularly Attorney General Fryberger, concerning religious status. The Divine Bhagwan's immigration outlook is far more hopeful if he is considered to be a 'religious leader'. So we've got to act more like a religion." Her slender shoulders shrug.

"You mean we're a religion now?"

"Of course," says Slowma. "You are standing in one of its temples and I am in fact a priestess. One of the higher ranking ones." She smiles sweetly and makes a brief curtseying gesture. "If we complete the mall on schedule I'm going to be a—what is it Arcana? It's a bishop or something, isn't it?"

"Acharya, Slowma. They'll make you an *Acharya*."

"But the Divine Bhagwan is against organized religion," counters Gilligan. "Like the guy who starts the religion may be enlightened but the priests always screw it up?"

"Oh don't worry," says Slowma with a cheerful laugh, "we're very much a disorganized religion. We'd never go against our Master's teaching which is to be spontaneous individuals, but we must bow down at the feet of the commune."

"You mean Deela's feet!" chirps the nearest of the architects. He is a rotund South African named Avibasso. He and the other bearded ones laugh.

"So, Chloe said you're a bricklayer?" says Slowma, assuming with some effort a more businesslike demeanor.

"An apprentice. They were exploiting me though. All I did was cut blocks on this huge noisy saw."

"That must have been hard on your ears," says Arcana sympathetically.

"What?"

43

"I said it must have been hard on your- very funny Swami."

Slowma is giggling.

"Construction experience, a sense of humor, I think we've got a crew leader here. Which project should we put him in charge of?"

"Maybe he should get a little experience first," says Arcana diplomatically. "Qavi Ralph could use some help at the welding shop."

"First rate idea!" shouts Slowma. "The welding shop it is. Qavi can show you the ropes. Only promise me one thing." She leans well across her desk; her eyes are milky pools of kindness. "Please be careful. Be careful with the tools. Be careful with the people. Construction can be very dangerous and the last thing we want is for anybody to get hurt. Watch where you step, watch out for nails, and be careful on the breaks, sometimes that tea can be very hot."

"Don't worry Slowma," he says in a friendly voice. "I'll be careful."

"I know you will." She flashes him a radiant, reassured smile. "Now you need to go to Robya for work clothes and Hippocrises for your medical check up." She glances at a large Divine Bhagwan clock hanging on the wall above her desk. The Master's gloved hands indicate five fifteen. "You can still make Robya. You can go to Hippocrises in the morning. Just take the Motor Pool bus. The first big building on your right is our airplane hangar, but for now we are using it for storage. Basmati will fix you up." As he is exiting, she arrests his progress. "Oh Swami Gilligan!"

"Yes?"

"Watch your back."

"My back?"

"Yes, we've had lots of problems with people's backs. They're not used to lifting things. Lucifia has been complaining there're too many workers, I mean worshippers, with back problems. Back straight, knees flexed. OK?"

44

"Oh. Right. I'll be careful." He throws this reassurance over his shoulder on the way out the door. He is grinning as he turns his steps towards Mahaclaptrap and the Motor Pool bus. *That woman is worse than my mother.*

4. Love on the Rack Tops

The commune's DC 3 is roaring in for a landing as Gilligan steps from the yellow school bus. It is a magnificent vintage plane, a replica of the one in Casablanca, donated to the commune by successful Hollywood producers who are dallying on the movement's fringes.

Wouldn't my father get a kick out of seeing this?

His mind flashes to innumerable car trips.

"Look Johnny. That's one of those new DC 9's. See how high the tail fins are set?"

Gilligan lights a duMaurier, his last one, from a crumpled box nursed all the way from Canada, through a stop at a Bhagwan centre in Santa Fe, then on to Los Angeles to meet Bala. Soon he'll be forced to downgrade to Yankee smokes. Parked near the airport's terminal (an office trailer like Chloe's) is the commune's Learjet. Like a dazzling white Pegasus it appears poised to leap into the skies from wheeled haunches.

The permanent hangar building, now used for storage, is cedar toned, with high narrow windows widely spaced along its length. It is three stories, with shallow gabled ends and translucent roof panels that mirror the pattern of the windows below. At the near end is a huge walled-in overhead door opening, more than large enough to accept the DC 3's wingspan. Beside it is a person-sized door. Here, he will receive his raiment for his upcoming worship as well as an assignation to new living space. This is just as well as his relationship with Bala seems to be foundering. *How could I have been so unconscious not to have seen her whole pregnancy trip? Was I just too happy to be getting laid again after losing Slipsma? What if she's preggers now? Oh well, if it hasn't happened to her by thirty-two, it's probably not going to. And if it does, she said I'd be off the hook. That's cool, I guess.*

Gilligan pauses to suck on his cigarette. Smoking indoors is forbidden at the Ranch and in all Bhagwan centers around the world. He spears his butt into a thoughtfully provided sand-filled tin can and steps into the cavernous hangar.

The place is quiet and cool. There is an office desk and chair in the southeast corner, to his right. Sunlight through a window casts a pale yellow rectangle on the gray concrete under his feet. There is pink insulation sealed by clear plastic on the walls and ceiling. Huge metal warehouse racks reach towards the roof. They contain blankets, pillows, cleaning supplies, clothing, foam mattresses, and, directly in front of Gilligan, many boxes marked with the titles of the Master's books: *The Sound of One Tea Bag Steeping; This, That and Whatever; The Way of the Fluffy Clouds; The Sound of One Ego Snapping...* all ready to be sold through the Ranch's Cuddly Shark boutique or via parcel post. Ceiling fans are set at regular intervals, on into the recesses of the warehouse. They turn slowly, blades in unison. Diffused light glows through the plastic roof panels, adding to a hushed, cathedral-like ambience.

There is no one in sight. He walks down the main aisle. The rows of storage racks tower over him on either side. *Has Basmati or whatever her name is already left? It's possible. There's no crime on the ranch. Doors are probably routinely left open. Maybe I should just help myself? Leave a note, be sure to sign it His Love...*

The light dims as he penetrates the hangar, leaving the brightness of the front windows behind. Everything is muffled coolness.

"Hello!" he ventures.

"I'm back here."

The female voice floats from somewhere towards the back of the hangar, to his left. He hurries past several rows of looming shelves. He spots a forklift in an aisle devoted to bedding and blankets. The forks are twenty feet off the ground. The large metal basket they support is even with the uppermost metal shelves.

"Hello there, I'll be right with you." The voice has an English accent. It is chirpy and pleasant. "I say, can you do me a favor?"

A face appears amidst the pillows on the top shelf. It is pretty-with pale white skin, rose petal lips and a beauty mark high on her right cheek. "Climb up into the basket."

"OK." Gilligan raises a hand in salute.

The basket is wire mesh, about three feet deep by six feet wide. He has no difficulty in clambering up the hydraulic mast. He straddles the rails of the basket, the bottom of which is covered with new pillows wrapped in plastic. Basmati stands opposite him on the top level of shelving, surrounded by more pillows which she pulls from the side of a huge box.

"Here, catch."

She tosses a pillow to him, then another right after, forcing him to drop the first one into the basket.

"That's it. Come on, we've got to fill that basket right up. We had another hundred people arrive today and they're rather short of pillows for their tents."

As she continues tossing, her motions give John Price ample opportunity to admire her, while maintaining his precarious perch. She is a diminutive young woman, but extremely shapely. Her breasts threaten to overflow the semi-circular neckline of her shift as she bends and moves about. After a couple of minutes, the basket is full.

"That'll do," she says.

She stops and gazes into his eyes for several moments. This is acceptable social etiquette at the Ranch, where much has been done to lower artificial barriers between people. If

48

there is an attraction there, some energy, why not just check it out directly without all the usual game playing? John Price, in the past, has preferred the games; his own might be called 'Let's avoid intimacy.'

But now he's an accepted summer worker, part of the larger whole. He is tuned into the commune. His pre-drive-by quickie with Bala, his crucial role in thwarting the assassination attempt, his brief, though uncomfortable inclusion in the Innermost Circle: all these things have buoyed his confidence. He resists the urge to tell the joke about the guy who dreamt he ate a giant marshmallow and returns her gaze. Her eyes are brown, a taupe shade much lighter than his own. She crosses her arms in front of her breasts. The curves of their white mounds appear above her neckline.

"I think you may be the one," she says smiling.

Her fingers begin stroking her upper arms, creeping onto the bare skin of her shoulders.

"I've been dreaming about someone dark and thin with brown eyes like the Divine Bhagwan. Yours aren't quite like his but they are really beautiful. I feel like you have something special for me." This is said in a matter of fact tone; a sexy mystical gleam is in her eyes.

"Well, I do have something." He reaches carefully into his pocket and produces the crumpled requisition form Slowma and Arcana gave him. She holds out her hand.

"Bring that over here."

Gilligan stands tall on the bucket's rails for a moment then leaps the few feet onto the metal platform. He slips as he lands, thumping awkwardly onto his bum. She plucks the requisition from his hand, pockets it. She straddles him and settles slowly onto his lap. Her breasts, her whole body, seem to be straining to escape from her smock.

"So," she says in her English lilt, her face very close to his, "how do you like the Ranch so far?"

"It's getting better all the time," he croaks. His hands have no choice but to settle on the tops of her luscious white thighs. Swooping down as smoothly as an expertly piloted plane, her lips land on his. Her tongue dive-bombs deeply into his mouth, then clings lovingly to the tarmac of his tonsils. She straightens up and grinds down on him, stroking the backs of his hands, then lifting them up and squeezing them over her breasts.

The buttons over those delightful mounds come apart as if by magic, Gilligan's hands fill with engorging glory. His thumbs stroke nipples which are the same rose petal pink as the mouth which he kisses again and again. The hang-ups that have hindered him in the past forgotten, he is caught up in the wonder of her body and the delicious sensations that are rocketing all through him. Basmati slides down his body and pulls off his shorts. She takes his erect penis in her hand and straightens it to perpendicular. She gazes at it admiringly for a few moments.

"How lovely," she sighs. "How perfectly lovely."

"Hullo! Babs? Babs dear, where are you?"

The hollow male voice is coming from the front of the hangar. Basmati raises her head, her right hand still gripping the base of his shaft. Her face has a look of annoyance on it.

"Oh bother!" she whispers peevishly.

"Who is it?" Gilligan raises himself up on his elbows.

"It's Lurchamo." She rolls her eyes towards the ceiling. "He's my husband."

She looks down at his member which now flops limply over her thumb.

"Well, that took some of the starch out of you, didn't it?"

She stands and quickly buttons up her smock.

"I'll be right there! You had better stay here," she whispers to Gilligan. She gives him a perfunctory good-bye kiss, pulls up her knickers, and turns away. She walks carefully along the edge of the huge warehouse shelf, and clambers down a ladder built into the structure on the aisle end.

With a fist of apprehension clenched in his solar plexus, Gilligan, adjusts his clothing and surreptitiously follows her. He remembers Lurchamo as the video guy in the helicopter and from the bizarre occurrences at Hemlock Grove.

If Basmati exposes me to that creep, I'll need some options.

He peers around a stack of bedding just in time to see her turn toward the sunlit desk he passed on the way in. With stealthy strides, he turns left at the second last row of shelving and creeps quietly behind the boxes filled with books. There are no sounds, no voices.

Is she whispering his location to her husband as he slowly unfurls the high-tech belt garrote he keeps for just such occasions?

He peeks through a narrow gap between two boxes. Lurchamo and Basmati are near the front desk, in a prolonged hug. *Of course.* The hug ends without a kiss. Perhaps theirs is one of the arranged immigration marriages that Gilligan has heard about. Seems quite possible, as Lurchamo's accent sounds Bostonian.

"So what have you been up to?" he asks as the hug ends.

"Dealing with a pillow shortage, actually. Lots of late arrivals for the Master's Darshan tonight."

Lurchamo looks around quickly, causing Gilligan to jerk his head back into the cardboard confines of his hiding place. "Listen," he continues in a lower voice. "Do you remember that case of electronics I brought here for you to stash?"

Basmati nods.

"I need it. We are stepping up surveillance operations considerably."

There is a note of joyful anticipation in his otherwise sepulchral voice as he says this.

"Oh," says Basmati going to the desk and unlocking a large lower drawer. "Because of the assassination attempt?"

"Partly."

His movements are attentive and precise as he takes the expensive looking burgundy leather attaché case and places it on the desk. He twiddles the notched unlocking wheels, lifts the lid, and gazes lovingly at the contents.

"Have you heard the latest?" he murmurs.

"Joke or rumor?"

"Rumor."

"You mean that the assassin is going to take sannyas?"

"No. That's old."

"Well?" Lurchamo is grinning, enjoying her anticipation. His teeth are long and thin. His eyes glitter as they glance around cautiously, causing Gilligan to again turtle his head swiftly inwards.

"Come on Lurchamo, I've got things to finish up here before dinner!"

"What's the most incredible thing that you could imagine happening right now?"

"Oh Lurchie dear," she chirps, "has Deela made you head of security?"

"No. No. Not to do with me. With him." Lurchamo gestures towards the framed poster of the Master which hangs behind the desk. "The latest is, and this is straight from Deela, that he's going to start to speak again. He may even speak at Darshan tonight. He's already begun talking up at Shangri Ooh Lala," adds Lurchamo with an air of significance.

"What's he been saying?"

"We're not sure," replies Lurchamo. "But we want to be. Deela is quite concerned."

He lifts from within the opened attaché case a small, button-sized microphone and holds it up for inspection in the light. He replaces it with a self-satisfied air and clicks the lid of the case shut.

"Now if you'll excuse me, I have to 'bug off'."

"You are so clever," says Basmati, taking his arm and walking him towards the door. "You know exactly what everyone is doing all the time, don't you?"

"As much as anyone can, my dear, with a little help from my friends." Lurchamo pats the case and turns the nether corners of his mouth slightly upwards. "I'll see you at Darshan tonight. Our usual spot in the front row. Ciao love."

Lurchamo exits. Basmati strides back to her desk to lock it. Gilligan does a fast reverse wiggle out of his cardboard corridor and hits the aisle running. He sprints back to the forklift and clambers quickly up to his original spot amongst the pillows. He hopes Basmati has not been too distracted by that bit of intrigue with Lurchamo.

"Hey Swami... are you still up there?

"Still here."

"Come on down then, I've got to get you your gear."

He peers over the edge of the platform. She's standing in front of the forklift. Her upturned face and the mounds of her breasts visible within her neckline are immensely appealing. He feels his heart begin to beat faster. His normal behavior would be to docilely come down and get his things, to do as he was told. But now he is an electric horseman riding the strange, sexy currents of the Buddhafield. He slyly reaches back with his left foot and hand, sliding and toppling a stack of pillows off the edge of the platform so they fall on and around Basmati. She is knocked off her feet amongst them, her simple dress askew. Gilligan leaps from the platform to the side rail of the forklift basket, hangs by his hands, and drops bravely to the pillow covered floor, landing beside her sprawled form.

"Just thought I'd drop in," he says with a touch of Bondian swagger. He kisses her insistently, passionately.

"You did that on purpose," she says. "You are a naughty fellow."

"Rather," he says, placing a British emphasis on the second syllable. "Now where were we, darling?"

5. Enlightenment Hall

It is the evening of the day of Gilligan's arrival and Master's Day Darshan, the highlight of the First Annual Universal Celebration. The sun has yet to set fully but the lights are all on at Enlightenment Hall as Gilligan approaches the Security Screening Station. The SS officers, as they are jokingly known, form a gauntlet that everyone must traverse before entering the hall. Two officers, dressed in crisp maroon uniforms with shiny badges and side arms, hold magnetic wands which they run up and down each of the passing bodies. Then two more SS officers, specially trained sniffers, check for the odor of perfumes, deodorants, aftershaves- anything that might set off the sensitive allergies of the Master. The final two (and most feared) in the gauntlet are psychologists, trained to spot lurking depressions or rages in the faces and/or postures of the attendees— any signs of "stuff" coming up which might be potentially dangerous. Therapists, Rolfers and other deep tissue workers are stationed nearby with portable massage tables to deal with such cases.

Spike, a drug-sniffing German Shepherd, is the final nose that must be satisfied if one is to obtain entry. There are, due to the limited number of canine peace officers, only two Security Screening stations, both on the south side of the hall. The north side, the side the Master approaches from, is protected by Little Snake Creek and peace officers stationed every twenty feet or so around the perimeter of the building. Some of these, alas, are unarmed trainees— there are only so many Uzis to go around.

Gilligan is one of the later arrivals, thanks to his Basmati-delayed dinner. The structure is capable of seating up to

fifteen thousand sannyasins on its close to five acres of linoleum flooring. Nearly one hundred disciples have as their daily worship the task of mopping the floor's huge expanse. The
Mopster crews have formed intricate dances, patterned
weaves of wet wigglings that cover every inch of linoleum.
The mops are shampooed, then hung to drip dry daily from
an ingenious clothesline which spans Little Snake Creek from
the rear of the hall to a huge, stainless steel pulley which juts
on struts, like a high-tech wagon wheel, from the far bank
near the Van Gogh Bridge. When spun, its tubular spokes
sparkle in the sun, while strategically drilled holes produce
melodic sounds, like hollow bamboos in the breeze.

Though the scene at the hall resembles, in its polyglot
cast and attention to security, something out of an international airport (albeit one where nearly all the passengers wear
shades of red and beaded malas in keeping with Master's re-
quirement for sannyas), the atmosphere is joyous. There are
jokes and laughter everywhere and the sporadic overwrought
squealings of long lost friends, such as Gilligan had witnessed
earlier that afternoon. The occasional anguished cries or explosive laughter of those being Rolfed on the spot by SS therapists punctuates and lends dramatic depth to the efferves-
cent atmosphere.

The evening air is soft, utterly comfortable after a very
warm day. The western sky is suffused with pink which fades
into a deep overhead blue. The setting sun hovers over the
horizon like a lantern. Enlightenment Hall is an island of light
in the falling dark, a noble ship floating above an ocean of ig-
norance. For Gilligan, the prospect of renewed discourses
from the Divine Bhagwan is like icing on a delicious chocolate
cake. On this day he has seen the Master for the first time,
played a central role in thwarting an assassination attempt,
been accepted as a Summer Worshipper, and successfully
made love with the smashing wife of a member of the Innermost Circle. Now, today, on Master's Day of the First Annual

Universal Celebration, he is about to hear the first public utterances of his Master in over a year.

How fortunate John Price Jr. Satyam Gilligan is to be part of these epic events! *On the face of this miserable, polluted, greedy cesspool of a world, is there anywhere that anything more beautiful is happening?* A feeling of gratitude, beyond anything he has ever felt for the parents who raised him, wells up in him as he contemplates the scene.

"Hey Swami Canada!"

It is Sergio Lamborghini, the bearded Italian giant, running a beeping wand over him.

"Hey," whispers Sergio. "You get ina trouble with the bigshots?"

"Oh no," says Gilligan. "Everything's beautiful."

"Thatsa great! Keepa smiling eh? Specially near the end of this line or they mighta Rolfa you. OK everyone! Letsa keep moving. We all wanta hear what the Master's got to say!"

Sergio Lamborghini's contagious laughter recedes behind him as a grinning Gilligan grooves on by sniffing noses, human and canine, into Enlightenment Hall. It is vast and open-sided except for the backdrop to the podium centrally located on the north wall. The curved roof is supported by a succession of white horizontal metal trusses which step up in a gradual slope, giving the roof a smooth, swooping shape, much like a flattened ski jump.

Gilligan is surprised by how full and empty it is. Empty in that there are huge areas of linoleum as yet unoccupied. Full because several thousand sannyasins are already seated in front of the podium upon which sits the Master's chair. The dais is polished marble, alabaster white with delicate obsidian veins emerging playfully and then fading back into the white. It is centered halfway along the length of the structure, with the back of the chair towards the creek. The Divine Bhagwan will soon be driven from Shangri Ooh Lala across the Van Gogh Bridge with Deela's Bronco and a Peace Force Jimmy as escort vehicles.

Many hundreds of sannyasins are standing; scores are dancing to the music that the commune's Big Snake Band, located just west of the podium, is playing. It is an upbeat rock anthem with a very catchy, almost familiar melody. Red, pink, and maroon garbed people continue to flow into the structure from the SS stations. The music crescendos and there is a great shout of joy as the Master's namastaying image appears on the giant projection screen above and behind the podium. This is the signal for the sannyasins, now numbering at least ten thousand, to take their seats, cross-legged or kneeling, on the gleaming white-patterned linoleum. Many of the older acolytes have brought pillows to cushion that all important root chakra.

The music stops. A wonderfully resonant male voice— it belongs to Kildaraj, the Divine Bhagwan's handsome and well-loved personal physician— states that it is now time for the Gauchamis. They are lead by Ma Chubaru, a famous singer from the Master's homeland. The hall's lights dim, except for those on the podium. As he chants with the others, Gilligan's hyperactive mind ponders:

If, as the Master teaches, all religions are variations of error, like whited turds left over from the hot shit that was once a living Master— and immigration- wise, the Master's chances of remaining in the good old U.S.A. are greater if he is demonstrably a religious leader and not simply a focus for weird, un-American cultish activities, then why don't we recite the Lord's Prayer? If we're going to play religious, why not do it with something that will help his immigration situation? Why use this confusing Gauchami gobbledy gook? Isn't it going to downgrade our image here in Ronald Reagan's America? Gilligan tries to ignore his negativity and come back into the moment, doing the Gauchamis. *That's my mind, swarming around everything, like a doubtful little bee... the nectar is here; drink while the flower is open!*

The vibes from the Gauchamis fill the hall, as thousands of voices sing, hum and drone together. This mass of sound floats across the creek, and up the slopes of the hills. It bathes junipers, sagebrush and rattlesnakes, vibrates among the boughs of the teenaged redwoods (each over sixty feet high and lovingly trucked up from California) that surround the Master's house, and settles into the ears of the Master himself.

Nivea hovers over him, yes, like a bee over a flower. In her hand, wand-like, is a pearl-inlaid long-handled brush which she glides through his hair and beard. The brush is said to contain only the softest bristles from the calmest boars kept at a Zen monastery high in the foothills of the Himalayas. It is said that Sosan himself used to feed the ancestors of those same pigs. Fully groomed, the Master steps into this evening's car, a 1976 twelve cylinder Jaguar XJ.

The last notes of the Gauchamis float into the desert sky. Running water gurgles from rapids under the Van Gogh Bridge. A triangle pings, a wooden flute sounds, joined by drums, tabla, and sitar. The music builds higher and higher. There is a great shout as the Master's car comes into sight on the road above Little Snake Creek. The Jag, flanked front and rear by the four-wheel-drives, trundles across the bridge, glides along the back of the hall and disappears behind the podium backdrop. The crowd shouts a giant 'Yahoo!', falls, then rises as one. The screen which displays the Master's au-tomotive approach goes blank, its white expanse lit from above and below by streaks of blue light. Everyone is on their feet, dancing and clapping their hands. The musicians, in-spired, bring their music to ever higher levels of excitement. The rim of a huge, brilliant orange moon emerges from be-hind the eastern hills. Auspiciously, this night, July 6, 1982 is the night of the longest lunar eclipse of the twentieth century. Celestial events are conspiring to dress the moon itself in the colors of sannyas. Another shout, a roar this time, as the Mas-ter steps onto the podium. He is wearing a gorgeous, azure, diamond-encrusted floor-length robe and a matching suede cowboy hat with a diamond studded hatband.

The Divine Bhagwan is in a mood to match his jolly and audacious outfit. He gestures with his hands cupped upwards for the sannyasins to continue their celebrating, which they do, the music ascending to a rhythmic frenzy. The Master bounces around a little himself, careful of his delicate bones, sending soft wavelets the length of his long white beard. He gestures to two or three women in the front row to join him on stage. They do, dancing ecstatically.

One is Gilligan's buxom buddy Basmati, but he is not interested in watching even her dance. He is too caught up in his own gyrations. His heart is beating with the shared joy of thousands; the trickle of gratitude he had been touched with a few minutes earlier has become an overflowing fountain. He feels cushioned, elevated, by a warm and loving silence, a high energy silence that penetrates his chattering mind, leaving it quiet except for a few words which provoke from his anguished heart more and more tears:

"Yes Bhagwan Yes. Yes. Yes."

The music stops. The Master is namastaying. Ten thousand pairs of hands responsively fold together. Ten thousand pairs of worshipful eyes return their Master's gaze. Ten thousand brains click into adoration mode. Ten thousand hearts are eased. They are captivated by the way they someday may be. The distant dream of enlightenment is, in this moment, as easily shared as gossip from a friendly neighbor leaning on a sun-drenched fence.

The Divine Bhagwan's folded hands and beatific gaze take in everyone as he scans the front, middle and back of the space from one side to the other. He turns and carefully, consciously, settles into the chair, becoming one with it. He crosses his right leg over his left. There is a generalized gasp, and some shrieks of delight, as mindfully, almost teasingly, he allows the sandal of his risen foot to disengage and—after hanging suspended for a long comic moment from the crushed velour encasing his big toe- drop to the marble surface with the ripe plop of genuine Gucci leather. He removes

60

from the voluminous sleeve of his robe a small stack of three-by-five cards—confirmation that he is indeed about to speak. On the cards are written questions submitted to him by sannyasins. He reads from the top card:

"The first question: 'Beloved Divine Bhagwan: You have been silent for so long. Why have you taken your guidance away from us? Are you not concerned that we will fall under the sway of evil forces?'"

The Master's eyes close for a long minute or two. Gilligan feels himself falling, heart beating, into the moment. There are the sounds of the rapids and mini waterfalls below the bridge, the occasional unsupressable cough. People who cough more than three times during Darshan are asked to leave. Sneezes are limited to two. Only one loud fart, though, and you are gone. This is discipline, mental and physical, in the presence of the Master. Gilligan's psychic freefall—becoming the sounds of the running waters, becoming the coughs—ends as the Master's eyes open and he begins to speak.

"Ma Anand Deela, this is a very good question."

The realization that Deela has asked the question shoots through the audience like a bolt of electricity. Ten thousand heads, containing ten thousand newly alerted brains, incline toward the Master in a wave, like ripened grain wafted by a breeze. Twenty thousand ears are flushed and warmed, however slightly, by enhanced attention. Initially, the Master's voice is hesitant, with a slight croak, as if rusty from lack of use. But as he warms up, it gains authority and musicality; his gestures broaden; his fingers form graceful mudras as they embellish his speech with wonderfully precise gestures.

"I do not know why I went into silence. It happened. It happened just as it is happening that I am talking to you now. I may stop again at any moment. I am open to any possibility. I allow my life to unfold without any interference from an ego. I speak. I stop. I sleep. I eat. I meditate. I watch television. I swim in the pool. I drive the cars. I have a cup of tea. This is what it means to be enlightened. It did not seem to me that I was silent for a long time. It seems like just yesterday I was talking to you at the Ashram in Spoona, and here I am talking again.

"But I am befooling you, for I have been silent the whole time. I was silent when I talked, I was silent when I was silent and I am silent now that I am speaking again. Listen to the silence that I am always speaking; hear the gaps between my words; feel the space behind them." Here he pauses and looks carefully at the question again. The huge soulful eyes again turn towards the audience.

"I have not taken any guidance away. It was never there in the first place. You people cling to what I say and try to follow it in the certainty that it must be right and good. You feel a little bit secure if you think you are being guided by a Master. If I open my big mouth it is only in the hope that it will bring you a little closer to the silence inside yourselves, to the insecurity and freedom of being your own guide. I do not interfere with anybody's freedom."

"You ask: 'Am I not concerned that you will fall under the sway of evil forces?' Deela. Get real please. I almost think you are joking. Of course I am not concerned. Concern and worry are functions of the mind and I don't have one! Evil itself is a function of the mind. I do not judge good and evil. I see only what is. I see you are trying to protect me Deela. You like to be my personal secretary and secretaries are good. You like to be my public face. You like to make trouble. That is why I allow you to act like my Pope. Most Popes are very boring, but I have one who needs to stir things up. I do not really care what you do. As long as I am here, just being, radiating bliss, I am doing my job. That is my job description: a bliss radiator. Speaking or silent I never break down; I radiate bliss twenty-four hours a day, every day of the year, with no holidays, no time off for good behavior! That is my function as the Master here in this commune. That is enough for me.

"I am a lazy fellow. I eat. I sleep. I meditate. I watch television. I swim in the pool. I drive the cars. That is enough. I am not a policeman; I am not your conscience; you need to find that for yourself, Deela. I will allow you to create the dramas that you need to move further down the path towards enlightenment, but I cannot play the roles you want me to play, I can only be who I am."

There is another pause here. Gilligan thinks he is going to move on to the next question. But the Master is simply allowing a story to come through.

"There once was a grandfather, a child, and a donkey who travelled together. They were very poor and went from village to village, begging. Their route followed a river and across every bridge was a town. As they crossed the first bridge, the child rode the donkey. 'Shame on you', the townspeople cried, 'to ride when you are strong and young and to force the old man to walk.' And they turned their backs on the visitors. At the next town the old man rode the donkey. 'Shame on you old man', cried the townspeople, 'to ride when the small child is forced to walk, to put all your weight on the poor beast when he would be better off carrying the child.' And these townspeople turned their backs on the visitors. At the third town, the old man and the child decided to try something new again. They hoisted the donkey onto their shoulders and started to cross the bridge. The townspeople laughed so hard at this sight that the old man lost his balance and the donkey was dropped into the river and drowned."

Here the Master pauses and looks out at the audience, a characteristic glint of mischief in his eye. "The moral of this story is: if you try to be all things to all people, you're going to lose your ass."

Laughter rumbles around the hall. He lets it die into silence. He leans forward with renewed intensity, again gesturing beatifically with his hands.

"It is up to each of my sannyasins to realize their freedom, to act from a place of courage, to be who they are and not who they think some one else wants them to be. You are actors in a great play, an unprecedented play. I do not for a moment take away your freedom to play the hero or the fool or the damsel in the tower or the castaway on the island or the Wicked Witch of the West. My choice is to play the guru. Yours is up to you. Now let us meditate together."

The elevated foot settles back into the sandal. The beautifully formed eyebrows, which had been moving expressively as he spoke, relax and settle, like birds nestling lovingly over their eggs. The Divine Bhagwan's eyelids are smooth and brown, the eyelashes a lustrous light gray. The right hand floats up, lifts and adjusts the cowboy hat slightly forward, Clint Eastwood style, as his eyelids, like great drawbridge gates, slowly close. At the same moment, the final snippet of the sun's glowing blood-red disc winks out behind the horizon.

Deela stays alert as those in Enlightenment Hall move into meditation. The lingering chime of a Tibetan bell is heard once, then again and again. Its sonorous vibrations finally die completely, merging into the sound of the running water below the Van Gogh bridge. Her silver sidearm loosened in its holster, she patrols with soft steps the front fringes of the meditative mass on the floor before her.

The moon, huge, orange, and now clear of the hills, floods half the hall, including the podium, in muted saffron light. She is crowded by heretofore discreet handmaiden stars revealed by the baleful influence of the eclipse which dims her brightness to a dull glow.

Deela is restless. Meditation always makes her nervous. Plus she is disturbed by the Divine Bhagwan's answer to her question. She was hoping for something a little more reactionary, like a restated need to guard against spies, potential assassins and sannyasins gone bad. A step-up in security at the very least. She knows that a fearful population is an easily controlled population. *Why did he have to speak again, now of all times? The commune is just beginning to take shape: the mall, the restaurant, the hotel, the disco, the casino — the profit margins there are to die for — all have either been begun or are in the advanced planning stages. The last thing we need is an onslaught of creeping spirituality and everyone sitting around with their eyes closed. And others will now have his ear. And hear his voice. Now he's a loose cannon, a monkey wrench in the machinery we've worked so hard to build up over the last year. I need to shut him up again somehow. There's the laughing gas... Kildaraj, Mr. Holy Serenity himself said he likes it maybe a little too much. That's good. Very good. We'll schedule plenty of dental work. Teeth can never be too clean. Maybe we could pipe the stuff directly into DB's room. Must ask Lurchamo about the possibility. A happy home life is best anesthetic there is. He's got his pool, his little frolics with the mediums. We could step those up too. Keep him mired in bliss in Shangri Ohlala. Mired in bliss. I like that. Thanks to that Dillard creep, we can tighten security tenfold, zero tolerance for anybody that so much as approaches him without express authorization from me. Then I'll just have to worry about the people in his house. Goody goodies like Kildaraj, Nivea and Shenilla. But we've got Lurchamo to keep an ear on things there. Chloe says we've got four million set aside already plus there's a lot more in the Foundation's safe, there for the taking. Loads of donated notes worth tens of thousands and diamond encrusted Rolexes worth millions. One more year and we'll be there — one hundred million dollars. Ommmm. One hundred millionnnnnn. One hundred millionnnn.*

Deela smiles as she mock-chants to herself. Silencing the Master by keeping him 'safe' in blissful seclusion in Shangri Ohlala would ameliorate many of her concerns. A few smaller festivals and one more Universal World Celebration and she, Chloe and Lucifia will achieve their financial goals, all now within reach thanks to the move to the West. The casino, scheduled to come on line the following Spring, along with the Foundation donations, would surely put them over the hump. Then there would just be their getaway to consider.

It will have to be a scorched earth policy. There can be no Bhagwan International Foundation left behind to chase after their money. So that means there can be no commune and no Divine Bhagwan. Well, he keeps saying that he has fulfilled the purpose of all his lives, that he's ready to die any moment. So much the better. He can move along and become a star or an angel whatever the hell it is you do once you've mastered the being human thing. Jail or deportation would work too. Either way, this place doesn't survive; they write off everything; we live happily ever after in Switzerland or The Bahamas or Ibiza. Deela allows herself a sigh. *It's such a big world. If he survives they'll probably start up again in India — land of zero opportunity. Still, Papa always used to say that death is the sweetest certainty — those that don't breathe cause no trouble.*

But that will be so sad. DB is such a doll. But he's never learned the value of a dollar, poor thing. All he cares about is creating his 'new man', so more people can be like him — utterly content, enjoying life just the way it is. A recipe for laziness if there ever was one. Well, let him talk — but occasionally. Maybe he'll inspire them to work harder and God knows they are enthusiastic, dedicated worshippers. One more year in this land of wealthy spiritual wannabes and we'll be home free. One hundred millionnnnn. One hundred millionnnn.

Deela surveys the alpha-waving throng before her. More has been accomplished by the sannyasins in a few months than even she had dreamed possible. But there is so much more to do. And she's got a spot on The Tonight Show next week. She wonders if there's any possibility of wearing her gun. At her feet are Kildaraj and Nivea, directly in front of the Master's chair. Deep in the crowd, highlighted by a white support post burnt to orange by the moonlight, is Swami Canada from that afternoon. He is beautiful, princely looking, particularly now with his face softened by the Master's presence. The fellow seemed harmless enough, docile even. But Deela had seen a gleam of urgency in his eyes that told her he would bear watching. That gleam, her father said, marked a person of great use or great trouble. Beneath Gilligan's lustrous lashes is a telltale sheen.

66

Aw, has the poor baby been crying? There's nothing like a shot or two of divine energy to soften them up, make them more malleable. He actually might look good polishing my bullets. I like them a little friskier than him, though. She makes a mental note that this one has potential uses and that he, if he ever wakes up, could be dangerous.

She continues to scan other faces, alighting first on one, then another, assessing risks, vigilant for opportunities. She learned this skill as her father's secretary, a role she embraced at seventeen, when her mother was diagnosed. She used to sit behind a small desk in the back of his office, watching the petitioners approach his massive one. It was he who brought the *Yakuza* to San Francisco in the early 1950's and made it flourish. "Watch with everything, all of you, not just your eyes," he'd say. His voice was like the growl of a tiger. She had learned very quickly.

"Chloe to Dayla, Chloe to Dayla".

Her Chief of Staff's voice is whispering into her earphone, which is connected to her Motorola by a braided white wire.

"Dayla! Dayla! Can you hear me?"

The silence in Enlightenment Hall is so profound that Deela dare not answer.

"Oh Christ! They must all be bloody meditating!" Lydia sounds very excited. "Hey Dayla, tap you're unit once if you can hear me."

Deela complies, lightly tapping the Motorola unit strapped to her waist.

"Have I got news for you! Guess who is in love? Come on, just guess!"

Deela taps her unit with staccato impatience.

"Oh. Rawt. You can't speak. We have reason to believe that our scrawny friend Dillard is falling for the beautiful Angelica. What do you think of that?"

Deela taps the unit once in approval. This information brings a sly smile to her lips.

Angelica. What a brilliant move that was, bringing her into the picture. That girl is a freak of nature. A seductress without any guile. She's the DB's favorite, for sure, after Nivea. He's got her practically living at Shangri Ohlala. But everyone loves her. Such sumptuous innocence. Assassin becomes sannyasin. The perfect headline, and just in time for Carson.

"Did you get all that?"

Deela taps once and the conversation ends. The meditation drones on and on, but Deela is now serene. Canny, cunning notions and possibilities rain down on her like a shower of crimson flowers.

The assassin turned sannyasin. We should be able to swing that for tomorrow afternoon. We can turn the little twit over to the authorities afterwards; he might even be remanded into our custody once he's done a little time. And he's the son of Alvin Dark, majority stockholder and CEO of Persephone shoes. That's just too delicious! The son of one of the shining stars of corporate America is rehabilitated by the notorious so-called sex guru!

Good story for now, but as time goes by that little runt could be the key to everything. Angelica's going to move on soon enough and break his poor little heart. Eventually it will penetrate his wormy little head that we've been using him. He got connections with those militia rednecks, The Million Friends of God's Country. The locals already think we are a godless cult bent on undermining the American way of life. And tomorrow we announce our intention to take over Heiferville in the October elections. We've already got a Zorro the Meditator Restaurant there and we'll break ground on the condos for our rich sannyasins next week. They just need some kind of leadership, someone who's pissed enough at us to make it his life's work to 'run us out of Dodge City'. Little 'ole' Dillard could be just the man for the job. Those forks I stuck him with are going to be a 'burr under his saddle' for a long, long time. Amazing how intuitively I just seem to do the right thing. Like Papa said, 'some are born to lead, the rest are sheep.'

Deela continues her quiet pacing, scanning faces and enjoying the somber light of the now fully eclipsed moon, as her mind contemplates schemes, future triumphs, and her ultimate, gloriously well-rewarded departure from the Ranch.

6. Breakfast at Macarena

It is breakfast the next morning. Gilligan's eggs are prepared by a smiling, ambidextrous, black swami merrily breaking and spilling to the griddle two yolks at once, cupping and spreading the shells in each of his large hands. His twin flippers move in conjunction over a griddle filled with as many as a dozen eggs frying or flying at once. He keeps up a steady patter as the sleepy sannyasins file by.

"How you like 'em, man? Sunny up? You got it. Got two easies ready to go, OK, they're all yours bro. Who's scared of the runnies? You don't wanna go with the yellow flow, you don't have to, baby. I got a couple solids right here. You want 'em darlin? OK, they're yours!"

Along with the eggs are homemade toast, fresh sprouts, clean unpeeled baby carrots, and potato fritters. There is a clatter of plates and a hum of conversation, punctuated by laughter. It is early, shortly after six in the morning, but the disciples who are commune members and summer workers are up and at 'em, fuelling up for a worship day that will run to seven o'clock that night. The cafeteria is clean, bright and spacious.

Through the large windows Gilligan sees Bala sitting at one of the many open air tables. Any impulse to approach her is squelched as she is joined by Yoyorod. The muscular, swaggering, oversexed Australian was the driver for the caravan of sannyasins coming up from L.A. Her stuff was gone when Gilligan returned to their tent after Darshan. Bala has moved on.

Oh well. She didn't want to be a summer worker anyway. Just on a quest for breeding stock. Guess that's her trip.

Gilligan made a half-hearted effort to connect with Basmati after the discourse but it was hopeless. Not only was she with Lurchamo and surrounded by Innermost Circle types, she didn't even glance in his direction. Like he was nothing to her, just another piece of tail.

"I hear you are going to be my roommate."

Newfyamo seats himself with folded hands across from Gilligan. There is an accusatory tone in his voice that twigs Gilligan's sensitive psychic antennae.

"Yeah, isn't it great? Basmati asked me if I wanted to be with another Canadian. I said fine."

"You said fine."

"Say, where is Fareezuryingyang, anyway?"

"It's near the vineyards and the dairy barn. Truck Farm bus."

Newfyamo looks displeased. He is from Cape Breton Island; how the Master came (apparently) to name him after The Rock is unknown. He is a lovable little farm guy smitten by wanderlust and a priest-like devotion to spiritual practices. Run over by a tractor at three, he was miraculously unharmed thanks to the impressive depth of mud at the homestead that spring. He became much quieter after the accident with a gravitas more becoming of a retired fisherman than a preschooler. To this day Newfyamo remains fond of pointing out the residual flat spot on the back of his head. His beard and dirty blond, centrally parted hair have grown and been bleached by the sun since he and Gilligan shared space at number 7 Wellesley Cottages in Cabbagetown. He worships outdoors, building steps into hillsides and helping with riparian projects along the creek banks. In Toronto, he was fond of seclusion and meditation, probably the most monkish in disposition of the men there. He was often teased for his resemblance, in stature, demeanor, and placid brown eyes, to the Master himself. Now, with the growth and lightening of his beard, the resemblance has been enhanced.

"I've got a lot on my mind these days, man. I'm not sure I need a roommate," Newfyamo says.

"Hey, man." Gilligan holds up his hands, his knife and fork pointing ceiling-wards above his still untouched eggs. "You must need me or I wouldn't have been assigned to you. It's the work of the Master, bud."

Newfyamo smiles briefly, reluctantly.

"Yeah. Guess I gotta go with the flow." He heads for the egg line.

Gilligan is puzzled. *Newfyamo has been on the Ranch for weeks now. He should be in a state of bliss. Maybe that tractor flattened his disposition. Plus there's the Maritime blood. He'd probably be happier on a fishing boat somewhere, being lashed by icy winds, slipping in fish blood, biting the heads off lobsters.*

He again eyes Bala and Yoyorod. They are feeding each other bushy forkfuls of sprouts. *Well, gag me with a spoon. How romantic. What the hell are they doing up so early? They must have volunteered for worship together. How sweet.* This is the end of this particular relationship for Gilligan.

Bala was there on his sannyas birthday back at the end of March – the day he got his mala and new name. Thanks to Deela's machinations, the Master had left Spoona earlier that month, precipitating an exodus of sannyasins from India to America where the much anticipated new commune would be established. His departure, though long-rumored, came as a surprise. So it happened that Bala arrived in India on the very same day the Master she came to see departed. Her return, hastily improvised one week later, included a layover in Toronto and a visit to the newly created Megadharm Bhagwan Meditation Centre at Number 6 Wellesley Cottages. John Price Jr. wearing red and very 'into' the Divine Bhagwan lived next door in Number 7 with a polyglot assortment of sannyasin and near-sannyasin misfits. Gilligan grins as he recalls that first conversation with Bala:

It was a sunny, warm day, an aberrant benediction for late March in Toronto. A group of them had just finished doing Dynamic Meditation on the Centre's backyard lawn. The meditation is a multi-stage ordeal of intense huffing and puffing, jumping and grunting on the spot, emotional release and spontaneous dancing. The technique is one of the Divine Bhagwan's unique creations, specifically designed to release the energetic blocks which typically plague the body/minds of Westerners. The meditation was intense and sweaty so naturally merited a cigarette afterwards.

Glowing and bare-chested, John Price retrieved his bright red pack of duMaurier's from his bright red jacket and settled into one of the two red Adirondack chairs that formed Megadharm's smoking temple. The other meditators laughed and talked as they filtered into the cottage. This tendency of people to laugh and talk post-Dynamic was irksome to John Price. *They've just spent an hour finding inner peace and they piss away the silence in quotidian chatter. Quotidian: great word. From Dickens, right? Yeah, Bleak House, quotidian ague. I should read some of that shit again. Wait no I gave that up to clear my mind, also known as the fucking Bermuda Triangle of trivia. Well at least I'm not yakking away like a gaggle of chickens — no, geese are a gaggle — chickens are what? A flock?*

His pointless internal chatter, stirred up by the Dynamic Meditation, was interrupted.

"You got a light?"

It was Bala, her brown skin flushed from exertion.

She settled onto the horizontally slatted, gently curved surface of the chair beside him, and leaned towards him with her elbows on its broad arm. She tilted her cigarette saucily, her ample, dark eyebrows raised, as if to say *What's with the blank look? I want this thing lit.* Her elbows pushed her breasts

73

inward, making them bulge over the sewn hem of her tank top. John Price, repressed Canadian lad that he was, responded strongly to the allure of her musky scent and the smoldering sexuality in the depths of her eyes: he got nervous. Very nervous.

"A light? Oh yeah, sure, no problem." He fumbled out his red plastic lighter, graced on each side by a full color picture of the Master and subtitled with the words **'SMOKING IS'** on one side and **'A MEDITATION'** on the other.

"Here," he said jauntily, "have a flick of my Bic." His third slippery thumb-stroke sparked a flame. She cupped her hands around his, although there was no breeze.

"So," he dragged in deeply, "how'd you like the dynamic?"

"I liked it. It made me horny."

He coughed violently, expelling blue-hued nicotine clouds from their rightful home in the tender alveoli of his lungs. They dispelled quickly, like haze from the transporter beam of the USS Enterprise.

"Really?"

He made an effort to settle back into his chair, coolly sipped on his duMaurier, despite the palpitations behind his scorched breastbone.

"Tell me –" she exhaled an aura of smoke around his head – "how does it make **you** feel?" She locked her eyes on his. They were brown with tiny, Doc Savage-like golden flecks. Her eyebrows were sexy, inquisitive hoods.

"That's a very good question," he said pompously. "I'd say the first thing I notice is a heightened sensitivity to the external world. I remember my first Dynamic last Fall. I was pretty tense in those days. It was at the old Madison Avenue centre in Toronto – they had these big blow-up MOM and DAD punching bags that you could really whale away on. I remember walking out of there feeling so real: gorgeous colors in the trees, leaves rustling on the street. I stepped in some dog shit. But I was in this calm space where, you know, shit is shit. I rubbed it off on a sewer grate. Instead of being disgusting, it was really beautiful."

He punctuated this monologue by working his jaw like a hyperactive goldfish, blowing a succession of smoke rings towards the sun-suffused haze of the sky.

"Wow." She leaned closer to him, admiring his classic Greek profile and long, thick eyelashes, mercifully not listening to a word he had been saying. "Why don't we go for a little walk?"

"You've got a bit of an accent there." He shifted in his chair, flicked awkwardly at some ashes that fell into his belly button. "American?"

"Californian. I'm from L.A."

She leaned very close to him, hanging over the arm of her chair onto his. She reached out with her cigarette-laden hand and began stroking his pony tail.

"I just adore Canadian boys," she said.

"All of them?"

His nervousness was mixed with excitement.

"No, just the sweet ones."

She traced the fingertips of her other hand over his chest, lingering playfully over his left nipple. Their eyes locked and they kissed deeply. There was the stench of singed hair.

"Holy shit!"

He whipped a hand around and patted his ignited pony tail vigorously. "Jesus. I hate the smell of burning hair."

"Sorry. It's a bit frizzy. I guess it got into the end of my cigarette."

"Yeah right. God it stinks."

"People." It was Ma Prem Pow, Megdharm's diminutive, ultra-cheerful centre leader. "The meeting and 'birthday party' are about to begin."

"Let's go for that walk," said Bala. "I'll wash your hair for you."

John Price was quick with his excuse. "Sorry." He indicated the meditation room from whence Pow called.

"It, um, sounds great- but today's my birthday. I'm getting my mala and new name."

Bala left for Los Angeles that afternoon, but not before extracting from the newly minted Swami Satyam Gilligan a promise to visit her at Stonedharm if he was ever in the neighborhood. As it turned out the centre expropriated his living quarters a few weeks later and his longtime girlfriend Slipsma returned from Spoona with Buckstar (a shady French Easy Rider clone) for a boyfriend. Swami Satyam Gilligan John Price Jr. was left with nowhere to live and no one to love. He decided to leave for the Ranch via L.A..

Bala lived in a huge communal mansion in an older section of Los Angeles, not far from the Shrine Pavilion of Oscar fame. Named Stonedharm by the Master, the mansion's older and more appropriate nickname was Ellis Island. It sheltered the homeless, the dispossessed, the gay, the stoned, the dealer, the artist, the con, and the crone. Gilligan and Bala fell for each other by the old piano in the massive living room, belting out sing-along chestnuts by Dylan, Denver and Young. It might be accurate to say that Gilligan, who sang with much energy and little nuance, passed Bala's audition.

The mansion's Bhagwan Centre was led by an out of control lesbian sannyasin named Clitiya. Her life was focused on her recently and expensively adopted Vietnamese baby girl. Gilligan, with already one big (or so he likes to think) strike against him, had gotten on the worst side of her by leaving the toilet seat up on a dark and partying night. Clitiya, up for a very early morning feeding, had fallen in and gotten stuck. Her cries, along with those of little Shantishiningpearl had awakened half the house.

Boyish and impressionable, he was boy-toy putty in Bala's hands. She was a lovely, fully grown woman – a part Mexican, part Native American, all California girl – who knew what was what. She did him good in elevating him to

Latest Boyfriend status. He emerged considerably from his shy-guy personality, adopting some of her earthy feistiness. Sexually, she was as competent and thorough as he was bumbling, and saccharinely romantic. There were, however, aspects of her behavior that, somewhere at the edges of the murky pool of his consciousness, troubled him. Like claiming her birth control method was vasectomy. And there was the shoulder stand thing which he dismissed it as one of her oddities, along with the way she ended showers with a blast of cold water and sucked it up her nose for 'cleansing'. Only people in a warm climate could indulge in crap like that.

She took him on a grand tour of her past. They saw her former boyfriend play in his rock band, putting Gilligan on notice that he was filling some rather large handmade sheepskin slippers which she produced for all her significant others. He was taken to her parents' home. Their swimming pool's wall was graced by a huge mural of Bala – complete with gap-toothed smile and a hibiscus in her hair. It had been painted by her most recently ousted boyfriend, a talented Chicano with a fondness for cocaine. He too lived at Ellis Island, though he no longer wore the slippers

So now me and Bala are done like dinner. Gilligan continues to muse as he observes Bala and Yoyorod through the cafeteria window. *She'd been trying to get pregnant the whole time. No doubt with all the boyfriends. Why didn't I see that? Because we were almost always stoned and she was great in and out of bed? Yeah. Let's see: Slipsma used me to get out of her marriage, Basmati used me for sex, Bala used me to get pregnant... what was the Master saying about being all things to all people? No wonder I was beginning to feel like a sugar cube, held over hot tea by silk-tipped tongs. Flirting with that teenager in the van was really a bit of inspired self-preservation. Amazing how sometimes intuition makes me do just the right thing. Now she's with Yoyorod - sniggering, swaggering Kangaroo that he is. If that's the type of fellow she wants, someone with no morals, who thinks only with his dick –*

then fine, she's welcome to him. They'll both be gone in a few days anyway.

He spears his first breakfast yolk. It oozes through the tines of his fork in a steamy yellow river. Dirty finger-nailed hands that are a mixture of tan, freckles and sunburn set down a brown plastic tray featuring sprouts and scrambled eggs.

"Something weird is going on here." Newfyamo speaks quietly.

Gilligan's attention drags back to Newfyamo. He breaks off a piece of whole grain toast and sops up some egg yolk.

"Weird?" he says as the warm yellow liquid squishes between his teeth.

Newfyamo leans forward, looks around briefly. "I found a secret tunnel," he whispers.

"You found a secret tunnel?"

Newfyamo nods while motioning vigorously with a clawed hand for Gilligan to keep his voice down.

"Yeah, yesterday afternoon."

"Where?"

"Down by the creek. Near the airport. I was stacking stones on the bank, you know, filling those wire cage things to prevent erosion. I went in among the trees to hang a rat. I'm squirting this bush and I notice a ridge in the sand. So I pee on it. The soil washes away and I see that this ridge is the edge of a board, a piece of plywood. So I try to pull it out. The whole bush lifts up! There's a manhole and a ladder leading down inside it." Newfyamo stands up in his excitement, urgently whispering the last sentence into Gilligan's ear.

"Really," says Gilligan.

There is a long pause, then a burst of laughter from the egg flipping area.

"It's probably part of the new sewer system," Gilligan says finally.

"Sure, but why disguise the entry with a bush?"

"Right." He cuts into his second egg.

"Have you told anyone about this?

"No, man. After the Darshan last night, I went straight to Yingyang and fell asleep." Newfyamo shoves a forkful of sprouts into his mouth and continues: "Is it possible that Deela and the Peace Force don't know about this? Maybe some of those wacko Christian fundamentalists are behind it. Like that guy who tried to assassinate the Divine Bhagwan."

"Don't know," replies Gilligan slowly. "The latest rumor is he's requesting asylum. Like he likes it here or something." Now it is Gilligan's turn to share some inside information. He pushes his tray to the side and leans towards Newfyamo. "Do you know a ma called Angelica?"

"Sure I know her. We're friends – kind of. She comes and works on our crew sometimes. She likes the sound of running water."

"Really? Do you know her in the biblical sense?"

"None of your business, nosey parker. Not that I wouldn't like to. Old and New Testaments."

"Well, she's been assigned to keep that guy Dillard company."

"You're shittin' me," says Newfyamo.

"I was there at Hemlock Grove when it happened".

"Whew. Strange. He's lucky. She's beautiful. Beyond beautiful, really."

Gilligan shoots Newfyamo a glance. "That wasn't the strangest thing though. You should have seen what Deela did to him. It was really fucking disturbing."

"Later, man." Newfyamo, jumps up, munching a last mouthful of sprouts.

"I gotta catch my bus."

"That's cool. No Darshan tonight so we'll meet at the payphones at nine. Then we'll go have a look-see at your tunnel."

Newfyamo pauses, is about to demur. Then his eyes gradually brighten.

"OK," he says.

The boys smell an adventure.

7. Welding Shop Worship

It is 9:30 AM, later that morning: teatime at the welding shop construction site. The heat of what promises to be a very warm day is beginning to be felt. Summer worker Gilligan, freshly cleared for worship by Hippocrises, approaches the welding shop site. He wears a red t-shirt, red shorts, red cotton socks and Ranch-issue steel-toed work boots coated by the dust which puffs up with each step he takes. He is eager to begin some meditative worship, ready to make his contribution to building the New Jerusalem.

This is the Palestine of Jesus, the Athens of Socrates, the India of Buddha, reincarnated. It is happening again, in gladness and joy just as at those other seminal, sacred points in the history of the universe. Now I will join the other disciples, my fellow chosen ones, in the cosmic dance of labor, the divine work of the ages.

The scene as he approaches the building site is less exalted than expected. In front of a makeshift steel-roofed hut, four men in various postures of recline are soaking up the morning sun. All wear work boots like himself. All are reading orange, brown and rust colored Louis L'Amour paperbacks with garish drawings of cowboys on the covers. None glance up at his approach. Gilligan stops. The dust settles around his feet.

"Ahem."

No response. There is the sound of one page turning.

"Um, hello. I'm looking for Qavi Ralph. I'm supposed to join the welding shop crew."

A gnomish, fully bearded fellow, whose dirty blond hair is streaked yellow by the sun, speaks up in an Australian accent. "Ralph's gone for a cruise. Teatime, mate." He jerks his thumb to indicate the hut. There is grumpiness in the tones of his voice.

"A cruise? You mean in a boat".

"Right. Yeah. In a boat! He's out on Lake Krishnamirth-less in our paddle wheel steamer!"

This provokes some chuckles from the other fellows, who continue reading. A second fellow, angular and tall, with John Lennon glasses, says, without looking up from his book:

"He's taken the pickup to get some supplies." This is Shaggyvan. He is lying on his back on a crude wooden bench to Gilligan's right, his copy of *The Sacketts* held at arm's length so it shades his eyes. "Swami, you're blocking my sun. It's tea time." This is said as the simplest statement of sacred fact, as incontrovertible as a rock.

"Oh, right. Sorry."

They're meditating! Of course. Teatime is a form of meditation.

Gilligan steps into the tea hut. The shaded interior retains some of the high desert's early morning coolness. There are plywood walls, makeshift trusses and the same metal roofing as is on the hangar building. A glassless window looks out over the construction site. A yellow strip of flypaper, dotted with victims, hangs in its frame. A recent captive, stuck above the film cylinder-sized container that plumbs the strip's coil, buzzes noisily in a futile effort to free itself. A short, pretty, slightly plump ma is bustling about.

"Hello, you must be our new worshipper." Her accent is English. "Excellent, excellent. Welcome aboard. How would you like your tea?"

"Just milk please." Gilligan believes his manners are excellent. His mother, conscious of taking a great leap upward from her Macedonian peasant roots, spent endless energy reminding him to say please and thank-you and may I be excused from the table.

"I'm afraid we have to make do with milk powder."

"That's OK." *We're pioneers here, prepared for the most inhuman of hardships.*

On the dirt floor to Gilligan's right is an oil drum which has been cut open to make a crude wood stove. A galvanized metal pipe, blackened around its base, runs up through the roof.

"Fancy a fag? You get one packet per day." The ma raises the lid of a shoebox.

Gilligan chooses a packet of Marlboros, a decent progression from his dear, departed duMauriers. *Dum dum da dum. Dum dum dum dum da dum. One step closer to cowboyhood.*

She offers Gilligan tea in a speckled blue metal cup. Tiny, loathsome chunks of milk powder swirl on its surface. He would come to know that this powder, bought in bulk by the ranch, would never dissolve completely no matter how assiduously, how passionately, how furiously it was stirred.

"Care for a book?"

She gestures to a shelf above the counter on which there is a neat array of paperbacks. There is a smattering of science fiction, a Tolkien, but the bulk are by Louis L'Amour; sagas of rugged cowboys finding their way in a forbidding landscape. Most are worn and faded, the titles barely legible in the wrinkled spines. He chooses a newer one. On the cover is a handsome, stubbled rider, lariat twirling elliptically overhead, bearing down with nostrils flared – both his and the horse's – on the reader.

"Thanks. I'll have a look at this one."

He feels a twinge of self loathing. So polite. Real cowboys probably say thank-you about once a year: *"Thanks Doc. If you hadn't come along and pulled that pitchfork outa my skull, there's no telling' what woulda happened. Got me a bit of a headache as it is."*

He hears the music of *The Good the Bad and the Ugly* as he steps back out into the bright sunlight. Doodle doodle doo.

Doo do do doo. Doodle doodle do. Doo do dooo. He pauses a moment, feet spread, tea steaming in his hand, the dust settling at his feet. He needs to look comfortably grizzled like the forms in front of him. Shaggyvan on his bench. Anugruffa, the Australian fellow, leaning against the tea hut, his work boots crossed. The other two fellows are on overturned five-gallon pails. One, named Smoothsill, is also blond, very tall and slender, taller than Shaggyvan. He is clean shaven, with a pleasant moonish face, small mouth and eyes like small blue ponds. The fourth man, whose name is Toasto, is brown-haired, and powerfully built with regular features and a beard that precisely matches the color of his hair. He looks quintessentially American. Just to Gilligan's right, stacked at the edge of the concrete slab that will support the future welding shop, is a stack of framed walls that have been built one on top of the other. It is on the edge of these that cowboy Gilligan figures he'll set a spell with his tea. *Wait for these hombres to get down to work. Reckon a man needs a little down time now and then.*

The board he sits on is loose, a top plate that has not yet been nailed. It slaps over onto its side. Gilligan loses his balance. He thumps down on his rear end then slides off the edge of the pile down to the slab. His hot tea sloshes out of the cup, all over his belly and lap.

"Shit!" he screams, jumping to his feet, holding his tee-shirt away from his body. "Jesus Christ that's hot!"

"Oh. Oh. Accident." Shaggyvan looks up. "You OK man?"

"The book. The book! Don't get any on the book." Toasto, who has something of a Texas drawl, jumps from his perch and snatches the paperback from Gilligan's hand.

"Oh, no problem. Dry as a bone. Man, I haven't read this one yet! You all right?"

"Yeah." Gilligan tries to keep his cowboy composure. "That board wasn't nailed on".

"Greenhorn," says Anugruffa, with a slight sneer. "He can't even take tea time without getting hurt."

"Aw, give him a break, Gruff," says Toasto, handing Gilligan back the book. "What's your name, Rook?"

"It's, uh, Swami Satyam Gilligan." He sips carefully at his teacup, now two thirds empty, though all the milk solids seem to have been retained.

Shaggyvan, the fellow with the John Lennon glasses, chuckles.

"You must be pretty new. The D.B. has really been getting into T.V. lately. One of my buddies got called Swami Rob, you know after Rob Petrie on Dick Van Dyke. I know another guy called Swami Anand Ponderosa. Then there's a welder named Swami Clint Eastwood."

"Ponderosa!" exclaims Toasto. "I wouldn't mind getting a name like that. Or Swami Anand Hoss. That'd be a good name for me, huh Smoothsill?"

The tall, angular Swami, glances up from his book and gives Toasto a brief, noncommittal half grin.

"From what I've heard from some of the women, Swami Little Joe might be closer to the mark," says Shaggyvan

Annugruffa throws back his head and guffaws. "Har! Har! Har! Har!"

"You're full of shit, Shags, no one said anything like that... did they?"

This last is said a little plaintively, eliciting more laughter from Annugruffa.

"Oh no, man, I'm bullshitting you. Except," he goes on slyly, "yesterday Saralee held up a one inch finishing nail and said," (he does a mock British accent) "I say, Shaggyvan, do you know who this reminds me of?"

"Haven't you boys got anything better to talk about?"

Saralee appears at the tea hut doorway. Her face is flushed with annoyance, masking some embarrassment. "Tea time is over in two minutes. Bloody idiots!" She flings the remaining contents of her own teacup in the direction of Toasto and Shaggyvan.

"Whoa!" shouts Toasto as he and Gilligan dodge out of the way.

"Women," sighs Shaggyvan, checking his glasses for droplets. "Can't live with them."

"Can't live without 'em," finishes Toasto.

"So," says Smoothsill, putting his book aside and stretching his entwined hands far above his head. "Break time's over boys. You must be Canadian, right?"

"Yeah, that's right."

Though Smoothsill's tone is mild, he feels defensive. Are these Yankees ganging up on him? Like most Canadians, part of him hates Americans. *They are bullying war mongers who know nothing about Canada and its far more equitable society. We let the Frogs speak their own language for Christ sakes. They have that attitude of strutting superiority even though they fucked up Vietnam.*

"Do me a favor, man." Shaggyvan is strapping on one of the tool belts that are hung on nails to the left of the hut's door. "Say 'out'. Say 'out' and 'about'."

"Out and about".

"Oot and aboot." chuckles Shaggyvan. "You're Canadian all right." He wears his tool-belt in a cool gunslinger style that causes the end of his long hammer to dangle just a few inches off the ground. He strides toward the stacked wall frames. "Pitter patter boys. Let's get at her".

Shaggyvan, Gruff, and Smoothsill, begin nailing the top plate which caused Gilligan's fall.

"We better get you some tools," says Toasto.

The tool trailer is a cleverly built little house on wheels. A side panel swings open and a leather tool belt is procured. He is given a tape measure, a combination square, a pencil, and a hammer with a pale yellow fiberglass handle.

"This one will do for now," says Toasto as he hands it over. "It's only twenty ounces but you've got your waffle head. Later, we'll get you a real hammer, an Estwing like mine. Once you know how to use one."

"Don't worry," says Gilligan gruffly. "A hammer and I are old friends. What's the waffle pattern for?"

Saralee joins them once she is finished in the tea hut. She is a competent nailer, though thankfully slower than Gilligan. A reggae tape by Third World called You Got the Power is cranked up on a battered ghetto blaster.

Exercise, music, sunshine. Working at the fabled ranch.

Gilligan's spirits rise. The lumber oozes sap, along with the scent of pine. The pleasant, warm sweat of honest exertion breaks out on the back of his neck and shoulders. He straightens, peels off his T-shirt, flings it so it drapes over the twiggy wires sprouting from a periscope-like conduit. Naked from the waist up, he re-grips his hammer, committed, surrendered to doing this Great Work, to building the New Jerusalem here in the high desert. He gives the budding blister under the little finger of his right hand only a mild glance. He will not ask Saralee for a band-aid. He will toughen his hands, bronze his skin and temper his soul here in this crucible of labor. He feels the great unchained spirit of Walt Whitman singing like electricity through his body.

"Uh, Swami? Gilligan?" It is Smoothsill, the tall, quiet swami, addressing him.

"Yo!"

"That's one of our no no's here. You need to put your shirt on."

"What?"

"Your shirt man," chimes in Shaggyvan. "You gotta wear one between ten in the morning and two in the afternoon."

"But I'm sweating man; this is some kind of joke right? I mean I'm into this!"

"Not just you man. Everyone. Too many people were getting sunburned, sunstroke. Couldn't worship. Lotta wasted energy. "

"Bitches rule number three-hundred and sixty-four," says Toasto. "You better put it on."

87

"Jesus Christ. All the Master talks about is meditation leading to freedom, being a spiritual rebel, and here I am forced to put on my t-shirt like a fucking baby."

He snatches his shirt from the wires. Stenciled across its front are the words Courage My Love. Display of his rippling bronzed torso will have to wait. His blister throbs with renewed tenderness.*I should grab some of those work gloves from the tool trailer. Or maybe Saralee has a band-aid.* He sees his upright pinkie held tenderly in her podgy fingers, those rosy English lips lowering towards it. *Kiss it all better...*

Across the road, a few hundred yards away, on a much larger site, the Motor Pool building is being laid out. A group of four sannyasins are setting stakes. He can tell, even from this distance, that one of them is a very shapely blonde.

"Hey Gilligan!" shouts Anugruffa. "You off on an island somewhere or what? Come and give us a hand!"

The crew leader Qavi Ralph shows up shortly before lunch. He is soft-spoken, in his late twenties, with a precipitously receding hairline. With him is the other female member of the crew, Boella. She is a striking ma of Indian descent, slim, with lustrous brown eyes and perfect skin. Her manners are reserved and excellent, as is her spoken English. Gilligan imagines she must be from a wealthy background, daughter of a Raja, that kind of thing. She has some of Deela's haughty bearing, but none of her innate ferocity. Ralph is hopelessly in love with her. He spends most of his time chatting and fussing around her as they unload more lumber, joist hangars and nails.

They raise the stud walls. Toasto holds a four foot level.

"Do you like it?" shouts Shaggyvan.

"A little towards you." Toasto eyes the level. "More, more, more man, a few inches. Whoa! Too far. Back. Back. Back. Back. Back. Okay, a little more. That's it. Nail it!"

This continues through the late morning hours, wall by wall. Gilligan cooperates, does his best. His nailing technique improves. Smoothsill and Shaggyvan are experienced carpenters. Though ostensibly the crew leader, Qavi Ralph, who was a bank teller in the outside world, defers constantly to the voices of experience. Toasto and Gruff are willing workers, plainly at home in what they are doing though without the depth of knowledge of the other two. They are also more talkative than the rest; Gruff likes to be right, while Toasto just likes to talk.

One wall is discovered to be inside out. Qavi seems delighted by the mistake, joking in a phony Indian accent. "Oh no!" He holds his hands to his head in mock drama. "Window should not be there Bubba. Must repair the damage. Turn that section around!"

The faux-pas corrected, Toasto and Gilligan are given the job of securing the anchor bolts whose silver threaded nubs protrude an inch or more through the bottom plates at four foot intervals. These must be washered, nutted, and tightened. A spongy layer of pale blue sill seal is compressed between the bottom plate and the concrete so its edge squeezes out like processed cheese from a sandwich. Gilligan tries to be alert and helpful, finger tightening the nuts for Toasto who follows with the wrench.

"We can take our time with these," says Toasto in his friendly expansive voice. "It will take them a while to suss out those roof trusses."

Qavi Ralph and Boella have gone off on another cruise. Shaggyvan and Smoothsill pore over plans spread on a plywood table in front of the tea hut. Anugruffa is adding more bracing to the walls. The slab is enclosed like a cage with the sap-rich studs forming the vertical bars.

"So" says Toasto. "You hear about the assassination attempt?"

"I was right there. I helped catch the guy."

"You're kidding me!"

"No shit, man. It was the first time I'd seen the Divine Bhagwan in real life. I'm namastaying, totally blissed out, and this skinny nutcase comes running out, shouting a bunch of God crap, and tries to stab him through the window. Then Deela showed up and fired her gun."

"Bet she enjoyed that." Toasto's wrench slips off the nut suddenly and whacks the stud beside it.

"It was weird, man. The guy was in some kind of frenzy. Like he expected Jesus to guide his knife right through that bulletproof glass and into DB's throat."   "Turns out he's our neighbor. Did you hear? He comes from the *compound*" – Toasto gives special emphasis to this word – "across the river. He's the stepson or something of the big cheese from Persephone shoes. Did you know that they're the fastest growing company in America? Lotsa money man. So did *they* want to talk to you?"

"Who?"

"The Bitches."

Toasto says this casually, glancing up at Gilligan to gauge his reaction.

"The Bitches?" Gilligan grins a little.

"Yeah, man. Here at the ranch you got your bitches and you got your cowboys. Cowboys wanna have fun and get things done. The bitches are mostly women. Women with power." He gestures with the wrench. "There is no bigger pain in this world than a woman with power. It's unnatural."

"Would... Deela be considered a bitch?"

Toasto bursts into an explosive laugh. "Wholly Jeez man, did you just fall off the turnip truck or what? She's the supreme mother of all bitches – her nails click when she walks across the floor, she's the bitchiest bitch of all the bitches, man!"

"But isn't she really close to the Divine Bhagwan? And she looks – appealing."

"You," says Toasto, "are greener than the grass on the sunny side of the septic tank! You got some heavy duty learning to do, boy! Heavy duty." Toasto pauses, the wrench snuggled around the nut to be tightened. "Deela's a fox, but the beautiful bitches are the most dangerous, man. Don't forget that. I don't know what the DB was thinking when he made her his mouthpiece and went into silence. She and her fellow arch-bitches Chloe and Lucifia just grabbed all the power. Everyone loves DB so everyone does what she says. If you don't, you're gone. Guess you weren't in Spoona man, but things were mellow there. No twelve hour work days. No Peace Force. No Uzis. I tell you, man, all she wants is to turn this place into a money-making machine!" Toasto laughs. "Maybe we'll take over as America's fastest growing company from Dillard's daddy across the river. That is if we survive." His mood dials back to somber. "The way she's pissing people off, always attacking President Reagan, trying to take over Heiferville, threatening to sue, what's his name, Fryberger, that attorney general guy, it's like she wants us to have enemies. It's distracting us from our purpose in being here. I mean regular guys like you and me only want one thing, right?"

"Right," affirms Gilligan. "We want to become enlightened."

Toasto cocks his head to one side. His eyes narrow. He looks at Gilligan suspiciously.

"Don't worry," laughs Gilligan. "I'm shittin` you. You mean we all want to get laid. Biology, right?"

"The other day," confesses Toasto, "I happened on one of the cleaners in a shower trailer before the drive by. Cute little thing with curly brown hair. I'd caught her eye once or twice at the disco. Man, neither of us said a word. I just jumped on her in one of the shower stalls. Must have lasted a total of twenty or thirty seconds."

"That long, eh? I admire your control, man."

"She just kinda smiled at me as I left. At least it looked like a smile."

"Are we talking about rape here, or what?"

"Naw. She was into it. Leant a guiding hand, you might say. It was a shared energy phenomenon."

Toasto's face takes on a more serious expression. "Then yesterday morning she comes up to me and says: 'I've got a riddle for you'. I say 'OK, what is it?' She says 'The sound of one hand?' I say 'Clapping?' She says, 'You got it. Better go down to Hippocrises.' "

"Was she a bitch?" Gilligan has moved to the next nut.

"Naw," says Toasto. "Witch. A spell-caster. Fuck up your mind." He mutters these last words almost to himself.

"So," says Gilligan studiously. "We got bitches and we got witches. Anything else?"

"Snitches," is the prompt reply accompanied by a laugh. "There seem to be more and more of them lately." He lowers his voice. "Trust me, even the stud walls have ears around here."

"Jesus Christ. How the hell do I know who I can trust?"

Toasto lowers his voice again. "You can't trust Deela. You can't trust Chloe or Lucifia or Patipaticake or Tootie, that hulking female brute who's Lucifia's secretary down at Hippocrises. Then there are loads of pawns like Lurchamo who have that upward mobility thing in their heads. You can't trust them either. Don't get me wrong, my friend. Almost all the people here are beautiful, sincere seekers who've given up a lot to be here. But you know what they say about a few bad apples spoiling the whole barrel?"

"Shit man. I thought we were doing holy work here. You know, building the New Jerusalem."

"We are!" Toasto reverts back to his exuberant self. "That's exactly what we're doing. But every garden has its snakes, man. Just watch your step while you are enjoying yourself. Welcome to the school of hard-on knocks!" He laughs again. "Come on grasshopper," he says, unhooking his tool belt. "It's time for lunch and drive-by."

When they return to work that afternoon, Gilligan is straddling the long wall of the stud wall cage, helping to fasten the roof trusses that Swami Ralph lifts in place with the forks of the Lull. Sixteen feet up seems precariously high on such a rickety structure, however well braced. His counterpart on the far wall is Toasto. Thankfully, with each truss they secure, their perches become a little more solid.

"OK Gills," says Toasto. "Get ready for another one".

The nickname sounds a little fishy. Still, it is a signpost on the road to acceptance by the rest of the crew. The truss is maneuvered into position, slotted into metal hurricane ties. Smoothsill, clambering amongst the superstructure of the trusses, holds a glossy wooden four foot level against the new arrival's vertical surface.

"You like it?" he yells to Toasto.

Toasto measures the distance from the end of the truss to the top p late.

"Nail it!"

"Nail it!" echoes Anugruffa.

"Nail it!" chimes in Gilligan, inching forward on the warm wooden surface. He isn't measuring anything, so he is strictly a backup chorus for the others. The yelling helps him forget his fear of falling. He produces from his pouch a one inch galvanized roofing nail. Though broad headed, there is minimal shank to grip and Gilligan's fingers are slippery with sweat. It is not as simple as it looks to pound this nail through the appropriate hole in the hurricane tie. He is startled by the raucous sound of a car horn coming from the airport road. It shrieks exuberantly on both the in and the out breaths: RAW CAW! RAW CAW! The nail slips and Gilligan gives his left thumb and forefinger a whack.

"Ow! Jesus fucking Christ!"

Now he is really sweating and tears come to his eyes. Fortunately he was only setting the nail and there is little damage- he'll get a blood blister later on. He shakes the hand out and resumes nailing. *Be tough. Be cool.*

"Hey man, what's with the horn?"

"It's Lionheart, he's second in command of Bang Pas Zoo, after Slowma," responds Toasto. "Also Shenilla's boyfriend, she's very close to Bhagwan, lives up at the house, Shangri Ohlala. Good people in there. Cool horn, huh? Whoa. Looks like he's coming this way. Look busy boys."

The RAW CAW RAW CAW of the horn sounds again as the approaching Jeep passes the motor pool site. The driver has his right arm raised high in greeting. Gilligan can see several worshippers waving back, including the attractive blonde he'd noticed earlier. At least she's as attractive as a golden topped shape seen at a distance can be. She's slim, but well rounded, and has a big smile. He can tell that much. The jeep, trailing a stream of dust that rises and suspends lazily in the high desert air, grows larger. The driver has a bushy reddish brown beard and is wearing a large maroon Stetson. RAW CAW! RAW CAW! The jeep skids to a stop. Lionheart pops out. He wears a Motorola, with an extra long antenna, slung low on his right hip. Gilligan hears the crackle of static and a burble of different voices.

"Ralphie!" Lionheart shouts. "Why the hell don't you turn your Motorola on? I've being trying to get a hold of you. It's embarrassing, man. The whole ranch can hear me begging you to answer!"

Qavi is in the Lull with Boella. She is ostensibly learning how to drive the machine. As the 'driving' at this time involves watching the men nail the trusses in place for many minutes at a time, it is difficult to see what exactly she is learning. Perhaps she is absorbing wisdom from the sun's rays as she tilts her lovely head back to receive them at more fulsome angle.

"Sorry Bubba," says Qavi in his Indian voice. "I was turning it on just an hour ago, and my name was not mentioned. It is off now to better instruct Boella on the workings of this infernal machine. Tell me, O fearless Master of construction happenings, would you happen to have a Beaddie in your possession?"

Lionheart grins. "You know I do you moochy bugger." He snaps open one of the breast pockets of his de-sleeved cowboy shirt and produces a rumpled packet of the Indian rolled-leaf cigarettes. He joins Qavi in a smoke. The hammering dies out from the latest truss installation.

"It's a natural," announces Toasto.

This is Bang Pas Zoo code for an impromptu break. Lionheart talks to Qavi in a low voice for a few minutes. Gilligan examines his thumb and finger. There is some discoloration where the skin pads have been pinched. Lionheart hops down from the lull. The man moves like a water bug. First one direction, then another.

"We need a few of you for a very special job," he announces. "The old man's place needs a boost. Smoothsill, you're with me."

"I'll go!" shouts Toasto.

Annugruffa and Shaggyvan quickly voice the same sentiment.

"Ralphie, I can't take all your best guys – we've got a job to do here, too. How about you, the new guy, what's your name?"

"Satyam, uh Gilligan," is the near croaked reply. His brain is whirl-pooling. *By 'the old man' does he mean – ?*

"Let me see your face, Swami." Lionheart scuttles to a nearby point on the slab as Gilligan obligingly leans in his direction. He tries to look trustworthy and guileless. *Relax the face. Soften the eyes.*

"You'll do. Gilligan, Smoothsill, and Toasto. You three are with me. Smoothsill you are now a crew leader and you two are his crew."

"But I told Slowma I didn't want to be a crew leader – ever," says Smoothsill, as he clambers down the extended arm of the Lull.

"That is very amusing Bubba," says Qavi Ralph, giving him a hand down into the driver's area. "I told Slowma the same thing just one month ago and look at me now – a crew leader also." He shrugs and mugs a silly beatific smile. "What to do? Surrender and be happy. You people are very fortunate. You are going to work on the Master's house in the very beating heart of the Buddhafield – yes, the very beating heart."

Toasto and Gilligan scrunch into the tiny back seat of Lionheart's jeep. With a lurch, some bumps, and several RAW-CAWS they back up into their own dust and are off. Gilligan watches the passing scenery, starting with the crew at the motor pool site. He spots the blonde immediately. She has a shovel, and is digging along with a couple of other workers, near the edge of road. As they approach, she is bending over, pulling something from the ground. She wears short red shorts and a wide-necked T shirt that falls away from one shoulder. At the sound of Lionheart's horn, she stands and waves enthusiastically. In her hand, wiggling in greeting, is a sharpened wooden stake. Her hair is golden; her smile is wide; her body perfect. Something in Gilligan's heart, like a country-sized chunk of the continental ice shelf rending and plowing itself afloat, lets go. He meets her eyes. They are sky blue and seem to be beaming something at him. A radiance. His mouth open, his hand raised in a zombie's salute like that of a wooden Indian, he, who has been nurtured to be passive, is seized by the need to act.

"Whoa! Wait! Stop! Stop! Stop! I know her! I know her!"

Lionheart sounds the horn again and again. "Sorry buddy, but I gotta keep moving. You can catch up with her later."

Gilligan stands up, turns, places his foot on the backrest of the seat, and gauges his leap. The blonde, quickly receding, has seen him stand up. She stands in the road watching his figure through the jeep's rooster tail of dust. But, before he can jump, Toasto tackles him around the waist.

"Hey! You're going to break your leg! What are you thinking?" He drags Gilligan back into his seat and holds him there until they are half way through Bhagwanville. Lionheart abruptly skids to a stop in front of Zorro the Meditator. He turns and faces Gilligan.

"You OK now?"

"Sure. Fine."

"Where you know her from?"

"Nowhere. Past life. Gotta be."

"Well, aren't you the romantic fool?"

"Yeah. Aren't I?" Gilligan sighs.

"Still want to go to the Master's house?" Lionheart puts the jeep in gear.

"You bet."

"You going to behave?"

"Yes, sir."

"She's one hell of a D1, I'll say that much," says Lionheart as he turns the corner from the Middle Way onto the Pathless Path highway.

"What's a D1?" asks Gilligan. "Is that like a ten?"

"Naw," says Toasto. "Though she's probably that too. A D1 is... there, you see that dozer there?"

Off to their right a smallish bulldozer is grading the site of the casino, which will be beside the new hotel. Its operator is a strong looking, brown haired, brown skinned woman who waves to them briefly, flashing large, equine teeth.

"That machine there is called a D3," continues Toasto. "A D8 is huge and a D10 is mammoth. We've got one working on the dam for Lake Krishnamirthless."

"So a D1 is – ? Gilligan is picturing a toy orange bulldozer he played with as a child. It had batteries and two levers, one for each tread. One lever forward and one lever back and the thing would go in circles, not getting anywhere, not pushing anything. He thinks of poor Dillard with the forks in his butt.

"A worker, excuse me, a worshipper, with a shovel. Doing holy work, you might say," Lionheart interjects. He laughs loudly at his own witticism.

Gilligan's toy dozer is replaced by the image of the blonde. *She had been waving especially to me. No doubt about it. And what happened there anyway? Trying to jump like that? I should have whipped off my mala and flung it back over my head. Then Lionheart would have had to have stopped. Now here's Enlightenment Hall and I'm going to cross the Van Gogh Bridge for the first time. Choices. Each one is a steppingstone on the path. I'll see her again. Maybe even tonight.*

A string of damp mops, fresh from cleaning the hall's linoleum acreage, is being wheeled out to dry on the line beside the bridge as they cross. Their heads of dangling grey hair sway in unison, keeping time with the thump of the jeep's wheels over the sturdy planks. The stainless steel tubular pulley on the far side, wider than Deela's coffee table, whirls and glitters in the sunlight. The holes in its fluted spokes sing a welcoming, multi-layered song as they enter the heart of the Buddhafield.

8. On and Off the Master's Roof

Gilligan is on the roof of the Master's house. He and Smoothsill are assigned to that lofty perch to enclose a small building's worth of air conditioning, filtering and purifying equipment that shields the Master's hyper-allergic lungs from contaminants. Their worship space overlooks the Van Gogh Bridge with its shining tubular wheel, Enlightenment Hall, and a good part of the Little Snake Creek valley which backbones the settled portion of the Ranch. Shangri Ohlala, assembled early at speed, consist of three large, conjoined trailers. With added siding, porches, rooflines and landscaping, the domicile's boxy origins are disappearing into contours harmonized with the surroundings. A larger building, whose capacious roof is a grid-work of skylights, forms a separate wing. This is the Master's indoor swimming pool. To Gilligan's right, beyond and well below the swimming pool, set at the base of the hill, is the Master's garage. Iceberg-like, it extends deep into the hillside, providing underground parking for the Master's sixty two (and counting) luxury and antique vehicles. These are overseen by the faithful Cheerstha, the Master's first-ever mechanic and disciple. Now humpbacked and ancient, he lives in a lozenge-shaped Airstream trailer within the garage's air-conditioned confines. It is said that he is a mere thread's breadth of a tightened nut away from full enlightenment.

Gilligan is blown away. To be teleported (albeit via Lionheart's jeep) to the Master's very house is beyond his wildest expectations. Here, in the calm eye of the Buddha-field, he feels walls of ego-stripping winds whirling tightly around him. He is conditioned by television, by suburbia, by

an overly protective mother and a cold, lovelorn father to do
what most do best: nothing beyond fulfilling one's ordained
role in life. His primal urges to hunt, to fight, to fuck, were
through much of his life channeled into facile cheering for
sports teams and the safe pleasures of masturbation. He fed
his self-importance with criticism of that which was happening around him: the rotten, usurious, greedy, wasteful, poisonous, polluting, uncaring, and above all stupid occurrences
that make up the wretched fabric of contemporary life. This
criticism was like a drug. It dulled his aching need for love by
focusing his attention on his own imagined superiority. But
deep down he knew something was wrong. He was wrong.
The soulless cancer he so readily denounced in the world was
in him, in his thoughts and the way they clouded the truth.
Ironically it was his thinking, his reading—Watts, Castaneda,
Fromm, Brautigan, Krishnamurti, Vonnegut, Robbins, Laing,
Rajneesh, Blake, Lawrence, Keats, LeGuin— that made him
aware of the need to be free of thinking. But how does
thought free itself from thought? This was where a Master
was needed, someone who knew the ways of being and presence. It was for this moment, these ego-stripping winds, that
John Price walked out of his very first class at a prestigious
law school five years earlier. He shrugged off his ordained
role as lawyer in favor of a quest. He became an actor, a poet,
an artist, a bricklayer, but his difficulties with these activities
highlighted a fundamental lack: he didn't know who he was.
Armed with the sword of spontaneity and the shield of irres-
ponsibility, his journey of self discovery brought him, as always, to this very moment.

Now, here on the Master's roof, the cable on his bag-
gage elevator is snapped. What is there to criticize? He is in
the heart of the commune, at the epicenter of the Buddhafield.
Overhead, a clear blue Oregonian sky. All around are fragrant
boughs of a hundred transplanted redwood trees- each one
brought on its own flatbed truck, then planted by horticultu-
rally inclined disciples in soil lovingly formulated to receive

them. Peacocks, electric blue, gloriously feathered, wander the grounds, free to strut wherever their avian hearts desire. Periodically appearing amongst the peacocks are women— bountiful, glowingly graceful women. They are the Divine Bhagwan's mediums, his masseuses, seamstresses, manicurists, milliners, upholsterers, cleaners and pool maintainers. They come and go from the house, wait and hover, chat and giggle, then float back indoors on a cloud of bliss. Though not as plentiful as the peacocks, they are every bit as beautiful.

If these creatures coming and going amongst the stiff, velvety brown trunks of the redwoods weren't distraction enough, there is also the ambience, the buzz, the holy effulgence that throbs through every moment at the heart of a Buddhafield. A divine energy that shouts rejoice! Play! Celebrate! Dance! Meditate pray fall down and give thanks for the glory and godliness, the energy and eternal delight of a living Master. Gilligan is now intensely aware of the beauty radiating from every molecule of existence. He rejoices in the silky sheen on the framing members and the glad coarseness of the cedar paneling they have the privilege of working with.

"Gills... Gilligan!"

It is Swami Smoothsill. He sounds annoyed. *How odd. He seemed so centered, so assured in what he was doing. Perhaps stuff is coming up for him...*

"You're nailing that on upside down!"

"Huh... what?" Gilligan stops. He steps back. He regards the panel, cut at some pains by Smoothsill just minutes earlier. The bottom of its gladly coarse surface is indeed exactly opposite in angle to that of the roofline below. *Did the poor fellow make a mistake?* He looks at the whole piece, the framed wall behind. Round peg. Square hole. Upside down. "Right!" he exclaims. "Right!" He lets loose a strained cackle of a laugh. "What the hell was I thinking?"

"Good question," responds Smoothsill. "But we need you to pay attention to what you are doing."

"Right on, man. Sorry. What's the best way to get this off?"

Smoothsill sends a flat, hooked steel tool clattering across the shingles. "Wonder Bar," he says.

Gilligan picks up the tool and has little trouble dislodging his work.

"Oh oh," says Smoothsill. "Could be trouble."

Gilligan is momentarily ready to defend his efforts, but sees that Smoothsill is looking to the south. Halfway between the tree line and the Van Gogh Bridge, are the Gateless Gates. These are marble obelisks that flank the paved road that leads from Enlightenment Hall to the Master's house. They are inscribed with the motto of the commune:

Life

Love

Laughter

One obelisk is complete. The other is being worked on by a humorless German Swami named Dozon who is applying the marble to a substrate of stacked cinder blocks. Beyond these are the Gated Gates, consisting of a red and white striped barrier arm, a security hut checkpoint manned by Uzi toting peace officers and a twelve foot high electrified fence ostensibly installed to keep the numerous deer who roam the ranch away from the Master's gardens.

Deela's white Bronco, the cause of Smoothsill's mildly delivered warning, is passing through the checkpoint. When even with the Gateless Gates, it pulls to the side of the road, engine running, headlights on.

"Smoothsill," whispers Gilligan. "What do you make of that?"

"They're waiting."

"For what?"

Smoothsill squeezes the trigger of the Skillsaw. Its fierce, sustained shriek drowns any possibility of conversation. Gilligan tries to be helpful, holding the panel (which does, in fact require a little more trimming) steady. The cut is finished with a mild flourish; the blade guard clicks into place over the fading spin of the carbide teeth. Smoothsill points with a free finger. Gilligan is momentarily mystified, then sees far on the other side of the valley, the glinting, golden shape of a speeding Rolls Royce.

"Wow." A feeling of excitement builds in his chest. "He's really moving."

"Right on. He was in the ditch twice last month. They used a D-6 to pull him out the first time. OK, Gills. You can nail this puppy on — right side up this time."

"Okee dokey."

Gilligan is eager to please. But the Master's approach makes it doubly difficult for him to concentrate. He stares at the cut plywood, trying to determine the best way to pick it up. The Divine Bhagwan's Rolls is trundling across the Van Gogh Bridge. Several brightly colored Enlightenment Hall mops dance up and down as vibrations pass from car to bridge to the clothesline. A ma appears from Enlightenment Hall and begins reeling the mops in, causing the huge tubular pulley wheel to glitter and sing in the sun. They will now be used, having been blessed by the Master's fleeting presence, to prepare the hall's linoleum pastures for this evening's meditations.

I must learn the secret of the Karma wheel, the mandala that turns round a still centre, sensitive to all vibrations, reflective of sky, earth, and the waters of life gurgling below. And in turning, the wheel sings, enriching the air and the souls of those who hear while fulfilling a supremely useful function: the drying of the hairs of the holy mops.

"Uh, Gilligan... That sheet's not going to jump into place just by your looking at it."

"Oh, sorry man. I'm spacing out a bit here."

"Just a tad, huh?"

Smoothsill gives him a wry smile as Gilligan wrestles the plywood onto the wall. The Bronco, the Rolls Royce, and a third vehicle — a Jimmy loaded with peace officers as a security escort, head up the road to the house. Gilligan finally sets the plywood into its correct position.

"Just tack her, Gills. Come on. We can go and greet the D.B. when he comes back from his drive."

The young men step to a section of the roof overlooking a cobble-stoned circular driveway, within the park-like centre of which is a large excavation partially lined with concrete. The mini cavalcade comes slowly up the road on the right. Back in April, on one of his earliest drives, before the building of the Gated Gates barriers, the Master, after speeding over the Van Gogh Bridge, accidentally ran over one of the free-ranging peacocks. It is said that the bird died enlightened. Its remains, once extricated from the grillwork of that day's Rolls Royce, were roasted or, more precisely, cremated. The ashes are buried in a place of honor in the foundation of one of the Gateless Gates, near the very spot the Master's spontaneous driving had freed its spirit from the obligations of many thousands of future lives. The Gates are being completed only now, after a long wait for the slabs of Italian marble which form their inscribed facing.

Red-clad people emerge from the house and nearby worship areas to greet the Master. Three swamis climb out of the aforementioned basin, which is as large and deep as a good-sized backyard pool. Two of them unhitch tool belts and lower them gently to the ground. The third is Lionheart, who has evidently been giving them instructions.

"Where the hell did they come from?" whispers Gilligan.

"I dunno," says Smoothsill. "They must have been working on the bottom of the ceremonial pond."

"An artificial pond, eh? I wondered what the hell it was."

"Oh yeah. See the archway there? That's where the ceremonial Yahoo! Bridge and Waterfall will be. The Master likes a short walk after he's been driving and he loves the sound of running water. So he takes a nice walk down along the pond and behind the waterfall. Everyone here to welcome him gets to do the Fallachami meditation when he disappears behind the water. He'll even be visible to the folks over in Enlightenment Hall."

Gilligan is curious to hear more details but the Rolls Royce, flanked front and rear by the security Jimmy and Deela's Bronco, proceeds up a gentle slope and bears left into the circle, foregoing the procession over what will be the bridged ceremonial Yahoo! Waterfall. The Jimmy stops well past Gilligan's position. Samurais take up positions on either side of the driveway, at a respectful distance from where the Master will emerge. Each has a hand on an Uzi. Two of them have long, sheathed samurai swords strapped to their backs. The Rolls glides to a stop opposite the house's main entrance, so closely below Gilligan's position that a good strong leap might carry him onto its roof. A curtain of silence descends as the ticking engine is quelled. A peacock wails. Sparrows twitter. Clusters of hushed, grinning sannyasins fold hands to chins in namastes.

Deela springs from her vehicle, trots to the Divine Bhagwan's driver side door, and opens it. Nivea emerges from the passenger's side with a fleeting look of chagrin, as if Deela is usurping one of her usual duties. She glides around the front of the Rolls to a position beside Deela, hands folded, her features now placid and welcoming.

The Divine Bhagwan disembarks from the vehicle slowly, his sandaled feet appearing first. Beautifully brocaded socks match his robe. On gaining his feet, he immediately looks up and namastes to the two young men. Gilligan is surprised; he had not expected to be noticed up there, let alone to be meeting the Master's eyes in a stunningly direct way. He is jolted, staggered. He feels something let go inside his chest. This man knows him, loves him, has in fact been waiting for him! He feels a sob heave up from his chest, catch in his throat, blur his vision. As when he first saw the Master enter Enlightenment Hall, he is swaying at the edge of a void.

The Divine Bhagwan, holding his namaste, turns slowly to his right and faces Deela and Nivea who are almost directly below Gilligan. The faces of both women are shining, beatific with smiles. Gilligan can see down the fronts of their flimsy red summer tops. Nivea's milky white breasts are bunching up with her namaste, spilling, swelling upwards into Gilligan's widening eyes. And he can see the pert outline of Deela's braless right nipple, squeezed up and almost out of her décolletage by the pressure of her elbows.

His Kundalini energy, doubtless galvanized by the presence of the enlightened one, begins to rise. A hard-on propels his shorts forwards into a sideways tent. With the Master directly below him, he can't forsake his namaste to adjust it. But it is damned uncomfortable and embarrassing. *What if he looks up again?* Gilligan moves his leg, hoping to ease the straining member past the point of textile tension, so it lies flat against his belly. He retracts his pelvis, lifts his right foot, and maneuvers the top of his thigh to nudge the knob safely upward. It is at this moment, when he is poised like a painfully shy stork in something akin to yoga's tree pose that his root foot slips. He bounces on his butt once before he tumbles off the edge of the roof onto the threesome below.

The Master, who dwells utterly within his surroundings, sees Gilligan coming. He takes one giant robe-swishing step backwards and turns to greet the worshippers who emerged from the bottom of the pond. Here is a man who will not be distracted by the sight of one of his disciples plummeting, legs splayed, towards his head.

Said plummeter's consciousness, in the brief moments he is airborne, flashes onto an experience he had during his formative years in Britishfield – a resolutely English suburb on the West Island portion of Montreal. He and his friends had been jumping off the low roof of Jim Crowfoot's garage. Crowfoot's 'old man', as they had stylishly referred to their masculine parental units back in the sixties, had encouraged the practice by placing a battered, gray-striped mattress in the landing area. A pilot, he enjoyed demonstrating how to land properly if one ever had to bail out. So in this real-life bailout, (or flail out) Gilligan's legs know, thanks to old man Crowfoot, that they must hit the ground rolling.

His feet clomp loudly on the redwood planks that front Shangri Ohlala's main entrance. He pitches forward violently, tucking himself into a ball. No NFL tight-end ever took out two opponents more cleanly and completely than his rolling body takes out Deela and Nivea. Both women sprawl forwards onto the authentic Parisian brickwork of the driveway. Gilligan winds up draped over their rounded contours like a limp squid. He tries to apologize into the small of Nivea's back, but can't speak or even breathe. The impact has, like the butt end of a hockey stick, knocked the wind clean out of him. The bodies below him are whimpering from hurt or sheer surprise.

A woman screams. The armed Peace Force officers approach at a run. The Master turns to his left and regards the tumbled jumble just as Gilligan manages to raise his head from its exquisite cradle.

"Hello Swami," says the Master with a chuckle. "Don't worry. Everything is OK".

"Thank—"

Gilligan's hoarse croak of gratitude is cut off as he finds he is talking into the business end of an Uzi sub-machinegun. The Peace Force has arrived.

"Don't move!" one of them barks.

"What do you mean don't move?" A raven-haired head jerks upwards. "Get him off me!" Deela is seriously displeased. She puts her hands under her shoulders and does half a push-up, thrusting her unwelcome passenger upwards. Gilligan finds his voice.

"I'm not moving. She's doing it! She's doing it!"

"Hey, itsa the Canadian guy! Don't worry fellas. He'sa harmless." The ubiquitous Lamborghini to the rescue. "Come on Swami Gilligan. Get-a up. We won't shoot you."

Gilligan gingerly regains his feet, relinquishing all contact with the female forms. Deela jumps up and turns on Gilligan with a snarl. "Arrest this idiot!" she shouts. "I want him off the ranch by sundown!"

"Heeyyy! It was an accident. I was up on the roof and I had a-a— that is, my foot slipped—"

"Never mind Deela," says a soft voice. "No one has been harmed. Are you ready to come inside Nivea?" The Master moves towards the house. Nivea brushes some dust from the front of her top. The heel of her left hand is scraped and bloody. She looks at it with some curiosity.

"Oh! Divine Bhagwan! There is someone here who wishes to take sannyas!" Deela's eyes are firing karmic darts at Gilligan as she speaks.

"Very good Deela," replies the Master. "Bring them into the house. I would like to go inside, before anything else falls from the sky."

There is a burst of laughter; the mood dials back to bliss as the Master carefully makes his way up the steps into the house. Deela hisses into her Motorola.

"Chloe. We're going into the house. Bring him in. Tell Lurchamo to have the video ready to roll. Over."

There is no crackle. No response. She taps the unit impatiently. Its antenna topples like a wet noodle and swings limply against her fingers, dangling from a wire. She utters a frustrated growl, and, holding the weighty device in her palm, raises it as if she would smite Gilligan upside his head with it.

"Yahoo!"

There is a rather haphazard Fallachami ritual as the Divine Bhagwan disappears into the house. Deela remains standing, her Motorola raised on high.

"Uh. Ma Deela..." Lamborghini's voice arrests her movement.

"The-a Master has-a speaka this guy..."

His eyebrows ride high for emphasis, as Gilligan trepidatiously regains his feet. To be spoken to by the Master is most auspicious. It is said to indicate multiple past-life connections and fitness for at least a mid-management position in the commune. Stiff-necked, Deela moves her head slowly from side to side and rolls her eyes skywards. She thrusts the Motorola into Lamborghini's free hand.

"Fix this!" Her teeth are gritted tightly. "Lionheart!"

The stubby uber-crew leader hands her his Motorola, and walks with her to the Bronco. Gilligan can hear Deela whispering fiercely to him while gesticulating angrily with her hands. When she is finished, Lionheart crooks a finger at him while turning in the direction of the concrete pond. Gilligan is being invited for a ritualistic hallmark of good leadership: a little walk with a little talk.

Meanwhile, Lurchamo emerges from the Bronco with a video camera on his shoulder. He whirls and aims it at the vehicle's open door. The gorgeous young Ma Angelica, looking riper than ever, steps out. She is followed by the scrawny arch-assassin. But Gilligan almost doesn't recognize him. Dillard is wearing red clothes! He is about to go into the Master's house and become a disciple of the man he tried to kill just over twenty four hours earlier. Angelica offers the plump bow of her mouth to be kissed. His face shining with happiness, Dillard Dark complies. Then he enters the Master's house. He is going over to the bright side.

9. Newfyamo's Tunnel

Gilligan works late at the Master's house. During his hurried dinner, he keeps a hawk-like vigil for the blonde from the motor pool site, but there is no sign of her. When his bus stops across from the Zorro the Meditator restaurant, he studies the diners carefully, but she is not among them. He doesn't understand why he tried the foolish grandstanding of trying to jump out of the jeep. He knows he's inclined to be impulsive, but that act was irresistible. In fact, resistance wasn't a factor at all. It just happened, like a magnet happens to attract iron filings. Whatever the case, there is a strong possibility she is gone. Many who came for the Master's Day culmination of the First Annual Universal Celebration have departed. Gilligan rationalizes his loss:

Someone who looks like that has a boyfriend already. She probably doesn't even speak English. Toasto did me a favor, stopped me making a fool out of myself. I mean, what was I going to do, drag myself up to her after breaking my leg in the fall?

The payphones are in a lonely spot, beyond the fringes of town, but well below the airport. Four of them stand in a Plexiglas criss-cross, sheltered by a shingled pyramidal roof. A pale pink glow above the western hills is a faint farewell from the day that was. A lone streetlamp, which provides illumination for callers, blinks on as dusk ends. It is from here that Gilligan will call his mother, who is alone in the suburban family home, every month or two. He and Newfyamo can hear the thump thump of the Stones' Sympathy for the Devil from the open-air disco several hundred yards away in town.

"Well bro, let's roll," says Gilligan.

The Americans on the crew, particularly Californians like Shaggyvan, call male co-workers bro. Gilligan finds this gratifying. A middle child, wedged between two sisters, he had always wanted a brother. Now he, in theory at least, has several thousand of them. As they walk up the road towards the airport Newfyamo voices some doubts.

"Uh, Satyam, is this cool? What if someone asks us what we're doing out here?"

"Don't worry man. Deela knows me. She and I are like this." Gilligan holds up two fingers conjoined. "Besides, I'm a crew leader with Bang Pas Zoo. I'm indispensable, man."

"A crew leader? You're shittin me! You've only been here a couple of days. Who'd you fuck?"

"No one. At least no one that important. Lionheart told me this afternoon. After I fell on Deela and Nivea."

"Yeah. I heard about that. But how does nearly killing two of his closest disciples qualify you to be a crew leader?"

"It doesn't. But D.B. spoke to me."

"No shit. What'd he say?"

"He said 'Hello Swami'. Then he told me not to worry. He said everything will be OK."

"Far out. That is so far out. So, they make anyone he speaks to a crew leader? No wonder so many of them are useless fuckheads. You should fit right in."

"Quit sucking up, Newf. With luck, if you worship hard, you might make it to my crew. Save the ass-kissing for then."

"So who's on your crew?"

They have left the lights of the town behind and are treading the freshly paved road in moonlight. Their shadows glide nimbly over the rocks and sagebrush clumps on the hillside to their left.

"Don't know, man. Maybe nobody. L.H. said he had a special job for me first. I've got to meet him at the horse barn first thing in the morning."

"The horse barn? Wow. Strange shit always seems to happen to you, man."

"I guess. Do you grok this moonlight, man? It's bright enough to read by. Lionheart said we're going for a ride. After we come back, I'll be in charge of the rock crusher."

Newfyamo splutters with laughter. "The rock crusher! You gotta be kidding me. Do you know what the rock crusher is?"

"Sure I do. It's a thing that crushes rocks."

"It's exile, man. You're right at the edge of the ranch, way north of the Truck Farm somewhere, with this huge noisy machine and a pile of rocks. It's in the middle of nowhere and they keep it running night and day. It's where they send people who've done something to annoy Deela. Now, what could you have done? Oh, yeah, maybe it was flattening her in front of the Master. Then I heard you wouldn't get off her!" Newfyamo is hunching over with laughter as he walks.

"Oh yeah, burst my bubble, you Newfie smurf shithead. Why don't you jump in the stream here and catch us a nice fresh cod?"

"I'm from the Cape, and as a matter of fact, we should be crossing this thing right about now."

Little Snake Creek is bubbling merrily along to their right. At this point in its meandering journey through the Ranch, it is shallow, stony and broad. The water moves quickly, babbling in a thousand moonlit voices.

"See the rock cages in front of those juniper trees? That's where we were working. Come on. Crossing's easy".

It is thrilling to cross the creek. The daintily rippled water, only a few inches deep, gives the effect of a horizontal slipstream. Moonlit reflections swirl around each of the plentiful stepping stones. Gilligan pretends a misstep would be a disaster, whisking him far away. The young men instinctively begin whispering once they reach the opposite shore.

Gilligan follows Newfyamo's squat figure up the waist-high cribbed rock embankment — part of the Ranch's extensive riparian improvements to protect against spring flooding. Through the junipers he can see some of the blue lights whose twin lines demarcate the airport's runway. In the distance, up the road to his left, is the future airplane hangar—the site of his blissful interlude with Basmati. A lone light pole outside the building casts a yellowish glow on the road. The windows and skylights are dark.

"It's right around here." Newfyamo stops. He mutters to himself, walks to and fro along the river's edge. He drops to his knees beside a sage bush and pushes it and the board it's on aside to reveal a manhole cover. Its circumference is inlaid with lettering clearly visible in the diffused moonlight.

"City of Portland?" says Gilligan. "What the hell is that doing here?"

"It's covering the secret passageway. How many other covers like this have you seen around the ranch?"

"None. But maybe it's part of the new sewage system. You know, the bubbling Pope Paul lagoons?"

"Yeah. Right. A sewage system that consists of one secret manhole cover near the airport runway. No way man."

The cover is heavy but pulls easily to the side. The scraping sound, to Gilligan's ears, overwhelms the gurgling roar of the creek. Embedded rebar rungs descend into the dark depths of a concrete cylinder. Gilligan dangles his feet over the edge, feels for the rounded edge of a step.

"You bring a flashlight?"

"No," answers Newfyamo nervously. "Maybe we should get one."

"Come on, man. Don't be chickenshit. I've got matches."

"What if there's a pile of shit down there or a body?"

"Puck puck puck," clucks Gilligan mockingly as he clambers down. He feels cool air wash over his legs and lower back. The moment he touches bottom, a light glares on from directly behind him.

"Get the fuck out of here man," he hisses at Newfyamo who has just begun his descent. "Someone's coming!"

Newfyamo's feet and butt scramble out of Gilligan's sight, revealing a circle of moonlit juniper boughs softly waving in the night breeze. Gilligan clambers above grade in time to catch a brief glimpse of Newfyamo's form running towards the embankment. He hears the sounds of receding splashes above the generalized gurgle. His friend has run right across the shallow creek, foregoing the steppingstones. Gilligan is about to follow but is stopped by the still displaced manhole cover and bush. He hears the parental voices: *put things back the way you found them.*

Besides, there've been no shouts, no sounds of pursuit, no bullets kicking up little puffs at my feet. Why leave telltale evidence that they have been snooping if they don't really have to?

But first he must observe the scene. Like the great Tarzan, Lord of the Apes, or his son, Korak the Killer, Gilligan the Cautious will hide in a tree and assess any enemy undetected. Juniper trees, ubiquitous at the ranch, are gnarly, scratchy affairs, growing wherever the high desert terrain allows a modicum of moisture to accumulate. Few would support the weight of a man, even a slender one. But, thanks to the groundwater from the creek, he quickly finds a suitably hardy specimen and clambers upwards. There are stubby, sappy nodules and hard little berries everywhere. As he settles in for his vigil, the dim light oozing from the still-open manhole goes out. Does he hear a faint click? He listens with every imaginary iota of his preternaturally acute simian hearing. Nothing. Moonlight, the murmuring of the creek and sticky fingers.

His descent is remarkably un-Tarzan-like. His hands stick. A branch breaks. He clings to the trunk, and, like the rawest of rookie firefighters, slides torturously down.

On the manhole ladder for a second time, he bolts upwards a step or two when the light comes on. But wait! He's certainly heard a click, the sound of a mechanism initiating the illumination. He glides soundlessly to the bottom of the rungs and turns, heart thumping, to face the light. A string of widely spaced bulbs, like those on movie marquees, recede in a dangling line. A tunnel, made of concrete culvert some six inches higher than his head is illuminated for about fifty feet, only to end in darkness. Moisture stains the bottom of its empty length like a guilty secret. Gilligan clambers up the rebar rungs and pulls the manhole cover an inch short of closed. Again he descends. He needs to see where this thing goes.

The motion sensors look like mini headlights with milky white lenses. The lights are thoughtfully set at the 10 o'clock position of the culvert to allow maximum headroom. Gilligan adjusts his feet to the dank, curved floor. A skein of earth scent is laced into the pervasive smell of damp concrete. He hears his breathing, the scrape of his shoes, and the clicks of the sensors as he approaches a new string of lights. Soon, anxiety clicks in. *How long does this thing go on? Crew leader or not, if I'm found skulking around the ranch after hours it won't look good. Newfyamo's probably on his way back to Yingyang. He's pretty tight-lipped. Probably wouldn't say a damn thing till I was gone for a week.*

He decides to employ Carlos Castaneda's Gait of Power. Breathing deeply, hunched forward, hands dangling low — a man of power never carries anything in his hands — with a relaxed peripheral gaze and long smooth strides, he whooshes through the tunnel. The heavy air ruffles his hair at the temples. The individual light bulbs, like sodium stanchions on a late night highway, sail smoothly past his head. He remembers being stoned, sitting in the very front window of Toronto's Yonge St. subway, grooving on the illusion that the dark tunnel, with its successive overhead crescents of light, was actually a well in which he was in a freefall down and down and down. Then the harshly lit bathroom-green tiles of Eglington Station would flood his view with a wave of banality. Now his heart pumps powerfully and his breath expels in rhythmic gusts, not unlike the *cool! cool! cool!* mantra of dynamic meditation. He throbs with exultation. This is meditation! This is alertness! This relaxed, yet total effort sailing through the unknown into the next satori, the next illumination!

There's another click which suddenly reveals a second tunnel veering off to his left. Gilligan stops so abruptly that he pitches forward onto his hands and knees. He hears something—a rhythmic pounding like muffled footsteps approaching! He jumps to his feet Tarzan-like, ready to gait-of-power the hell out of there. But Tarzan's jungle reflexes are a tad overwrought and the top of his savage, but nobly shaped head smacks into the corner of the overhead sensor, sending him once again to his hands and knees. Ahead of him are divergent strings of light illuminating separate concrete tubes. The rhythmic pounding, enhanced by a dented skull which a light probe reveals is oozing blood, resolves itself into music. He can't make out the tune which sounds like it is coming from the distant shore of a lake. He is under the dance floor of the disco.

He regroups, chooses the passageway to the right. The one to the left can be saved for another journey. The knock on th`e noggin has drastically sapped his enthusiasm. He remembers exploring similar culverts in Britishfield. He and his buddies joked about being engulfed by giant turds if all the toilets flushed at once. Or about being eaten by hordes of sewer rats, a la 'Willard'. Or of somehow surfacing in Paula Buckingham's house. She, whose breast size—orange or grapefruit—was the subject of some animated, echoing tunnel discussion. These thoughts muddle his still tender cranium as the disco sounds fade. He passes a last string of lights. His shadow falls across a set of rebar ladder rungs leading upwards. This fork is at an end. He grips the cool, rigid bars of rust-hazed steel and begins to climb.

Another steel manhole cover lifts and scrapes easily to the side. There is a waft of warm desert air and the sounds of Bhagwanville's night life. Shrieks and yells of celebration. A school bus pulls away. And, louder than ever, the disco, featuring the twangs of the opening riff of Van Morrison's 'Brown Eyed Girl'. Gilligan wishes he was there now, trying his luck at the meet market. Maybe that blonde would be there. This grand tunnel adventure has yielded only a throbbing head and a profound sense of disorientation. *Why can't I see anything?*

His eyes adjust. He is still confined in a cylinder, a larger one, with walls of black plastic tarpaulin instead of concrete. Above his head, framed by wooden joists, is a recessed plywood circle sized like the manhole he stands in. Insight hits Gilligan with an impact as formidable as that of the light sensor a few minutes earlier: He knows where he is and where the trapdoor above his head will take him. If the fork in the tunnel was under the disco and he came in an easterly direction, he must be under Hemlock Grove! He is so certain, he doubts the wisdom of standing up and seeing for himself. *Why take a risk to know what's known?* But the heady lure of confirmation causes him to reach up and push gently.

The hatch, composed of plywood, Styrofoam and carpet, lifts soundlessly. As Gilligan's head pokes upwards he is inundated by a gale of raucous laughter. Some of the cackling mouths are less than an arm's length away. Above him, illumined in reverse, is the photo map of the ranch built into the black, circular glass top of Deela's massive coffee table. He is at the hub, the very nerve centre of a nefarious karmic web.

Dark human shapes, like shades from some underworld, hover above him. One has the head of a bird, an ibis with a long, pencil-thin beak. It is poking directly towards Gilligan's upturned eyeballs! There's a sustained sniff as the straw traces a line that runs directly between Gilligan's eyes. He jerks his face, upturned as if in supplication, back into the shadow below floor level. There is more female laughter, cackling and howling like hyenas over a carcass. The heads bob back and forth. A finger smushes down and rubs in a circular gathering pattern, then melds with an unseen mouth. The shadowy shapes are those of Deela, Chloe, Lucifia, Patipaticake, and Tootie- Lucifia's massive sidekick and secretary. They are sniffing themselves into an ecstatic cocaine-fuelled frenzy.

Gilligan's mind flashes back to a warning given to him back in May by Alchemendra, the legendary group leader whom Deela has recently declared 'persona non grata' at the Ranch.

Is this what he meant about something being rotten? Not that I'm philosophically against drugs. Spiritually evolved beings, like Don Juan in Carlos Castaneda can use them for higher purposes. Maybe that's what's happening here?

He gives his head a shake, sending waves of pain cannonading between the boards of his brain, echoing like pucks in an empty arena.

Ow. Fuck that hurts. Maybe this isn't really happening. Maybe I'm really lying where I hit my head in the tunnel, slowly being overwhelmed by radon, argon or some other weird sewer gases. They're mixing with the Buddhafield vibes, causing toxic hallucinations.

He touches a finger to the dent in his head. It is very tender and moist with blood. *Real enough.* He sucks the finger clean, mirroring the actions of the bitches above.

"Fellow bitches—" It is Deela's voice accompanied by more laughter. "Welcome to this special meeting of the Innermost Circle. First, a special thank-you goes to our dear Lucifia who has managed to procure our celebration powder. Snort mindfully ladies!" With the subsequent round of applause, two more shadowy ibis forms descend and sniff powdery lines.

"You'll be pleased to know, my sisters," Deela continues, "that the media hit from our "assassin sannyasin" has been beyond prolific. "Thanks to our shiny new 'fax machine' that the ever-useful Lurchamo suggested we invest in, both AP and Reuters have picked up the story! It will be in every major newspaper by morning and the guys who came from Portland TV to cover the assassination are coming back again. We're mocking up some 'before and after' pictures of Swami Prem Dillard that I can hold up when I'm on Carson this week. We are talking a publicity blast of hydrogen scale proportions! Do you realize what this means, my sisters?"

"That we all get to be on the television?" Chloe asks in her unmistakable Australian twang.

"No. No. No. I'd love to share the spotlight, of course, but I've explained this many times, Chloe. You are an Aussie, Lucifia is German. With that annoying little snot Fryberger on our tails about immigration issues, we can't afford to give foreigners too high a profile. Patipaticake and I are the only legal American's among us. As she rarely says much of anything, it falls upon me to carry the load for the rest of you. Fortunately I've been blessed, perhaps beyond my unsurpassed managerial acumen, with oratorical abilities far beyond the pallid pale. Pallid pale? Does that make sense?"

There is a moment of baffled silence, some scraping on the glass tabletop, and the sounds of four straws sniffing.

"Where was I?" continues Deela. "Oh yes, what all this media attention means, my pretties, is that we are realer than ever. Our brand profile is now etched into the brains of North Americans. So we are going to add another celebration festival! Every seeker in America is going to want to come and see the Enlightened One who produced the '*Miracle of the Assassin turned Sannyasin*'. The therapists, the restaurant, gift shop and especially our temporary charitable casino (isn't it grand that we've been designated a religion and can legally run one?) must all be ready ready ready to rake rake rake it in! It needs to happen this December, during Christmas season, when all the 'spiritual' types out there will either want to avoid, or recover from, having to be with their families."

"Vat vill vee be celebrating, Deela?" asks Lucifia, enunciating the syllables of 'celebrating' in a way that indicates it is far from her favorite activity.

"Who cares? We'll think of something. Patipaticake, that can be your job. My dear, dear sisters, my fellow mellow Innermost Circle-ites, I believe that our three-year plan to reach our financial goals, thanks to my brilliant handling of the Dillard situation, has just been reduced to one year. At this time next year, after the Second Annual Universal Celebration, we shall all be relaxing on a beach in the Bahamas, blissfully counting our one hundred million dollars."

"But Dayla," says Chloe, "how do we get away with that money? We'll need to take the Foundation's safe at Mahaclaptrap, or at least what's in it — the big note donations and the diamond Rolexes. Even if we get them, how do we stop the Bhagwan Foundation from coming after us for it? I mean Kildaraj and Nivea and them in Shangri Ohlala are still on the Board of Directors and —"

"Fear not, my Aussie rose." "I am always considering the end game before my opponent has decided on a gambit. And dear Papa taught me to always, always have an escape route in place from the beginning. Getting out will not be a problem." Deela drums on the table above Gilligan's head for emphasis. "As for the Foundation, if you will recall, our plan is to leave this place in a state of irreparable chaos, where no one will be in a position to come after anybody — ever. Here's the deal: the bigger we get, and the more I push their buttons, the more worried and angry the rednecks in this State become. We've already bought up half of Heiferville, and tomorrow's paper will proclaim Madma is running to be its mayor. Once we take that teeming metropolis over, as we will, we'll move on to Wacko County. It is dreadfully underpopulated, don't you know? A few thousand more American sannyasins here, combined with historic voter apathy out there, and we take over the county too. Who knows? I may run for sheriff. That gun n' god crazy militia group the Million Friends of God's Country has already been muttering about bulldozing the Ranch. I've got them on simmer right now, but give me time and I'll bring them to a boil. One delightful little nugget is that besides being the son of one of the most powerful men in the State, our assassin sannyasin is currently a god-fearing member of those very same Million Friends. No doubt he was trying to be quite the crusading hero, or martyr or whatever with that assassination attempt."

"But isn't he one of us now?" The voice is high and piping.

That must be Tootie. I remember her from Hippocrises. She's huge, as big as Lamborghini. Why is it that so often the biggest people have the highest voices? Part of Gilligan is grappling to make sense of Deela's discourse while another part of his mind is drifting amidst trivialities, wanting only to go to sleep.

"For now, Tootie. But that won't last. Angelica, innocent, sexy saint that she is, will be loving to anyone she's near, but that Dillard creep is heading for a few months in jail. Trust me, she won't be 'there' for him when he gets out. And hell hath no fury like an assassin sannyasin scorned."

There is more laughter.

"So you see my pretties," Deela goes on, "it is all orchestration and timing. We turn up the heat slowly, carefully. When the stove's on fire, when the commune is attacked, that is the time that we seize the moment, and, as our redneck friends would say, skedaddle."

"Dayla, you are a genius. It is an honor and a privilege to be your co-conspirator."

"But what if—"

"Lucifia, hush. Chloe, you were saying?"

Gilligan's head feels like it's spinning like Linda Blair's in *The Exorcist*. In danger of losing his footing on the ladder, he closes the hatch above him and clambers down to the base of the shaft. The lights click on, blinding him, making the backs of his eyes hurt. He buries his face in his arms and crumples into the fetal position at the base of the ladder. With blood still oozing from the wound in his head, he loses consciousness and, as the lights click off again, he falls into nothingness for more than an hour. When he awakens the bleeding has stopped, but a massive headache remains. He is unsure if what he thought he heard was real or a dream. He wants it to be a dream. He moves as quickly as he can back down the tunnel, forgetting all about nonsense like the Gait of Power.

10. Hoodoo Canyon

Eight horses came with the ranch when it was purchased by the commune in the fall of 1981. They are housed in a small barn, about half way between the Truck Farm and the cafeteria, not far from Gilligan's and Newfyamo's abode in Fareezuryingyang. Gilligan's horse, given to him for his morning mission with Lionheart, is named Bear. Bear was so named because as a foal he lost the upper third of his ears to frostbite one cold New Year's Eve. The former owners of the Big Snake Ranch, the no-good McStonehead brothers, got so damn drunk down in Bend that they failed to barn the horses. It is said the McStoneheads now live in a hotel in Vegas, gambling and drinking away the millions that the 'red people' overpaid them for their land. Their legacies are the horses, and the name of Little Snake Creek, which the Divine Bhagwan decided to retain.

Bear is wending his way along a dusty path that leads to Hoodoo Canyon, which is located on ranch property some five miles south of the Bhagwanville town centre. Lionheart apparently chose to take Gilligan on this mission because of his bricklaying experience. They must select stones with which to cap the rim of the ceremonial Yahoo! Waterfall and to face the ceremonial Yahoo! Bridge in front of the Master's house. Hoodoo Canyon, named for the several totem-like obelisks that crowd its northern end, is a sacred site of some renown in shamanistic circles. Accessible only by horseback or helicopter, it is part of the lore of the Ranch. It is said that Wovoka, the well-known turn of the century medicine man, regularly did the ghost dance there, as did his predecessors through the ages. It is fitting that the stones for the enlightened Master's ceremonial waterfall, the centerpiece of Shangri Ohlala, should come from the holiest heart of the high desert. Such a fact will certainly merit a mention in the brochure for next year's Second Annual Universal Celebration, which promises to far eclipse the first as a cosmic happening.

It is mid morning. The long ride is not uncomfortable for Gilligan, who at age fourteen spent two weeks at a dude ranch in British Columbia. His attitude then, thanks to his natural affinity for riding, was a rare deviation from the usual sullen, hormonally-charged resentment of that age. He actually enjoyed himself, as he is now. On the other hand, Lionheart's stiff-backed posture, and the frequency with which he stands up in the stirrups, indicates that he'd be much more comfortable in his jeep. For the first half hour of the ride, until they move out of Motorola range, he constantly issues instructions back to Bang Pas Zoo. Now, his apparent discomfort does not preclude him from belting out, again and again, to the sunlit hills through which they've been threading their way, the only cowboy songs he knows: *Home on the Range* and *Sweet Baby James.*

It is at the painful nadir of a particularly flat note that Bear spooks. The handsome bay gelding shoots ninety degrees off the path at a gallop, stopping well up a steep hillside so slippery with gravel that Gilligan is forced to dismount and walk him back down.

"What the hell made him do that?"

Lionheart, who was well ahead on the path and has returned, hoarks and gobs.

"Dunno, pardner. Rattlesnake, I reckon. These hills are full of 'em."

Irrepressible, dwarfish, with his fulsome rusty beard flecked with grey, Lionheart could, by appearances, be anywhere between thirty and sixty years old. He reminds Gilligan of a human stump—one that has sprouted fresh-sapped branches from a hundred knots. He is, in fact, forty four. A helicopter and fighter jet pilot in Vietnam, he spent two years air-lifting the wounded out of the jungles and rice paddies of the Mekong delta. He flew one of the choppers that hovered over the embassy's rooftop during the Americans' final, graceless exit from Saigon. He came home to Texas, shell shocked and strung out, to find his wife had a daughter by another man and was doing very well thank-you. He took a job doing construction in Libya for a couple of years, then headed back to the Far East to find himself. He ended up in Spoona in the late seventies and, after a year of dynamic meditations, was drug-free and in love with Shenilla, the British milliner and medium to the Divine Bhagwan.

"Holy shit!" Gilligan scrambles back atop Bear. He forgot about the rattlesnakes.

"Come on, man," laughs Lionheart, "it's just the other side of that pass."

The pass into Hoodoo Canyon is, at times, not much wider than a horse. It feels cool and damp deep in the shadows of rock walls which tower up to forty feet high on either side. At times, the stirruped toes of Gilligan's work boots scrape the unyielding surfaces to either side. When they emerge into the sunlight, his eyes are dazzled.

The canyon climbs in front of them like a rough, broad staircase the size of side by side football fields. The 'stairs', which are gradients of gravel and rock, incline and slope inwards in a rough 'V', forming a rude channel that the horses traverse the bottom of. It is here that spring floodwaters exit and find their way to Little Snake Creek and the Big Snake River. The upper third of the canyon is a single broad ledge from which sprout, bathed in the gold of the morning sun, eight magnificent hoodoos. The tallest is perhaps thirty feet high, the smallest the height of a man. These totemic pillars, formed from volcanic tuff capped by basalt, stand in a ragged semi-circle. They remind Gilligan of chivalrous knights in golden helmets, gathered to fulfill a sacred quest.

In the forefront of the hoodoos, set like an altar in a nave, is a massive flat boulder, the same tawny color as the backs of Bear's ears. Seated on this boulder are two men: one dressed in white; one dressed in red. One bearded. One clean shaven. They sit as straight and still as the hoodoos casting shadows behind them. They are deep in meditation. Having tied their horses in the shade, Gilligan is half way to the sunlit ledge when his eyes confirm what his heart already knew. The man dressed in white is Alchemendra. From his previous encounter many weeks earlier in the month of May, Gilligan knows worlds of dangerous possibilities are about to open. As they approach the two meditating figures, his mind flashes back to his last encounter with the famous womanizer and magician:

It was early Sunday evening, May 16, 1982, the end of Alchemendra's workshop at Buck Lake, on a retreat property northeast of Toronto. Somewhere in the western gloom the sun hovered. A windless May rain, severe enough to subdue the black flies, pattered on the forest's leaves and drummed on the overhanging deck. The lake's far shore was a gauzy outline of fir trees clambering up the horizon. The renovated barn was constructed of stacked firewood mortared together to form walls half an arm's-length thick. Its hayloft, floored with gleaming maple, was a spacious studio where the workshop took place. The former stable area below contained sleeping areas, kitchen, and bathroom facilities. French doors opened from the studio to the deck, under which Gilligan and the others waited. Workshop participants gathered at the lower entrance in a lumpy V formation. At its apex, a dazzling white Lincoln Continental limousine purred contentedly, headlights on dim. Wipers swished every nine seconds. Gilligan swayed with the others, singing sannyasin songs to the strumming of Newfyamo's guitar. All felt great. All were waiting to say farewell to the man who had been their infuser of spirit throughout the weekend workshop.

Alchemendra had been` a mildly innovative British therapist before becoming a sannyasin of the Divine Bhagwan. It is said that during a discourse back in the old days in Spoona, the Divine Bhagwan stopped in mid-sentence to suddenly shout: "Alchemendra! The goose is out!" Alchemendra had a verifiable satori in that moment. He became a dazzling group leader, an energy phenomenon that began to think it might actually be enlightened.

Energy was the key. Energy trapped, repressed in the musculature, in the dormant cells of those who were unconscious had to be released. It was kept there by thought, by recurring thoughts of anger, jealousy, worry, guilt, and shame, thoughts that the thinker, by and large, was not conscious of. These thoughts wound around the repression over and over like the filaments of a spider's web, binding the energy in a Promethean trap. The Divine Bhagwan had showed him that mastery of his own energy, of the elemental vibrations of his body, allowed him to reach directly into the trapped energies of others and release them. Alchemendra further realized that the group leader's ability to seduce every beautiful woman in sight was gratifyingly helpful to the flow of energy within the group dynamic.

At Buck Lake, Alchemendra worked with pure Shaktipat, a direct energy transfer from Master to disciple. He'd arranged participants in formations- you here, you there, place your hand between his shoulders, touch her hips very lightly... he pressed here, touched there, incanted affirmations, guided relaxations... rock anthems would swell from a badass ghetto blaster on cue as blissful energy would seemingly flow through the room.

Only seemingly because Satyam Gilligan John Price was mired at the end of the energy formation lines. When those around him were falling to the floor in bliss, he was contemplating the scene with a mixture of bemusement and anxiety, unsure whether to topple with the gang or perhaps assume a middle way and just go to his knees. Occasionally he felt a little something; once he even sobbed briefly when a needle of joy pricked his heart.

Alchemendra struck Gilligan as being more affable than imposing. He was a handsome man, perhaps in his mid fifties, with long hair-a style becoming somewhat outdated in sannyasin circles. Since the Master's move to America from India, the 'now' style featured a clean shave, short hair, and an entrepreneurial fervor to make good in Ronald Reagan's America. Alchemendra's beard was also long, much like the Master's, though of a reddish hue. The eyes, framed by bushy brows encroached by grey, were hazel, and bespoke an exceptionally keen intelligence. He seemed to John Price surprisingly approachable, as if he were ready to share an important secret meant just for him.

Each participant experienced a one on one conversation with Alchemendra as part of the group proceedings. As Gilligan stood before the man at the apex of the group 'V', something had happened in his belly. It was an inner vortex, akin to anxiety, but far more delicious. He felt urged to action, like a child that sees others playing.

"So Satyam Gilligan," Alchemendra said. "How is it going?"

"Right now, pretty good."

There had been laughter from the group.

"You are obviously not lacking in intelligence." The tone of Alchemendra's voice was resonant and pleasing; the cadence patrician and distinctly English. "But you are defensive. I knew you were defensive the instant you walked in that door."

There was a long pause. Solemnity slid into the atmosphere of barely suppressed mirth like a front of low pressure.

"So what are *you* going to *do* about it?"

Alchemendra had emphasized the 'you' and 'do' in a way that seemed to thump into Gilligan's solar plexus. He was suspended, strung out on his feet in the middle of the room, a blossoming muddle of conflicting compulsions. The question hovered, like an insistent hummingbird probing his flower of uncertainty.

"Well?" said Alchemendra very gently.

"That's a deep subject."

Laughter cannonaded off the walls.

"You are funny. Why is that?"

"I guess... so people will like me."

"Ah. Otherwise they wouldn't?"

"I don't know."

"Does love need a reason?"

"In theory, no."

More laughter.

"Of course this," Alchemendra fingered his mala, "and these red clothes, aren't a theory are they?"

Gilligan had no riposte. He felt like he was being scourged with a whip of feathered silk.

Alchemendra smiled at him radiantly. "They are an adventure, aren't they?"

"Yes."

After this conversation something let go in John Price Satyam Gilligan. He began to enjoy himself, to trust what was happening around him and within him. The only negative workshop notes were sounded by boyfriends or husbands whose narrow viewpoints caused constrictive karma. Transcendent energetic adventures, if a couple has the courage to let go, can only enrich a relationship once the overflowing distaff half returns. Alas, some failed to understand. One very large Swami from Australia threatened to push Alchemendra's nose down into the region of his second chakra. An ugly scene was avoided as the ma in question stood by her man, rubbed his chest and called him 'her big ape'. She forwent the energy phenomenon experience, however transcendent.

Gilligan's highlight was the post dinner entertainment on Saturday night. Toronto's Megadharm centre presented an impromptu Wizard of Oz skit. Ramastan, Newfyamo, Droopbshant, and Suredear dazzled as Scarecrow, Cowardly Lion, Tin Man and Dorothy while Gilligan, his ponytail released under a conical hat, did a star turn as the Wicked Witch of the West. Cackling through the fireside romp thawed some of the highland chill that had been bred into his bones. Two of the youngest women, glomming onto him as a surrogate androgynous rock god, chased him round the hearth at the performance's close, eager to tug at his hair and steal his hat.

At the end of the workshop, the group wedged in anticipation outside the Buck Lake portal sang along with Newfyamo's guitar:

We all move like big fluffy clouds
blown by the breeze of a flute
Home to you....
La lalalala lalalala lalalala home to you...

It reached a crescendo and stopped. All closed their eyes. Hands folded into the namaste. Alchemendra was coming. Gilligan could feel it. He opened his eyes as the magician appeared in the doorway wearing white cotton pants, a snowy white sweatshirt, and a white silk jacket. A white painter's cap perched atop the flow of ruddy hair. Fronting the sweatshirt and cap was the stylized image of a goose in flight. His mala (the wooden beaded necklace with the picture of the Divine Bhagwan in its locket) if he was wearing it, was underneath the sweatshirt. His hands folded together in Namaste. An 'oh my god' and a few collective groans sounded above the rain.

Alchemendra up to then had been wearing red, like themselves a disciple of the Divine Bhagwan. White was a Master's color, one the Divine Bhagwan had worn exclusively until his burgeoning discipleship had upgraded his wardrobe.

A few of the 'older' sannyasins turned and walked away into the rain. They didn't look back.

Satyam Gilligan was astounded by Alchemendra's blasphemous change in apparel. The two discerning swee- thearts, who had been so taken with his wicked witch, ran to Alchemendra and threw themselves sobbing at his feet. Evi- dently they were easily moved. White sleeves rose, a hand set- tled on each of their heads; their sobs turned to sighs. The white wizard moved towards the car, leaving the supine teens whimpering ecstatically in his wake.

Gilligan found himself stepping forward with new- found temerity.

"So what's with the white clothes?"

"Ah yes. You've noticed the clothes. Impossible to miss I suppose. I choose white because in the new frontier I'm one of the good guys... not a bad girl."

He brought his thumb onto Gilligan's third eye, his face very close, and whispered:

"Remember this: there's something rotten in the state of Oregon!"

If he had been somewhat numb to the influence of Alchemendra's magic earlier, Gilligan was now struck head on. Warmth pierced his chest. Like a teabag hitting hot water, a core of preciousness unfolded tendrils of sensitivity from his chest throughout his body. He staggered against the bark of a cedar deck post. His cheek to the moist, fragrant roughness, he grinned, goofily contented. Alchemendra moved on.

Ma Prem Pow, the Toronto centre leader, her face over- cast with concern, held open the Lincoln's rear door. The re- maining people, stunned, but grateful, moved with the car, touching its windows in farewell, their hair beaded up with droplets. Gilligan remained at his post, his beautiful post, lost among the gray shades that flowed like milling crowds over the surface of the dimpling lake. The Lincoln glided away, noiseless on a carpet of wet leaves. Gilligan slid down, squatted knees to chest, and watched rivulets finding their way home along a million and one pathways.

In the present, in Hoodoo canyon, before Gilligan and Lionheart get too close, the clean-shaven man in red whose features are shadowed namastes briefly to Alchemendra and even more briefly to Gilligan and Lionheart. He pulls the hood of his sweatshirt more snugly around his chin and disappears amongst the hoodoos and their shadows. His figure is tall and elegant, and niggles with familiarity.

"Someone doesn't want to be recognized," he whispers to Lionheart.

Shh." Lionheart puts his forefinger briefly to his lips, then holds it upright, truncating Gilligan's inquiry.

"Hey man, where the hell did you get the suit?" Lionheart shouts at Alchemendra, who has stood up to greet them. The erstwhile group leader is wearing a white, double breasted Armani suit complete with a Western style bowtie cinched with a diamond clasp.

"I got it in Toronto, actually. A store on the Danforth. Hello Satyam Gilligan. Or should I perhaps call you Hamlet?"

Gilligan feels a jolt of energy strike him in the breastbone. Alchemendra is grinning broadly at him as he embraces Lionheart who has scrambled up on the stage-like ledge.

"Hello Alchemendra. That's still your name isn't it?" Gilligan feels he is grinning stupidly.

"Yes. Though barely. Excommunication by Pope Deela appears to be looming."

"Oh yeah," says Lionheart. "Those bitches would feed me my own nuts if they knew I was meeting you."

"Of course they would. I was in the neighborhood on some corporate business (Alchemendra gives a jaunty little tug on his lapels) and thought I'd touch base with my old friends, and one newer one."

Alchemendra winks briefly at Gilligan then puts an arm around Lionheart and strolls with him towards the hoodoos. He lowers his voice, but not so much that Gilligan cannot overhear.

"I've heard, through a certain Swami Buckstar, that Deela and company have obtained a considerable supply of cocaine and God knows what other drugs. We both know it's just a matter of time before her power trip blows up in her face. I don't want the old boy to be blown up with her."

"Sorry, man," replies Lionheart. "We tried to slip you in to see him. I was even willing to drop you down with the 'copter when he was out on his drive, but Deela and the samurais have been riding shotgun with him every day. She'd arrest you for sure. All that time he was in silence, Deela has been consolidating her power. Shenilla says that even those who live in his house, where there are no security guys allowed, are getting paranoid, thinking they're being spied upon.

"That wouldn't surprise me." says Alchemendra. "As I mentioned, I've lucked into a corporate job quite nearby, since Deela ordered all sannyasins to stop attending my workshops. It shouldn't be overly long before I'm back in the neighborhood."

He wheels and strides towards Gilligan. "And what about you, rabbit ears? Have you heard what we've been saying?"

Gilligan nods as the magician squats on the ledge above him and holds his gaze with his piercing hazel eyes. "You're right about the drugs." Gilligan is almost whispering. "I've seen them in action."

"Indeed," says Alchemendra thoughtfully. He continues to gaze. Gilligan has the sensation of falling into the moment. He feels the sun move a notch up the sky, warming his ear and cheek. Beyond the walls of the canyon behind Alchemendra, there's the sound of a chain saw, or a dirt bike starting up.

"You have a role in this," Alchemendra says softly. "Let it come to you. Make good choices." He stands and gestures towards Lionheart and the faint sound of the revving motor. "I've got to go."

A quick embrace of Lionheart, a brief salute to Gilligan, and Alchemendra disappears amongst the hoodoos. Gilligan notices his running shoes, as dazzlingly white as the rest of his ensemble, have small, crimson lights in the heels, which glow with every step. Lionheart hops down from the dais.

"What was that all about?" Gilligan could not have been more astonished if the hoodoos had started dancing.

"What was what all about?" Lionheart looks as serious as a soldier ready for battle.

"That! Him! Did he want me here for some reason? And who was that other guy? He looked kind of familiar..."

Lionheart again holds up the forefinger. "Loose lips sink ships." His grave look hasn't changed. "Nothing happened here. Nothing. Right?"

The questions clawing at Gilligan's lips gradually retreat to his brain, where they will keep a restless vigil for many months.

"Right," he says finally.

"Now," says Lionheart. "Let's pick out some rocks! We'll stack 'em up there, near the base of that hoodoo. I'll be landing the chopper in that clear area."

They head for the north-facing wall of the canyon, where the rocks are strewn plentifully, and pleasingly mottled with the greenish, sickly sweet hues of lichen and moss. For the rest of the morning they stack the rocks, speaking only when the work demands it.

11. The Rock Crusher

It is Gilligan's first day as crew leader of the rock crusher. He has told no one of what he saw from below the map table, nor of what happened in Hoodoo canyon. Both events are shrouded in a miasma of dreamlike implausibility doubtless enhanced by the whack his noggin took in the tunnel. So too his vision of the blonde ma at the motor pool site. He had even asked Lionheart about her again, but he said she was not Bang Pas Zoo and must have just been volunteering for the day. As near as he could tell, she was gone, back to Sweden, or wherever it was she was from. He renewed his resolve to remain in the moment, to trust the universe to unfold as it should and to at all costs remain at the Ranch, to be a part of the Buddhafield.

As it happens, his crew at the rock crusher consists of one very appealing, but very dangerous young ma named Vavaloma. The very same Vavaloma whom his van from Stonedharm in L.A. picked up hitchhiking on an Oregon highway. The eighteen-year-old whose very overt 'friendliness' had precipitated the end of his relationship with Bala. She is wearing, as is Gilligan, standard rock crusher garb consisting of a zippered red coverall, hardhat, steel-toed work boots, and orange headphone-type hearing protection.

The control room of the machine, accessed by a steel-ringed ladder, is small, warm and noisy. A fine rain falls outside. The controls they oversee are stark: red and green punch buttons the size of a teacup's bottom located twelve inches apart on an inclined panel. One for stop. One for go. Large windows all around the booth allow the occupants to monitor the crushing process as it happens. A ramped conveyor belt runs from one huge steel hopper up into the maw of a second, located below the window above the control panel. To the rear another longer belt escalates the finished product— gravel, crushed by steel rollers and sifted by screens— and dribbles it in a pebbly stream onto a conical hill. Dump trucks deposit rocks to be crushed and pick up finished aggregate from any of the three piles created by the crusher. A front-end loader stands ready to service the trucks.

Traffic has been sporadic thus far. The rain, which began the night before, has muddied things up, slowing work on the dam and roadway projects. Gilligan's main tasks are to start and stop the machine and to watch the hoppers, making sure that rocks don't get jammed and fail to fall to the crushing wheels below. Jams are dislodged by prodding the recalcitrant rocks with long metal bars.

Gilligan is explaining this to Vavaloma when a dump truck arrives, allowing them to do some hands-on training with the prods. Now, in the vibrating control room, sweaty and damp from their exertions in the warm summer rain, Vavaloma unzips her jumpsuit to navel level, revealing pert breasts encumbered only by a loose fitting pink undershirt. She is a sexy little package, with blue eyes and long crinkly blond hair that is tucked up under her hardhat for safety around the machines. She has rosebud pink lips and adorable little white teeth. But she comes with a serious warning label.

Lionheart, when he dropped her off in his mud splattered jeep, said something about a threat from her father, who threatening charges for the abduction of a minor. Somehow he was in thrall to the absurd notion that she'd been brainwashed by a cult. She'd been assigned here, to the outer limits of the ranch, as a precaution. Lionheart specifically warned him about hanky panky.

"This one is totally out of bounds, by order of the legal department. No sex. Pretend you are British." Lionheart had winked before hitting the horn for a parting RAW CAW.

Now, high in the cramped control room, Vavaloma's headphones vibrate in concert with the demi-globes of her breasts. Gilligan notices her luscious salmon-pink lips are moving. She is talking to him. He gestures non-comprehension. She slides across their shared bench, lifts his headphones a crack, and brings those lips close to this right ear.

"What do you do for excitement while the machine is running?"

Her breath is like warm, enlivening rain on his cheek. Her right hand is on his leg.

"Oh," he says brightly, Lionheart's warning still fresh in his mind, "I've got a book."

He indicates *Beezlebub's Tales to his Grandson* by George Gurdjieff which is sitting on the ledge above the control panel.

"Or I watch the rocks. In fact," he says, starting to get up, "I think I see a few have fallen off the belt. I better go get them."

Her hands on his shoulders stop him. She kisses him on the mouth.

"You're so cute," she says. "You were in the van and here you are again. There must be a karma connection there. I can't decide whether to fall in love with you or not."

A feeling of apprehension well beyond performance anxiety fails to prevent him from kissing her back.

"All these vibrations are making me horny," she says with a distinct absence of shyness. "Let's do it here while we're watching the rocks."

"Uh, sounds good, but I'm afraid I can't have sex with you. Orders from the boss."

She is unzipping his jumpsuit, deftly traversing the folds and moguls on the slope to his groin. He puts his hand on hers and an overly earnest expression on his face.

"Vavaloma. Really. I can't have sex. I've gotten some special warnings about it."

"Fine." Her tongue is stroking his earlobe. His protective headphones are dangerously discombobulated, his red hard hat askew. "We won't go all the way then," she whispers. "I promise."

He is being seduced more easily than a foolish school-girl— by a foolish schoolgirl. Her hand frees itself from his limp effort at resistance. Her slender fingers, adorned by pink nail polish badly in need of a touch up, plunge into his under garment like an Olympic tower diver, and encircle his rapidly stiffening dick. Gilligan, along with unspeakable pleasure that makes him gasp and yield his earlobe more deeply into the warm Jacuzzi of her mouth, feels a twinge of real resistance within his usual hung-up smog— courtesy of the transplanted Victorianism that hovered over his childhood like the odor of rancid cheese. He will rebuke this misguided teenager, tell her in no uncertain terms that they cannot, dare not, go against the wishes of the duly appointed authority figures within the ranch hierarchy. But, as her cascade of blonde curls tumbles from beneath the hardhat and headphones which clatter onto the wine-dark floor of their booth, he realizes that what they are about to do is not having sex at all.

It is mere play. A spontaneous conversation. Sex, real sex is unquestionably the act of intercourse itself. Not going all the way, is, for heaven sakes, just harmless frolic. Not sex in the biblical sense. No, this is more tantric- a spiritual joining, a Vulcan mind melding of energies. Vavaloma is unquestionably a very spiritual entity...oh God yes, very very spiritual—oh yeah, right at the head of the class when it comes to—

Gilligan's thoughts, exalted to steep and lofty heights by Vavaloma's spirited exertions, are sucked back to earth as the door to the control room is flung open and a man wearing a powder blue Persephone track suit is framed in the door-way.

"Mandy!" he screams. "What in heaven's name are you doing?"

His words are clearly audible, though the din from the crusher has doubled with the opening of the door. Mandy's fine head comes up and she peeks over her shoulder.

138

"Daddy?"

The man grabs Vavaloma and wrenches her to his side. "Come on. We're going home."

"No. I want to stay here," she pouts.

"Excuse me, sir," says Gilligan, getting to his feet while adjusting his clothing. "I don't think you have the right to—"

"The right!" screams the man, turning on Gilligan and pushing him hard in the chest. "She's sixteen years old you piece of shit! Sixteen!"

The last word is almost sobbed as the man turns again towards his daughter and the door. Vavaloma is crying. Gilligan puts his hand on the man's shoulder.

"But she—" he begins.

The man, whose name is Mr. Jones, explodes with a burst of superhuman strength. An accountant by trade, he is not large. His lanky body is hunched at the shoulders; there is a distinct paunch under the folds of his sweatshirt. But, like a mother who miraculously lifts the rear end of a minivan that is crushing her child, adrenaline, testosterone, and other endocrinal fluids course through his limbs. He turns on Gilligan with a primal snarl, grabs the open folds of the swami's coverall and flings him backwards up and over the control panel into the safety glass window which, impacted by Gilligan's helmet and shoulders, breaks into a thousand tiny cubes. An unseen membrane holds it together, embracing the contours of Gilligan's body in a bulging, translucent mosaic. But then, like the rink-side glass of long ago under Maurice Richard's skate, it dissolves and falls, allowing Gilligan to tumble backwards over the window ledge into the rock crushing hopper below.

Darkness. Glimpses of gray sky. Bouncing and jouncing. Drizzle on eyelids. Headache. Gilligan is vaguely aware of motion, of being bound, wrapped from feet to neck in the smell of wet rubber. He is being transported. The metal bed of the vehicle thumps his back with every bump. It stops. He hears voices.

"Who the hell is this?" Gruff. Unfamiliar.

"I don't know. He... fell. Back at the machine. I think he took a knock or two from the stones. He was lucky there were just a few left and that the grate held. I couldn't just leave him there."

Familiar. Vavaloma's father.

"So this is a cultist," murmurs the first voice. "I've never seen one up this close before. Well, leave him where he is. Let's get the truck on the barge."

There's a lurch and a bumping up of wheels, front then back. A metal gate clangs shut. The headache is so intense that he doesn't want to open his eyes or move his head. Drizzle turns to rain, pattering Gilligan's forehead in a steady rhythm. He is floating, wafting in a slow eddy on the sounds of the rain. Rivulets of water run down his face into his ears. There is a spattering and pinging of droplets on rubber and metal. He is turning slowly on the bosom of a river, the great heart of an engine beating below him. The rain, like the rapid pats of a massage therapist, is pummeling his headache and his consciousness down and down through the bottom of the boat into cold waters where rainbow trout are suspended-— waiting their chance to jump and glisten in the morning sun.

There is a dead baby with the trout. Its eyes are frozen open. He is afraid they will be eaten away, with minnows swimming through them, but they are wide and blue and beseeching. There's deep sadness, an urge to help, to resuscitate. With an infant, you put your mouth over both the tiny nose and mouth. Watch the little chest expand with brief puffs of air. He'd learned that by the blue waters of a pool, practicing on a baby-sized doll. He reaches out, tries to hold the podgy arms. But the baby's skin is cold and nubbed, like the uncooked chicken from his mother's fridge. The child slips from his grasp, floats slowly away. The sad face and blue eyes turn to reveal a precious white baby's bottom— like from a diaper commercial. Bubbles emerge from the base of the pristine crack, farts in the bathtub.

Now he is playing golf with his father and other men, his dad's friends from the country club. But he can't tee it up. The golf ball is made of soggy bread. It slumps over the tee and topples off it. He has to hit it now because the men are already on their way down the fairway. He tries and tries but it is hopeless. The men are now far off on a distant green. He thinks he hears his father calling him, but knows he is really addressing someone else. A thread breaks. Frayed ends float downwards. The sound of rain. Darkness

12. Persephone's Office

Gilligan wakes up in a huge circular office filled with light. Someone is talking, but not to him. His headache has receded to a dull pain that coats his skull like hair. He touches a tender swelling just above and behind his left ear. It is a more toxic cousin to the one on top of his head, the seventh chakra clunker suffered in the tunnel a couple nights earlier. He wonders vaguely what became of his red hardhat, which in fact is in pummeled red shreds at the apex of the three quarter inch aggregate hill back at the rock crusher.

He is reclining at the pillowed end of an upholstered leather couch which bends with the circumference of the room. The leather, fragrant and reddish brown, reminds Gilligan of his father's lazy boy chair—one of the few items that went with him when he and John Price's mother separated for good some five years previous. The room, which is the top floor of a renovated barn silo, is round, and perhaps forty feet across. It is encircled by windows bright with late afternoon sun.

He sees a vista of hills, buttes, and mesas receding into the distance. The rain has yielded to a high blue sky castled by white nimbus clouds that are bellied with a tinge of grey. Centered in the window beside Gilligan's head is the peak of a Victorian farmhouse with a cast iron weathervane in the form of a nude woman poised to throw a spear. It is remarkably graceful—a huntress, Diana or Athena—according to the best information the marijuana-muddled mnemonics from his university years is able to retrieve.

He tunes in to the voice that is speaking: It is powerful, with resonant timbres in the lower registers. In its tones, cadences and vocabulary, it implicitly bespeaks the supreme importance of both the medium and the message.

"Yes. Hello. It's me again. Yes, Mr. Dark, from across the river. Listen, Miss Chloe, I've spoken to your security people and they are unable to help me. Everything, it seems, short of when one dares to sneeze, has to go through Ms. Deela... Oh, really, she has rules about that too, does she? You've been very kind Miss— ... all right, Chloe; I understand she's busy, but one of your people has been injured and is here in my care. I'm attempting to facilitate his return to you... Very well. I'll hold."

The man, who has been hidden by the high back of his leather swivel chair stands and begins to pace. He is trim, in his mid forties. He wears faded bluejeans and a bright blue golf shirt emblazoned with the Persephone diving bird logo. His hair, a uniform silver gray, is cut short. It contrasts with lush, coal-colored eyebrows. These, combined with Paul Newmanesque blue eyes, give him an aspect which is pleasant, unsettling, and remarkable.

"So, you've joined the land of the living." He flashes Gilligan a brief smile, revealing large, perfectly aligned, white teeth.

"I guess so." Gilligan, struggles to sit up, but feels woozy and must lie back.

"Take it easy. We're quite sure you have some form of concussion. You've taken a few whacks on the old cantaloupe. I'm in touch with your people right now."

Gilligan feels a twinge of discomfort on hearing Chloe referred to as 'his people'. Somewhere deep inside of him, under his layers of passivity, perhaps inspired by his interlude with Lionheart and Alchemendra, part of him (unknown to himself) is preparing to go to war with the bitches.

"I'm Alvin Dark," continues the man. "You're at the Executive Research Center for Persephone Shoes International. We own this spread" — here he gestures towards the rounded hills, mesas and buttes extending to the horizon beyond the window on Gilligan's left— "most of which is across the river from your commune. Certain circumstances have caused you to be, for the time being, our guest."

Dark, who continued his pacing, now approaches Gilligan. "Do you remember how you got here?"

Before Gilligan can answer, there is a crackling from a speaker on Dark's desk.

"Dayla will speak to you now," comes the Aussie twang of Chloe.

"Excuse me a moment please," says Alvin Dark. The man is brisk, but genuinely courteous. He returns to his desk and picks up a handset tethered by a whip-thin retracting cord.

"Miss Deela," he says, "it's a great pleasure to finally speak to you."

Even from some fifteen feet away, Deela's angry tones can be heard. Dark, in self defence, removes the handset to a position two or three inches from his ear. Gilligan is able to make out the words 'kidnapping', 'trespassing', 'illegal', 'sneaky', and 'big fucking lawsuit'.

"But... but Miss Deela... you have to understand that... Really Miss Deela your man here... All right your *swami* here isn't a prisoner… No. No... She is with her father now... Yes that's right... No, he can leave whenever he wishes, it's just that... No, we haven't hurt him, apparently there was an incident involving your machinery... some safety glass broke according to Mr. Jones... Certainly, Miss Deela, feel free to call the FBI... As far as I know Mr. Jones is on his way to Vancouver right now... Yes she is... Yes... Willingly... quite willingly, yes... She broke down crying here in my office and hugged her father... She is his daughter, Miss Deela and, I was told, just sixteen years old... He seems fine though he likely has a mild concussion; there are two wounds on his head though one seems older... I was only told that he fell into some machinery...Yes, I did ask, but was told it was better if I didn't know... Mr. Jones, or rather his lawyer, over the phone...It's a free country Miss Deela. You can sue us if you wish, although Mr. Jones' lawyer mentioned something about possible charges involving the abduction of a minor..."

Here Alvin Dark holds the receiver away from his ear for several seconds. He looks at Gilligan with raised eyebrows that bespeak astonishment tinged with mild amusement.

"Ms. Deela," he is finally allowed to continue, "I appreciate your point of view on this, I do, but perhaps we can move on to another subject. I am given to understand that you have a son of mine in your commune. If I understand the reports correctly, he attempted to assassinate the Bhagwan, and has now joined your religion. Is that correct?"

Dark has wandered to the far side of the circular room. His handset's tether stretches as taut as a fishing line that's hooked a marlin. "So there was a hearing this morning? He pleaded guilty but the commune pressed for lenience? Interesting. No... no... no, Ms. Deela, I am not proposing any kind of trade or swap. Dillard is a free man, just like your uh swami here... I just want your assurance that he has not been harmed. He is a bit emotionally unstable and... yes... yes... that's good I suppose... Listen Ms. Deela, I have a suggestion: I will make our barge available to you for crossing the river. I'm sure you're familiar with our dock and parcel of land adjacent to your farming area? Send whomever you like to pick up your- swami here and I will see that they are safely returned to your property. Or, if you would do me the honor of coming yourself, then I would be pleased to offer you a dinner this evening, if you like. We have an excellent chef on the premises... yes, Ms. Deela, I understand your people are strictly vegetarian... oh, seafood is OK for you then... and you don't mind fowl if its well prepared...filet mignon, only if it is free range? Yes, understood... no emu meat though, OK, we'll keep that in mind. Woody does a roast duck that is out of this world. How many shall we expect in your party? Three or four? That sounds delightful. We'll look forward to seeing you tonight...fine...bye for now.

Alvin Dark walks slowly and thoughtfully back to his desk. There is a faint clicking sound as the telephone's extension wire reels in.

"You hungry?"

Gilligan nods.

Dark punches a button on the telephone. "Woody, send us up a plate of cheese and crackers and of couple of cold beers, will you please. Wait a sec— beer OK?"

Gilligan nods enthusiastically.

"Hey!" he exclaims when a tray bearing bottles, frosty mugs and assorted edibles is brought by a large, athletic looking young man wearing blue jeans, a Persephone t-shirt, and a freshly scrubbed smile. "Northwest Passage! That's the stuff we get at the Ranch!"

Several minutes pass as Gilligan munches and sips away. Dark continues moving about, shuffling or signing papers, nibbling from the tray, pacing back and forth, thinking. Gilligan has soon eaten everything, even the pickles and olives. He is wet-fingering salty cracker crumbs when Dark wheels his office chair into the curve of the leather couch, and sits down.

"Do you feel well enough to talk?"

Gilligan nods as he tilts his mug's bottom skywards.

"Another beer?"

"Sure. Thanks."

"Tell me about this Ranch of yours. I am curious about it."

"You mean in regard to what happened to your son?"

Gilligan's solar plexus tightens with guilt.

"My son," spits Dark, rising from his chair and pacing, "is a grown... person and free to do what he likes. Frankly, he's weak. He'll fall for whatever goofy idea is out there— first he was a pothead hippie, then a born-again Christian redneck, and now I gather he's become one of you people, wearing red clothes and beads and worshipping someone's picture around his neck!"

Gilligan is about to explain that the one hundred and eight beads on the mala symbolize all the different methods of meditation and that the mala locket with the Master's picture is simply a reminder that enlightenment is a possibility each of us wears, but Alvin Dark ploughs ahead with Dillard's story.

"Two years ago he walked into Portland campus, and announced to anyone who would listen that he was my son." Dark produces a Persephone monogrammed hankie from a pocket and blows his nose violently.

"Turns out, he was right. Way back, when I was a pup starting out in sales, I bluffed my way into a high-powered seminar in Las Vegas. I'd had a few drinks in one of the room parties. She was a chambermaid, stocking linen in a storeroom. It just— happened. Next morning, on my way to checkout, I passed her with my luggage. She was pushing the towel cart. She winked at me. Then I forgot about her completely.

"She raised him in Vegas, sometimes working nights as a hatcheck girl and doing god knows what else. No wonder he's such a screw-up. She figured out who I was a few years ago when she read my autobiography." He jumps up and strides to a nearby bookcase. He plucks a volume from it and tosses it to Gilligan. **'Alvin Dark's Light of the Sole'** is the title boldly lettered above his host's hugely smiling face. Nudging into the frame is a Persephone running shoe with its patented pressure activated heel-light glowing rosily alongside Mr. Dark's pearly whites.

"Have you read it?"

Gilligan shakes his head. He remembers Alchemendra walking away in Hoodoo Canyon, heel-lights aglow.

"Keep it as a souvenir. It explains the seventeen secrets of success."

Gilligan is about to ask what they might be, when Dark continues.

"So there he is, confirmed as my son. He has nowhere to go, no calling, no vocation, no talents or skills, a failure in school. His mother ended up marrying a Toyota dealer from Boise Idaho and has young children with him. The psychologists on my staff—I've got bearded Jungians coming out the yingyang— tell me Dillard is suffering from absent father syndrome, that he's a weak little loser because he didn't have a 'Dad' there to initiate him into manhood. So the guilt's on me. I got him a place to stay. I gave him an entry level job punching shoelace holes in Portland. He couldn't 'hack it' there, so I brought him out here to work in product development. The next thing I know he's talking about being 'born again' as one of the 'soldiers of the Lord'. He got involved with a local group of fundamentalist militia types, called the Million Friends of God's Country. They believe in a Christian America where everyone bears arms and loves Jesus. Those who do neither are infidels in their world view. Needless to say, they hate the fact that the Divine Bhagwan and your group are here even breathing their good air. I'd lost touch with Dillard for a couple months until I saw him in the news the other night. The kid isn't afraid to take risks; I'll say that for him." Alvin Dark airs out a large sigh.

"I suppose I'm not much of a father, Mr. Gilligan. I've got a billion dollar company that's making stupid amounts of money even as I speak. Persephone Shoes, soon to be Persephone Athletics, is my real love. And the world needs the jobs, the commerce."

"Right," agrees Gilligan astutely. "Everybody needs to eat."

"And to work! It is my belief that we humans need work like we need water. Humans without work are like body parts without blood: they begin to fade, then rot, then erupt into sicknesses that are a blight on the rest of us— addictions, cancers and cults."

"Now hold on," declares Gilligan, "we are not a cult."

"I didn't say you were," says Dark smoothly. "I'm not in a position to judge, though just the other day I took a meeting with one of your ex-members. He says he can improve the productivity and happiness quotient of our workforce. Intriguing fellow, all dressed in white. We have another meeting tomorrow. In fact, I'm thinking of hiring him as an advisor for an upcoming trip to the Far East, which he is quite familiar with. We are looking in to seriously reducing our labor costs by shifting production in that direction. But I know so little about your commune and your—uh- Master." He leans forward, clasping his hands between his knees. "I want to understand."

Gilligan is gratified to have the attention of an older, more powerful man. With the tiny bubbles of two Northwest Passages now exploring his bloodstream, his headache is subdued; he is feeling expansive, loquacious, and benign.

"The first thing to understand," he begins, "is that the Divine Bhagwan is an enlightened being."

"Enlightened, or just full of it? How can you tell?"

"Grace. Presence. The feeling of a light going on somewhere deep inside you when in contact with that person."

"What's with all the cars? How many does he have? A hundred?"

"Just sixty-two or so, I think, at last count. All gifts from wealthy disciples. All in mint condition. Some go back to the nineteen twenties, but he doesn't drive them much because the suspension is poor-hurts his back. Rolls Royces are his favorites."

"Tell me about the work you do over there."

"Well, first of all, we now call it worship. The divine Bhagwan says that work, done with full, loving awareness, is a form of meditation. Also, he's applied to be a landed immigrant on the grounds that he is a religious leader. So it was decided that to be more like a religion, our work would be called worship."

"But isn't that just a manipulation so he can get what he wants?"

"Oh no, man. Don't think that!" protests Gilligan. "No one manipulates anyone at the ranch. The Divine Bhagwan is all for freedom, for everyone being as spontaneous as possible. Our religion is against religion."

"And how often do you, uh, worship?"

"Twelve hours a day. Seven days a week. Seven in the morning till seven at night. Longer in crunch times. We do have breaks for meals, tea-times, and drive-by."

"Really," says Dark. "How much do they pay you?"

"Nothing," chirps Gilligan cheerfully. "In fact, there's a lot of people who *pay* a hundred dollars a day for the *privilege* of worshipping at the ranch."

"They pay a hundred bucks a day to work twelve hours a day seven days a week! Where can I find workers like that! That's unbelievable!" Dark, almost spluttering, begins to pace again. "Why in the world would people do such a thing?"

"To be in the Buddhafield."

"To be in the Buddhafield?"

"To be in the Buddhafield."

"This Buddhafield sounds like it has made you people into slaves— working to glorify some guy whose got—what? —five million dollars worth of cars?"

Gilligan sighs tolerantly.

"The Buddhafield is a field of energy that surrounds an enlightened being. The nature of energy is, as William Blake observed, that of eternal delight. One just wants to dance, sing, rejoice, celebrate that the Master has come and is willing to share the great secrets with us."

"So you dance through your work for twelve hours a day?" Dark's voice is tinged with cynicism.

"Yeah, more or less."

"Could it be that the essence of why you work twelve hours a day without pay, doing a lousy job like running a rock crusher, is that your needs are taken care of? Is it that as long as you do what you are told, you don't have to worry about anything? Not like in the big bad real world out there?"

Gilligan drains his mug. "You're starting to sound like my father, man."

Dark takes the mug and heads for a fridge built into the bookshelf. Satyam Gilligan John Price feels there is some truth in what his host has just said. *I have been getting what I need at the ranch. The food is good, the work/worship challenging. I'm even a crew leader (though I guess I may have screwed up my first command) with some real responsibility. And, with so many beautiful, energetic and spontaneous young women there from all over the world, even I, with my tendency to feel shamed, repressed and nervous around women, stand an excellent chance of getting laid on a weekly, if not nightly basis. Yeah, I'm getting what I need. But isn't there something more to it than that?*

Dark returns.

"There's more to it than that," begins Gilligan.

"I'm listening." Dark settles into his chair.

Gilligan ponders as he pours another Northwest Passage into a fresh frosted mug. He is careful to tilt his mug and ease the liquid down the glassy inclined slope, a demonstrably Canadian distinction. The pale yellow brew is not as piss-poor as most American brands. What he has imbibed to this point has not only cured his headache, it has soothed the prickly edges of the defensive reactions which normally characterize his behavior. It should be noted too that part of Alvin Dark's winning formula (covered in chapter 4 of <u>Light of the Sole</u>) is the ability to inspire confidence by listening in a caring manner. As the wise salesperson knows, 'they don't

care what you know unless they know you care'. Gilligan enjoys a three gulp swig from the mug.

"The 'more' that there is to it," he proclaims after a self-
satisfied sigh, "is the quest." His own voice sounds strangely
familiar to him. "It is the urge that seeks transcendence, time-
lessness and grace. It is the wish for wholeness, atonement
and love. It is driven by a passion for truth, rapture and beauty. It is the mother of courage and the father of creativity, the
soul of optimism and the visionary gleam that ignites the fires
of exploration and discovery. It is the first function of our
deepest core: the wish to transcend, to become one with God,
to know boundless peace and freedom for ever and ever,
Amen."

Gilligan again tilts his mug.

"Amen," says Dark, smiling. "Though some might ar-
gue that the first function of our deepest core is to be fed, I
agree completely that this 'questing urge' is a good thing. But
I'm an individualist. I don't understand why you need a Master and a commune to experience it."

"You don't. Even when we calcify into responsible, con-
formist adults, there are still occasions when one feels the
emergent mystery of existence, whether it is in the glory of
sunset or while making love. Maybe one morning the toast
pops up and we go, 'Aha! That's it!'"

"I've had that happen," says Dark. "But only with raisin
toast."

"What the Master and commune do," continues Gilligan, "is increase the possibility and probability of such experiences happening. This is the magic of the Buddhafield. This
is why we feel compelled to be at the Ranch." Gilligan takes
another fulsome sip of his beer. He is beginning to feel sleepy
again.

"But what about *your own* purpose?" asks Dark. "What
about your vision, the goals you strive for in your life?"

"My mind is a bundle of desires, dreams, and petty
negative jealousies. Adding goals to this mess would just be

adding new voices to a cacophonous choir. Only when my mind stops, and I understand who I am, can I possibly fulfill my destiny."

"I disagree," responds Dark. "I think it's by striving to define and then fulfill our destinies that we find out who we are. As I say in my book, a person who has no concise mission statement that focuses, or is a touchstone for where he is going in this life, is a lost soul adrift with the tide."

There is a period of silence. Gilligan finishes his beer. He is hanging for a butt. But there are no ashtrays in this place. Down to earth vices have no place in the Olympian world of Persephone Shoes. Maybe smoking is permitted only in certain locales, like the smoking temples at the Ranch. He yawns as he contemplates Dark's lack of understanding. But then, the concept of no-mind is a difficult one for westerners to grasp. He tries to think of a way of putting it more clearly. But nothing comes. He wants to take a nap.

"How did you come to be involved with the Divine Bhagwan?" asks Dark.

"It pretty much just happened." He makes an effort to sit up more alertly. "I was searching for something I guess. I'd been involved in an Edgar Cayce group in my last year at university. That brought me to the Fifth Kingdom bookstore where I found myself drawn to one of the Divine Bhagwan's books. In it, he talked about meditation, all one hundred and eight methods. Then when I went to acting school, I worked part time at Whole Fools Trading Company down in Cabbagetown. They were really cool people. They loved the same stuff as me: Smoking dope, music, dancing, spiritual seeking. I guess I was pretty sexually uptight and inexperienced and there were some really beautiful women sannyasins around there. I had managed to remain a virgin till I was twenty one and then I just had Daphne for a few years after that. She was into Bhagwan too, but we were breaking up. Plus my mother..." Gilligan stops. There's a pain in his chest. He's forgotten what he was going to say. He's very sleepy. Must be the beer giving him heartburn.

"Sorry," says Dark. "What were you going to say?"

"Oh nothing," blurts Gilligan. "It's just that my mother had had some schizophrenic episodes around that time. Delusions. Catatonia. Shock treatments. Nothing too serious. She had a lot of hostility towards my father. I don't think they were all that compatible, if you know what I mean. When she booted him out, she was yelling that she wasn't going to go to hell for him. My Dad was packing, putting his underwear on his dresser. We looked at each other and we both started crying at the same time."

Tears, wrung through the rusty anvil in his chest, are squeezing from the corners of his eyes. Sobs threaten to break out as the image of those sadly stacked skivvies lingers. Gilligan lifts his now empty mug to his mouth in a desperate attempt at controlling his emotions. But they march on, like lemmings over a cliff. The dregs of his Northwest Passage dribble down his quivering chin. He inhales a couple of drops, begins choking violently and honking through his snot infested nose. The memory of his father leaving has bitten him unawares in a most tender spot.

Alvin Dark rolls his chair silently backwards and ambles towards a box of Kleenex. Gilligan remembers what Bala once said to him. They were alone in the communal shower at Ellis Island, with the morning Los Angelene sunshine slanting in amongst the falling sparkling droplets: *"You haven't cried like a baby since you were a baby."*

This touches off the 'insights' of his amateur Inner Therapist: *Is this a breakthrough? Or a breakdown? Will I be able to feel things now?*

The sun is low on the horizon, bathing the landscape in splendidly theatrical crimson light. It renders the white Kleenexes that Dark tugs from the box as pink as rose petals. He pulls two, then a renewed bout of sobbing prompts him to bring the whole container back to the hunched over sannya-sin. Finally, the emotional storm passes. Gilligan takes the proffered tissues and blows his nose vigorously. He remembers his father, child of the depression that he was, objecting to him using two Kleenexes for one blow. His mother, true to form, had defended him. "His nose is different. He needs two dear."

*To her, my nose was special. To that cheap Scottish bastard, Kleenexes, like electricity, were money draining away. He doled out crumbs of affection — no, crumbs of **attention** — to his eager, starving children like each glance was a quart of blood.* Gilligan is ready to kill his father — who is ignoring him even now, forsaking his generous invitation to visit the Ranch in favor of a pleasure jaunt to Pebble Beach with his shapely new wife. *Talk about screwed up priorities! And then his idiotic warning about the commune being potentially another Jonestown. What crap!*

Gilligan symbolically blows his mother's holy effulgence all over his dad's face. He looks briefly, futilely, around for a garbage. Dark does not hold out his hand like his mother would have. *"I'll take that dear."*

Alvin Dark is standing by the window. There is the faint sound of oversized tires on gravel.

"Here come your friends. Wow. That is some striking looking woman! Does she always carry that gun?" The concern in Dark's voice is several notches above mere apprehension.

Gilligan completes another nose blow and lifts himself up beside Dark at the window. "Don't worry," he says. "Hey! There's Lamborghini! He's a peace officer and a really good shit. He's afraid of guns."

"Who's the other woman?"

"That's Ma Chloe. She's the — uh, president I think — of the commune. She's very... straightforward."

"Great," murmurs Dark. "Major decision makers are here. Maybe we can talk some business, but not with those guns. If you'll excuse me, I'd better go meet them. Will you be joining us for dinner?"

"No thanks, man. I think I'll just crash here for a while if that's OK."

"No problem. You have a good rest." Dark heads for the spiral stairs beside the centrally located elevator.

Gilligan sees Dark emerge below. A silver dollar-sized thin spot is highlighted at the crown of his head by the final fiery beams of daylight. The renovated silo is climate controlled and Gilligan, a good twenty feet above, cannot hear what is being said. He sees Dark shake hands with Deela, Chloe and Lamborghini. Their long shadows stretch all the way to the building he stands in. There are smiles and some brief phony laughter, typical of business people who wish to appear to be harmlessly human, at least on first impression. Then there is a more intense discussion halfway between the Bronco and the house. Gilligan can see Deela's pretty features are frowning darkly. At one point Chloe tugs Deela's sleeve and turns as if to go back to the car.

"Wait," murmurs Gilligan, "you can't just leave me here."

Deela stands firm, arms folded, listening to what Dark has to say. Finally, she undoes her gun belt and hands it to Lamborghini. He returns to the Bronco and settles into the back seat in the manner of one who is ready to wait. Alvin Dark, the epitome of the new American entrepreneur has a fortress of solitude that is a gun-free zone. Gilligan steps back from the window as Dark, Chloe and Deela turn towards the house. He is very tired. So weary, that even his nicotine craving has faded to a minor print in the swirling gallery of thoughts, emotions and bodily aches that are his life museum of the moment. He lies down, zips his coverall up to his chin. Overhead is the curved glass dome that is the roof of the silo. It is artfully conjoined by a web of interlocking metal tubes painted in Persephone's signature athletic blue. The diving swallow trademark, in broad, stained glass inserts of a complementary crimson hue, is fashioned into the curves facing every quarter of the compass. They blend nicely with the darkening sky which erupts here and there, near and far, with clusters of pink clouds forming feathered buttes, hills and canyons that mirror the reddening landscape below.

But Gilligan has no eyes for those skies. His lids are closed. The Persephone blue tubes have become the metal triangles of Buckminster Fuller's domed American pavilion at Expo 67. He is fourteen, and, thanks to his father, has a season's passport to all the exhibits. He's on La Flume- an ersatz hollow log which screams down a long wet chute only to plop into the spray-filled resistance of the ancient pond below. The log settles and floats, rocking gently with giggles. This is La Ronde, the play area of man and his world. It ushers John Price Jr. Satyam Gilligan into a deep, peaceful sleep.

13. Strange Bedfellows

Deela leans back from her meal. The dinner is remarkably good—fresh duck with a hard, tasty crust, grilled and garnished with lemon and coarse pepper. To the side are onion curls, flat fried potatoes, and slabs of red, green and yellow peppers that are crunchy and flavorful. And the duck is delicious. It is marvelous to eat something substantial again, something that has pulsed with the blood of life. Maybe she is a carnivore at heart. Chloe certainly is, judging by the way she tears in—snatching up bones and enthusiastically gnawing them clean. And she had been knocking back the California white wine with a typically Australian disdain for moderation.

Deela carefully takes another sip of her first glass. She prefers the razor's edge of chemical highs to the murky bonhomie provided by alcohol. Besides, not having her gun at her hip makes her feel wary. The dinner has gone well. Too well. Alvin Dark proved to be a disarming host in more ways than one. He even sent an extra large dinner to Lamborghini out in the Bronco. Nice touch that. Her father, long before the police stormed into their office and murdered him before her eyes, had told her, "If you want loyal people around you, make sure you feed them well." She notices with a faint sneer of repugnance that Chloe, responding to Dark's interest in the ecological initiatives at the ranch, actually seems to be flirting with him. She is expounding on the riparian projects underway along Little Snake creek:

"The key to controlling the creek is the Krishnamirthless dam. Now that we have that finished, the big sluice gate allows us to control the flow while the little one at the Truck Farm allows us to fine-tune the irrigation. We've also been planting trees— more than two thousand so far— and laying in rock cribs along the banks. This is going to control the flooding in the spring and allow us to have plenty of water for farming in the summer. Now that, combined with our new sewage lagoons—"

"Chloe—" says Deela sharply, "I'm sure Mr. Dark doesn't want to hear every detail of our business. We need to get to the point of our little visit here. Mr. Dark, we don't like trespassers and spies on our land. And we don't like those who aid and abet those who trespass." She puts the tips of her long, beautifully manicured and polished nails together. "Do I make myself clear?" She levels a fierce, threatening gaze at Dark.

There is a silence of several moments. Chloe slowly lowers a bone she's been chomping to her plate. Dark leans back in his chair and crosses his arms. "Ma Deela," he says at length. "Such hostility and condescension in response to our hospitality is disappointing. I'm sure security is a grave concern for you and your commune. It is something I quite possibly can help you with. I'll tell you what. If any more requests like that from Mr. Jones come my way, I could consider telling them to address their inquiries to the commune's Peace Force. Would that be helpful?"

Yes it would," says Deela, with a hint of pout.

"Fine, we will make it so."

"For our part Mr. Dark, we are not interested in breaking any laws- in fact, we are proud to say that Bhagwanville is completely free of crime."

"Now, as for your... Swami Gilligan, whom you haven't even asked about—"

"Nor," interjects Deela, "have you asked about your son, the assassin."

"Touché madam. How is Dillard?"

"He suffered some scrapes and scratches after the assassination attempt. Nothing serious. It seems that the state Attorney General, Mr. Fryberger—who, quite frankly, is a little creep that hates our guts—has taken a personal interest in his case. He's ordered a psychiatric evaluation, and seems determined to keep him from rejoining us at the Ranch. Since he is now Swami Prem Dillard, we've not pressed charges. My lawyers say he will likely get a few months in prison on charges the state will bring."

"I see. Well, your swami is fine and resting upstairs in my office. I can keep him here till tomorrow if you like and have the company doctor come in and look him over."

"One of our own doctors will examine him. And I will be asking our legal department for recommendations as to how to proceed."

"Must," queries Dark, "every second sentence that comes out of your mouth be some kind of threat, veiled or otherwise?"

"I want to be clear and honest," sulks Deela. "How else would you have me be?"

"I would have you be a good neighbour. Someone who is willing to listen. Someone who knows a good thing when she hears it."

"Are you saying you have something good for me, Mr. Dark?"

Deela leans back in her chair and crosses her arms, mirroring Alvin Dark's posture. Her breasts swell into the scoop of her neckline. Now she is the one flirting. Dark grins, meets her eyes.

"I believe I do."

"Go ahead. I'm listening."

Chloe resumes her assault on the vestiges of her bird.

"Having learned something of your operation over there," begins Dark, "I believe I see an opportunity for a remarkable synergy to occur, a win-win situation for all of us. Peresephone needs labor. Cheap labor. We are moving full bore into the athletic apparel business and are currently scouting locations for factories in the Far East. This is an enormously expensive process. My proposal is that we hire your commune as a manufacturing subcontractor for our products. We supply the building, the materials, the equipment, the management. We can even supply the land. We own a few hundred acres on your side of the river, adjacent to your Truck Farm, where the barge that brought you here docks. Supplying the labor is where you come in."

"Wait, you can't use our people for your bloody sweatshops!" Chloe splutters some morsels of duck back onto her plate.

"Chloe! Eat your dinner!" Deela's knife-like voice softens to silk. "What, Mr. Dark, do you propose our cut would be?"

"My people can go over the numbers with your people. My rough calculations indicate, with a medium sized factory, a cash flow to the commune of about $100,000 per."

Per year?"

"Per month."

Chloe gives a low whistle.

"Plus, I'm given to understand that people are lining up to pay to 'worship' in your commune. That could make our enterprise doubly profitable for yourselves."

"Not for ourselves, Mr. Dark."

"Call me Alvin."

"Alvin." Deela leans forward over the table. "Ours is a spiritual commune. We are striving to develop an oasis where our Master's vision of a New Man can take root and grow. Only if humanity itself undergoes a fundamental change, a change of heart, if you will, can this planet be saved. We are instruments of a larger purpose, part of an experiment that will ultimately allow humans to fulfill their destiny as responsible stewards of this planet. We will consider your proposal."

"Will you be discussing this matter with the Divine Bhagwan himself?"

"Goodness no," says Deela blithely. "Our Master has no interests in such mundane matters. Such decisions are ours to make."

"Now you're talking, neighbor. I suggest we start with a small pilot project and keep publicity to a minimum." Alvin Dark smiles and raises his glass.

"Well mates," says Chloe, cheerfully raising her newly filled glass. "Here's to strange bedfellows then?"

Three wineglasses come together with a satisfying clink.

14. Gilligan Gets it Up the Ass

After a brief post-dinner tour of the Persephone complex, Gilligan returns with Deela, Chloe and Lamborghini in the Bronco. Still woozy, he slumbers through the brief ferry ride, the drive through the Truck Farm and on up the valley to Fareezyuryingyang while Deela and Chloe excitedly whisper cash-flow in the back seat. Lambhorghini is kind enough to help him to the tent he shares with Newfyamo, who is duly miffed at being awakened at the ungodly hour of ten PM.

The next morning, unimpressed by the rock crusher debacle, Lionheart sends him back to the welding shop crew with nothing more said about Hoodoo Canyon or Gilligan's flamed-out crew leader status. With the same crew of Shaggyvan, Toasto, Ralph and the others reunited, there is the yelling, the joking, the swearing, the smoking, the gossip, nails to be driven and lumber to be lifted. In the evening there is food to be eaten, Northwest Passage draft to be drunk, and the Queen of Spades (the Bitch) to be avoided in nightly card games of 'Hearts'. Then it is on to the disco to dance and dance and the hope of 'going home' with someone pretty. Concerns about the real bitches recede to the back burners of Gilligan's mind as he immerses himself in the moment to moment pleasures of the Buddhafield. For a few weeks he becomes stronger and more skilled with each passing day. His heart (unburdened to some extent by his meltdown in Alvin Dark's office), like the iced-over skin of a lake in spring, begins to crack here and there, admitting a measure of warmth and light to the cold waters below. Then he gets sick.

He begins to feel bloody shitty and to find blood in his shit. Sapped of energy, he can do little more than help out in the tea hut. He is sent to Hippocrises and Lucifia prescribes him sulfur pills in the hope of fixing the problem cheaply. But the condition worsens and now, after a week of intimate acquaintance with the Welding Shop site's outhouse, he is back to seek further remedy. Unfortunately it is Lucifia, rather than the kinder, gentler Kildaraj who is on medical duty.

Her mandate is to keep the Ranch workers healthy and fervently worshipping, not moping around her health centre. She is far from pleased to see this slender, doe-eyed Canadian who always seems to be underfoot back in her examining room with the temerity to tell her that her graciously rendered sulfur pill cure did not work. Expensive antibiotics are not to be needlessly squandered, so she is subjecting Gilligan to a rectal examination.

"Zis vill not be pleasant," warns the Teutonic tyrant. Her bedside manner, that of a thoroughly unlovable Colonel Klink, already has Gilligan thinking of her as Ma Mengele. He is bent forward from the waist, his pants around his ankles. His hands grip the cold edge of a stainless steel counter that is redolent of antiseptic. He hears, just off the edge of certainty, the sardonic words "for you" added with quiet glee to the end of Lucifia's sentence.

Conjecture is banished by a baleful, violating, thoroughly unbearable whump of pain that spreads from his asshole into his bowels, which feel simultaneously pummeled by a dozen frozen sledgehammers. A spoiled child, Gilligan's pain threshold has never been particularly high. And this whump is just the overture to an 1812 symphony of torture yet to come.

"You need to relax," commands the good doctor. "You Canadians are nearly as tight-assed as ze British."

"Ha ha." Gilligan tries to comply.

The device she is thrusting resembles a giant white dildo with a miniature searchlight lensed into its bulbous tip. It ploughs another centimetre into his anal rectal region. He expels a tragic moan that resonates as from the shit-coated walls of hell.

"Oh come on Swami," tsks Lucifia. "It is not zo bat".

"A walk in the park," gasps Gilligan.

He has no time to reflect on the political irony of a Canadian getting fucked up the ass and pretending to like it. At least in this case the fucker is a German and not American.

"AAAARRRGH!"

He gags, then almost throws up, passes out, and begins sobbing for mercy all at once, as the device slides to full insertion.

"Vat do you say Swami ?You zink maybe now you vant to become gay, mmmm?"

Gilligan can only groan and grip the counter which has become slippery with sweat from his fingers.

"Ooo Swami, you should see this," murmurs Lucifia. "Zee tissues are very red. You haff an infection!"

There is a brief sucking sound and subsequent pop as she removes the device with an unnecessary flourish and tosses it clattering into a sink to the right of Gilligan's hands.

"Now vee vill haff to give you some antibiotics. Zey are very expensive." Lucifia shakes her head ruefully as she says this.

She has dark hair, pale skin and small pretty features which are somewhat incongruous atop a lanky, large-boned frame. Sneering annoyance is her default demeanor. She pushes her glasses further up her nose and begins writing a prescription.

"Can I stand up now?" asks Gilligan with some trepidation.

"Of course you can stand up!" she shouts at him. "Unt pull up your pants! Vat are you vaiting for? A colonic rinse? Zis is not a fucking spa vee are running here! It is a health centre, Swami, a health centre! Zere are other people vaiting who need treatment! Now take zis-" She viciously rips off the top page of the pad- "and give it to Tootie at zee front. You vill haff to spent a veek in Mydad to recover."

As Gilligan slinks out of the room she goes to a cupboard, clicks open a plastic canister, and tosses down a couple of little white pills: mood enhancers. Lucifia's father was an unrepentant low level functionary in the Nazi party. His anger and disappointment at the Reich's failure (compounded by his wife's irksome defection to East Germany in 1958) had been transferred to his children.

Lucifia, bright enough to become a doctor, had been the lucky one. She happened to be on the floor at the Bhagwan disco in Hamburg in 1979 when Chloe, on some bad mescaline, had a seizure to the beat of 'We are Family'. Lucifia treated her, then nursed her back to health. The women formed a bond beyond friendship and Lucifia was only too happy to accompany Chloe back to Spoona and a lofty position in the commune.

At the front desk Gilligan has to wait. A tall Italian wearing new work boots is being admitted. He's a festival-goer who has lingered for further weeks as a paying worshipper. His face is flushed and he sways from side to side. He has a wallet open against his chest and is peeling off one fifty dollar bill after another. His hands are also flushed.

Ma Tootie, who accepts the bills with a bored look on her face, is an imposing specimen, all of six feet tall and well over two hundred pounds. The arms emerging from the sleeves of her pharmacist's smock are like legs of raw mutton. On her left forearm is a tattoo of a naked woman entwined with a snake. Lucifia's long-time cohort, she too was there at the Hamburg disco in 1979. It is said that she can powder pills simply by rubbing them between her thumb and forefinger.

"More?" inquires the Italian.

"More." Tootie's voice is like an old-fashioned train whistle.

Her outstretched hand fills with several more bills. "OK," Tootie finally pipes, tapping the edges of the stacked bills on the counter. "The doctor will see you now.

15. Swami Snakebite

Mydad, the illness recovery trailer, is about halfway between the recycling depot and Hippocrises on the westerly portion of the Pathless Path highway. It is a place devoted to speedy recovery through the generous application of tender, loving boredom. All ill worshippers (forbidden to stay in their tents, trailers, or A-frames) are funneled here, where they are given nothing to do except get better. Attached at its rear is a large sundeck made out of re-jointed lumber, a product of the recycling depot just down the road. Here, Gilligan is meditating. He sits on a cushion in the thin ridge of shade afforded by the eave of the trailer. He can feel the warm radiance of the afternoon sun reflecting off the decking in front of him. Until he got sick, Gilligan was enjoying his crew and the worship too much to even think of meditation, though perhaps the element of danger, which results in enhanced attention to the here and now, makes hammering nails or negotiating slippery rooftop trusses meditations in themselves. Now, with nothing better to do, he sits, his system chock full of antibiotics, hoping that his stools will eventually firm up.

Aside from his ongoing need to use the bathroom, he enjoys his meditation more than ever before. Something loosened in him over at Persephone. Mr. Dark listened to him, listened to him in a way his own father never could. Divested of some of his anguish, Gilligan now feels ready to cut his old man some slack. John Price Sr. had helplessly watched his wife drift into a mental illness that within a few years tore his marriage apart. Then his only son joined a cult. *Guess he was lucky to re-marry a younger chick who wanted to do stuff with him.* Gilligan is beginning to see that his father is after all just a guy: an older version of John Price Jr., stumbling through life in his own way.

But I don't want to stumble. I want to walk on my own two feet. With awareness.

Swami Gilligan moves his consciousness into his feet. They are bare; his running shoes lie on the deck in front of him. It is a pleasant sensation as his toes protrude from the shade of the trailer behind him into the warmth of the afternoon sunlight. He remembers his breath and feels the weight of his bones and his body. He's eaten what lunch he can, and craves a cigarette. His thinking mind revs up with the onset of this desire:

I must try to quit. That's the thousand and first time I've said that to myself! What was that Professor Shroyer used to say at Western, every time he lit up while teaching The Marriage of Heaven and Hell or whatever? Oh, yeah, "Stupid self destructive habit."

It is Gilligan's chest area, the lungs and heart, which feel the lack of physical affection throughout childhood. *Guess the expressing affection thing was one of Mom's issues.* This hollowness was compounded when at puberty there was no bar mitzvah, no confirmation, no being hung from his tits by bear claws to mark his passage from carefree innocent to worthy young warrior. There were, however, cigarettes, sold freely to him or any other kid at the local Esso station in Britishfield. The place that had provided oral gratification through Sweet Tarts, sour grape gum, and jawbreakers, conveniently offered du Maurier, Rothmans and Export A for more of the same, in the form of a palpably false signal that a transition had been made to adult concerns and adventures.

He remembers La Ronde at Expo 67. He was thirteen. He and his friends had been denied access to a ride for having bare feet. The brutal attendant had painfully twisted and bruised his upper arm. Johnny Price had smoked a cigarette to recover, perched atop the metal-piped gate barrier of another ride. A man with a moustache, doubtless a father watching his own kids, had turned to the skinny kid with tear stained eyes, and asked, "Why do you smoke?" He'd had no answer.

Fuck. Thinking about this shit is not meditating. Watch the breath.

He straightens himself and makes the effort. He feels telltale cramps in his belly, all is still not well with his digestive tract. There are faint hammering sounds coming from the recycling centre up the road. Dishes clatter in the kitchen. A bird chirps from one of the juniper trees on the wall-like hillside in front of him. The hammering stops. He is feeling the beginnings of incontinent looseness in his bowels again. *Maybe I should go before —*

"Oh Swami." Ma Taroo's voice sings out from behind the screen door to his left. "I hate to interrupt you but it's time for drive-by."

Drive-by. This day's only chance for him to catch a glimpse of the Master. Since being spoken to by the Master, Gilligan feels blessed, connected, known. Where there was trepidation, unworthiness, and fear that his guilty core would be exposed by looking into the Master's eyes, he now has a shining teaspoonful of confidence in his breast that the man behind the wheel is a friend. He cannot miss drive-by.

I wonder if I'll have time to —

"Better hurry Swami. We're running a little late."

Gilligan pulls himself to his feet. He feels a little dizzy standing up in the sun, then gets his bearings. He hears the front door close and the receding giggles of the mas. He pulls on his running shoes and hurries after them. There will be only a small gaggle of sannyasins on this stretch of the road. An excellent opportunity to connect with the DB.

The half dozen people from Mydad are in a line, chatting, leaning, looking to the right for the oncoming caravan. Gilligan takes a spot on the end to the left. Up the road, a hundred yards or so, is the lineup from Hippocrises. It is perhaps fifteen people long. He can discern the large-boned, bespectacled figure of Lucifia and also recognizes Swami Kilda-raj, the Divine Bhagwan's personal physician. The man is tall, handsome, and possesses other annoying qualities, such as a deep and sonorous voice.

Gilligan leans forward and looks to his right. Sure enough, atop the nearest rise in the road, glinting through heat mirages, shine the headlights and stainless steel bulk of the oncoming tanker truck. But there is something else that catches his eye, something that causes his heart to pound like ocean surf in his ears. At the nearest end of the waiting line of recycling depot worshippers, little more than one hundred yards away, is the blonde he'd seen at the motor pool. *She's still here!* She is again wearing short red shorts and an off the shoulder t-shirt. She leans forward and back, her hands clasped to her chin, plainly excited by the Master's approach. The tanker truck looms larger. Gilligan watches the gorgeous one bend her legs into the spray, enjoying the brief coolness. Then the truck blocks his view, and is soon upon them. The water spatters his own legs.

Now comes the great silence. The Master speeds be-tween groups then slows to a relative crawl, making brief eye contact with each disciple. His driver's window is down: a pleasant rarity. The back of his left hand waves slowly, his Rolex glinting. Gilligan namastes, meets the eyes, feels a stab of joy pierce him from heart to vitals. Then there's a puff of smoke from the exhaust as the D.B. guns it all the way to the Hippocrises group. The red Peace Force Jimmy follows, striv-ing to catch up. Gilligan's heart beats wildly. There are sighs, a couple of sniffles from his line, aftereffects of the Master's energy. Once past the Hippocrises group, the Rolls accelerates again and whisks out of view around the shoulder of a hill.

YAHOOO! The shout goes up and is echoed from the other groups on the road, then again from the surrounding hillsides. Gilligan falls to the moist pebbled surface of the road and, for a moment, lets an absurd what-the-hell release of delight wash over him.

He is first on his feet and walks quickly up the road towards the recycling depot. He hardly knows where he is going or why. Then he sees heads begin to lift and realizes:

Of course. The blonde. I'm getting closer to the blonde. Where have you been, you minx? Here at the recycling centre the whole time? If I hadn't been sick, I would have found you sooner...

Something else is happening. Something unfortunate. The YAHOO! fall has jolted his bowels even looser, and with every step he is in increasing danger of crapping his shorts. He tightens his sphincter and tries to walk more quickly.

"Hey Swami! Where are you going?" Manoo and Taroo, the giggling custodians of Mydad, have realized that one of their charges is going AWOL. "You can't just wander off, you know! Oh my God! Why is he walking like that?"

Gilligan does not dare to turn or shout an answer. He tightens up his butt even more. This gives him a mincing, pigeon-toed gait, with a very odd wiggle. From the rear he looks like a Chaplinesque wiener dog. The laughter of Manoo and Taroo has spread to the entire group behind him. The growing wave of hilarity does not deter him. Eyes focused on the blonde, impelled by forces he will never understand, he continues speeding towards her. She is getting up from the road. Her top has climbed upwards, revealing the white skin of her slim waist. She stands and smoothes her top, begins brushing grains of gravel from her breast with the backs of her fingertips. Gilligan, in the moment as never before, perceives in slow motion: fingers, breasts, firm resiliency, the round softness of her revealed shoulder, blonde curls warm in the sun. He even sees the redness of sunburn and peeling skin on her nose. A few freckles. Blue eyes. Then she is pointing and smiling. At him.

Bubble fart. Squirt. He has lost control halfway there. He stops. Dead. He puts his hands behind his back in an agony of embarrassment. He makes a brief, ludicrously contorted attempt to smile back. Pulls a hand free and gives her a stiff waist-high wave. Her point turns into a brief, puzzled, wave. But she wears a big, beautiful smile. His heart soars, the high tide of his blood crashes in his ears. He hears the laughter and calls to return behind him. Something dribbles down the inside of his right leg.

Shit. It's coming.

He has to make a run for it. Like a spooked thoroughbred, he bolts to his right, down the stony embankment of the road, across the ditch, and around the corner of a small hill. *I'll cut through to the back of Mydad and hit the bathroom before anyone else returns. Damn! But at least now I know where to find her!*

He runs, wantonly leaping bushes and sliding down slopes. His shoes fill with sand and pebbles. His underwear fills with stinky, blood-tinged gravy. The steep hillside behind the Mydad deck comes into view; he just needs to veer to his right and traverse a few score more yards to get to the back door. He thinks of how he will dive onto the toilet while simultaneously dousing his underwear and shorts in the sink. He leaps a particularly deep gully.

He hears the rattling sound in mid air, feels his foot land on something soft. His ankle turns; he falls forward; he feels a stabbing, bruising pain in the back of his right calf, as if he had been shot with a nail gun. He groans and turns, sees the snake, diamond-backed in the dust and so like the colors of the ground it is as if the desert floor itself has writhed to poisonous life. The reptile slithers in amongst some rocks, and Gilligan is alone. Twin puncture wounds in his leg ooze single, glossy pearls of blood.

He has shit himself for real now. Terrified, he groans, struggles to his feet. He thinks of still making it to the bathroom, then telling them what has happened. But Mydad is not in sight. Just the steep hillside looming to his left and a sloping ridge straight ahead. His eyeballs hurt; throb in their sockets.

Rattlesnake bite. What are you supposed to do? Suck out the poison. Can't reach it. Tourniquet. Stop it from reaching the heart. He rips off his t-shirt, ties it above the knee. He sinks back to the ground. With a kind of dull wonder, he realizes he can no longer feel his leg. He can't move his toes. He hears the faint sound of laughter. *I've always been a loner. Self sufficient. The kind who'd crawl into a shady corner and die. Stoic, like a good cowboy.*

But now there's too much to live for.

"HELP!" he screams. "HELP! HELP! HEEEELLLPP! I'VE BEEN BITTEN BY A RATTLESNAKE!"

Within a minute he is surrounded by friends. Manoo, Taroo and a couple of his fellow patients. One is a hulking Swede who is badly sunburned. He had fallen asleep while reading Louis L'Amour at lunch time. The white rectangle of the opened book is a reverse brand angled across his chest. He picks Gilligan up under the shoulders while others take his feet.

"Holy shit, this guy is a mess."

"Ewww—right. Set him on the deck. We can hose him off before bringing him in."

Gilligan feels himself being lifted and carried a short distance. He is gently lowered onto the hot boards of the deck.

"Take it easy Swami, we're going to give you a bath."

He is sprayed up and down with water that is surprisingly warm. He begins to relax, almost luxuriating in it. Suddenly the water turns cold as the sun-warmed portion in the hose runs out.

"Ahhhgh! Stop! Stop! It's too fucking cold!"

He tries to get up and run away.

"Hold him down guys," says Taroo. "We've got to get all of it."

He is pinned down, told to hold still. He looks back over his head at the Swede.

"Hell of a vay to vake up eh Swami?" says the big fellow.

The man's large white teeth are framed by a florid, peeling, freckled, brown-patched face—a mishmash of recovery from sunburn. A halo of blond curls encircles the face. Gilligan remembers the blonde's puzzled wave, her big smile. She recognized him from his antics in the jeep. He is sure of it. A smile of his own tugs the corners of his mouth upwards as he succumbs to the rattler's venom and the world fades away.

"How are we doing?"

"I don't know about you Doc, but my whole leg is paralyzed."

Gilligan has to make an attempt at impressing the Divine Bhagwan's personal physician with his wit. He is back in Hippocrises, in the same room as his near disembowelment by the notorious Lucifia. He is prone on a gurney, wearing fresh shorts and t-shirt provided by the kindly mas of Mydad.

"This antivenin should have you feeling better in short order," says Kildaraj tapping a syringe that he holds up to the light.

Gilligan has been feverish, chilled, nauseated, sweaty, and scared. Interspersed amongst these sensations, like cactus flowers in the desert, are moments of lucidity, unfolding one after the other, like the petals of a lotus.

Perhaps snakes truly are the great teachers of myth, the facilitators of change, the high priests of the animal kingdom.

"Do you think this means something?"

"Does what mean something?" Kildaraj probes for a vein in Gilligan's leg.

"Being bitten by a snake, here in the Buddhafield?"

Kildaraj smiles. To Gilligan, the smile looks beautiful: like the 'flowering of consciousness' the Divine Bhagwan has said a real smile should be—not the salesperson's smile or the

175

empty 'I am a good person please don't hurt me' show of teeth more typical of smiling in the 'real' world.

"It means one thing," says the doctor, deftly inserting the needle. "You were a bloody fool to be running around in the sage like that. What in the world were you thinking, old boy?"

Gilligan does not immediately answer. He is caught up in wonder that such a large needle going so deeply into his flesh caused no pain. *Does venom, like death, cancel out pain?* Plus, he's never been called "old boy" before. It's a finely delivered personal touch that briefly evokes in him a sense of how fine, how noble, the best parts of the British psyche truly are. Gilligan feels the blood throbbing into the tourniquet around his leg.

Kildaraj washes his hands in the sink. "So, why were you running over hill and dale?"

"At drive by," confesses Gilligan, "I saw this blonde up in the recycling depot line up. She was-"

"Beautiful? Very sexy looking?" Kildaraj nods. "I believe I know the one you are referring to. She's been worshipping at the recycling depot."

You keep the fuck away from her! Gilligan has to restrain himself from actually shouting at him. Instead he says:

"The more attractive they are, the more nervous and stupid I seem to act around them. I had no idea of where I was going or what, if anything, I was going to say when I got there. Do you—happen to know her name—or anything?"

"Sorry, old boy, I know nothing about her. But what in the world made you stop and run off the road?"

"Diarrhea. The blood soaked kind. I've had it for weeks. I was taking a shortcut to the bathroom. I suppose I should have gone behind a bush or something."

"I see. But antibiotics should have cleared up that ailment in a few days."

"Lucifia just gave me some yesterday."

176

"Yesterday!" Kildaraj's handsome face briefly twists into a snarl. "Isn't that just bloody typical?" The face resumes its demeanor of god-like tranquility. "Don't worry old boy." He pats Gilligan on the shoulder and turns to leave.

"Doc?"

"Hmm?"

"Hoodoo Canyon. That was you, wasn't it?"

Kildaraj's eyes widen in recognition. He soundlessly locks the door to the examining room and turns both taps in the sink on full. He sits alongside Gilligan's prone form and whispers next to his ear.

"I don't know how much he said to you, but the man you know as Alchemendra and I go back many years, well before the Divine Bhagwan. I've known him to show remarkable foresight in the past, so please heed him when he says that, with the Master speaking again, it is only a matter of time before Deela's machinations get the better of her. When that happens, we will all, including the Divine Bhagwan, be in great danger. There are people here you can trust. Lionheart and myself are among them. And, as unlikely as it seems, Alchemendra says your karma is to play a pivotal role when the time comes. When it does, your ability to 'Trust' will be our secret weapon. Remember what I've said here, because it will not be repeated."

With venom, antivenin, antibiotics, and painkillers coursing through his bloodstream, Kildaraj's words filter into Gilligan's mind as through sifting, bypassing, overlapping panels, each level rendering the words more hallucination than reality.

Did I just hear what I thought I heard?

The taps are turned off and the door is swung wide.

"With all that's happened, old boy," says Kildaraj in a loud voice, "you're looking at another two weeks in Mydad. That leg is going to swell up a great deal. But don't worry. You should come out at the other end better than ever."

Gilligan feels himself being turned over and transferred to a rolling stretcher. The tubes in the fluorescent fixture over his head are preternaturally bright, glowing in primary colors like light sabers. He closes his eyes and falls quickly into a sleep that will seem to last for days.

Gilligan is sitting up in bed, reading a Louis L'Amour book while the air-conditioner drones below the room's window. The 'view' is two sage bushes on the hillside that walls in the rear of the Mydad trailer. His two weeks end today. The bulk of his time has passed in sleep, fever, dozing, trying to meditate, or in some combination of these. His body has been dealing with the effects of the snake venom, the bowel infection, the antibiotics, the antivenin, and the concussive bonks he received in the tunnel and rock crusher. The last two days he's felt better and gone to drive-by again. The blonde was not to be seen. He hears the sound of boisterous laughter coming from the front desk. A chubby hand reaches in and knocks on his open door. Floating in behind it on another gust of laughter is Ma Slowma, the chief of Bang Pas Zoo.

"Hello Swami Gilligan," she warbles. "How are you feeling today?"

"Hello Slowma." He dog ears his book and plops it on top of a low mound of similar titles which grace the bedside table. "Not too bad, thanks."

He smiles back at her. He feels nervous, guilty. Why the hell is she here? Has she found out about his excursion down the Hemlock Grove tunnel?

"Well Swami," she says brightly. "Do you feel ready to return to worship?"

"Oh yeah. I took a shit this morning that was—" Gilligan opens his fingertips in front of his mouth in a gesture signifying tasty perfection— "the perfect ripe banana. I offered to let Taroo see it but-"

"Gills!"

"Right. Sorry".

"You are needed back at your old crew— with Qavi Ralph. They're close to finishing the Welding Shop. You can eat at Macarena tonight and start with them in the morning."

Gilligan's heart swells with no small measure of delight. After being brought up to excel as a student, to become a clever lawyer or businessman, he now feels a joyous, visceral attraction to working with his hands. Plus there's the fun of seeing his fellow crew members again.

"Oh. One more thing Gilligan. It looks like you have friends in high places! This was sent to you out of Shangri Oh-lala, the Master's House."

She hands him a small, neat envelope.

"Bye Swami."

Slowma floats her boat-like way out the door. She is buoyed by a rising tide of female laughter as she approaches the front desk. These sounds swiftly fade to the background as Gilligan's studies the envelope in his hand. It is a pale tan color, made of grainy paper whose faint topography can be felt under his fingers. An exquisite rust-colored line-drawing of the Master's profile graces the upper left hand corner. A nearly illegible scrawl in fine black ballpoint reads: *Swami Snakebite*. He grins, then realizes the envelope has already been opened, neatly slit along the top edge. The note inside is still there. Same classy stationary. Same physician's scrawl:

> *Swami,*
> *Blonde is Dutch. Name Seatrice.*
> *Left the Ranch a week ago. Sorry old boy.*
> *K.*

Gilligan carefully places the note back in the envelope. He folds and tucks it into a side pouch of his red nylon backpack. He gets his few things together. There is the tingling sensation at the base of his nostrils that happens when he is touched. It sends extra moisture to his eyes. He begins to hum to himself, not wondering why or by whom the note was opened. He is buoyed in spirit by a diamond-bright notion, un-thought, but felt in some deep crevice of his gut: *she'll be back.*

16. Dillard on Parade

It is a month after Gilligan's release from Mydad, midday at the motor pool building. All of Bang Pas Zoo, perhaps a hundred sannyasins, are called to a meeting by Deela. The newly erected roof—the building is a huge structure designed to accommodate several buses and trucks at once—provides shade from the late August sun. During Gilligan's 'sick leave' the welding shop has been largely completed. The last few days, he and the rest of the crew have been working inside, hanging drywall away from the hot sun. Now fully healed, with lunch safely in his belly, the motor pool's concrete pad, poured just two days earlier, radiates subtle warmth as it cures beneath his outstretched legs.

Beside him is a new crew member named Fleuritima, a petite Quebecois woman who was assigned to him as a work partner. She and Gilligan were teamed as drywall screwers all morning. It was cool to be her ostensible mentor, to feel that he had acquired real skills that he could pass on to newcomers. And she was cute and fun to be with.

A long table is set up in front of the crowd. Behind it sit Chloe and Slowma. Their faces are serious. Deela, wearing a sleeveless velour jumpsuit and her gun, paces back and forth in front of the table as she delivers her harangue:

"We all know that there is no crime in this commune. Isn't that right?" People in her audience nod and murmur assent. "Since there is no crime in this commune we have to say that what happened last night is either an act of misguided playfulness or temporary insanity. Or, maybe, there are some people here who are criminals pretending to be sannyasins!"

"What in the world happened Deela? Was someone killed?"

The drawling masculine voice coming from the rear of the assemblage is a familiar one.

"No Toasto. No one was killed, but they easily could have been! Some idiots, or terrorists, thought it would be a funny late night prank to park the Ranch's septic pump truck in front of my house at Hemlock Grove! These same idiots didn't put the truck in gear or use the right brake or something. When a member of the Peace Force tried to start it early this morning to move it to a safe distance, it started rolling backwards down the slope. Poor Lamborghini couldn't stop. It smashed right into our brand new five star restaurant! Half the patio is destroyed!"

"I hope nothing spilled outa the truck," someone whispers from behind Gilligan.

"Yeah," he whispers back over his shoulder. "That'll cost you a star or two right there."

There are some suppressed giggles all around him.

"It's not funny!" screams Deela. "This is damaging! It is damaging to the commune! It is damaging to our image! It is damaging to the Divine Bhagwan!"

"People," says Slowma in her earnest singsong, her hands clasped in front of her on the table. "We need to remember why we are here."

"Slowma's rawt," echoes Chloe.

"We have a pretty good idea who did this," intones Deela, scanning the assemblage with a venomous stare. "Don't think that we don't. I don't care how good you are in construction. If there is any more crap like this—you call us the bitches—well this bitch bites and I'll bite you harder than any snake. You'll be back digging ditches in the outside world, no more big, important sannyasin in the Buddhafield. Hear that cowboys?"

There's a long pause as she scans the audience with her hand on the silver butt of her gun. Gilligan imagines her opening fire, 'Wild Bunch' style. Blam! Blam!Blam!Blam!Blam! Qavi, Smoothsill, Anugruffa, Shaggyvan, Toasto and himself crumpling dead in slow motion. The shit truck prank was Shaggyvan's idea, after a Saturday evening spent successfully forging and liquidating beer tokens at Macarena cafeteria. It seemed like a good idea at the time, more fun than the usual games of 'hearts'.

"One more thing, people," Deela continues, "something far more positive for our commune. We have someone here who has come all the way from Portland on his day pass from prison, someone who was in the news a couple of months ago, and will be again tonight. Chloe."

Chloe picks up a Motorola from the table in front of her and speaks into it briefly. A scene that Gilligan witnessed almost eight weeks earlier is reprised, as Lurchamo, hefting a video camera on his shoulder, backs out of Deela's white Bronco which has been idling at the edge of the site— very close to the spot where Gilligan first saw the blonde, Seatrice. He is followed, as he was before, by the sumptuous Angelica, who is dressed in shorts, tank top, and in what might have been some pinup calendar photographer's idea of sexy accessories, work boots and work gloves. She is followed by Dillard, who wears a red coverall. The skin of his face and hands looks even pastier than Gilligan remembered. His hair has grown longer and dangles over his ears like greasy worms. Dillard's eyebrows are set lower on his forehead and his lips are drawn into a very tight line. It appears prison has not been kind to him.

"Swamis and mas," proclaims Deela, "I want you all to welcome the assassin turned sannyasin, Swami Prem Dillard! The prison took his mala away, but we are told he'll get it back when he is released in another six to eight weeks. Dillard came all the way here to see his sweetheart, Angelica, and of course the Divine Bhagwan. He'll just have time to see the drive-by, then our Peace Force officers will escort him back to Portland."

"They'd better escort him to drive-by too!" Gilligan yells these words before he can think the better of it. The audience laughs and even applauds. Since his return from the rattlesnake bite, he is markedly less shy about speaking out.

Deela takes the quip with good grace. "Don't worry people. What's that Sufi saying the DB likes to quote? 'Trust in God, but tether your camel.' Swami Dillard, you are one camel that we are going to keep a very close eye on." Deela looks at her watch. "I have to go and lead the drive-by, people. Dillard, say good-bye to Angelica now. You're going to have to come with us."

Dillard, who has been standing with an arm around Angelica's shoulders leans over to kiss her. She, who has been standing with her arms crossed, offers him her cheek. Sergio Lamborghini and another peace officer escort him back to the Bronco. There is a smattering of applause from the assemblage. This increases as Deela waves to the crowd and shouts "Remember why you are here!" before getting into the Bronco which speeds off towards Shangri Ohlala.

Chloe stands up. "Remember his face, everyone! We wanted you all to see him. Sure he took sannyas in the heat of the moment, and maybe to save his skin. When he does come back, we want you to all know who he is, so if he worships with you, you can keep an eye on him. Rawt?"

There are murmurs and declarations of assent from various portions of the crowd.

"Rawt. Thank-you. Slowma?" Chloe nods to the head of Bang Pas Zoo.

Slowma stands up. She wants the meeting to end on an upbeat note. "Uh, people, let's sing 'Remember' before we go."

She begins to sing the music group favorite in a voice that is touchingly sweet and clear.

> *"To help us drop fear*
> *To help us draw near*
> *Oh Divine Bhagwan*
> *We remember, we remember, we remember why we're*
> *here!*

This chorus, like most of the commune songs, has a simple, infectious melody which is repeated again and again. Everyone joins in and it lifts the spirits of all present, except perhaps for Chloe, who continues to sit at the table with hands folded. Her eyes, like strobe lasers, dart from face to face. Her mouth is set in a thin, suspicious line. Evidently she is not quite ready to forget the sacrilege of the shit truck escapade.

As resonations from the song fade from under the steel roof, Slowma says gently, "OK people. The Master will be driving by soon. Take the time between now and then to think about what has been said here, think about why we are here."

There is an approving murmur as everyone gets up to go.

"Oh," says Slowma, "I want to talk to and hug all the crew leaders. Worship safely guys!"

Gilligan wanders with Fleuritima along the creek bank downstream from the motor pool. They are laughing about the 'shit truck' meeting... chuckling over Deela's vindictiveness and Slowma's soft heart.

"I think she'd be happiest if we were snuggled together in a nice warm nest and she could tuck us all under her feathers where we'd be safe," says Fleuritima.

"Yes, or if she had a hundred tits she could nurse us with simultaneously. Whoa! Wait a second."

Below them, walking barefoot along the shallows of the further shore of the creek, is another young couple. One, the

185

young woman, has a shape that Gilligan could easily recognize from twice the distance: the superbly well-rounded Angelica. Her companion, with whom her fingers are loosely entwined in the manner of lovers, is of a familiar stature and bearing. One that is reminiscent of the Master himself.

"Hey Newf!" Gilligan shouts.

The man's head turns. It is unquestionably the limpid-eyed visage of Gilligan's tent-mate. Newfyamo.

Well, the little bugger certainly can keep a secret.

Newfyamo raises and waves his free hand in the manner of one giving a friendly greeting, albeit with significant changes. His hand is reversed, and his middle finger, and only his middle finger, is firmly extended skywards. Clearly, he would like some quiet time with Angelica. Over the last few weeks they have somehow become an item.

"Hmm," says Gilligan. "I think there is a certain sannyasin assassin who wouldn't be too pleased to see what we are looking at."

"That girl is much better off with your friend. That assassin is *mechant*—wicked," says Fleuritma. "He gives me the creeps. Come on." She takes Gilligan's hand. "Let's find a place to wait in the shade."

17. The Epic Cruise Begins

It is now full on into Fall of 1982. The days, though sunny, have been shorter. Chilly, even frosty mornings give way to pleasantly warm afternoons and increasingly cool evenings. As the sun climbs the sky, outside worshippers peel clothes like layers of an onion, followed late in the workday by the same process in reverse as floodlights brighten work scenes. The welding shop is complete and being used as the commune's Friday night movie theatre. The first feature, shown on big screen through the VCR technology that was so instrumental in introducing the Divine Bhagwan to American TV and movies, is *Conan the Barbarian,* as requested by Toasto. Down the road, the carpentry shop is being retooled as a temporary casino.

Qavi Ralph's crew is disseminated: Smoothsill to the new downtown mall site; Toasto and Shaggyvan are building a bridge at the Truck Farm, with Toasto as crew leader. Qavi Ralph drives a lull fulltime. He is in recovery from his now broken romance with Boella. Anugruffa joins Gilligan on the mud crew for a few days but then is summoned to work with Dozon on the foundation slabs for the permanent casino, a grandiose structure due to be completed for the Second Annual Universal Celebration in July of 1983.

Gilligan is happy to be indoors mudding in the Motor Pool building. The building consists of a large central amphitheatre flanked by balconies which access second floor offices. Taping and finishing the drywall joints is a challenge, a new skill to be mastered. He loved working with Qavi's crew, even developed considerable proficiency. He can nail green vinyl sinkers with a tap and a couple of blows and, after an embarrassing attempt at cutting with the blade in backwards, he knows his way around a jigsaw. The art of finishing drywall, the spreading of glossy white mud to smooth seams and corners, appeals to him. It has some of the sculptural appeal of bricklaying, where the mortar can assume an infinite variety of interesting shapes before yielding to that required by function.

The motor pool building has made massive progress since the 'meet the assassin' meeting. Because the First Annual Universal Celebration was a huge financial success, a smaller festival is planned for December to celebrate, as duly researched by Patipaticake, the birth date of the Master's father. The festivities will be held in the warmth of this specially modified motor pool building. To this end, the huge bay doors at either end, large enough to accommodate buses and the biggest of the ranch construction vehicles, have been expanded outwards some twenty feet, with added steel roofs. Temporary walls with double layers of thick polyethylene film have been added. The extensions will enclose a stage for the commune's rock band at one end and be used for extra seating at the other.

The head of the mud crew is Narzesh. He is a tall, slim fellow in his early thirties. He has a neatly trimmed moustache and goatee. With his sandy hair and waspish good looks, he is apparently coming off a previous life as a swashbuckler in the court of Louis XIV. Narzesh runs the motor pool crew as his own little Shangri-la, with himself as the high lama. He seats himself in a lone chair in the centre of the amphitheatre and from there dispenses instructions via Motorola or through minions who ferry back and forth from their worksites. He seldom raises his voice except in good natured jest, loudly teasing someone or other to the amusement of all. He maintains a light atmosphere -informed by the unspoken understanding that everything happening is a total joke. Nevertheless, every person wants to help make it a joke they can be proud of. Narzesh often shares his chair, which is of the metal, school auditorium variety, with some curvaceous sweet young thing or other who sits on his knee and acts as his assistant. He is known to disappear on 'cruises' in the Motor Pool pickup truck for hours at a time, often in the company of his current assistant. Gilligan, despite his earnest attempts at meditation (long since abandoned) back at Mydad, lacks the equanimity to resist jealous and envious thoughts regarding Narzesh's seemingly privileged position.

One extremely blustery day, after Gilligan is on the crew a couple of weeks, Deela, Arcana, and a couple of the architects arrive on to check the progress of the work. Deela has been off the ranch for considerable stretches the previous two months, making media appearances and collecting funds from Bhagwan Centers around the world. Unfortunately, her belligerent style and the widespread, but unproven suspicions that foul play may have been involved in the recent Hieferville election, with the mayoralty being won by Madma in the midst of a bizarre stomach flu outbreak, has turned popular opinion, particularly in Wacko and the neighboring counties, decidedly against the Ranch and the Divine Bhagwan. She and the architects are touring several projects to assess the progress made in her absence.

It is afternoon tea time and Gilligan is in the outhouse taking a crap. The blustery November weather suddenly turns vicious, with sideways blasts of pelting rain, and wind gusts which cause the plastic structures jutting from the bay doors to belly in and out like sannyasin diaphragms in the first stage of dynamic meditation. The polyethylene sheeting, billowing and flapping like the sails of a schooner in a typhoon, snaps the grid-work of the west bay's enclosure. The plastic walls are crushed like a drink carton in the hands of a schoolboy. They shred, tear and gather themselves into a mini tsunami of plastic, nails and kindling that rolls down the length of the building.

Narzesh, Deela, Avibasso, Arcana and another architect are in the middle of the amphitheatre as this happens.

They watch the shredded mass, shaped like a giant horizontal cigar, roll towards them at a frightening speed. Narzesh manages to sidestep it, then watches it bowl over Deela and the architects, who, with understandable shouts and screams of fear, are knocked on their backsides and engulfed. But he can't worry about them. He knows the enclosure at the far end is now at risk.

"Get away from the bay!" he screams over the howling wind and the cries for help from his visitors.

Waving his arms like an over-exuberant umpire, he runs towards the farther, as yet intact, wall of plastic. The funneling wind has thrown bits of insulation, plastic, mudtape and packaging high into the air where it flutters like confetti. The balconies fill with red-clad workers drawn by the rending crash. The plastic-covered grid at the east end bulges like an overdue pregnancy. Vertical two-by-fours bend like drawn bows. For a few seconds it appears the wall will hold, but it cannot. Bounding satellites of the original oblong plastic cylinder- which has stalled mid building, bogged down by the weight of more than one overfed architect- bounce up and into the straining membrane, repeatedly battering it.

"Holy fuck," whispers Narzesh.

He runs towards the bay, not heeding nor perhaps hearing Deela's demands to be freed from the plastic. He has vague ideas of somehow holding the wall in, whipping up some planks to reinforce it. But the bubble bursts like overblown gum from a child's face, and another mass of sticks and plastic is ejected from the building with the force of projectile vomit.

It is the outhouse which bears the brunt of this bundle. Moving at the speed of the tumbleweeds that are chased by the winds from the surrounding hills, it crashes directly into the plywood structure which topples like a cowboy taking a shotgun blast to the chest.

Gilligan has just finished his final wipe and is peering down at the scrunched homespun ranch issue tissue to ensure

190

that it is sufficiently unsoiled, when his refuge is toppled. His booted feet flip upwards and clunk against the door above his head which splinters inwards. There is a scraping sound, a feeling of motion, and the snapping and flapping of plastic sheeting. Fortunately the structure does not crumple. It is merely pushed by the impact, surfing on the gravelly soil for a yard or two. In its wake, the open hole half-filled with crap, piss, and toilet paper, is mercifully covered with plastic and other debris. Gilligan is uninjured by the mishap and is struggling to pull up his red coveralls when Narzesh flings open the door and stands astride the opening above him.

"You OK?" he demands. He teeters, struggling to keep his balance as the wind buffets him from behind. The bulk of the ball of plastic has bounced off the outhouse and continues rolling and tumbling in the direction of the welding shop.

"Yeah, fine," says Gilligan, as nonchalantly as he can under the circumstances.

"Give me your hand. Gaa!! What the fuck is this?"

The discombobulated swami has managed to proffer the hand which still clutches the toilet tissue.

"Sorry man, I didn't know what to do with it".

"The other hand then. Jeepers creepers what a disaster!"

Gilligan is hauled from the outhouse, desperately adjusting his clothing and flicking away the offending tissue while trying not to fall back in. There is a good deal of unsuccessfully suppressed laughter from a small knot of witnesses to the outhouse escapade. But not from Narzesh, who knows he must now face the wrath of Deela who stands with arms crossed amidst the wreckage of weeks of worship.

Part of the fallout from the Motor Pool fiasco is that Narzesh, while still barely maintaining crew leader status, has his driving privileges revoked. Two days after the storm Narzesh hands Gilligan and Morris (a chubby Kiwi carpenter) the keys to his beloved crew truck (a nearly new Ford Ranger) along with a long 'shopping list' of needed supplies. He issues dire warnings (fated to be duly ignored) to return swiftly with all the supplies and a completely unscarred vehicle. So it is that Gilligan and Morris have the opportunity on a lovely late Fall day to take an epic cruise of the Ranch.

Their first stop is Sariputput, the repository for all pipes and plumbing. A short drive from town on the road to Hippocrises, it consists of a boxy two-story building and an oversized garage, both clad in green metal siding. The roof-line of the latter sags in the middle despite being brand new. Such aberrations, the fruits of the labor of inexperienced work crews, are scattered about the commune.

The larger building's front door is flung wide open and from within a male voice can be heard singing the chorus of "Oklahoma!" with full-throated joy. The building is cool and drafty, as all the doors and windows are open to the day's fine weather. There is a small office space to their right and crowded rows of steel shelving stacked high with pipes, fittings, sinks and toilets.

"Hello!" shouts Morris over the 'waving wheat that sure smells sweet'. Hello!"

The singing abruptly stops.

"Omigod!" exclaims a voice from on high. "Some real live men have come to pay me a visit!"

Cantilevered above the back end of the building is a large mezzanine on which are stacked more shelves and pipes. Standing midway on the mezzanine, his hands grasping a green metal railing, is a thin fellow in his early thirties. He has longish sand-colored hair and a large, thoroughly groomed handlebar moustache. He wears a red coverall which is dazzlingly clean.

"Don't move a muscle, gentlemen. I'll be right down!"

Eschewing a nearby staircase, he vaults the railing and grabs a metallic gold fireman's pole, which he slides down, completing a graceful double revolution in the process. His free hand circles skywards, the fingers turned upwards in a theatrical mudra. As he lands he brings his hand down with a flourish:

"Greetings! I'm Swami Flamhir. What can I do for you two?"

"We're here for some supplies," says Morris implacably. "Where's the list, Gilligan?"

"Gilligan!" exclaims Flamhir. "*The* Swami Gilligan? He of the 'dropping in' on Deela from the Master's roof? That was just so precious and hysterical! And the DB spoke to you, didn't he? I heard all about it! Say? Why aren't you a crew leader?"

"That's a bit of a long story —" begins Gilligan.

"Too long for right now," interjects Morris, thrusting the supply list into Flamhir's hand. "We've got to keep moving along or Narzesh will have our asses."

"Ooooh, I love it when you talk dirty," simpers Flamhir.

Morris glowers at him. The ruddiness typical of the big fellow's cheeks has spread to the rest of his broad face. He is flushed and looks ready to bite the teaser's head off.

"Fine fine fine fine fine fine," acknowledges Flamhir, studying the list intently. "You want lots of scaffolding I see. Back your truck up to the shed. Now tell me Swami," he nearly circles Gilligan like an eager puppy as they walk towards the shed, "did he really say 'Thanks for dropping in'?"

"He said 'everything's OK.'"

"Everything's OK?" The phrase appears to delight Flamhir intensely.

"Everything's OK? Well, that sums up his message in two words, doesn't it? No need for any more discourses!"

He throws back his head and releases a raucous, cackling laugh. Morris is grinning and shaking his head as he backs the truck up to the shed. A still laughing Flamhir raises the overhead door. As it waggles to a rollered stop, Morris cuts the engine of the truck.

A chugging sound comes towards them on the road from the direction of town. "Mail!" screams Flamhir, throwing his hands over his head. "Mail! Mail! Mail! I've got mail!"

Dancing with excitement, he buzzes past them and flits to the edge of the road. "Oh it is! It is! It is! It's Sumpads!"

At the mention of the name Sumpads, Gilligan's interest is aroused. Sumpads is a young woman of some considerable power and notoriety at the Ranch. She is in charge of Mercurata, the Ranch's mail division. It is said that she is an accomplished speed reader who personally peruses each item of mail received by anyone in the commune. Those containing donations or suspicious contents are funneled directly to Chloe or to Deela herself.

"It's her! It's her! Right here, sweetheart! Bring it to me!"

The distant chugging quickly grows to a formidable growling. A Harley Davidson motorcycle with a lidded sidecar swoops into view. The driver, Sumpads, is a particularly impressive feminine specimen. She is a steroidal version of Gilligan's fantasy ideal of slim, but well rounded. She wears tight red leather pants and a matching jacket. A broad, golden zipper bisects the sturdy, finely formed mounds of her breasts. Said zipper is open to her solar plexus; her breasts thrust and climb within the leather like spirited stallions in a starting gate, barely restrained by the overmatched straps of a cotton tank top. Her legs are sculpted pistons, straddling the machine masterfully, as if it is they that orchestrate the rhythmic poppings and rumblings of the engine between them. She pulls to a stop, wordlessly extracts an envelope from a satchel at her side, and hands it to Flamhir. Her left boot taps down on the gearshift and she pulls away.

"Wait a minute!" exclaims Gilligan, stepping forward. "Don't you have anything for us?"

Sumpads speeds off without a glance, the rumblings of the Harley echoing off the hills.

"Guess not, eh?"

He had wanted to engage the mailperson in some sort of repartee, mostly to get a better look at those astonishing tits. Sumpads indeed has a body that seems lifted from the pages of Conan the Barbarian. It is said that she can crack Brazil nuts between the cheeks of her exquisite rock hard buttocks.

"Is she always so chatty?" he asks.

But Flamhir isn't listening. "Oh swamis, swamis, this is important."

He is holding the letter in two hands, by its edges, like a phonograph record.

"Can you just give me one moment please?" He squats on his haunches in the sun, leans on the warmed metal siding of the garage.

"Oh, how thoughtful," he says sarcastically. "It's already been opened for me." He draws a single folded sheet of powder blue stationary through the slit in the top of the envelope, unfolds it, and begins to read. "Oh my God," he mutters after a few moments. "Oh my God!" This time louder. "Oh, God please no!"

Flamhir is overwhelmed by choking, wracking, sobs. He holds the letter away from himself at arm's length, pinching it by a corner as he weeps between his knees. Its contents are at once precious and horrible. Gilligan and Morris look at each other. They are not comfortable. They want to be kind. But they still need their scaffolding. The sobbing, which is truly wretched, continues. They sidle over to Flamhir. Morris squats down beside him.

"Is there anything we can do, mate?" He puts a hand on the stricken swami's shoulder. Flamhir shakes his head. "That's fine then, fine. We'll come back a little later."

Gilligan and Morris shuffle somewhat guiltily back to the truck.

We should be comforting the guy. Offering some support.
"Swamis! Wait!"

Flamhir is holding out the letter, eyes red, tears dripping off his moustache. "Read the rest to me. I can't see," he pleads.

"Sure, mate," says Morris gently. He again squats down and begins to read:

"Beloved Flamhir, I have some terrible news: I have AIDS..."

"Just the next paragraph, please" urges Flamhir and again buries his face in his hands.

"OK Let's see. 'They don't know much about the disease, except it is thought to be caused by a virus and transmitted by mixing bodily fluids. The bible thumpers are calling it a gay plague but my doctor says they're discovering straight cases as well. Frankie, or Flamhir, I never thought I'd regret mixing a single drop of anything with you but now you are at risk. Please see a doctor at once.' That last bit is in big capital letters, mate," interjects Morris, and then continues reading:

"'I am very tired now. Don't come and see me. I mean it. You are better to be near Him now. I would come there but it is not possible. I hope to write you again soon. Please know that I love you and am with you always no matter what happens. Love and his blessings, Garnesh.' That's it."

Flamhir sits head bowed in his hands for another few seconds. "Thanks Swami," he finally says in a whisper. "Go ahead and find what you need. I'll write up your order in a few minutes."

"Sure mate," says Morris. He beckons Gilligan to follow him into the garage amongst the racks of pipe. They leave Flamhir sitting disconsolately in the sun, the letter at his feet trembling gently in a very mild breeze.

18. The Quarantining of Flamhir

The sounds of the recycling centre are a busy mélange of hammer rat-a-tat tats, explosive hisses and thwacks of air guns, and the screeches of recalcitrant nails being pulled from knotted wood. Coveralls have been tossed aside since late morning and there is much laughter and banter among the sannyasins as they work in the sunshine. One crew is taking apart large plywood platforms that supported summer festival tents while another, using compressed air nailers, is reconfiguring them into shingled panels which will form the roofs of the insulated A-frame structures that are to be the new living standard at the Ranch. (Gilligan himself will, it is said, soon be mercifully released from the nocturnally frigid tent he's shared with Newfyamo in Fareezyuryingyang to a new A-frame in Walt Whitman Grove. The diminutive Maritimer, seldom seen in recent weeks due to his romance with Angelica, was assigned an A-frame ten days earlier.) A huge ghetto blaster sits on the centre table thumping out Bob Marley's *No Woman No Cry*. Many of the sannyasins are singing, even dancing along as they work.

A woman collecting nails in a bucket is slim with curly blonde hair. Seeing her from the rear Gilligan's heart leaps to his throat. But when she turns, her lips are thin, her teeth small. *Not her.*

"We need some two-by-fours for the motor pool," shouts Morris above the music.

"Help yourself," says the woman with the bucket. She indicates several piles of sorted lumber not far from the entry to the complex.

Morris and Gilligan back up the truck and begin laying the lumber on the rack along with the pipes they have brought from Sariputput. They eye each one down an edge to make sure it is not warped. A yellow school bus roars up from the direction of Hippocrises and discharges a single passenger. The tall swami lingers at the side of the road, watching the bus disappear in the direction of town. He looks at his watch. When they finish loading, he is still there, legs spread, arms crossed, waiting. Gilligan climbs up on the cab to secure the load with some bungee cords. From this vantage point he recognizes the one who waits. It is the kind doctor Kildaraj. Gilligan yells playfully:

"Hey Doc! What the hell are you doing? Waiting for a taxi or what? Hey Doc!" He stands straight up on the roof of the truck, waving his arms. "Hey, it's me, Snakebite!"

Kildaraj remains, standing impassively, looking down the road towards town. He gives no sign that he has heard Gilligan. Impulsively, the latter jumps on the hood of the truck, then thumps onto the ground. He jogs towards the doctor. The rock-crusher gravel, which tops this and similar clearings at the ranch, crunches under his feet. He is about halfway when he again shouts, "Hey Doc, Doc!"

Kildaraj whirls suddenly and motions him away.

"Go on back," shouts the Doctor. "You can't be here!" His voice is strident, almost angry.

Gilligan stops in his tracks. "Sorry," he says automatically. "I just wanted to thank you for the note. It's me, the snakebite swami."

Kildaraj's hazel eyes connect with Gilligan's for a moment. There is a flashing hint of a smile. "Right old boy," he says. "Right." He goes on fiercely, "Now for God's sake, go directly back now. Hurry!"

Gilligan is puzzled, mystified, and curious as he ambles back to the truck, head bent forward, hands behind his back. He watches his shadow take the sunny sparkle from the small stones as it passes over them.

"There's something fucking weird going on here," he mutters to himself.

"The only weird thing here," says Morris, who is suddenly in his path, "is you! What in the name of the sweet baby Jesus are you doing jumping on the truck like that? Look at this!"

He indicates the dusty imprint left by Gilligan's work boot when he leapt from the roof to the hood of the truck. "What the hell were you thinking? Narzesh is going to have our balls when he sees this!"

"Right," says Gilligan. "I saw Kildaraj there and wanted to thank—" He is rubbing the spot with the hem of his T-shirt. "Look it's coming off."

"It's fucking dented!" shouts Morris. "You can't wipe off a fucking dent!" The normally taciturn Kiwi is losing control. His face is red and his eyes bulge menacingly. "Look at it."

"Uh, yeah, right," concedes Gilligan. "It does look like a bit of a dent there. But, uh, pop the hood, maybe we can bang it out from the other side."

"We'd bloody well better." Morris jerks the hood release inside the cab. Gilligan fumbles with the safety. His companion's aggression has made him nervous. His hands are sweaty. "Aha!" he shouts triumphantly and lifts the hood high. But it slips from his grasp and slams shut. Morris is back beside him.

"Gaa! You're unbelievable!" He stomps back towards the cab.

Gilligan runs his palm over the hood. "No fucking worries mate," he proclaims. The dent is gone. "There," he smirks at Morris. "Fixed. Just the way I planned."

"Well, I'll be a son of a gun," says Morris joining him. "It is too!"

"Come on mate." He pushes Gilligan's shoulder. "If we time it right, we can hit Macarena for tea time." They settle in and start to roll.

"Slow right down," whispers Gilligan. "Check this out."

Ahead of them a familiar vehicle, Deela's white Bronco, is pulling up to where Kildaraj stands. It is followed by a red Peace Force Jimmy. Swami Lamborghini emerges from the Bronco. He carries a bundle to Kildaraj, who pulls something over his head. As they trundle closer, Gilligan can see that the doctor's face is now covered by a respirator. Gilligan has a heavy feeling in his solar plexus, as if he swallowed the rusty head of a sledgehammer.

"Stop here man," he blurts. "I've got to check the load. I think I forgot to tie those studs at the front."

With an exasperated sigh, Morris lifts the gearshift into park. Gilligan climbs back up to his perch on the truck bed and pretends to fiddle with the bungee cords. He sees that Kildaraj, still wearing the respirator, is wrestling his fingers into surgical latex gloves. Then Lamborghini helps him into a disposable surgeon's gown. Its jade color stands out against the surrounding shades of red like a lesion on healthy skin. Lamborghini snaps a glove on his own left hand and uses it to open the door of the Jimmy. With a brief hands-up gesture Gilligan reads as exasperation, Kildaraj slides into the back seat beside another figure. Lamborghini peels off his glove, tosses it onto Kildaraj's lap, and kicks the door shut. He jumps into Deela's Bronco and drives back towards town. The red Jimmy with Kildaraj in it enters the compound and heads straight towards Gilligan.

He drops all pretence of bungee preoccupation and slides to the ground. He waits with one hand clasping the strut of the passenger side's rear view mirror. The Jimmy looms up. It is as spotlessly clean as any of the Divine Bhagwan's own vehicles. The driver is masked, and gowned like Kildaraj. The car is moving at a very careful speed and the driver's black hair and pallid skin tone are quite visible. The weight in Gilligan's gut somersaults as he realizes the driver is Lurchamo and simultaneously has a look at the passenger in the rear seat beside Kildaraj. Poking from each side of the man's mask are the coiffed curls of a large auburn moustache. It is Swami Flamhir who is being taken away.

The Jimmy rolls by them and grinds up a road that is little more than a dirt trail scratched between two hills. Gilligan watches it disappear behind the hill to the right. Two hawks circle lazily above the hilltops, riding the air currents. They cry out repeatedly; piercing, keening sounds easily heard above Bob Marley and the recycling centre's hammers. He slowly swings open the door and gets back into the truck. Morris turns up the stereo. It is playing a song about a mystical stairway. The cries of the hawks follow them out onto the road.

The boys don't talk as they head back towards Sariputput. The queasy feeling in Gilligan's solar plexus does not go away. Seeing Flamhir being carted off like some sort of space alien has deeply disturbed him.

If Kildaraj is involved, there must be some kind of real threat. The commune can't become infected with this AIDS thing. But is it that contagious? And if it is, could he and Morris be infected? They were near Flamhir when he was crying. Morris even touched him. Hadn't the tear-soaked letter said something about bodily fluids?

Gilligan edges closer to his passenger side door. He studies Morris out of the corner of his eye. The rotund Swami seems fine. Face flushed. *That's normal.* He is singing softly along with the tape. Gilligan rolls down his window all the way. *Can't have too much air circulation.*

"Slow down man."

He has just seen a familiar figure emerge from a sparkling-white full-sized van parked near the front door of Sariputput.

"Pull up beside them. I know that chick!"

It is Slipsma, his girlfriend for three years when she was known as Daphne. Four more women emerge from the van. The rear doors are flung open and mops, buckets, cleaning solvents and neatly folded bundles of red rags are marshaled. Each girl is fitted with a respirator and plastic gloves. Slipsma directs two of the cleaners into the main building and the others into the garage, the scene of Flamhir's emotional meltdown just an hour or so earlier. This scene is carried out without the usual joking and giggling that accompanies any Ranch activity. There is an undercurrent of nervous apprehension that suggests the women have been told there is a certain level of danger in what they are doing. Gilligan jumps out of the truck and greets Slipsma. She is tucking the blonde bouquet of her hair into a kerchief as he approaches.

"Hey!" she smiles. "I didn't know that was you. The sun was reflecting off your windshield. How are you?"

They share the customary Ranch hug. She is wearing a spiffy red jumpsuit that looks like it has been freshly pressed. Gilligan notes her delicate wrists, high cheekbones and fine grey eyes. Her initial inquiry, which he answers with a nod and a smile, is followed by another:

"What are you doing here?"

"I'm on a run with Morris here. We're getting supplies for the crew at the Motor Pool. How about you?"

"Oh, Deela wanted me to supervise this job personally. There might be some kind of bug that could be dangerous to the Divine Bhagwan. We're disinfecting everything."

"Supervise?"

Gilligan tilts his head, gives her a look of wide eyed incredulity. He has heard that Slipsma has become something of a super cleaner. Her exploits with bucket and mop, Ajax and rag, vacuum, broom and squeegee are the stuff of Ranch legend. It is said that she can go into a filthy shower trailer equipped with nothing more than a moist towelette and emerge twenty minutes later leaving everything spotless, including the towelette. It is also said that if Nivea should ever fall ill, Slipsma would be given the honor of cleaning the Divine Bhagwan's toilet.

"Yes," she giggles. "I've been named Lead Facilitator for Tydass. Deela just told me yesterday."

"Well, congratulations. I'm impressed. What happened to Madma?"

"Madma's moved to Bhagwanpuram, which is going to be the new name for Heiferville. She's beginning her job as mayor there." Slipsma seems to be choosing her words carefully, as if she knows a great deal more and can only risk divulging a certain amount. "You'll read all about it in the Totally Positive Times this week."

"I see," smiles Gilligan. "And will the news of your promotion be all over the front page?"

In her time with Buckstar, Slipsma allowed herself to develop an aura of goddess incarnate, an emanation indicating that the soles of her feet float inches, if not meters, above the dross earth of mere mortals. To this she adds a sharp-scaled patina of officiousness, a 'we are now on the record' tone when she asks:

"Were you boys *here* earlier?" She is looking at the scaffolding and pipes on the Ford's rack.

Gilligan feels a surge of defensiveness.

"Yeah. We swung by a while ago and picked up some stuff."

"Did you go inside?"

"Just for a second. What we needed was in the garage there."

Music comes from the main building. It is *Heart of Gold* by Neil Young.

"Sit down, Satyam." She indicates the ledge of the van floor where the sliding door is open. He complies. There is no doubt who is in charge at this moment. She puts her red Persephone-shoed foot on the ledge beside him.

"Nice shoes."

"Thanks." She gives him the briefest of smiles. "They're new."

The shoes are striated with reflective metallic threads that give them a disco look. He is ready to tell her he knows the guy who made them, but she continues.

"You need to tell me what happened here. You and your friend there could be at risk."

"From what, the new fag disease?"

Slipsma's eyes widen in astonishment. "How in the world did you know about that?"

"Oh, I have my ways," he says smugly. "You aren't the only one with friends in high places, you know."

She turns and walks in a slow circle with her arms crossed. Neil Young wails. Morris turns the truck engine off. Her 'Phonies' crunch on the gravel. When she replaces her foot on the ledge, her eyes are moist.

"Did you touch him, come near him at all?"

Officiousness is gone from her demeanor. She is scared and worried—for him. Gilligan is touched. Suddenly she is the tender college girl who happened to love him, who shared many of the barely articulated yearnings of his smothered heart.

"No," he sighs, "I didn't. You know me. Homophob-ic."

"How about him?" She indicates Morris in the truck.

Gilligan's belly contracts.

He must tell her. For his own good.

"Not really."

"Not really?" she whispers. "Listen, Satyam, it's just precautions at this point; you can imagine what a deadly *sexually* transmitted disease could do to this commune? We know it's only spread by bodily fluids. Chances are you are both totally safe…"

"He was crying," Gilligan whispers.

"Who?"

"Flamhir. He got a letter. Morris read it to him. He patted him on the shoulder. That's it. Listen. We gotta get going. It was nice to see you." As he gets up he squeezes her shoe. He walks towards the truck. The knot in his belly has moved up to flood his heart with emotion. It gushes upwards, tingling his nostrils and watering his eyes.

But what? Why? Morris will be OK. No. It was squeezing the shoe.

Settling into the sun-warmed vinyl beside the oblivious Morris, Gilligan remembers:

She'd married a good guy, a tall, unusually ambitious doper, the assistant manager at the Odeon Carlton Theatre, on his way to becoming a lawyer. It was the mid- seventies; the Poseidon Adventure was playing. Gilligan, an usher, was friendly with Daphne and Tim. They'd smoked dope and played chess in the box office after closing.

A couple of years later, he ran into them at Western University where Tim was pursuing his lawyerly ambitions and the friendships were renewed. But by the end of the school year John Price and Daphne Binns were chastely in love. She married, he a virgin. Ideas, ideals, fears, repressions and sexual tensions clogged the air, along with the pervasive scent of cannabis. In the face of a reality as palpable as an elephant defecating in the middle of a theatre's crowded lobby, nothing was acknowledged. Finally, one day in May, she came to help him paint his new flat. They were so excited and scared by what they knew had to happen, that every ten minutes one of them had to pee. It turned into a paint and pee session. While snacking amidst his wretched drop-sheet covered student furniture, John Price allowed his left hand to reach out and stroke her running shoe. They ended up in bed, and, after some coaxing, she managed to deflower him. John Price, led by that left hand, had taken his first tottering steps towards adulthood. By falling in love, over the next few years they emerged from their cocoons together- she from her ill-advised marriage and he from his own parentally ordained future as a lawyer. Flitting romantically amidst the flowers of new experiences: music, poetry, vegetarianism and sex on playground equipment in the depths of soft summer nights, they found great chunks of themselves in each other. But the luster faded, as it must. From behind a facade of fealty, she began cultivating her escape from him. Said escape and his own desire for more freedom were effectuated by her trip to the ashram in Spoona while Gilligan remained in Toronto's Cabbagetown.

"Morris?"

The big fellow, his window rolled down, is tapping his meaty fingers on the door frame in time with the music. He nods.

"They seem to be making a big thing out of this Flamhir disease. Do you think you might have caught it?"

Morris laughs.

"Caught it? No fucking way mate! It's transmitted by sex. It said so right in the letter. I patted him on the shoulder. I didn't give him a fucking blow job!"

"Yeah man, you're right. Still you know the powers that be can tend to overreact sometimes."

"No fucking worries mate. Come on, let's enjoy our cruise. There aren't going to be many days like this one!"

He turns up the music and resumes his drumming with more vigor. Reassured, Gilligan lets out a sigh, and settles back into his seat. He watches the rounded hills roll by, and the sunlit mesas revealed beyond them. The anguish in his chest eases. Five years later he is finally letting go of Daphne's foot. He also realizes that his former beloved is now one of the ruling bitches of this wondrous commune.

19. Why Gilligan Came to the Ranch

As their pickup truck trundles along the Pathless Path highway towards Macarena, Gilligan recalls the last time he had a real conversation with Slipsma. It was back in Toronto, in Cabbagetown, almost five months earlier, the morning of May 14, 1982. He was squatting amidst sundry neglected perennials in the garden behind Number 7 Wellesley Cottages, gazing at two scrawny marijuana plants. They were thriving, in a top-heavy, over-watered fashion, next to a dusty bleeding heart in full bloom.

Do I harvest them now? Better smoke them before they are ripped off or — God forbid — even confiscated.

Anti-drug rumblings were echoing from the loftiest nags of the Bhagwan movement: Deela and her celestial lieutenants. Illicit activities by disciples could not be allowed to harm the Divine Bhagwan's application for resident status in the United States. The religious right, sensing a threat from the "sex guru" and his commune, had brought considerable political pressure on all levels of government to deny him a visa. With Megadharm, the new Toronto Bhagwan centre now next door in Number 6, confiscation was an alarming possibility. Gilligan sighed and plucked both plants, shallow roots and all.

"Still enjoying your gardening, eh?"

Slipsma, whom he'd known for much longer as Daphne, was standing on the worn, silvered sundeck. Chosen during her recent months in Spoona as a medium to the Master, she'd tasted the ineffable, whilst he — the former boyfriend--remained a mere flake of flotsam twisting in the eddies of her wake. Slipsma—which means Exalted One (she had narrowly preceded the sitcom stage of disciple namings) —returned from India via Toronto to 'clear' things with Satyam Gilligan, whom she'd known for much longer as John Price. He had written to her more than once, whining about missing her.

On the home front things did not work out the way John Price had hoped. Despite his involvement in the Divine Bhagwan's so-called sex cult, and despite being employed (until recently) in the grooviest natural foods store in Cabbagetown, he was having problems making it with other women. Not that there weren't opportunities. Opportunities were knocking as regularly and insistently as the clapper on a recess bell. The problem was himself. His insecurity and prickly, defensive heart. He was interested in making love without the love; in fantasies becoming real, without the reality. Like a head of lettuce cut off from its roots, his psyche crawled with wormlike fears of impotence, of latent homosexuality, of being always unloved. Daphne had been a locus of emergence for the liveliness of an otherwise barren soul. The removal of this focus had left him bereft.

Slipsma had graciously returned to him in the aforementioned 'sharing' mode. But it was no use. They didn't 'connect' despite her willingness to share the superb flow of tantric energies she had become a vehicle for at the Ashram. The morning after she arrived, after a less than fruitful night in Gilligan's loft, the phone rang. It was Buckstar. Gilligan watched her heart leap into the phone. It was a cosmic coincidence, an amazing surprise! She and Buckstar never planned anything. It was wonderful the Way their lives and spirits had simply flowed together. And now he was ready to flow up from Florida on his brand new Honda Gold Wing Innerstate motorcycle, so they could share the same 'space' again. What bliss! John Price saw that though he was supposedly reborn as Gilligan, with Slipsma he was just a piece of old history.

Everyone but Newfyamo, who had heard something of his shady dealings back in Spoona, was impressed by Buckstar when he arrived. Tangled blond hair. Cool French accent. Buckstar had grown up on the beaches of Cannes. He knew beautiful people. He played Gilligan's guitar much better than the owner ever could. They had some fun sing-a-longs. Buckstar and Slipsma spent every moment together, in utter harmony, seldom speaking. Interminable hugs, quiet whisperings, more interminable hugs, as if they shared their own finely tuned ecstatic wavelength. Gilligan nursed his self pity the whole time. Now it 'felt right', at least to them, that they would ride off into the sunset to New York City. Buckstar had some friends there, some unspecified business, and who knew? Perhaps the call would come from the Master to join him though Buckstar, tainted by a known attachment to drug dealing, was unlikely to be invited.

Slipsma was coming to the back yard to say a final good-bye. Back less than a week from India, her slenderness had been enhanced by a bout with amoebas. With her halo of long blonde hair like unto spun gold, Gilligan now thought of her the same way she did: as nothing less than a goddess. Her raiment that day was pink leather hot pants with a matching leather vest over a pink T shirt. On the shirt was a large image of the Divine Bhagwan with the words ENLIGHTENMENT COMES TO AMERICA. A new pair of pink cowboy boots and a glittering pink motorcycle helmet under her arm completed the ensemble.

"Nice outfit," said Gilligan.

"Thank-you."

"Heading down to Dallas to try out as a cheerleader?"

"Very funny."

"Where do you get the money for all these new outfits?"

"Buckstar is quite wealthy and very generous."

"And what happened to your tooth? It's fixed isn't it? But you still move your lips to cover the gap while you talk. Let me guess: Buckstar's dentist? I guess you are happier with a real man."

His tone was distinctly petulant.

As part of the 'clearing' process, she had 'shared' with John Price the tape of a session she'd had with Kabbalah, the Spoona ashram's famous astrologer. In it, she'd referenced her new liaison with Buckstar as evidence of Saturnian evolution, since Buckstar was a man, whereas John Price, whom she'd been with for close to four years, was more of a boy. Since then, John Price/Gilligan had sulkily persisted in proving the correctness of her evaluation.

At that moment, stuck by the needle of his petulance, her aura of ineffable preciousness was momentarily lost. She seemed about to curse and swat at him, the way she had in the old days on certain monthly occasions when her delicate nerves would fray. Instead, she closed her eyes and took a deep breath.

"You don't need to do that."

"What?"

"Put yourself down."

Satyam Gilligan looked at her blankly. He folded the leaves of the pot plants and stood up to put them in his pocket.

"You *are* so much Satyam, but you don't act on it!" Slipsma put her hands on his shoulders. "Believe it or not, in many ways you are more fun, more intelligent, more sincere, and way more sensitive and wholesome than Buckstar. But you don't show it because you don't know it. Just be and do."

She gave him a longish hug. He was touched and a bit stunned by what she'd said. *Can she really believe it?* But though her words stayed with him, her blonde halo was being tucked into her helmet. Her leather-clad butt disappeared around the corner of the cottage. He heard the expensive purr of a motorcycle, some laughter, then the sound of the motor dwindling as, gearing up, it bled into the traffic sounds of Toronto. He gazed at a knot in the deck below his feet. It looked like a rhinoceros with a thick, upraised horn.

This was the moment he decided to leave Toronto for the Ranch, to do whatever it took to be with the Master. But first he needed funding for Alchemendra's Buck Lake workshop which began that very evening. He would have to visit his mother.

He made the journey to Denlord Estates in North York later that morning. As he walked towards what was once the family home, he congratulated himself on his decision to leave for the Ranch as soon as possible after Alchemendra's workshop. His bricklayer's apprenticeship session ended the next week. He would receive a decent check. He could postpone the next session indefinitely.

It doesn't matter. At least I'm my own man, not another cog in the organized madness, the frenzy of selfishness that is the modern world.

His mother's house featured a swooping roofline and beige fieldstone facade—a big subdivision seller, as the neighborhood was littered with them. Doctor Purtz, their neighbor, still driving with the generous nose pointing nearly straight upwards (it always gave John Price's Dad a chuckle) sifted past Gilligan in his elegant grey Mercedes. The doctor lifted his hand in a measured wave as he recognized John Price. The eyes widened, the head and nose turned. The thought "What the hell is the kid doing wearing beads and red clothes" furrowed the highly trained medical forehead.

Is the tinted window going to glide down? Will the doctor speak to me?

No. He remained sealed off from the lovely May day by the air-conditioning. But his routine was off track. He stopped short of the garage and waited a moment for the automatic door to open. Normally, he would have glided in there all in one motion, like plankton inhaled by a whale.

Gilligan tossed his cigarette butt to the curb and cut across the lawn to the asphalt driveway. It was patterned in shadow by the leaves of the maple tree and the ellipse of his basketball hoop still nailed to the trunk, though grown with the tree somewhat above the regulation ten foot height. He stopped, crouched, and sank an imaginary baseline jumper.

"Swish," he said in a loud whisper that resonated with the fluttering leaves of the poplars behind the house.

He pushed the doorbell to set Ralphie off, just for fun. He opened the door with his key before his mother could get all worried about answering it. Ralphie whimpered with joy, wagged his tail furiously and reared up with paws on Gilligan's chest in frantic efforts to lick his face.

"Hi Ralphie, how you doing boy? Are you a good dog? Yeah, he's a good dog!"

He grabbed the mongrel beast by the luxuriant fur below its ears and wrestled playfully.

"Hi dear. How are you?"

His mother sat in her usual spot on the left side of the striped gold loveseat, whose back was badly faded by the light from the bay window. Needles clicked as she worked at knitting a scarf. It was about a foot wide, close to twelve feet long, and bright red. It was for him.

"I'm fine Mom, how are you?"

"Oh fine, fine. I'm fine. I'm knitting you a scarf." Her forehead was furrowed in concentration. She wore a pink housecoat and matching bunny slippers. "What's new, dear? Can I get you something to eat?"

"Oh, not too much- Ralphie..." John Price said this in a special tone of voice that drove the dog into whirling paroxysms of anticipation.

"I'm going to do a workshop up north this weekend."

His mother was a petite woman, prematurely aged by the nervous breakdown and subsequent shock therapy that had precipitated the break-up of her marriage three years previously.

"Is it an acting workshop?"

"Sort of. Ralphie? Do—?" The dog became more excited, running back and forth in a manic relay between Gilligan, who had stepped into the living room, and the front door. He slid ludicrously as his momentum buckled the beige floor mat and his nails scraped on the foyer's tiles. Ralphie was an engaging mutt with long, shiny fur, jet black save for the snowy white bib, feet and tail tip. He'd served for years, as pets often do, as the focal point for the affections of a non-affectionate family.

"I guess you could say," he continued to his mother, "that the workshop is geared towards helping us act more naturally." John Price/Swami Satyam Gilligan knew from his brief, failed acting career that acting naturally was not his strong point. He yearned to be more spontaneous.

"Will you stay for lunch, dear?"

Marian paused in her knitting and looked up at him hopefully.

"Sure Mom, but I've got to be back downtown by four o'clock."

"Should I scramble you some eggs or would you like a sandwich?"

"Eggs sound good. The workshop's two hundred and fifty bucks, Mom. Is there any chance you could lend me the money?"

"Of course dear, I'll give you a cheque."

"Ralphie? Do you want to go for a walk?"

The dog yelped his assent and redoubled his frantic antics. John Price opened the door. There was a staccato clatter of nails; the mat ejected inward under hind paws. Ralphie became a black and white sniffing streak, here and there, then ecstatically to the trunk of the maple tree where he cocked his leg.

"See you later Mom."

"Ok dear. Be careful. Watch out for the cars."

Jesus Christ,it's a short crescent in a fucking subur— and *I'm twenty five years old— good thing she missed that close call with Purtz— I know. I know. I'll always be her little boy. I guess I should allow her that.*

"Come on Ralphie, let's go in the ravine!"

When he returned from his walk (during which he managed to smoke the morning's meager marijuana harvest) Marian was sitting in the same spot on the love seat, knitting. A tuckered out Ralphie lay in a yellow patch of sunlight on the broadloom. He rolled his eyes towards John Price and thumped his tail in greeting.

"Your lunch is ready. I was starting to worry, especially when Ralphie came back by himself."

"Yeah, sorry about that. I was thinking about something and he wandered off."

"You used to be so smart in school dear, but I think you may think a little too much."

They ate lunch in front of the TV. MASH was on. Gilligan chuckled copiously. His mother brought him dessert— tinned fruit cocktail—and handed him a Time Magazine.

"Lizzie gave me this to look at, Johnny. It has an article about the Divine Bhagwan. They say he's running a sex cult."

"Oh Mother, that's such crap! They are just trying to sell magazines."

He scanned the article carefully, laying it on the table in front of him as he spooned the fruit cocktail.

"... .taxes owed in India.... owner of scores of Rolexes and several dozen mint condition antique cars... officials stress he is in America as a tourist... bones broken in therapy groups... sex as a path to enlightenment... the Bhagwan has left no stone unturned in merchandising... .reportedly half a million disciples from all over the world..."

"Would you like a cup of tea before you go, dear?"

"Sure, but in the living room, okay Mom?"

He snapped off the TV which had just switched commercials from Ktel to Vegamatic. "Die, Cyclops!" he muttered.

Gilligan settled onto the plush beige carpet beside Ralphie, rested his head on the dog's warm flank. Ralphie crooked one paw, lifted his head inquiringly and then stretched out again with a big sigh. The patch of sunlight he'd been sleeping in had moved, so only the shaggy white tip of his tail remained illuminated. Satyam Gilligan sighed too.

"It's a weird life, Ralphie boy, isn't it?"

Between himself and the kitchen stood the solid mahogany dining room set. John Price remembered their last Christmas dinner there, the first one without his father. He sat at the window end of the oval table, with Granny opposite, in his dad's place. She was a peasant woman from Macedonia. Fifty years in Canada, she had not learned to write nor speak English, remaining hunkered down within a flimsy fragment of the Canadian cultural mosaic. She buried her vice-riddled husband several years ago, had howled out his name three nights in a row. The sight of her grandson, sitting there across the table all grown up with his ponytail and red clothes, had tickled her. Her daughter for years had said he was brilliant in school and was going to be a lawyer. The old woman had chuckled, then laughed from her belly, a silent aching laughter, beaming it into his eyes.

"Johnny, Johnny, Jesus Christ Johnny," she said over and over again.

Gilligan remembered how dumbfounded he'd been. His grandmother was a creature of the earth, a natural, grounded woman. *What was so funny?*

"Have you heard from you father?" asked Marian as they settled in with their tea.

"Not since my birthday. He had us to their new condo for dinner."

"And how was Dale?"

"She was great. She gets along well with Lizzie and especially Jean, what with them being almost the same age and all."

Her knitting needles began to click steadily. John Price imagined the scarf growing, snaking out towards him, wrapping itself around his neck. He looked at the marble-topped coffee table. For years John and his sisters had been forbidden to come anywhere near it lest they crack the marble. Now, as always, the circular heirloom supported three objects: a squirrel-sized, seated golden poodle, a green-streaked heavy glass ashtray, and a wooden gilt-painted cigarette box. Gilligan opened the latter and gazed into it the same way someone who isn't hungry opens the fridge and then closes it again. It was empty.

"Mom, don't you think it's time you got out of this house? I mean six-thousand square feet of living area is a little big for one person. Dad's not going to come back."

The needles continued clicking.

"I know that Johnny. I'm not waiting for your father to come back. I've got to think of Ralphie. Ralphie and Immaculata."

"Ralphie can go with you. Ralphie and Immaculata for that matter. Though God knows why you're paying her forty dollars a week to come over here and have lunch."

"She's been coming for eleven years and she still cleans."

"Yeah, right, she helps you clean out your fridge. She's taking advantage of you. Why can't you see that?"

"Was your lunch all right?"

"Yes, Mom. Fine. The eggs were good."

The needles click.

"Have you seen the doctor lately?"

"No, dear. He says I'm stabilized now."

"What about the psychologist? You should be talking to someone."

216

"Dr. Schindler says balancing the chemicals is the most important thing."

"Dr. Schindler," said John Price contemptuously. "Him and his Italian loafers and his brand new Mercedes sports car—he's nothing better than a drug pusher Mom."

Marian glanced at her son. She stopped knitting and reached for her cigarettes. Gilligan pulled out his DuMauriers. Cigarette smoke swirled, ignited to a gleaming blue by the sunlight. The golden poodle coruscated on the table.

"Have you heard from your father?"

"You asked me that already, Mom."

His mother, as always, sucked on her cigarette from one corner of her mouth and then blew the smoke ceiling-wards from the same corner while holding the cancer stick daintily high between her fingertips. There was something grotesque about the procedure, as if she were playing at being a gangster and a princess all at once. He blew a couple of smoke rings, watched them illuminate into haloes as they hit the sunlight.

"I'm sorry dear. I mean did he say anything else?"

"He said he'd like to burn the Bhagwan tapes I've been lending you. He thinks I'm screwing you up. I told him that to me it was like putting flowers in someone's room."

"Well dear, I have to admit a lot of it is over my head. I really don't understand what he is saying most of the time. I'm not smart like you dear."

"Mom, have you thought about what I told you on the phone? About using my new name?"

She looked at him dully.

"You know, Swami Satyam Gilligan."

Marian nodded and shook her head as she drew on her cigarette. She exhaled through the corner of her mouth.

"I don't know dear. It seems a bit strange to me. The first two names I could never remember, and Gilligan—your sisters both think it's ridiculous."

"It **is** ridiculous, Mother, that's the whole point."

He leaned forward, animated, gesturing with his hands. "All of life is pretty ridiculous. The new name helps me to let go of the past and see things in a fresh way."

His mother put out her cigarette and resumed her knitting. There is some emotion in her voice. "What do you mean the past? Is your family what you want to let go of?"

"Well, in a way, yes. I mean all that bourgeois crap to be a lawyer, get rich, have two-point-five children, it just seems so empty. What you raised me to be is not who I really am."

"We did the best we could, dear."

The knitting needles clicked faster than ever. Satyam Gilligan didn't know what to say. He had a nice buzz going and then went and upset his mother.

"There is something else, Mom. We're building a new commune in Oregon. I'm going there."

"Is Daphne going with you?"

"No, Mom. She's back from India. She's got a new boyfriend. He has a big motorcycle."

"Motorcyles are dangerous; I hope you never get on one, Johnny."

Gilligan stubbed out his cigarette in the hefty, clean, glass ashtray, foregoing the smaller one that he'd shared with his mother up to that moment.

"When, dear?"

"I don't know. Soon. I can't go there directly because you have to be invited. But there are Bhagwan centers down in the States. I'm going to get as close as I can. I kind of know someone in Los Angeles, a girl named Bala. There's a center there, a really cool old mansion where I can stay for a while. I mean my whole life revolves around this guy. I think I should at least meet him."

His mother stopped knitting, looked directly at him. Her eyes were moist.

"You go then, Johnny, if that's what you need to do. Just be careful."

"I will, Mom. Thanks. Oh. And do you think I could have that check for the workshop? I'll make it out for you."

"Oh course dear. I've got my purse right here."

He swiftly filled out the paperwork and crossed to the loveseat to kiss her on the cheek.

"Bye dear."

"You take care of yourself, Mom."

The dog had moved to its spot on the matt in front of the door. His tail wagged as John approached.

"Scuse me Ralphie, I gotta go."

He kneeled to hug the dog, nuzzling its silken ear.

"You're a good dog, Ralphie. The best," he whispered.

As Satyam Gilligan walked past Dr. Purtz's house, tears welled up in his eyes. He had to wipe them away.

Good old Ralphie. I really love that dog.

20. The Truck Farm

The Truck Farm, a flat few hundred acres in the easternmost region of the Ranch, fills a pregnant bend in the Big Snake River. Emptying through the navel or *hara* centre of this belly is Little Snake Creek which emerges onto the Truck Farm plain from the valley that is the spine of the Ranch. Once into the farmland it deltas menorah-like into irrigation channels which converge into an oblong pond that drains through a small set of locks into the river itself.

The epic cruise of Morris and Gilligan brings them to the crest of the last rise before the Pathless Path highway descends to the level of the farm. They have managed to quadruple what should have been a fifteen minute drive by dawdling, soaking up the sunshine, and doing some sightseeing. The eat-work-drive by-work-eat-disco-sleep routine is so involving, that many sannyasins see little of the Ranch, other than their worship areas, the cafeteria, the disco and their lodgings. To ameliorate this situation, Slowma has promised a day off after the December festival, to usher in the New Year with a special bus tour of the entire Ranch for all Bang Pas Zoo members. In the meantime, for a lucky few such as Gilligan and Morris, there is cruising.

After the encounter with Slipsma, there was a stop at the site of the new casino. There, the dour Dozon, along with Anugruffa, were wiring mesh reinforcement for the incipient slab. Gruff, who is of a naturally garrulous disposition, was happy to see Gilligan, if only to have someone to talk to. Do-zon is typically about as communicative as the concrete blocks he worked with.

They then stopped for a peek at the natural waterfall about half a kilometer upstream from the Van Gogh Bridge. There the banks of Little Snake Creek are high, well over ten feet. The falls, though modest, were beautiful in the sunshine, disgorging into a swimming hole the size of a very large hot-tub. Such is the unusual warmth of this November day that immersion was tempting.

"Wow, that's amazing. Did you know that the artificial one, the ceremonial Yahoo! Waterfall we're building in front of the Master's house is even higher?" said Gilligan. "But this is a great place to bring a chick."

"Yeah," adds Morris. "For a picnic. Speaking of which mate, it's tea-time. Why don't we stop at Macarena? It's a touch out of the way, but there might be cake."

"Cake, you say? This is a moment when we should ask ourselves, 'What would Slowma do?'"

"She'd say 'Let them eat cake'," shouts Morris.

It was there amidst the waterfall's thousand voices that the epic nature of their voyage sank into the young men's souls.

"You realize," said Gilligan, as they settle into the truck, "that this cruise may well qualify us for the Beetle Bailey hall of fame?"

"Beetle who?"

"Never mind. Drive on MacMorris. To Macarena we go."

Macarena was paradise. Lovely fresh coffee and leftover chocolate cake from Hemlock Grove. Sun streaming through the windows; sparse crowds; relaxed conviviality. Buxom Abreatha and sexy Greek Neato warned Gilligan that a new beer token system was coming. Numbered tickets would henceforth replace photocopied designs that certain

Bang Pas Zoo workers had been known to replicate by hand.

"Why in the world are you telling me this?" he says huffily. "Talk to the Australians and the Kiwis. They're the ones who are beer crazy. Right Morris?"

Morris, his mouth full of cake, mouths some incomprehensible slander against the Australians. Neato sings *Some Day My Prince Will Come* as she and Abreatha giggle their way back into the kitchen. *What,* thinks Gilligan, *do they think I'm some kind of Prince?*

The last stop for the sojourners before the Truck Farm is Koubiya, the Ranch's dairy farm. On the opposite side of the road and the creek from the tent enclave of Fareezyuryingyang stands the large barn that supplies the milk needs of the entire ranch. A renovated holdover from the Big Snake days, it takes advantage of a large natural clearing and easy access to the creek for pasturage and drinking water. Each day scores of gallons of raw milk are produced and consumed by the commune. Morris, who grew up on a sheep farm in New Zealand and is fascinated by anything to do with food, eagerly insisted on the visit. City boy Gilligan humored him and enjoyed the sights, if not the smells, within the complex.

They fed the two giant emus who are guardians against coyotes for the chickens and the gloriously plumaged roosters whose piercing cock-a-doodle-doos awaken Gilligan every Fareezyuryingyang morning. The cruisers, succumbing to an onslaught of dedication, decided to pass on visiting the horse barn, which is another five minutes off the Pathless Path. Gilligan would have loved to visit Bear, but the afternoon is beginning to wane. He senses that Narzesh is likely already wondering where the fuck they are.

Morris managed to score some fresh hardboiled eggs, which he is happily peeling and eating as they arrive at the upper edge of the Truck Farm. The view is splendid. The golden autumn sun, nudging towards proximity with the hilltops behind them, pours light over the scene like a beneficent god. The creek, pond, and irrigation ditches shimmer. Fields of dead corn stalks are a burnished golden brown. One field is highlighted with orange and yellow pumpkins and gourds. In the distance, the great bend of the river sparkles blue and serene. On its further shore, off to Gilligan's left, elevated amidst gentle rises, like a church in the European countryside, is the research centre for Persephone Shoes. The glass dome of Alvin Dark's silo-office reflects bright beams, as from a lighthouse. Down the hill to their left is an old clapboard barn with a circular driveway. This is where the trucks come for the produce and the school buses turn around. To the right of this, on a barren, level field, someone is peering through a transit level on a tripod. A hundred or so yards away from him, looking like a misplaced scarecrow, someone else is holding an elongated numbered stick.

Gilligan recognizes the rotund figure at the tripod. It is Avibasso, one of the architects who just a couple of days earlier was leveled by the giant plastic cigar at the Motor Pool. He is an older South African whose disenchantment with Apartheid blossomed into a spiritual quest after his wife died of breast cancer.

"Come on," says Gilligan. "Let's go see what Avibasso is up to."

"Hey man, what's happening?" he calls out as they drive up.

Avibasso straightens up from the eyepiece. "Well, well, well," he chortles. "If it isn't the Crapper King! Let me shake your hand!"

At this he attempts to hold out his hand but bends over double with gales of laughter. "Give me your hand, and you hold up this shitty piece of toilet paper. I tell you the look on Narzesh's face was worth all the shit I've been put through these past couple of days. Ha ha ha!" He regains his composure and makes a notation on a clipboard that hangs from the tripod. "Now what can I do for you gentlemen?"

"We're on a cruise," says Morris. "We've got to get the Wackerpacker from Toasto."

"Well, keep going," says Avibasso motioning the stick-holder to another position. "He's building a bridge across the creek, just before the pond. They're going to need it for access to the new building. See where those machines are working, beyond that smoke there? Hmm. Those bridge boys must have had one hell of a teatime campfire."

In the distance across the creek to the east and south of them, working in a sunlit haze of dust, a huge grader and a backhoe can be faintly seen and heard.

"They brought those machines cross country from the Rock Crusher. Hell of a trip."

"What are we building?" asks Gilligan.

"Technically, our neighbor is building it. It'll be a kind of factory to make money for the ranch. Putting bloody shoes together for Persephone, then shipping them across the river on the barge." Avibasso's tone as he says this indicates that he does not approve of this entire project. "And it's a total bloody secret so don't tell anyone. I don't know why I'm bloody well telling you. They'd have my balls for it."

"Is this part of it?" asks Gilligan.

Avibasso laughs again. "What this is—or at least will be—is a vegetable washing building."

"You're kidding," says Morris. "It looks like it's going to be huge."

"It is. Didn't you hear?" The architect lowers his voice to a mysterious whisper. "Due to the divine influence of the Buddhafield, we are now capable of producing huge vegetables. Carrots as big as you are, like Findhorn's."

"Really?" says Gilligan. "You're—"

"Right," interjects Morris. "And cucumbers nearly as big as my dick!"

"Ha ha ha ha! Ha ha ha ha! Go on now you two. I've got work to do. Maybe you can worship here soon enough.

It's got to be ready for next year's Universal Annual Celebration. We're expecting twenty thousand people for that one!"

Gilligan and Morris move on. The shadow of their truck, with the elongated shapes of the pipes and lumber on the roof rack, extends over the cut off cornstalks. The road, now little more than twin ruts and a green grass meridian, is dry and smooth aside from the occasional puddle. Off to their right a crew of sannyasins is loading freshly dug potatoes onto a flatbed trailer. These will be used for flat fries at tomorrow's breakfast.

Ahead appear silhouettes of two pickup trucks, and the familiar outline of a house-like tool trailer, the same one that issued Gilligan his first hammer. A plume of smoke rises to their left. The smoke is caused by the fact the new bridge is on fire.

One of the trucks belongs to a welder, a tall, excitable Polish fellow named Swami Clint Eastwood. Standing on the midpoint of the bridge, which consists of wide planks laid across steel girders, he and Toasto, back-dropped by dense gray smoke billowing from the juncture of bridge and shore behind them, are in a heated, arm-waving argument. Somehow, unknown to Swami Clint Eastwood, sparks from his torch have ignited dry grass under the bridge. This mere smolder, during a lengthy sun-soaked tea time on a small beach by the river, had a chance to gather strength to the extent the planks themselves began to burn.

"Hey Toasto, what's happening, man!" Gilligan shouts as he and Morris skid to a stop before the bridge and jump out of the truck.

Toasto's countenance lights up. "Hey, Gills. How you doing buddy? Say, do you guys mind going under the bridge here and giving Shaggyvan a hand? We got a bucket brigade going."

"Never mind Toasto!" a familiar voice shouts from under the bridge. "It's out."

A five gallon white plastic bucket is flung up from the creek bed and, with a hollow thump, sticks an upside-down landing in the middle of the bridge.

"Hey Shags!" Gilligan peers over the bank. "Let's see you do that again!"

Shaggyvan clambers from under the bridge and stands on the further shore. He is an odd sight: his red jeans thoroughly drenched from the knees down, his granny glasses fogged to the point of opacity. These he takes off and wipes on a dry portion of his shirt. Steam from the extinguished fire gathers around him like a wizard's cloak.

"What the hell are you doing out here?" asks Shaggyvan.

"Cruising. We need your Wackerpacker."

"It's in the back end of the tool trailer," says Toasto. "Everything OK under there, Shag?"

"The fire's out but three planks are burned almost through. We'll have to replace them."

"Beautiful," says Toasto. "Just beautiful. We put them in this morning and now we've got to take them out again. You—" he turns on Swami Clint Eastwood the welder, "can stay and help us. This is your fuck-up!"

"Crew leader is responsible for job site," says the Pole calmly. "Would be liking to help you but must go to casino site for girder welding. Goodbye. Thank-you for nice tea time." The lanky welder strides off the bridge and jumps in his truck, which has large acetylene and oxygen tanks strapped upright against its cab.

"One welder in the whole damn commune and he has to be a Polack pyromaniac!" shouts Toasto at the retreating vehicle, kicking dirt after it in frustration.

As Swami Clint Eastwood's truck rolls past Avibasso's survey station, another vehicle approaches from the opposite direction. RAWCAW! RAWCAW! The sound of Lionheart's horn floats across the sunny haze of the fields.

Toasto throws his hands up in the air. "Now that's just great," he exclaims. "How in the hell did Lionheart find out about this so soon? Did you two use your Motorola?" he asks Morris accusingly.

"Don't have one, mate. It was all Narzesh could do to let us use his truck."

The open jeep continues to approach very quickly, sounding its horn again and again. The driver, dressed in red, has no hat, and no beard!

"Wait a minute," mutters Toasto. "That's not Lionheart."

Shaggyvan jumps on top of the upended bucket. "You're right man," he says, shielding his eyes from the sun. "Who the hell is that?"

The jeep tears towards them at an alarming rate. It swerves back and forth across the road, nearly bucking out of control. Gilligan sees the driver has long dark hair, and is very thin. He knows him.

Lurchamo? No.

"Gaa!" he shouts, turning and running back towards the others. "It's him! The assassin, Dillard! He's back!"

"Well how about that?" exclaims Toasto in his down home voice. "Looks like he's stolen Lionheart's jeep. We'd better stop him."

"Block the bridge!" Shaggyvan, still atop the bucket, is waving his arms at Morris, who is leaning against the truck, carefully peeling another one of his boiled eggs. "Block the bridge!"

Morris nods. He walks over and plants himself, still peeling, in the middle of the roadway to the bridge.

"Not like that you idiot!" yells Shaggyvan. "With the truck! With the truck!"

"Oh, right mate." Morris hurries over towards the truck.

RAWCAW! RAWCAW! The rapidly moving vehicle is just a few hundred feet away and it is obvious that Morris will not be in time.

"Stop!" shouts Toasto. He moves to the front of the bridge, waving his arms widely over his head.

"Halt!" shouts Gilligan. He moves in front of Toasto, one armed raised, gesturing authoritatively for the jeep to pull to the side and stop.

RAWCAW! RAWCAW! The jeep keeps coming, as if impelled by the gusty breath of the devil himself. They hear its tires scrape on the gravel road as it swerves. RAWCAW! RAWCAW!

"Holy fuck boys." Shaggyvan is still on the bucket. "He ain't stopping!"

RAWCAW! RAWCAW! Gilligan can see Dillard's face clearly now. He is gaunt, unshaven, his shoulders hunched vulture-like around his mouth which is fixed in a maniacal grin. His black hair, near shoulder length now, wafts free from his head as if they were the heavy strings of a dank mop. His eyes are black pits of negativity, fixed like dark lasers on their goal: run these godless sinners over!

"Jump!" screams Toasto, as the Jeep bounces and roars towards them.

Gilligan, Toasto and Shaggyvan jump sideways like so many bowling pins tumbling to their next reincarnation. Surging adrenaline adds bounce to the springs in their legs. They splash one after the other into the creek several feet below. The jeep, which barely slows enough to gain the bridge, hurtles over the plastic bucket which has fallen to its side. It is gobbled up under the front fender and scrapes then crunches as the front wheels of the vehicle fall through the burnt out planks. Its momentum halted, the jeep nosedives and rears up on its front end, flinging Dillard Dark cleanly over the windshield and onto the other bank. The jeep plunges completely through the fire-weakened planks and topples into a near vertical headstand. It remains impaled, headlights submerged and elevated rear wheels spinning.

Dillard Dark's body, in a half tuck position, describes a long, gentle ellipse as it soars some thirty feet in a slow motion somersault before tumbling and bouncing along the ground for an equal distance. He is saved by the softness of the roadbed, which is loose gravel and sand awaiting compaction. He comes to his feet and groggily wiggles each extremity. Intact enough, he faces the sannyasins who are still extricating themselves from the creek's waters. He removes his mala and begins twirling it over his head.

"Y'all can have your graven image back!" he shouts and flings it in their direction. It clatters on the upended rear of the jeep, then nestles within the hub of the spare tire. "And y'all can have your red clothes back too. I don't need them anymore! I know all about you people!" He pulls his red sweatshirt off and flings it down. His trousers follow. His underwear is mercifully left in place. "Most of you are just sad, or stupid or running away from something! Y'all had me going there for a while. I was blinded by love, love for a no-good Jezebel, but I'm on to her and all of you now! You don't believe in God or any damn thing! And you don't know what love is neither! You just want to feel you're better than normal people like me! Well I'm not sticking around to get used and walked over! No one walks over Dillard Dark, you hear me? No one!" He screams out this last phrase as he turns his spindly, acne-splotched body and runs in the direction of the Persephone complex on the other side of the river.

"Shouldn't we try to catch him?" asks Shaggyvan, as Morris helps him out of the creek.

"Running's not my strong suit," says Morris.

"Naw," says Toasto. They are all panting from the surges of adrenalin. "That's not our job."

"Yeah," adds Gilligan. "Plus you know DB always says, 'hard to get here, but easy to leave'."

"Everyone might not feel that way," says Shaggyvan. "Listen."

Echoing faintly down from the valley, drawing closer every moment, is a sound never before heard on the Ranch: a police siren.

"Well," continues Shaggyvan, pointing to the elevated rear end of the Jeep, "As far as sannyas goes, I think he just resigned his commission."

"Look!" Toasto points towards the river, where a head pasted with black hair is the fulcrum of long white arms flailing towards the Persephone shore. The current moves Dillard quickly downstream, towards the complex. It appears he'll be swept past the glittering white buildings long before he reaches his goal. He disappears behind the rise of land on which the machines grading the shoe factory site continue to churn away. They cast long shadows over the rippled earth, towards the arc in the river where Dillard Dark's furiously swimming body was last seen. Though hundreds of yards away, their vibratory temblors are enough to upset the delicate balance of Lionheart's jeep. With creaking and groaning sounds much like the Titanic once cast over the dead calm North Atlantic, it slowly begins to topple. Moving as one, Toasto, Gilligan, Shaggyvan, and Morris tiptoe quickly off the bridge. The toppling stops at a Pisa angle. The sound of the siren draws nearer, though no vehicle is yet in sight.

"This," says Gilligan in a voice that feels, as never before, very much like his own, "is going to mean trouble."

21. Father and Son Reunion

Alvin Dark is alone in his office. It is a Sunday evening ritual he's embraced during his sojourns at the complex: take an early dinner; send everyone home; be alone and think. He enjoys the company of his thoughts, particularly on a night preceding a long journey. His thoughts are very good to him. They are his friends.

The son of a Portland tailor, though an indifferent student, he was always relentlessly inquisitive. After quarterbacking his team to the state championship in his senior year, he took a job in a bowling alley in addition to helping his father in the shop. By the age of twenty he'd worked his way up from pin-boy to manager. Endlessly handing bowling shoes over the counter made him curious. Why did so many regulars prefer a certain pair, the shiny ones or the ones with the brass eyelets? When the alley received a shipment of replacements, on a whim he grabbed some leather laces from his father's shop and put them in a few of the shoes. He found he could charge a premium for them: five cents an hour more. *Distinction,* he thought. *People want distinction.* It was a thought he held close as his career spiraled upwards throughout the sixties.

This evening, contemplating the muted November sunset through the curved sweep of the silo's windows, Dark's thoughts and eyes turn to the red people across the river. As silent as distant insects, the grader and the backhoe at the new factory's site finish for the day, stopping side by side amidst settling dust.

That Deela charged us a pretty penny for the use of those. But she knows as well as I do that I'd pay way more to get my own machines and operators out here. The deal we forged is a sweet one. She'll even provide construction workers from foundation pour on-wards. Once it's up and running it'll be a huge win for both sides. Too bad it's never going to last, particularly with the bad blood they've been stirring up around here. Regardless, it'll be good to get that building in and be ahead of our planning curve. To bad we couldn't manage another personal meeting before I go. Interesting woman. Something of the evil enchantress about her.

Far to left of the factory site, just the other side of the red peoples' pond, the early evening's second pillar of smoke begins to rise. Alvin Dark grabs his binoculars. A jeep, im-paled in a bridge, is burning. A number of men are scooping buckets of water from the creek and throwing them onto the blaze, which consists of black smoke pouring from the engine area. A bright red peace force Jimmy is on the scene, along with a number of other vehicles.

Well how about that? I thought I heard a siren when I was eating my dinner.

Ding! It is the silo's elevator, which Alvin never uses. He grips the binoculars more tightly, ready to fling them as a weapon if necessary. The door slides open. There, shivering and hugging his elbows tightly, a picture of goose-bumped misery in soggy pink underpants, is his only son, Dillard Dark.

"Dillard! What the hell?"

"Hello Daddy."

Alvin Dark pulls a yellow, green and red-striped Hud-son's Bay blanket from the cupboard beside the elevator. He touches up the thermostat heat and sits Dillard down on the same curved leather couch that Gilligan occupied three months earlier.

"What the hell happened?"

"I swum the river. I escaped from the red people."

"Escaped? I thought you wanted to be there. What about your girlfriend?"

"She ain't my girlfriend. Never was neither."

"I checked with the facility" says Alvin. "They said you were released and were going back to the Ranch on their bus."

"I did. I got there and-"

"And what?"

"They acted like they didn't know what to do with me. Same as Mom. Same as you."

"Look Dillard, I've done my best to find you some solid work, but this being a father is all new to me."

"Ain't your fault. It's mine. I let the devil touch me. He took my soul." Dillard says this with a passionate hiss, as he stands up and begins to dry himself with the blanket. Alvin Dark pulls celery colored Persephone sweat togs from another cupboard and tosses them on the bench beside his son.

"They left their mark on me too," continues Dillard. He tosses the sopping pink underwear into a trash bin, turns and displays the scars on his bum. They are very pink against his pasty skin, and angled towards each other like eyes that have been stitched shut.

"Good god," says Dark. "How did-?"

"Doesn't matter. What matters is that the devil touched me. They brought me into his house. It was across a bridge and between two hills. There was no furniture. Only his chair. I knelt down and touched the devil's feet. Cloven hooves in sandals. Then I fell into the devil's eyes. They gave me the necklace and he said my new name was Swami Prem Dillard. He touched me here-" Dillard points between his eyebrows, to the mystical third eye. "Rubbed me here with his thumb. I felt like I was falling, or floating, and burning, my body, my fingers, everything, burning, but it didn't hurt. I felt smart, smart all over. Like I'd do anything, anything to keep feeling that way. That's the devil's trick! The devil makes you feel good! But it didn't work. I'm on to them now. I was lost but now am found. The road to redemption lies before me."

Dillard's voice has been steadily rising in volume as he says this. He has been moving about as he speaks, his body galvanized by the recollection. Now he drops the blanket and, naked, moves with upraised arms to the windows overlooking the commune.

"It didn't work! Do you hear me, devil? I'm on to you and the slaves toiling in your pits! Like that temptress disguised as an angel! Faithless, betraying, Jezebel!" As he says this last he slaps the window vehemently with his upraised palms.

"Dillard!" Alvin Dark moves quickly and grabs the young man by the wrists. "You're smudging the window!"

"No!" Dillard struggles to free himself, but his father twists his wrists, induces pain that sits him back down on the couch.

"Are you going to behave now? Are you? Are you?" Alvin wrenches Dillard's wrists outwards, bending them back for emphasis. Dillard screams loudly as pain shoots up his arms and into his shoulders. Finally he relents.

"OK. OK. I give. I'll be good." He fixes a malevolent stare on Alvin. There's a new depth of rage in those eyes, something oily and combustible that causes a queasy turning in Alvin's gut, like the sight of maggots under an old log in the forest.

What the hell happened to the kid in prison?

"Good. Now please. Get dressed." Alvin tucks the sweat togs into Dillard's chest.

There are a couple of minutes of silence as Dillard dresses and father and son collect themselves. Alvin takes a few Kleenexes and wipes Dillard's handprints from the window. After a few minutes of pacing, he sits beside Dillard on the couch.

"Look Dillard. I'm sorry. I don't want to be hurting you like that."

Dillard, now fully dressed, stares down at the carpet. Clearly the kid is at some kind of crossroad. Alvin Dark's instincts, fine-tuned through scores of intense negotiations, tell him to wait. The next words must come from Dillard. Night-time shadows begin to shroud the Persephone complex.

"I was going to ask her to marry me," Dillard finally whispers.

"You were—who?"

"The girl. Angelica. She was so beautiful. The first one who ever—she dumped me Daddy, dropped me like a lump of shit she'd picked up by mistake. But don't you worry, I know whose fault it was; I know it was Lucifer's work. He sent a demon to possess her, to wrest her from me. But there will be a remedy. There will be redemption."

Dillard's hair, drooping over the collar of his sweatshirt in snaky tangles, infuses the material with river water, deepening the celery color to a swampy green.

Alvin Dark stands up and begins pacing again. He turns on the hooded flex-light on his desk. *Damn his mother! Had him at what? Seven months? Probably on coke the whole time.* He moves back beside Dillard.

"Listen buddy, I know you've had a bit of a rough time. I'm going away tomorrow, probably for a few months. We're scouting factory locations in Southeast Asia, India, maybe even China. I've retained a new guy. He was kicked out from across the river, too."

"I wasn't kicked out. I escaped."

"Anyway, this Alchemendra is going to show me a place in Thailand where they teach Zen Archery. He says it is the ultimate in goal-setting. Two weeks ago he did a one day workshop with our Portland management team and more than a dozen creative improvements came out of it."

"That's real exciting, Alvin. For you." Dillard blows his nose.

"Listen Dillard, how would you like to hold the fort here while I'm gone? At least until you feel better about things? I'm pretty much shutting the place down, but maintenance is still needed. I was going to have Bill do it, but he has his hands full coordinating that building across the river."

Dillard unclasps his hands. He wipes his eyes and turns to face his father. "You mean it? I'll be in charge of this place?"

"Well, there's not much to be in charge of—"

"I'm going back to Jesus, Daddy. I'm going to be a soldier of the Lord again."

Dillard stands up and paces thoughtfully towards the windows facing the river. "This can be our command center."

"What was that, son?"

"Bible study center. We did some Bible study in prison, Daddy. I'd like to carry Christian activities like that on here while you're gone."

"Super. That's a definite win-win. I know the place will be taken care of and you'll be sorting things out."

"Yeah. Super. But you know what they say, keep close to thine enemy." Dillard peers towards the Ranch. The area around the bridge is floodlit and a small bulldozer has appeared, a D3 to pull Lionheart's jeep out of the bridge.

"You're not going to do anything foolish again, are you?" asks Alvin.

"Naw. I've learned my lesson. This time I'm going to be real smart. But mark my words Alvin, I will not rest until that devil is dead!"

Alvin Dark laughs. "Dillard, that guru is a good thirty years older than you. You just be patient and you'll see him dead soon enough."

"Oh I'll be patient." Dillard pulls his hands into his sweatshirt sleeves and leans on the window. "I'll be damn patient. Don't you worry. I'll be very damn patient."

Alvin Dark sighs, then claps and rubs his hands together. He stands up.

"Good! You can stay in your old room downstairs. Now, if you'll excuse me, I've got some work and packing to do. I've got a long journey that begins tomorrow at the crack of dawn. And Dillard, I'm really pleased that you came back and that we could — connect like this."

Alvin crosses the room and extends his hand to his son. Dillard, still brooding over the scene across the river, doesn't notice him for a few long moments. Then he turns and his right hand slowly emerges from the recesses of the sage-colored sleeve. It feels cold in Alvin's fingers. Cold and dry, like the skin of a snake.

"One more question, son. He called you Swami Prem Dillard. What does the 'Prem' mean?"

"Love," Dillard says with a snarly grimace. "It means love."

22. Seasons Change

The fallout from Dillard's great escape is of a kind with the Ranch's first snowfall- quiet, with only minor accumulations on the higher ground. There is no publicity of the event. The Totally Positive Times, which had trumpeted the "assassin sannyasin's" conversion, never mentions that Dillard has left the Ranch. He fades from the collective consciousness, like a mosquito bite that has lost its itch.

For Gilligan, the big event of the moment is that he, one of the very last, is finally allowed to move from the frozen confines of Fareezuryingyang into a brand new A-frame. The desert nights in late November are often well below freezing. Gilligan had taken to sleeping in his clothes with Newfyamo's abandoned bed foam piled on top of him. Once cozy in this insulating mound, he would fashion a kind of tunnel to his nose; an invigorating lifeline to the stark, crisp air. In the mornings, with the tunnel rimed stiff, puffing fog with each breath, he would wriggle out from under the mound, and make a hasty, stiff-gaited lunge for the shower trailer, which was kept, in the name of communal economy, only marginally warmer.

His new digs are relatively fabulous. His A-frame is located in a housing area called Walt Whitman Grove. The Divine Bhagwan is an admirer of the long-bearded poet who, along with Blake, Van Gogh, and Yeats, is said to have had satoris—glimpses of enlightenment. In terms of published books, the Master noses out Whitman by three-hundred and seventy-four to one. Gilligan, along with the A-frame, has acquired a new sense of belonging. Though still nominally a summer worker, it is clear that he is destined to remain at the commune over the winter.

As the days of the December Master's Father's Birthday Festival draw near, the expanded Motor Pool building is somehow being completed on time. The architects go back to the drawing board and the blown-out plastic walls are replaced with corrugated translucent roof panels. This festival, though much smaller than the First Annual Universal Celebration, will nevertheless be a significant money-maker for the commune, particularly with the temporary casino now ensconced in the carpentry shop.

Narzesh gathers the mud crew on a goof-off day of finishing touches. There are only three left. Gilligan, Esperanto-a tall, confused and very funny-seventeen-year-old who could easily pass for twenty-five—and Fleuritima, the sprightly French Canadian ma whose path Gilligan constantly seems to be crossing. Gilligan likes Fleuritima. She is a cheerful, compact brunette, with fetching full lips and a wide smile: Aquarian qualities that he instinctively finds attractive. He has warm feelings for her that are a chakra or two higher than the typical adolescent lusts that he's heretofore been ruled by. He has not as yet 'gone home' with her. He senses it is coming, but bulwarked by the roots of their friendship, he is content to let that flower open in its own time. He is, in fact, more content than at any previous time in his life. It is the worship mostly, along with the beneficent aura of the Buddhafield, which is drawing him out of a morass of self-involved thinking into the wider world. He approaches every work day with the earnestness of a good student. By paying attention to what he is doing he acquires proficiency and, along with it, the respect of his peers. He evolves into a very good mudder, quick and neat in plastering seams and corners. Narzesh keeps him around until the end of the job because of this.

For his part, Gilligan lost some of his immature awe of Narzesh during a shouting match they had when he finally returned the crew truck after the epic cruise with Morris. Narzesh was waiting on his truck, steaming, late for his dinner. Gilligan dropped Morris at Macarena. He had not even come to a full stop in front of the Motor Pool when Narzesh accosted him: "Where the fuck have you been?"

From there, the conversation went steadily downhill, like small pebbles of dimwittedness dislodging larger boulders of stupidity from a mountainside of testosterone-steeped righteousness. Gilligan, instead of being filled (as he might have been a month or two earlier) with all-Canadian contrition, found himself to be unrepentant.

"For a cruise. Just like you do."

"Like fuck I do!"

"Like fuck you don't! Like that time you disappeared with that Mala chick, you know the German with the cutie-pie hat, for- how long was it? Oh yeah, four and a half fucking hours!"

"Fuck you!"

"Fuck you!"

"Fuck YOU!" Pause. "Was it really four and a half hours?"

"Four hours twenty three minutes to be exact. We were timing you."

"I remember that day. We went down by that waterfall. You know the one upstream from the Van Gogh?"

"Course I do," grinned Gilligan. "It was on our itinerary."

"You are an asshole. Gimme my truck and get outa here!"

"Fine." He proffered Narzesh the keys. "And be careful of the hood. It dents easily."

Gilligan left the encounter feeling even more therapeutically enhanced than after Alchemendra's workshop.

"People," Narzesh now tells the assembled crew. "Slowma has issued new worship assignments while the Birthday festival is going on. Fleuritima, you're to report to Slipsma at Tydass. You've been promoted to cleaner. Esperan-

240

to, you'll stay here, but you are now on the paint crew with Kalus and Shamsheer- two beautiful women, a little older than you, you should learn a lot." He wiggles his eyebrows suggestively. "I'll give you a little tip here, buddy. Make sure you clean your brushes at the end of the day unless you want to find out what your left nut tastes like".

"Copy that, Boss," says Esperanto with a brief salute.

"I'm going to join the crew building the new mall, and Gills, you are to report to the Cuddly Shark Boutique. I hear they want someone creative to decorate the windows."

"The boutique! I wanna work on the mall, man. I'm a Bang Pas Zoo guy."

"No, you're a boutique 'guy', at least during the festival. Surrender swami. You just might like it. Lots of nice looking mas there." This time he does the eyebrow thing to Gilligan.

"Fuck you," moans Gilligan dismissively.

"No, fuck YOU!" Pause. "You've no choice. So have fun."

Gilligan can't help but chuckle at the mocking reference to their earlier altercation.

"So let's go people. I'll give you all a ride into town. I have to return the truck to Bang Pas Zoo anyway."

Before she leaves the truck Fleuritima gives Gilligan a lingering wet kiss on the cheek. It ignites an ache deep in his chest. He decides to join the mall workers for tea time. He needs a smoke.

23. Incident at Big Snake River

"A case of champagne to anyone who goes swimming in that river!"

The challenge is issued in the cockney tones of Shanosserpan, a British Bang Pas Zoo stalwart with twinkling eyes and a magnificently overlarge proboscis. Said proboscis, cultivated in the rugged soil of the English working class, sniffs the opportunity for some rollicking good fun.

It is New Year's Day, 1983. The Master's Father's Birthday Festival ended over a week earlier. Gilligan not only survived, but enjoyed his tenure at the Cuddly Shark Boutique. After five months at the Ranch he feels like he now moves with the flow of the Buddhafield's currents. The Dutch blonde, Seatrice, did not appear for the festival. She, along with his misgivings about Deela and the 'bitches' running the commune, have been put on the back burners of Gilligan's mind. So too his concerns about his mother. Part of him regretted not being 'home' for Christmas. She sent him the scarf she'd knitted, all twenty-four feet of it. He wears a piece of it now, with other sections gifted to Fleuritima, Shaggyvan, Newfyamo, Toasto and Slowma. He reminds himself to phone later and wish her a happy New Year.

Such distractions aside, he is absorbed in the moment to moment life in the commune. A life that features good food, the Master's discourses, dancing in the disco at the end of a hard day's worship, as well as a blossoming romance with Fleuritima. Slipsma had been quite taken with the French Canadian's energy, competence and upbeat personality, and continues to be reluctant to release her from Tydass. Thus, she is not on the bus as Shanosserpan, Gilligan, and the entire Bang Pas Zoo membership are rewarded for a hard year's worship with an afternoon tour of the ranch. The Truck Farm, the riverside fringes of which they are currently jouncing over, is their last scheduled stop before heading to Macarena for dinner.

The weather has turned truly cold after a long spell of wet and mild. The road consists of mud and matted grass frozen into the deep ruts left by the last tractor that dared to brave the previously pliable terrain. Though occasional snowflakes bite at the windows, the bus is warm and convivial. Seats are crowded with bodies happy to have a break from routine, and to imbibe views of the great projects they have collectively undertaken. The Big Snake River, perhaps two hundred meters wide at this point, is a steady black flow. Within the oily darkness of the water, occasional chunks and slabs of white ice slide silently by.

"O.K. people," calls Slowma, from the front of the bus. "We're going to stop for a bit here, stretch our legs." She has not heard Shanosserpan's challenge amidst the din of desultory conversations. "You've all heard of Persephone shoes? That's their research centre you can see across the river!" The glass domed silo, with its surrounding trees denuded, looks closer and more exposed than when Gilligan last saw it.

"And over there, across the creek, is the site of the factory that we're running as a joint project with our neighbors! And, on this side of the creek where those orange stakes are is the site of our future vegetable washing area!" Slowma has a way of making everything she says sound like the best imaginable news.

Most of the bus's occupants disembark. They stand, hands thrust in pockets, arms crossed, shifting their weight from foot to foot. Snowflakes swirl amongst them and dance above the river's surface.

Shanosserpan again announces loudly, "A case of champagne!"

Shaggyvan, who is standing on a rock peering into the dark, swiftly moving waters, turns and says, "You're serious, a case of champagne?"

"Yes," proclaims Shanosserpan "a case of champagne to the first person who goes swimming in this river!"

"You're on," says Shaggyvan, removing his glasses and handing them to Gilligan.

"No Shags, noway. No. No. No." Slowma, grasping what is happening, talks as if to a puppy.

"It's for a case of champagne." Shaggyvan spreads his long arms wide as he utters this irrefutable justification. Shaggyvan now has a girlfriend. Captivated by his low-slung hammer, she had, at every drive-by break, made the long trek from the carpentry shop site to the welding shop, in order to stand beside him in the roadside line. A tall, well-built Texas gal, she had cut quite a figure, day after day, making the lonely ten minute walk along the dusty road, gradually looming larger. Shaggyvan had shown no sign of noticing her at first, but Texas persisted. Soon they were talking, sharing meals, taking each other home. A case of champagne would insure Shaggyvan any number of very happy nights through the dark winter days ahead. He pulls off his sweatshirt and toes off his work boots. His pants follow, leaving him clad only in drooping pink-tinged underwear. His skin, aside from his hands and face, is pallid; summer's blushes and brownings long since gone.

"No, Shaggvan, no! You can't do this. No!" Slowma makes horizontal chopping gestures with her hands.

Shaggyvan steps gingerly onto some shoreline rocks, then in up to his knees. Without ceremony, nor a glance at the joking, giggling onshore crowd, he slips headlong out into the river and swims a few strokes a foot or so beneath the surface, his body a long ghostly fish. He scrambles goose-bumped and shivering, back up on the rocks.

"This was not a good idea," intones Slowma, as the Bang Pas Zoo workers applaud, tease and congratulate him.

A spout of water suddenly erupts from beside the rock Shaggyvan is on. A loud, fearsome, bang echoes up and down the river.

"Whoo hoo! Hey boys, I found some nice bright red targets over here!"

The voice is coming from across the river. A bearded man, dressed in a red and black checked lumber jacket is waving a rifle over his head. Above him the remnants of a blue-grey puff of smoke are swiftly being dissipated and carried downriver by the breeze.

"Everybody in the bus!" screams Slowma. "Now!"

Toasto runs into the water in his boots and plucks Shaggyvan off the rocks, lifting him awkwardly to shore. Everybody scrambles up the bank and through a thicket of juniper trees, behind which the bus is fortunately out of sight. There is no talking. Just a few frightened grunts and whimpers. Gilligan has the presence of mind to scoop up Shaggyvan's clothes and boots on the way. Once amongst the junipers, he turns and crouches, peering back through the foliage. Four men can be seen gesticulating, shoving each other playfully. There is the faint sound of drunken laughter. All but one are dressed in hunting gear and carry rifles. All but one are large and bearded. The other is slight and wears a hooded black jacket. His balled hands are thrust deeply into its pockets. Even from this distance, Gilligan knows that the hooded figure, last seen swimming across this very river, is Dillard Dark, in cahoots with the gunmen.

Shaggyvan narrowly avoids being asked to leave the ranch as punishment for his utter disregard for the commune's welfare. His protestation that he and the other crew members were just having a 'little fun' is dismissed as selfish and egotistical. Shanosserpan is told that if he made any attempt to pay off the shameful case of champagne wager, he would certainly be asked to leave. Both swamis do prolonged stints at the rock crusher and are subsequently assigned, ironically enough, to the crew building the permanent casino.

24. 'When the Healing has Begun'

It is night shift at the mud crew, late March in the high desert. Snow on the ground and a full moon in the sky. There is a 'crunch' on to finish the hotel in time for the spring 'tourist' season. The mud crew has grown since the early days with Narzesh. It has split into day and night shifts and is very much in demand as building after building is finished in the burgeoning commune.

The hotel, like the permanent casino across the road, is a top priority project. Two stories high, built in a quadrangle to enclose a courtyard garden, it will be a haven for the many older, wealthier sannyasins worldwide for whom a futon on the floor has lost its cachet. Hour after hour, day after day, room after hotel room has to be beaded, taped and mudded, allowed to dry, mudded again, the walls sprayed with stucco, and then troweled into a pleasing, irregular topography of flattened islands.

The need for speed leads the commune to invest in the latest in automatic mudding and taping equipment. Gilligan is running the bazooka, named after the military hardware of the same shape and size. It applies drywall tape with an underlying bed of mud. A nifty lever can be cocked and sprung, to automatically cut the tape at the end of a seam. A second lever causes a small plastic wheel to pivot over miniature goalposts at the business end of the bazooka and neatly crease the tape that goes into a corner. Other crew members follow the 'bazookiere' and smooth the tape flush against the wall.

The bazooka's tube is filled with liquefied mud from a pumping station manned tonight by Sumpads, the Ranch's erstwhile 'mailman'. Her Harley grounded by cold and snow,

247

this is her third night of pitching in to help with the crunch. She gradually lost some of her flinty aloofness as she got used to working with the night crew. This night, as Gilligan comes to fill the bazooka, she seems to put on a little show, just for him. She is wearing a thin orange cotton jumpsuit, unzipped to expose maximum cleavage. Having her fasten the mud-feeding tube to the end of his proffered bazooka is exciting enough. But when she begins pumping the long handle her breasts writhe under the jumpsuit like captive electric grapefruits trying to climb into the warm Florida sun provided by the halogen work lights which stand on high tripods, like Martian sentinels.

"Go for it Swami," she says, disengaging the tether.

He stands there foolishly for a moment. *Go for what? Oh yeah, the work.*

"It was beautiful while it lasted. See you in a while." He hefts the bazooka and heads into the hall.

"I'll be ready," she calls after him.

His timing is good. The crew is just finishing coating the seams he put down on his last run. Fleuritima is there, young Esperanto, and Bhadakarma, an American swami from Buffalo. Bhadakarma is stringy and short. He has a mass of unruly brown hair and a scraggly beard that fails to hide a number of acne-related complexion issues. He is twenty seven, very close to Gilligan's age, and is possessed of an antic, manic sense of humor that makes him fun to be around.

"Hey man, you're right on time," he shouts as Gilligan strides in and applies mud-coated tape to the nearest virgin corner. "What happened? Couldn't think of an excuse to hang around Sumpads?"

"Yeah. She was begging me to stay but I had to get back here before you started any fires."

"Fires?" asks Fleuritima. "Why would he start a fire?"

"He's from Buffalo, Cheri. They actually have fuel trucks that follow the fire engines around because they never have time to stop for gas. Firemen just turn on the news to find out where they should report for work.

"Well, at least we have some excitement in our lives, man. What's the big event in Toronto? The Orange Parade? Someone burping?"

"We don't burp. We're too polite."

"Polite, or uptight? You people aren't comfortable letting a fart without written permission."

"That's unfair! I've phoned in for verbal permission many times."

"Pllffffffbbb!" Esperanto is posing in the middle of the room with lifted leg, using his drywall blade to waft the odor in Gilligan's direction.

"Well, I'm from Texas," he announces, "and we shit whenever, wherever and on whoever we want. And we shit big. Real Big."

"That's so childish," says Gilligan, serious faced, continuing to work.

"Really infantile," agrees Bhadakarma. "You should be ashamed".

"You're all idiots," says Fleuritima.

"Yeah," says Bhadakarma, "and we've got all night to prove it. Hey! Lets do a play! We'll call it Long Day's Journey into the Night of the High Moon."

"I'll be the gunslinger," says Esperanto. "My turn to use the bazooka, hombre."

"No way man." Gilligan snips the tape with an authoritative cocking of the cutter. "I'm on a roll here. Besides, I gotta go back and get at least one more refill, so I can die a happy man." He sidesteps a glob of mud that Fleuritima flicks at him and does a seam, then another. He works from the base of the wall upward, snipping the tape as the bazooka bumps the ceiling. Fleuritima jumps in and smoothes the tape, then applies a coat of mud. She flexes her blade over the edges of the mud bands, feathering them so they'll be invisible under the stucco. She hops aboard a small stepladder to finish the upper portions of the seam. Esperanto, meanwhile, is attending to the corner. Overgrown teenager that he is, he easily reaches its most remote heights.

"Come on Bhads, let's go!" Esperanto prods Bhadakarma, who is still toying with names for his imagined impromptu play. Bhadakarma wipes his blade on his coveralls and moves to join his comrades, saying in his drollest Churchillian voice, "It is a far far better thing I do, than I have ever done before!"

Gilligan knows he's got to work hard to keep ahead of this crew. If they overtake him and have to wait for something to do, they will tease him mercilessly, particularly young Esperanto, who will implore him in his deepest cowboy voice to put the bazooka in the hands of a real hombre. In the many wintry weeks of doing this, they have all become adept. Fleuritima is possibly the best of them all; though too small to handle the bazooka, she is quick and fine with the blade. The sight of her agile form, working cheerily beside him, causes a portion of Gilligan's heart to warm, like a crackling trashcan fire in a wintry streetscape.

The two of them have a love affair. It began slowly and grew once she was finally released from Tydass in early Februrary . Thirtyish, she had a year or so before broken off one of those long term quasi-engagement relationships which go nowhere. Her ex-boyfriend, a rising functionary in the Parti Quebecois, lived in a world of ideas and causes which did not include her need for love and spiritual fulfillment. She is not particularly Gilligan's 'type' physically; their lovemaking was more enjoyable than passionate. But, he felt more for her in his heart than he had for any of the sannyasin women he had had the good fortune to be with since Daphne. There was very little of the using and being used that had characterized his relationship with Bala. He smiles to himself as he hits another corner. What was it she had said last night?

"Slowma said she sometimes feels like crying when she's around us."

250

It was true. He's felt a little bit of it, a cracking feeling in his chest, something timeless, like the appeal in a baby's eyes. Something perhaps very close to the real reason for being at the Ranch.

The worship winds into the small hours of the morning. The full moon, the instigator and purveyor of lunacy, is well into its western descent. Bhadakarma is waiting for Esperanto to return with a full bazooka. He restlessly begins to flick some of the mud from his blade onto a blank wall. The globs and striations spattered across the grey smoothness please him. This is art. He picks up a larger gob and begins brandishing his blade like Zorro.

"En guard!" he shouts at the wall. "I must warn you my friend, that I am ze finest mudder in all of Oregon!"

Esperanto, similarly infected with night madness, has discovered that the bazooka's release mechanism could effectively be jammed open with a small screwdriver. His visit to Sumpads yields a batch of mud that can spurt like a handful of ejaculate over a distance of several yards. On returning, he wastes no time in testing his newly refined weapon by firing a wad across the room. Gilligan, tiredly finishing a corner, feels it slap against his neck, and ooze down the back of his coveralls. He turns around slowly.

"Oops. Uh, sorry pardner, I was just testing this here machine out and it uh, kinda got away from me."

"No problem, buddy." Gilligan scoops a handful of the cold, white icing from his collar. He faces Esperanto, legs shoulder width apart, hefting the glob of mud in his hand like a pitcher waiting for a signal from the catcher. His voice is measured and calm.

"You know what, I'm not even going to wing this at you though you definitely deserve it. It's late. I'm tired... and very disappointed. But you are young and childish," he sighs. "Best to let it go." He strides dejectedly through the doorway. Once out of sight, he dashes down the hall several doors where Sumpads is set up with the mud pump.

251

"Excuse me."

He steps in front of her, lifts the handle to fully prime it with mud, and races back with it to Esperanto.

"Die Texan Dog!" he screams.

He pincers the handle together as forcefully as he can, sending a snake-like gush at Esperanto's head. The young man is able to dodge it easily.

"I knew it!" Esperanto brings the bazooka to bear on Gilligan. He closes in for a sure shot but slips on the detritus of Gilligan's volley. The mud from the snout of the bazooka smacks harmlessly into the ceiling. It dangles there briefly like a sleeping bat before plopping down to the floor.

"Fire!"

Bhadakarma and Fleuritima simultaneously fling trowel-fulls of mud at Gilligan, scoring direct hits. Esperanto, suspecting treachery, has cleverly recruited them to his cause. Members of the troweling crew two rooms away, hear the commotion and are quick to join the fray. They gleefully and lethally fling mud from the ends of their long, flat finishing trowels. Sumpads shows up looking for her pump and immediately becomes a target as the guys can't wait to wet her ample curves. Soon mud is flying everywhere, bodies are smeared, couples and groups fall to the plywood floor wrestling and laughing in mock battle. The painters and even a wayward plumber show up. Those watching in amusement are promptly splattered and forced to either retreat or join in the melee. The hilarity and messiness crescendo as a booming authoritative voice cuts through the din.

"What the fuck is going on here!"

The tall figure of Narzesh appears in the doorway. He is still crew-leader of the mudders, and the overall foreperson for the night shift. It is he who is responsible to Slowma and Deela for what goes on. He is known for running a fun workplace but now his face is red and he looks pissed. Everyone stops where they are, dripping in mud, entwined on the

252

floor, or in mid fling. There is the sound of panting and suppressed giggles.

"You think this is funny? I'm taking down all your names. Then, we're heading to Hemlock Grove, as you are! We'll let Deela decide what to do with you, once we've finished waking her up."

Gilligan, along with every muddy soul in that room, feels something vile sink from his throat into the pit of his stomach. *Why is Narzesh acting like such a prick? Deela is going to freak!*

Narzesh, still in the doorway, turns to someone in the hallway to his left.

"Donger, hand me my pencil." A widening grin spreads across Narzesh's face as his 'pencil' turns out to be the huge wand and nozzle of the stippling machine, all hosed up and ready to fire. The tall crew leader lets out a prolonged war whoop that swiftly turns into maniacal laughter as he sprays all and sundry with the sticky white pellets and worms of stipple that fan out from the nozzle in a wide swath.

Worship-place bedlam ensues. Shrieks, screams, splattings and an abundance of laughter float from the eastern quadrant of the hotel skywards into the cold, moonlit Oregon air.

Later, at five-thirty in the morning, the moon madness spent, Gilligan is alone on the second floor balcony. He is slicing off the glowing end of his cigarette with his six-inch taping blade. The burning edge has encroached upon a red line encircling the cigarette's paper halfway down. It is a Kent Menthol, a flavoring Gilligan has always found repulsive. The fiery head cleaves off neatly. The courtyard below is composed of frozen late-winter mud gouged and ridged by various construction vehicles into a still-life gelatinous sea. To Gilligan's right, mired past the tops of its treads, is an abandoned mini bulldozer. With a scraping ping he flicks the cold stump of the smoke from the top of the rail in the direction of the Bobcat. Its end is smudged with lipstick.

"I am a good and worthwhile person," he says. "On April 10, 1983 I will stop smoking for ever."

He has changed brands and drawn the halfway lines on each cancer stick as part of the Ranch's Smoke While you Quit program. The program is run by an older sannyasin named Ted. Ted is dying of lung cancer.

Gilligan sighs, leans forward on the rail. There is a brilliant full moon. He reflects on the power of that disc, now scraping the roof line to his left. Influencer of tides, menstruation, and moods. A boom box is playing in the quadrant across the way. It is a song by Van Morrison, *When the Healing has Begun.* He feels the lipstick on his mouth, the mascara on his eyelashes. He glances through the window behind him. The crew is still in full hang-out mode: reclining with eyes closed, chatting quietly, reading. There is Bhadakarma, lying in a squared circle with Esperanto, Fleuritima, and Narzesh. They are chatting and giggling sleepily, heads resting on bent elbows, their teacups and snack plates beside them. As Toasto would say, 'Its a natural'.

They've had a wild night, the discipline of work gradually devolving into thoroughly loony behavior. After the mud fight, the cleanup, which happened to coincide with their "lunch" break, had morphed into a free-for-all make-up session with the mas delighting in applying eyeliner, lipstick, blush and mascara to the faces of the swamis. Bhadakarma's face has been painted with lipstick, mud and wall paint into that of a ludicrously smiling clown. Dry work clothes had somehow been procured for everyone, while a nearby laundry trailer had been commandeered, washing and drying coveralls that had been transformed by the fray into slagged-over strait jackets.

Gilligan takes a deep breath in and exhales a long plume of white vapor. Though the moon remains visible within a huge misty ring, snowflakes begin to fall. They plummet through the still air as if following taut fishing lines. Soon he is witnessing a thick downfall of fat white flakes. They fall like stones; no fluttering, no deviations, just a fast plunge to the mud below. There, despite their bulk, they dissolve, as if the congealed mud formations contain some residual warmth from the engines of the machines that created them.

Gilligan has a vague impulse to call out to his comrades. The spectacle of the moonlit snowfall is unearthly and beautiful. But he's immersed in the scene and caught in the spell of Van Morrison's music. It continues to float and pulse throughout the courtyard, a song about healing, and dancing under the stars. He stays and listens, removes his cap, so the snowflakes nestle, gather, and melt down into his hair, cooling the warm dome of his scalp. His thoughts settle with the snow. He licks some flakes from the blade of his taping knife. The steel is cold, wet and alive under his tongue. Tomorrow is his 'sannyas birthday', a year to the day since John Price Jr. first met Bala , then received his mala and new name from the Master. But he has no plans to go to Hemlock Grove for his celebratory piece of chocolate cake. Deela, Chloe and the others are sleeping dogs that he is for now happiest to let lie.

25. Swami Ted

It is Smoke While you Quit day. April 10, 1983. Muckiness prevails throughout the Ranch. Little Snake creek flows in a near torrent, challenging the riparian improvements lovingly made by Newfyamo and crew over 1982's long, hot summer. Here and there grass beds are washed out; rocks are dislodged from their retentive cages; but overall the work is good and the creek banks, aided by the modulation afforded by the dam at Lake Krishnamirthless, hold.

It is in the near-completed permanent casino that Swami Ted has gathered the dozen or more worthies who have participated in the program. The casino is an airy building featuring a vaulted pyramidal ceiling, a configuration favored by Avibasso and the other architects. Plush carpeting of a sage green intended to instill a peaceful, relaxed feeling in the clientele also serves to remind the commune's administration that here, as no where else, money will certainly be made. A large circular area under the pyramid's peak remains carpet free, allowing the surface of Dozon's concrete slab, as smooth as buffed marble, to show through. Here is where the circular bar will dispense essential lubricants for the profit making machinery.

It seems that certain sannyasins had merely participated in the Smoke While you Quit program to spare themselves hours and days of working in the mud and cold. It is said that some took up the baleful habit with renewed gusto the very evening of the day in which, as good and worthwhile people, they were to have their last cigarette. The Smoke While you Quit program had, in certain quarters, been renamed the Smoke While you Fuck the Dog program. The canine fornicators, their brains doubtless fogged by carcinogens, had made the mistake of admitting their duplicity within earshot of spiritually-minded stoolpigeons whose lines of communication, like the filaments of a spider's web, instantaneously brought the matter to Deela's attention. The wheels of retribution, unlike those of justice, turn swiftly. All participants in the Smoke While You Quit program from the beginning of time through eternity's last gasp are now deemed to be ineligible to receive the free communal cigarettes.

There may be those who wonder why a spiritual commune, allegedly devoted to meditation and the development of an entirely new form of awakened human being, would allow its residents and world-wide disciples to indulge in alcohol, gambling, tobacco and various forms of profiteering. Such doubters are victims of the negativity that is at the core of the ego's power. As William Blake said, it is the road of excess that leads to the palace of wisdom. The stony path of self-denial leads only to the narrow-windowed temple of righteousness. To get beyond, one must first go through! Therefore, the Master would say, if you must smoke or drink, do it with awareness. Be aware of the fibrous artificiality of the filter on your lips, the noxious heat of the smoke entering your lungs, the dulling narcotic effect on your brain. Awareness, awareness in the here and now, is the only gateway by which to transcend all kinds of stupidity, including indulgences in sex, tobacco and alcohol. Through paying attention, moment by moment, to the stupidity of one's actions, intelligence arises, naturally allowing its lack to fall like ripe fruit in the Autumn sun.

For Swami Ted, such nuances do not matter. The cancer burning through his lungs has set his heart on fire. He has seen, in fact been smitten by, an evil in the world. He is determined to end his days in gallant battle against it. Not against the cancer within him, though he does what he can, but against the cancerous behavior of these adventurous, spiritually minded, and, for the most part, still young sannyasins. He strides back and forth along the arc of the seated assembly as he speaks.

"When we started this six weeks ago we were declaring war. A war that had to be fought on many fronts. A physical

war against our bodily addiction. Today, if you have been following the program— 'light' cigarettes of a brand you don't
like, smoking them only halfway, then your body has begun
to wean itself from nicotine addiction. Other important battles
have been fought on the inner landscape of your minds. The
affirmations and hypnosis work to defeat the illusion that cigarettes, like your Mommy's breast, are your friend. Have you
been watching other people smoke? Watched yourself in the
mirror?"

Heads nod.

"And?"

"Really ugly."

"Anyone here find it looking cool and beautiful?"

No. Nobody did.

"Some of you have had your last cigarette. Some of you
may want to have one last crack at it. But this will not be a
fond, lingering farewell. It will be a death blow for an enemy
already softened up by mortar fire, whose resolve has been
weakened by weeks of psychological warfare, whose supply
lines have been cut off. Your last cigarette, should you choose
so, will be a form of aversion therapy." He produces a cigarette and holds it up in front of him. "You will take a cigarette.
You will break it in half like this. Throw away the filtered
end." He tosses it backwards over his head. It rolls to a stop
on the concrete. "Stick the other end in your mouth and light
it. Now take the longest, deepest drag you can and hold it in.
If you don't puke immediately, do it again. And again. Three
times. You may not throw up. A lot of you will. I guarantee it.
That's why you are going to do this in the bathrooms. There
are lots of toilet stalls. And don't force yourself to puke. You
don't have to. You'll feel plenty bad enough for the therapy to
work. Trust me. Any questions?"

There aren't any. There is little chatter as people head
for the washrooms. Gilligan remains behind. He will not do
the aversion therapy. He hasn't had a cigarette since the once

he tossed onto the congealed mud of the hotel's courtyard. And puking is not his thing.

I wonder if the master has ever puked. He must have. Everybody does. When an enlightened person pukes, does it smell good? Would it be a kind of nectar, something to be saved and sold in tiny, artful bottles? People preserve his hair, his clothes, his cars, why not his puke?

Swami Ted produces a cushion and settles in to mediate at the front of the room. The split between pukers and abstainers is about fifty/fifty. Gilligan looks at Swami Ted's face. Classic military. High forehead. Piercing eyes. Craggy skin. Steel gray moustache and eyebrows under a thatch of white hair. A demeanor that bespeaks discipline and commands respect, a compact, square-jawed man of fifty plus. He piloted an F-15 during the Vietnam War, then worked with NASA in the astronaut training program for many years. Divorced, then diagnosed with lung cancer, he successfully gave up the habit, but too late. His impending death motivated spiritual seeking, which led him to the Divine Bhagwan. He's chosen to use his remaining months to help others avoid making the same colossal mistake he has. Gilligan exhales a deep breath. The pink tinge of Ted's complexion is undercut by a gray pall. The cheeks, beneath the vibrant burliness of the eyebrows, are sallow. Here is the face of a man at whose doorstep death thumps insistently for entry.

The meditators smell burning tobacco. Each feels the craving for a cigarette. Retching sounds come from the women's washroom. Then from the men's. Cravings recede. Toilets flush. Steps scuffle across the carpet as returning sannyasins settle in to meditate. These sounds are repeated again and again until all pukers are purged and there is silence.

"This brings our smoke-while-you quit program to a close," says Ted after some time. "It's too late for me, but you people—for the most part—" Here he pauses and grins at a couple of the participants who are on the plus side of fifty— "you all have a long road ahead of you. If you stick with what we've completed here today, that road has just gotten longer, and I hope, wider and smoother too." He raises his palms together in the namaste salute. Swami Ted's gray eyes, normally glowing with cold fire, are soft and moist as he clasps his hands in front of his heart. Gilligan, to some extent still lost in meditative thought, is a little surprised to feel a tear on the side of his own face. His own last cigarette was smoked many days earlier, on the hotel balcony, as the snow began to fall. He will smoke many more in the next few years, but only in his dreams.

"Is Swami Gilligan here?" The stubby, bearded form of Lionheart is in the doorway. Gilligan raises his hand. "You're in trouble Swami. Slowma wants to see you at Bang Pas Zoo right away."

"O.K." Gilligan's hand lowers slowly and settles in front of his suddenly trepidatious belly. The last time he saw Slowma was after that wild night shift with the mud crew at the Hotel. She and Arcana had shown up at 7 AM. He remembers how Slowma's bovine eyes had widened on seeing his lipsticked and mascaraed face. Gilligan, with his working experience at the Ranch, is reasonably certain that Lionheart is just yanking his chain by saying he was in trouble. Months ago he would have been fair game to his own gullibility. But he is overcoming his mother's peasant mentality, one which views the world as incomprehensible and dangerous, a place best ruled by those who are born to do so. He is learning to see things as they are. Lionheart, the son of an electrician who regularly consumed two mickeys of vodka a day while working a union job at General Motors in Lansing, Michigan, embodies a common working class philosophy: funny is good. He told Gilligan he was in trouble as effortlessly as his father would have sent a young apprentice to go and get a left-handed wrench.

Swami Ted is making farewell rounds, hugging the women and shaking hands with the men. "Congratulations, son," he says to Gilligan. His grip is strong and fierce, as if transmitting a jolt of desperate, defiant energy. It is the second last time Gilligan will see him.

26. The Unbearable Heft of a Moto-rola

With twenty-two separate construction projects underway at the Ranch, space is at a premium in the Bang Pas Zoo office. Most are dead-lined for completion by the Second Annual Universal Celebration scheduled for the first week in July, a mere ten weeks away. Slowma, endowed by nature with a surfeit of gregarious, nurturing qualities, has, with each new architect 'hired', seen her desk positioned ever more closely to the entrance door. There, at least, she can greet and love up any and all who enter.

"Swami Gilligan, how are you?"

Gilligan feels reassured by the regard beaming from her eyes. He is definitely not in trouble. He returns her hug with real warmth.

"Go and talk to Arcana, sweetheart," says Slowma. "We've got a job for you."

Arcana is a pint-sized Canadian ma from the west coast. Though perky in demeanor, she is as level headed and contained as Slowma is sloshing over with good will. Together, along with manly exhortations supplied by Lionheart, they keep Bang Pas Zoo running with a surprising degree of cheerfulness and efficiency despite the variegated characters, languages and skill-sets among its worshipforce. Her blue eyes gaze up at Gilligan's from under straight reddish-brown bangs. She has faint freckles on her nose of a similar hue.

"Gills, have we got a job for you! What do you know about washing vegetables?"

"Vegetables?"

"Yes. Legumes. Carrots. Parsnips. Radishes. Beans. Tomatoes. Zucchinis-"

"Tomatoes are a fruit."

"Really?"

"Well, technically anyway. At least I think I read that somewhere."

"Hnh. They still need to be washed. Also peas and po-tatoes—"

"Tubers."

"What?"

"Potatoes."

"They're-?"

"Tubers."

"Not to be confused with tube tops like you happen to be wearing."

"Gills?"

"Arc?"

"Shut-up. Now go see Avibasso. He'll tell you all about it."

Avibasso, whom Gilligan and Morris encountered at the Truck Farm during their epic cruise, is the jovial epicenter of the cadre of bearded architects that infest Bang Pas Zoo headquarters.

"You've got it easy, lad," he says, gesturing towards the blueprints spread out on his desk. "Not much to it. A mildly sloped metal roof on metal trusses set on metal posts. You ever work with steel before?"

"No. Though they had us do a bit of welding in brick-laying school."

"Perfect. I'm sure that's why they chose you. The slab may be a bit tricky. You've got to include these trenches here see? That's where the water from washing the vegetables will go. It will all be reclaimed here at this end and then sent back to the fields through a network of pipes. Nothing wasted. You done much plumbing?"

"None."

"Perfect. Here, here, and here will be giant fiberglass bathtubs that we're going to build to wash the vegetables in. Now, that will be a tricky business. Let me guess. You've never worked with fiberglass before either?"

"Wrong. I've owned a few, maybe more than a few, hockey sticks that were definitely reinforced with fiberglass."

"Super. For a minute there I thought you might not be qualified. Hopefully there will be some members of your crew who know what they're doing." Here he raises his eyebrows inquiringly at Arcana.

"Oh yes," she says quickly. "We're going to put Toasto with you for the first bit, and we've got an older Australian swami, Samcroco, who's had a great deal of construction experience."

"Toasto! But he's already a crew leader. He should be running things, not me."

"Wrong, Swami." A pixie frown briefly flashes across Arcana's features. "Toasto has had some—uh—difficulties as crew leader, what with the burning of the bridge and then that unfortunate incident with Lionheart's jeep."

"Not to mention the toppled crane at the new Macarena site," interjects Avibasso.

"Speaking of the Truck Farm," says Gilligan, "has anything been heard of that Dillard guy who crashed Lionheart's jeep? He was among the rednecks that took a shot at Shaggyvan."

"He's no longer a sannyasin. I can tell you that much. Deela gave him the Alchemendra treatment." There is a touch of exasperation in Arcana's voice as she says this.

It was during Gilligan's snakebite illness that Deela announced, before the entire commune gathered in Enlightenment Hall, the excommunication of Alchemendra. His transgressions: being out of uniform, giving out 'goose' names, and allowing his own picture on brochures to be far larger than that of the Master. "He will," she said, "from this day forward go back to being Charles Paxton, or whatever his name is. Sannyasins will no longer have anything to do with him. No workshops. No meditations. No healing sessions. Nothing. He has betrayed our Master!" Deela's voice became extra shrill at this point. She went on to excommunicate a masseuse who had written a tell-all book alleging the master used laughing gas recreationally, and liked to frolic with certain female sannyasins. Excommunication, sneeringly and publicly delivered by Deela, was as feared by sannyasins as it once was by medieval scientists.

"Weren't we going to press charges and sue the Million Friends of God's Country? That's who those hunters were, weren't they?" Gilligan pursues his inquiry about Dillard. He can't believe such a reckless and ugly act went unpunished.

"Our favorite attorney general Mr. Fryberger has dismissed our complaints, saying the fellow was legitimately shooting at a duck," says Avibasso, raking his fingers through his beard. "Alvin Dark has disavowed any knowledge of their actions, though he does admit he's been away, and will be away, on what he called 'retreats' for a number of months. He has been working with the spiritual teacher formerly known as Alchemendra, believe it or not. Rumor has it that Dillard Dark has become a Colonel or something in the One Million Friends of God's Country. He's something of a prodigal son to them, returning from the Devil's clutches, and all. They say they've got quite a militia, and he's determined to 'finish what he started' at the First Annual Universal Celebration. They've got a few dangerous god-fearing ex-Vietnam types who know how to use weaponry. We, on the other hand, have the godly ones like Lionheart and poor Swami Ted. The 'Friends' have made public threats, well received threats, to bulldoze us out of here. Heiferville, which we are trying to rename Bhagwanpuram, has not gone over well with the locals. There've been some strange stories about people getting sick during the election there. Council people who could have swung the vote the other way. *Sixty Minutes* has even done a story on it. No charges have been laid though — yet." Avibasso's cheery countenance has turned very grim.

"Wow," says Gilligan, "so Deela and them may have actually poisoned — ?"

"That's enough negative chatter people," says Arcana. "Gills, how many crewmembers do you think you'll need for this job?"

"Crewmembers?"

"Yes. People to help you. Deela wants it done yesterday."

"Yesterday?" Gilligan's mind and emotions are knotted up. A headache, which had been lurking in his back-brain, surges to the frontal lobes. He pushes the thought of having a cigarette away. There is nothing like awareness of pain to highlight awareness of thought.

If I don't think of them, I won't need one. But his mind, as minds do, instantly moves to another problem: *The ranch threatened by Dillard and some kind of militia? Ex Vietnam types? That must have been them, on the other side of the river. Gun-crazy Americans. Intolerant aggressive assholes. Killing their own kids at Kent State. How much easier to do here, nice red targets. Ironic that there are so many Jews here, and Germans, for that matter."*

"Gills? Hello? HOW MANY CREW MEMBERS WILL YOU NEED?"

"How the fuck should I know? I've had one crewmember ever, and she was abducted by her father! I've never been in charge of anything and know dick-all about construction. I was an apprentice bricklayer for six months. My bricks, according to my shithead Irish boss, went 'up and down like a whore's pants.'"

Avibasso and Arcana look at each other. They are amused and a little embarrassed by Gilligan's outburst.

"Well," Avibasso clears his throat, "good to know there'll be a steady hand at the helm."

"O.K.," says Arcana. "Let's go with six members on the crew then. You'll have Toasto, Samcroco, and we'll throw in a few summer workers."

"Summer workers?" shouts Gilligan. "I'm a summer worker! From last summer! Why in fuck's name are you putting me in charge?"

"Because we like your attitude," says Avibasso, working hard to keep a straight face.

"There are no whys here," says Arcana calmly. "There is just what's happening. You don't have to do it if you don't want to."

"I don't?"

"No."

"If I say no, won't that be seen as a lack of surrender?"

"Not by me."

"By who then?"

"No one...probably."

"Deela?"

Avibasso stifles a guffaw.

"Gills—" Arcana puts her small, lightly freckled hand on his arm. "The commune needs you. All those vegetables and tubers..."

Avibasso, desperately squelching his own mirth, ducks behind one of the inclined drafting tables. There is a long pause.

Gilligan finally says, "Do I get a crew truck?"

Avibasso pretends to talk into a Motorola which has been standing sentinel at the edge of his desk. "Hemlock Grove, come in. Cancel that excommunication order. Over."

"No," says Arcana. "But you do get a Motorola. If you need supplies, just radio for them. Also we've got buses running out to the Truck Farm all the time."

Long pause. Big sigh. "O.K.. Fine. I'm surrendered. When do I start?"

"Toasto and Samcroco are forming up the slab as we speak. Here's your Motorola. You know how to get to the Truck Farm, don't you?"

Arcana slides the device from the edge of Avibasso's desk into Gilligan's hands. "Have fun swami."

"Our Swami Gilligan, with his own real project and crew. You can do it Gills!" Slowma drenches him in emulsions of human kindness, as he trudges by her and out the door. The Motorola feels like a lead brick; the heavy, unknown weight of responsibility in his hands.

27. Gilligan in Love

It is a spring morning at the Truck Farm. Warm sunshine, welcome after a night of rain, is occasionally occluded by cottony nimbus clouds. White birds flock to and from clusters of stunted weeping willows and junipers that hedge the Big Snake River. The water is turbid and swift-moving from the spring rains. It would be a pleasant hike down there, past fields of soybean, corn, tomato seedlings and fallow grassland tingeing green. But today the mud spoils any prospect of river idylls: the ghastly, treacherous, boot-sucking, tractor-eating, livestock-killing sludge that can turn road and field alike into quagmires. It is a springtime bane for all of Wacko County's ranches.

A crew leader for almost a week, Gilligan forthrightly admits his experiential shortcomings to the more seasoned construction worshippers on the site, particularly Toasto and Samcroco. While gracefully allowing them to make all construction decisions, he contents himself with pondering crucial calls such when tea times can take place. Now, as directed by Toasto, he walks a plank laid over the mud to an island of stones just offshore from the incipient concrete slab for the future Truck Farm Vegetable Washing Facility. When done admiring the view, he swings a-ten pound sledgehammer, whacking a staked batten board into the stones. From it will be stretched a string line to delineate pillar locations. His lungs, recently freed from the miasma of cigarette smoke, burn with newfound intensity from the exertion. He lifts the sledge high over his head, wondering if the tool is too big for the job, as both he and the batten board are sinking through the stones at an alarming rate.

RAW CAW! RAW CAW! The sound of Lionheart's horn wafts across the valley. Gilligan's mind flings back to the day of the bridge fire and Dillard's escape from the commune, then to the first time he met Seatrice's eyes: his futile attempt to jump from Lionheart's jeep as that same horn sounded. He gives the board a final whack that sinks it to the hilt, then shields his eyes to observe the oncoming vehicle. It is a small red Datsun pick-up, tracing a dustless path down the wet gravel road. Lionheart's jeep was junked after the bridge incident, but his trademark horn was salvaged. This he blows again and again.

Wouldn't stop singing on the way to Hoodoo Canyon. Won't stop blowing that horn. Gilligan grins and shakes his head over Lionheart's irrepressible nature. The truck slides to a stop at the far end of the site. As the site's crew leader, he must meet the boss and see what's up. But being an inexperienced goof-up, his Billy boots are now solidly stuck in the mud. Ever resourceful, he thumps the fat head of the sledge into the gravel in front of him. He leans forward on the nub of the hickory handle and, pressuring downwards, manages to extricate his right foot. Unfortunately his rubber Wellington is no longer on it. His red socked foot circles in the air a few inches above the shaft of the boot.

RAW CAW! RAW CAW! Both doors of Lionheart's truck open, like bright red wings.

"Fuck Lionheart! This is not a good time," Gilligan mutters.

He leans mightily on the hammer's handle, stepping with the socked foot onto the soft gravel. Though temporarily dry, the mound quickly compresses, and his foot begins to sink, as does the hammer, whose head is engulfed by the mud below. The handle is disappearing like the periscope of a submerging U-boat. He wrenches upwards with his left foot which slithers free, leaving its boot also up to the rim in the thick black mud. He steps onto the stony mound. Abandoning the impaled sledgehammer whose thick handle end now protrudes by a mere eight inches, he nimbly negotiates the length of the coarse plank laid between the mound and the stony, mesh-overlaid dryness of the slab base.

Watch out for slivers. His mother's voice. He'd caught a doozy sliding with his sisters on socked feet on the hardwood hall floor back in Britishfield. Immersed deep in the ball of his left foot it had come out weeks later on a river of pus, softened into a spongy wooden worm. He stops for a moment, puffing. He watches the rooster-like, chest-forward form of Lionheart emerge from the pickup. A diminutive, dirty blond, mildly bow-legged swami jumps out of the passenger's side. The sun swoops from behind a cloud, igniting the glistening thread of the roadway winding up the valley into the brown hills that crowd the horizon. The new swami is talking animatedly to someone, gesturing comically. Lionheart magisterially surveys the progress of the work on the site. A blonde ma emerges from the truck. She is smiling. She is laughing. She is gorgeous. It is Seatrice, the girl of his dreams, come to be a member of his crew.

Gilligan, his socks still reasonably dry, navigates the gravel-bedded rebar mesh between himself and the group from the truck. Lionheart comes to meet him, expecting a report on the progress of the work. The sharp-edged, three-quarter-inch stones biting into Gilligan's feet are unnoticed, as with every step, his eyes absorb the truth that the new arrival is indeed the blonde vision they'd been smitten by many months before. As they continue to drink her in, his optical intake valves blow significant gaskets. Hormones squirt all over the tissues of his heart, causing it to beat more wildly with every step, gushing supercharged blood into his head, which froths into a veritable jacuzzi around his floundering brain.

Lionheart is talking. Gilligan hears nothing. Seatrice continues to laugh at the little swami. She's wearing maroon jeans and an-off-the shoulder velour top under a thin nylon jacket. Blonde curls cascade all over the lovely contours of her exposed collarbone. Her lips are full, her teeth white, her smile wide.

"Swami!"

"Huh?" Gilligan finally stops, turns to face Lionheart.

"Where the hell are your boots?"

"Boots? Yes. Right. Boots. They're, uh, stuck in the mud. Over there."

"What size are you?"

"Uh, ten is good," responds Gilligan.

"Sweetam! Grab a pair of boots, size ten or larger out of the back of my truck will ya? Good thing I threw a few back there this morning. There'll always be a few dopes losing their boots in mud like this."

"Aye, aye chief. Right away sir!"

Sweetam is unquestionably Scottish. The little swami scrambles into the back of the pickup. Seatrice, for a moment, is alone. Her large blue eyes meet with Gilligan's. He feels like she is beaming something at him. Alien energy? Friendship? He is grinning stupidly. Her eyes go down to his feet, then bulge with humor as her hand comes to her mouth, stifling laughter.

"Hey Blondie! Come give us a hand up here. I'll be all day!"

Her eyes linger on Gilligan's just a moment, as she turns to help Sweetam.

"Got a couple of D-1's here for you Gills. Throw a piece of plywood down beside where your boots are stuck. You should be able to pry them out with a two by four. Toasto's still here, that's good, and that old Aussie there, Samcroco. They know what they're doing. Lean on 'em. You'll get the hang of it. These two (he jerks a thumb in the direction of Sea-trice and Sweetam) are totally green, but they're both will-ing—you're hoping *she's* willing, I can see that; Jeez, you could at least *pretend* to listen to what I'm saying?

"Sorry, yeah, plywood, got it."

"Eureka! Perfect size elevens!" Sweetam is standing on the bed of the pickup, waving Wellingtons on high.

"They'll do. Bring 'em over. If you are not done here in a few weeks, the entire commune will be eating dirty vegetables at the next world celebration. So no pressure here, Gilligan. Let me know if you need more people. People, we've got." He claps the rookie crew leader on the shoulder.

"Come on you two! Bring the boots and meet your new crew leader.

Sweetam there is Scottish and blondie there is... what are you honey, German?"

"Not German, Dutch. And my name is Seatrice."

Seatrice walks over with a look of displeasure on her pretty face.

Gilligan's heart is like a jackhammer in a cubby-hole. Her hair, parted down the middle, cascades to her shoulders in a tumult of waves and curls. That under her jacket one of those shoulders is naked, that those ample, firm breasts under that thin layer of velour are obviously unencumbered by a bra is... distracting.

"Come on chief! I can't stand here holding these things all day!"

Sweetam drops the boots dangerously close to Gilligan's toes.

"Right. Right. Sorry. Sweetam is it?"

He slips into the boots. *Lionheart is a life-saver.*

"Right chief, Sweetam it is. What are your orders?"

Gilligan straightens up to his full crew leader height.

"And how do you say your name again?"

"Seatrice."

There's a husky quality to her voice; her accent is strange to his ears. She rolls the 'r' and seems to put four syllables into a word that should only have two.

"Seatrice," he says, mimicking her.

"Seatrice." She corrects him.

"Seatrice?"

"Seatrice."

A crowd seems to have gathered around them. Sam-croco, Toasto, Swami Clint Eastwood the welder, Sweetam—even Lionheart has not left the scene. They all laugh with every attempt he makes.

"Ah, Seatrice."

More laughter, louder than ever.

"Well," he says, smiling hopelessly. "Whatever your name is, welcome to the crew." He steps over swiftly and hugs her, his nose luxuriantly tangled in intoxicating curls, his hard-on pressing into her lower belly. For a couple of moments, he feels a yielding in her body, her breasts warming and rising into his chest. Then she gently disengages him, her face flushed with embarrassment.

Sweetam leaps into the act, spreading his arms wide, draping himself over Gilligan, feigning soppy emotion. "Ach, thankye soo much for the warm welcome. Every new crew person made to feel sooo welcome. It brings a tear to me eye, it does.

"Come on people, let's get to work!" Gilligan extricates himself from the Scotsman's grasp. "We gotta be done by next week, if not sooner." He's found, in his few days thus far as a crew leader that he has an affinity for telling people what to do, though there's always a faint spark of surprise when they comply. People herd back to their tasks, raking gravel, cutting, fitting and tying the stiff mesh grids. When the concrete pours, the mesh must be lifted to the mid point of the slab's thickness, giving it a steel backbone. There are also trenches to be dug, the future drainage for the vegetable washing tubs. This is where Gilligan sets Seatrice to work. With her big smile and graceful, bountiful body, she has suddenly become the sun at the centre of his solar system. His brain tissues, soaked in a sea of pulsating, drum-beating hormones, refuse to function normally. Exulting in his role of crew leader, he comes over to show her how to dig.

"See, I use my foot to push the shovel into the ground, like this."

"Like this?" she asks. Equipped with work boots, she pounds the spade in deep with her heel, then flings the dry earth far out into the surrounding mud.

"Yeaaah. But spread your hands a little wider. Like here and here."

What total bullshit. I just want to touch her hands.

"Gilligan! We've got to set the rest of these lines! And where's the sledgehammer?" It is Toasto, waiting to continue with the batten boards.

"O.K. man, I'm coming. The sledge is over by that batten board. It may be a little stuck."

He turns his attention back to Seatrice.

"Do you think you can somehow manage without me now?"

"It's going to be difficult," she says flinging another shovelful. "But I was raised on a farm, so hopefully I'll learn eventually. Despite my handicap."

Handicap?"

"Yes. You know. Being a foolish blonde."

He pushes a stray golden strand back from her temple. The sight of her luscious lower lip warms his own mouth. The tip of his tongue feels hot.

"You don't seem all that dumb. And your English isn't bad."

"Why thank-you. I guess all those years at university are paying off."

"What was you major?" He continues to stroke the hair on her temple.

"English literature."

"Oh. Mine too."

"Gills! I'm sinking out here!" Toasto is trying to pry the sledge from where Gilligan left it impaled in the mud.

"Put down a piece of plywood first! Jesus Toasto! I've got a crew to run here."

"A crew to run; he's got a crew to run!" It's Sweetam, piping up again, mocking him.

"Get to work!"

Gilligan can only act angry at the little Scotsman. The guy is incredibly funny.

"Right chief!""And don't call me chief!"

"Sorry, chief."

He stands there, a hand still on her shovel handle. Her blue eyes are bottomless. He's smiling like an idiot.

"Bye."

"Bye."

He wants to keep talking to her. One more word.

"Gotta go now."

His voice is husky. He's lost.

"Bye."

"Bye."

His feet aren't moving, but his head does. He leans down and kisses that luscious mouth, briefly and passionately. For just a moment, she kisses him back, as naturally as a sizzling wave embraces the wet sand of the shore.

"Hey you!" she says, pushing him away without violence, a look of astonishment on her face.

As if the kiss were the puffing release of a docking clamp, he steps back, gives her a shrugging, smiling look of 'I don't know what the hell I'm doing'. As he walks away, he feels the springiness of the mesh under his feet. The grid seems to undulate, like the long swells of a great lake. His fingertips are tingling. His tongue is thick in his mouth. Toasto's bearded figure, standing with hands on hips out by the batten board, looks very small, as if seen through the wrong end of a telescope.

"Jesus Christ," he mutters.

He stops walking, brings his fingers to the bridge of his nose. Their tips are throbbing. He feels blood gushing beneath the skin of his nose, propelled by the bass drumbeat of his heart. He pivots on the marinating balls of his feet and looks behind him. Seatrice has just flung a shovel-full of gravel. In a girlish stance, the shovel held loose against the front of her thighs, she smiles at him, shakes her head softly from side to side. Radiant, dazzling sunshine shreds through the person he was, lifting him like summer's dandelion fluff high in the warm evening air. In a moment of exalted, rarefied lucidity, his life's priorities, formerly an ever-shifting jumble—like a mound of rats crawling over and over each other in a futile quest for dangling cheese—resolve themselves into one prime directive: he must be with her.

28. Operation Big Snake

The attraction between Gilligan and Seatrice is instantaneous and brilliant, as if separate shreds of matter and anti-matter wandering through the cosmos had happened upon each other and imploded into a star. What remains of Gilligan's old consciousness becomes something like a brave new world circling the bright sun of his relationship with Seatrice. And he is brave, even brazen in his pursuit of her. Where he once might have been diffident and nervous, he is self-assured and confident. There is a rightness, a wholesomeness in the feeling that allows him to let himself go. He would dare anything, risk anything to be true to the bright new sun that is gifting him with such a solid center of gravity.

It is his huge good fortune that Seatrice is engulfed by the same romantic tide as he. Whether it is chemistry, matter meets anti-matter, or just one of Nature's minor miracles like cell mitosis or the creation of diamonds, she feels and is subject to it as much or more than Gilligan. His dark good looks, dreamy brown eyes, and slim angular body fit what might be her fantasy ideal just as her curves and blond curls do his. Gilligan is ridiculously turned on in her presence, instantly becoming charming, witty, gallant, and as friendly as an over eager puppy. Her body is a revelation. He loves to watch her walk; his eyes constantly go to her, drinking in the lines of her form and the charms of her face: blue eyes alive with intelligence, full pink lips, a wide, white-toothed smile and a pert nose that sprouts darling freckles when reddened by the sun. The love sparking in him makes her laugh, softens her heart into mush. Their spirits jive, as if each can show the other vistas previously unimagined. Waves of romantic joy seem to rise out of the ground and carry them on crests of unfolding events they have no control over. They delight in each other's company.

Seatrice is an old-school free spirit. She grew up on a dairy farm near Zunderdorp in Holland, a few kilometres north of Amsterdam. She received the benefits of both higher and lower educations. Higher at the University of Amsterdam and lower in the feeding, calving and mucking out of the stalls of her parents' dairy farm. She was an only child, a rarity in Holland in the late nineteen fifties, but her parents, Jan and Betsy, were determined not to spoil her. Along with farm skills, she was taught how to sew, knit and cook. Gifted with extraordinary physical beauty and a sunny disposition, she knew little of the loneliness of an only child. Indifferent to Amsterdam's rampant drug scene in the late seventies, she cultivated her facility for languages at the University while working as a very popular bartender. It was her love of dancing and a sincere questing spirit that brought her to Bhagwan's Divine Disco in the heart of Amsterdam. Feeling an instant connection with the DB, she spent the summer of 1980 in Spoona and became a sannyasin. On returning, she began a romance with the Amsterdam centre leader, a graphic artist named Arpesh. When she met Gilligan, she knew what she had with Arpesh was over, though it broke both their hearts after two happy and exciting years. He left for Amsterdam forthwith, understanding that though she gave her heart freely, she did not give it lightly. This thing with the Canadian was not just a passing fancy. Seatrice wasn't made that way. Gilligan was spared a painful parting from Fleuritima as her mother in Sherbrooke had fallen ill and she had returned to Quebec in early April.

Buoyed by love, with Seatrice as Gilligan's constant lover and companion, the building of the Truck Farm Vegetable Washing Facility proceeds with near-effortless joy. Within a week Toasto is called to help craft the giant circular bar in the Permanent Casino. Samcroco, the gruff Australian carpenter has no interest in being the 'bloody foreman' so Gilligan steps more and more into the role of true crew leader— making construction decisions, ordering supplies in a timely manner, and assigning worshippers (the crew's ranks are swelled by summer workers to as many as twelve) to suitable jobs. His hands have acquired strength and deftness after nearly a year of daily construction worship. It feels good to pass these skills on to others: "Loosen your grip, let the hammer swing. That's it! See, you're letting the tool and gravity do more of the work." He learns to read plans, and more importantly, to read people. He learns to give them guidance, along with the space to make a few instructive mistakes. Mostly, with his own heart constantly rejoicing in being with Seatrice, he encourages them to enjoy their work. None are paid; some are paying one hundred dollars a day for the privilege of being there. All are learning that in the Buddhafield being in the moment and enjoying the task at hand are better than resenting the boss while enduring drudgery for the dubious rewards of deferred gratification. And how often, when the pension is finally attained, does the tendency to resent, practiced for so many years, remain? Gilligan thinks about such things in these halcyon Truck Farm days. The weight of responsibility, which he initially shrank from and resisted, turns out to be something like a bag of seeds that, once hefted and planted, can yield solid nourishment and expanded horizons.

The day when the job is finished comes all too quickly, though barely on schedule. It is, as it happens, Canada Day, July 1, 1983, the eve of the beginning of the Second Annual Universal Celebration. The sloping roof, the steel pillars, the huge, rock-hard fiberglass tubs, all painted a glossy white to ward off the sun are completed on schedule and according to plan. Gilligan, just as Narzesh did back in December, disseminates the crew to new assignments, most of them temporary positions to help feed, entertain, enlighten and lighten the wallets of the throngs arriving for the Celebration.

One of the perks of leadership is that he's managed to keep Seatrice with him for the duration of the job. Over the eight weeks she had become a de-facto second in command, smoothing some of Gilligan's more impulsive and arrogant tendencies with level headed sweetness. It is close to 7PM, the last hour of the last day of his assignment. They are enjoying a sandwich dinner in the new guard tower near the river. He has ceded the Vegetable Washing Facility to the farm worshippers who are tractor-tugging a flatbed wagon full of carrots and cucumbers into the receiving area, the first to receive the necessary ablutions from the facility. The guard tower was ceded to himself by Narzesh, the erstwhile d'Artagnan of the mud crew who, as a former fireman, has been assigned to a beefed-up Peace Force for the duration of the Second Annual Universal Celebration. He told Gilligan, without saying who she was, that he had an important 'meeting' at Macarena. Would he be good enough to 'hold the fort' for him for an hour or so? Gilligan, planning a last, romantic, summer's evening picnic by the river with Seatrice, was only too happy to accept the fine view and enhanced privacy offered by the guard tower which is a stubby affair built on thick pressure treated posts about ten feet off the ground. Built after the Shaggyvan river incident, located between the pond and riverbank, it commands a clear view of the entire belly-shaped bend of the Big Snake River.

There has, despite rumors of a 'military buildup' by the Million Friends of God's Country, been very little to guard for a number of months. The shoe factory, its shell completed early in the New Year, has stood idle since then. The noble social experiment, poised to soar to unknown heights of profitability, was forced to shut down when a German swami mentioned the factory to his father who happened to be a vice president of a certain rival athletics manufacturer with a world-wide presence. There was some high level huffing and puffing about Persephone Inc. benefiting from unpaid slave labor. The commune's financial people did their best to point out that child labor would not be used and the commune and Persephone Inc. had created a win-win situation from which everyone benefited— the consumer most of all with lower prices. But there were howls of protest. Persephone's union members in Portland took to the streets with wildcat strikes, which were quickly supported by workers all over the country. Government officials were roused; safety inspections demanded; immigration and insurance issues raised. The project was quickly and completely abandoned. The building now awaits the return of Alvin Dark who has spent months in the Far East, buying and creating future factories and, under the tutelage of his Senior Consultant Mr. Charles Paxton (better known as Alchemendra) was re-creating the entire manufacturing process using energetic principles loosely based on Feng Shui. It is said that the two of them, referred to by certain wags in Head Office as Lancelot and Galahad, were recently seen at Mt. Baldy outside Los Angeles, drinking one hundred year old Scotch with a well known Zen Master. Dark the Younger, aka Dillard, had also been noticeably absent from the Persephone complex on travels of his own, drumming up anti-Bhagwan support in church basements all over northeastern Oregon.

From where they recline on the floor of the guard tower Gilligan and Seatrice can hear the distant rumble of the tractor mingling with the burble of Little Snake Creek as it dribbles over the pond's sluice gates. After a dinner of peanut butter and particularly luscious jelly sandwiches, they are naked and exploring the tastier areas of each others' bodies. With Seatrice, sex is playful, spontaneous, adventurous and athletic; the hang-ups and nervousness which previously plagued him are gone, like night vapors dissipated by the rising sun. He is deeply involved in ministering to her from behind, she with her arms folded atop the thick half-wall of the tower, when she suddenly exclaims, *"Potverdorie!* I'm seeing a floating head!"

Gilligan, whose own mind is floating on a creamy sea of savory sensations, congratulates himself on inducing such ecstasy that the lucky girl is experiencing hallucinatory visions. She reaches back and tugs at his pony tail.

"Gilligan, look!"

He pulls himself to his knees and they together peer over the thick pressure-treated timber of the tower's sidewall. Directly across from them, on the further shore of the river, is a low dike of tufted green grass, constructed for spring flood protection of the Persephone property. Floating atop the tips of the grass is a head, a man's head, clad in a red baseball cap. The head is heading in the direction of the Persephone complex several hundred yards downriver. But it is staring in their direction. Even from this distance, of well over a hundred yards, Gilligan can see that the eyes, located above a scruffy, dirty blond beard, are very wide. The head stops. The head turns and shouts to the rear.

Gilligan can't make out what is being said. He realizes the blonde head of Seatrice, her curls tumbling over and around her lovely naked shoulders, jutting above the half wall of the guard tower, with his own darker visage peeking around it, must look odd. The floating head grows larger and taller, acquires a neck, and shoulders which are clad in army style camouflage. Gilligan hears the knocking sounds of a diesel engine, straining its way up a hill. The metallic snout of a black cannon appears. It obscures the view of the man, thrusting well above the crest of the berm. Twin sets of deeply ridged treads appear, then a wall of metal that obscures the man entirely. The cannon grows to an ominous flagpole, stark against the blue sky, then topples forward until the black-eyed hole of the barrel is pointing directly at them. The roar of the tank's engine revving its way to the top of the slope, swoops apocalyptically across the river, causing a mild trembling in the guard tower's structure.

Seatrice, while growing up in Holland, had the places and stories of WWII bred into her. Her uncle hid fugitives from the Nazis. Her mother witnessed an allied paratrooper being shot to death. The Panzers had clattered over the cobblestones of her father's village. The sight of the tank across the river terrifies her. She pushes abruptly backwards from the wall, sending their two naked forms sprawling unceremoniously to the floor.

After exchanging a frightened look with Seatrice, who is frantically putting on her clothes, Gilligan crawls over to assess how much danger they are in. The tank at the crest of the dike has been joined by two jeeps, also an army green color. Each contain two men, and a second head has poked its way out of the tank, joining the first one. All are dressed as weekend soldiers, in combinations of street attire and army issue camouflage. All but one. A slender figure, standing up on the passenger side of the jeep to the right of the tank, is dressed in black jeans and black t-shirt. Despite the stringy hair, now grown to shoulder length, and the darks wisps of a longish, faintly messianic goatee and moustache Gilligan easily recognizes the pallid countenance they belong to. It is Dillard Dark, the prodigal son returning with enhanced firepower.

"Sinners!" Dillard's voice is high-pitched and reedy. It sounds like Daffy Duck talking through a kazoo. "Filthy, perverted sinners! I was lost, but now am found! The day of reckoning is near! Sodom and Gomorrah will fall! Come out of there with your hands held high in the air!"

"Yeah, especially the blonde! She can come out first!"

This is yelled by the man whose head and torso protrude from a hatch in the front deck of the tank. Gilligan sees that the other men, with the exception of Dillard, are laughing. The shoulders of the jeep's driver are shaking behind the windshield.

"Could you hand me that please?" He indicates the Motorola, which is murmuring and cackling softly within its leather holster. Seatrice has just uncovered it amongst the clothing. Her hand trembles as she hands it to him.

"Don't worry," he says. "They aren't going to do anything."

But his own hand is unsteady as he takes the device from her. His heart is thumping the walls of his chest like the fists of a demented inmate in a padded cell. His fingertip is slippery with sweat as he switches bands to Channel D and pushes the call button.

"Lionheart, come in please. Do you read, over?"

"Lionheart here, what's up? Over."

"We're at the Truck Farm, in the new guard tower by the river. There are some kind of soldiers across the river. They've got a tank. They have weapons pointed at us right now. Over."

"Who the hell is this? Over."

"Satyam Gilligan. Repeat. There is a tank. Its cannon is pointed at us right now! Over!"

"Jesus Christ. Listen Gilligan, stay put. I just finished fuelling up the chopper for drive-by tomorrow. I'll notify Deela, and do a fly-by there for a look-see. Maybe pull you out of there. Over."

"Roger that, Lionheart. Gilligan over and out."

He leans against the half wall. He has managed to dress himself while talking on the Motorola. Seatrice has snuggled up to him with her head on his chest. He can feel her heart pounding.

"Let's run," she says.

"We can't. The helicopter's coming. We'll be safer here for now."

On the central pillar of the tower is a black rotary dial phone, fortunately hung low enough to be out of the line of fire. Gilligan snatches up the receiver. Below it is a laminated list of all the extensions on the Ranch. He dials 07 for Macarena. It is answered on the first ring by Abreatha.

"Yeah, Abreatha, listen it's Gilligan here; I need you to do me a huge favor. Find Narzesh and tell him to get back to the Truck Farm immediately... Yeah, it's an emergency, no question... No, just tell him to come. Thanks. Bye." He hangs up and settles back beside Seatrice. "Got to give him at least a chance to cover his ass. It won't look too good if he's not here when these assholes start their holy war."

A surge of anger possesses him. He turns and peeks again over the half wall. Two of the men are talking, apparently joking. One of them lights a cigarette. Dillard remains standing in the jeep with his arms folded. *I can't just lie here hiding while those goofballs laugh.* He stands up. His sweaty hands grip the top rail. His legs feel weak.

"Hey Dillard," he shouts. "You can't do this. It's against the law."

Dillard spreads his arms wide.

"Do what? We ain't doin' anything—yet!"

"You threatened us!" Gilligan screams. "Does your father know you're doing this? I happen to know him personally, you know!"

"My Daddy's away. We're using this land for our games."

"Games! You call this a game?"

"Sure enough. War games."

"We need to talk. Our leaders are on their way."

"Oh, you want to parlay do you? We're on our way across the river now. Meet us at the pier." Dillard motions to the tank driver and the other men to move back to the road.

"Come on." Gilligan opens the trap door that is the exit from the tower. "I've got to head over to the pier and talk to these goofballs. Go to the vegetable washing building."

"No. I'll come with you."

"Baby, it's not safe. Lionheart and probably Deela will be here soon. God knows Dillard might take a shot at her."

"No. You are safer if I come. They'll behave better."

"Maybe so. Maybe not. In any case, I'm your crew leader and I'm telling you to go back to the site!" Gilligan, for the first time in their short relationship, is getting pissed off at her.

"The crew's over. I'm staying with you."

"Fuck, you're stubborn."

She takes his arm. "Get used to it, Swami."

They remain arm in arm until they cross the locks at the base of the oblong pond. The pier on the Persephone property is a good half kilometer beyond them. On the far side of the river the tank and jeeps are, for the time being, out of sight behind the dike. Gilligan hits the send button on the Motorola.

"Lionheart. Come in. Lionheart. Over."

"Lionheart. What's up? Over."

"They're crossing the river. Repeat. They are crossing the river to their shoe factory property. It's Dillard. He says they want to talk. Over."

"Roger that, Swami. I'm good to go here at the airport. We're waiting on Deela to arrive from Jesus Grove. Channel D is open. Over."

"Deela here, Swami." Deela interjects with a very quick, staccato rhythm to her voice. There is a pause.

"Go ahead Deela."

"Who the hell is this anyway?"

"Swami Gilligan down at the truck farm. The officer in the guard tower had to—answer the call of nature. I covered for him. Over."

"Gilligan. It's been so long! I have a job for you Swami, an offer you won't be able to refuse! But for now don't say anything to the invaders. I want to speak with them personally."

Another pause. "Roger that, Deela. Gilligan out."

Seatrice and Gilligan walk hand in hand across the remainder of the Truck Farm's 'belly' to the bay where the Persephone pier fingers out into the river. On the further shore, Dillard and the men, from a similar pier are maneuvering the tank onto the barge. The ferry, though almost completely filled by its bulk, takes the weight surprisingly well and is soon chugging towards the pier where Gilligan and Seatrice wait. Dillard and three of the men, all of whom have rifles slung over their shoulders, ride alongside the tank, on the gunwales of the barge. As they approach, Gilligan can see that Dillard has a large knife sheathed against his right leg. Its bone handle is identical to that of the weapon that lodged in the window crevasse of the Divine Bhagwan's Rolls one year earlier. The barge docks beside the pie but no attempt is made to offload the tank. Dillard hops onto the pier and raises his arms to the sky.

"Praise the Lord! Praise the Lord! The chariots of our righteous war can cross the river. Don't worry sinners! Sherman there will stay where he is—for now. We come in peace. We come with a message."

Gilligan and Seatrice stand well back from the pier, intimidated by the tank and the armed men. "Can you wait?" asks Gilligan. "Our leader is coming in a helicopter any minute now."

"Your leader!" Dillard balls his fists stiffly downwards as he shouts. "If you mean that psycho bitch who stabbed me, she ain't no leader! Satan! Satan hiding behind a white beard! He's your leader! He's the false God! He's the one whose day of reckoning is at hand!"

"That's it?" asks Gilligan. "Is that your message?"

"No, this is!" So saying, Dillard whips the knife from the sheath and holds it skywards in front of him. Seatrice lets out a brief yelp of apprehension as Gilligan pushes her behind him. Dillard stays rooted to his spot on the pier. He holds the knife aloft like a religious talisman. The blade glints in the July evening sun. "It has come to our attention," intones Dillard, "that certain brainwashed American citizens are being held in your compound against their will. Release them or we, the Million Friends of God's Country, along with our friend Sherman here, shall be forced to effect a rescue operation that could prove... damaging."

"Rescue operation! No one here needs to be rescued!" Gilligan takes a step or two forwards, his arms spread wide. Seatrice claws him back to his original position."

288

"Release our people!" shouts Dillard, drowning out Gilligan's protest. "Release them, or Operation Big Snake Storm commences at fourteen hundred hours tomorrow!"

29. The Bitches' Bash

It is Canada Day, the evening of July 1, 1983 and Deela
is in a mood to celebrate. Not because it is Canada Day of
course; the existence of the socialist, multicultural tundra to
the north means nothing to her. The reason for rejoicing is
something of far more substance and value: the achievement
of one's personal financial goals. Said goals do have some
Northern resonance however, for it is in four copious, overlarge and over-stuffed hockey bags, manufactured in New
Westminster, British Columbia that more than one hundred
million dollars in communal profits and donations, principal-
ly heisted by Deela, Chloe, and Lucifia now sit under the
monstrous glass-topped coffee table in Hemlock Grove.

This is not to say that Deela has not experienced some
nail-nibbling worry in recent weeks. When the Master began
speaking again a year ago, she knew that her power as the
supreme pipeline to his wisdom would be drastically cur-
tailed. It was her good fortune that he decided to limit his
speaking engagements to festival times only. Utilizing the ex-
pertise of Lurchamo, she had monitored his other conversations as closely as possible, lest those close to him in Shagri
Ohlala, like Nivea, Shenilla or Kildaraj, should poison his
mind with negative information. Members of the Bhagwan
Foundation, particularly the aforementioned Dr. Perfect, had
evidenced increasing suspicion around suspected financial
improprieties concerning the commune's operation. He even
suggested an independent audit be done by sannyasin accountants from outside the Ranch. Then Dave Fryberger, the
nosy weasel who happened to be Oregon's Attorney General
seemed intent on investigating the alleged poisonings during

the Heiferville election as well as immigration issues around the Divine Bhagwan's prolonged stay in America, publicly claiming that the sannyasins were more of a dangerous cult than a bona fide religion.

She has steered the communal ship through some dangerous seas. This evening, gathered around the Hemlock Grove coffee table that conceals their booty, are her sisters in crime: Lucifia, Chloe, Patipaticake and Tootie. Champagne, cocaine and chocolate cake are available in abundance. Tonight they will party, and plot how they can best take the money and run.

"Why don't we just take the money and go? Like right now?" Chloe punctuates her question by inhaling a generous line of white powder cleverly positioned over the image of the Van Gogh Bridge on the black glass of the table top. "We take the Learjet, be in New York tonight and Switzerland tomorrow."

"Chloe, my dear, how many of the Divine Bhagwan's sannyasins are there world-wide?" Deela asks.

"Truthfully?"

Deela nods patiently.

"Fifty thousand, maybe sixty."

"Yes, and if we leave just like that, each and every one of them is going to know what we've done. Our own Peace Force officers, our lawyers, accountants, our ex-soldiers (who are in every country worth going to in the world) backed by Bhagwan Foundation International, who will soon discover the 'withdrawal' of all the diamond Rolexes and other fabulous goodies that Chloe and I made from the Mahaclaptrap safe last night, will not rest until they hunt us down. That is why it is best that we leave when this place is in a state of, shall we say, creative chaos. A chaos so complete that our departure seems natural and warranted. A chaos that preferably leaves the Foundation in ruins. A chaos where our little burglary, once discovered, could be attributed to almost anyone. Besides, I'm afraid that I personally suffer from James Bond

Syndrome: I don't like to leave a situation without first blowing it up real good."

After the requisite laughter dies down, Lucifia says, "Zee removal of Kildaraj vould be a significant step in zee correct direction." The tall *fraulein* is drinking from one of the fluted glasses she insisted be procured along with the champagne. "Zere may be an 'accident' at Hippocrises zis very evening."

"What a shayme," says Chloe, wiping her nostrils with the back of a knuckle.

"And how many busloads of street people have we now brought to the Ranch?" asks Deela.

"Eight," says Patipaticake. "Three each from Los Angeles and San Francisco and two arrived from Chicago yesterday. All American citizens. If the county elections were held tomorrow, we'd stand a good chance of winning."

"Alas, alack, my dream of wearing that bright shiny sheriff's star will have to be back-burnered. But some of those people must be unstable, even dangerous. Capable of doing, or at least being blamed for, some very disruptive things, burglary no doubt among them." Deela takes a generous sniff herself, directly off the runway of Bhagwan International Airport. "Also, my dear sisters, my fellow bitchin' bitches, Lucifia and I have come up with a rather brilliant plan to provoke the Million Friends of God's Country into providing us with the ultimate disruption: an attack upon our Ranch. Thus far they've been rather slow to get their collective asses in gear."

"But wouldn't that put the Divine Bhagwan in danger?" Tootie, after downing three fluted glasses, pipes up with the question.

"Not if Fryberger arrests him first on immigration charges. And I have it on good authority, my dear sisters, that just that may happen as soon as tomorrow afternoon. What could be the more perfect disruption than the arrest of the Divine Bhagwan, or God forbid, his crucifixion by some sort of invading Christian god squad?"

"That would be too awful," says Tootie.

"Of course," says Deela. "Awful for all of us. But our pain may be a benediction for the rest of the world. Look at Jesus. He never made it big till after he was dead. I mean at his death he just had twelve disciples. Inspired by the Divine Bhagwan's martyrdom, our fifty thousand could spread his message, the message of the possibility of Enlightenment to every country in the world, which could well be a turning point in history, the ushering in of a new Golden Age for this world."

"Well we'd have plenty of gold anyway," says Chloe through a mouthful of chocolate cake.

"That is so deliciously crass, Chloe," says Deela, raising a glass of her own. "I'm rather perversely proud of you."

It is at this moment that Patipaticake, now back at the kitchen counter holds up Deela's Motorola. "It is Lionheart calling in on Channel D," she says. "Something about a tank on the other side of the river down at the truck farm."

Deela makes an 'I'll be right there' gesture, then stands and raises her arms towards the ceiling in jubilation. She veritably prances over to the picture window as if she would embrace the hills, the windings of Little Snake Creek, the Van Gogh Bridge and Shangri Ohlala which are all bathed in yellow evening light. "A tank? You mean Dillard and his rednecks are making their move! Why oh why," she exclaims, "am I so perfectly synchronized with the great Tao? Can it be that it is I who makes—no not makes—who *allows* these things to happen? Is that my gift? Perfect timing? Verily, verily, the universe is unfolding as it should. Now girls, if you'll excuse my self-congratulatory rapture, I have a call to take."

Deela takes the Motorola from Patipaticake as the others upbraid Tootie for helping herself to an outrageously large piece of chocolate cake.

"Take all you vant," sniffs Lucifia. "Get even fatter! Break more chairs!"

"That chair was a piece of junk, a piece of junk!" sing-songs Tootie in her curious falsetto.

"Zat was a state of the art medical receptionist's chair ordered directly from zee catalogue for two-hundred and fif-ty-seven dollars! Crushed on zee second day!"

"It wasn't crushed!" wails Tootie. "Just bent, just bent!"

"Ladies!" Deela interrupts, clapping her hands sharply together. "Fortune smiles. We have work to do. Lucifia, that happened to be Swami Gilligan, the perfect patsy we dis-cussed earlier. The time has come for his lady love to get sick. You and Tootie are with me; we're going for a little helicopter ride. Come on, Tootie. Let's go! No. Leave the cake here. Yes, all of it. Good girl. Patipaticake will save it in the fridge for you."

"Deela," says Chloe. "Do you want me to notify the media about this?"

Deela pauses at the door and considers. "*Sixty Minutes* is already on its way. They're doing a piece on the Second Annual Universal Celebration and the 'alleged local tensions'. Quietly let the other biggies know that something's brewing: *Time, The Washington Post, New York Times.* Leave the *Orego-nian* out of the loop for now. We don't want any meddling by the local authorities until the time is right."

Lamborghini catches more than a whiff of champagne as the three women climb into the Bronco.

"The airport, Sergio. Drop us at the helicopter, then head down to the Truck Farm. I want the Peace Force and the Samurai's down there as well. Tell them to use their sirens. We're moving into crisis mode, Code Red until further no-tice."

"Code-a red it is, Deela! I've-a always wanted to use-a this thing." So saying, Lamborghini slaps the flashing red cri-sis-light onto the Bronco's roof and turns on the siren. As they leave Hemlock Grove and go past Mahaclaptrap welcome center and the Zorro the Meditator restaurant, hordes of sannyasins newly arrived for the festival part before them like the proverbial Red Sea, their faces strobe briefly to the color of their clothes as the light swirls. Some, recognizing Deela in the front seat, wave enthusiastically or even Namaste. Her nostrils still tinkling to a chemical tune, she gives them a kind wave and a brief smile of benediction as the Bronco turns onto the airport road and picks up speed.

Gilligan and Seatrice are halfway back to the guard tower by the time the helicopter clatters over the Western hills. The Sherman tank remains on the barge, which is now tied to the pier on the Persephone side of the Big Snake River. Dillard and his cohorts are gone. Preceding the copter is the dust shrouded shape of a pickup truck, jouncing its way along the dirt trail to the guard tower. It is driven by Narzesh, who, still in Peace Force uniform, has managed to cadge the vehicle from some pal or other at Macarena and return in an extremely timely manner. He waves to the approaching Gilligan and Seatrice before he mounts the guard tower ladder and resumes his post.

The chopper sets down in a fallow nearby field. The evening sun burnishes the dust cloud it kicks up with golden orange glow. The shapes of Tootie and Lucifia, one like a brick and one like a stick, emerge from the cloud and bear down swiftly on Gilligan and Seatrice. Lucifia strides directly in front of Gilligan and stops well within the normal Westerner's 'personal space' barrier. Gilligan instinctively takes a step back. Her breath is a distasteful blend of cigarette smoke and champagne. She removes her glasses and stares contemptuously down at him through overlarge pupils.

"So Swami Tightass. Vee meet again. I'm afraid zere is a medical emergency. Vee haff to quarantine your sveetheart. Tootie. Take her away."

Seatrice shrieks as Tootie wraps a fist the size of a grizzly bear's paw around her upper arm. She claws to no avail at steely digits the size of hot dog wieners. "Ow! That hurts! Let me go!"

Gilligan, hearing his Beloved in pain, is galvanized into clear, cold rage. He flings Lucifia aside like a matchstick doll, sending her sprawling to the ground. Dealing with the gargantuan Tootie, who is of comparable heft and strength to any NFL nose tackle, is another matter. He too claws at those intractable fingers, then karate chops Tootie's forearm with all his might. It is like plinking a jeweler's hammer into a frozen side of beef. It does annoy her, however, and she takes a backhanded swing at him with her free fist. Unluckily for him she connects, and deeply, with the softest section of his midriff. The wind leaves him in a sickening rush. He collapses, doubled up in agony, unable to speak or even breathe as Seatrice is half dragged, half carried into the waiting helicopter. The dust having settled, he can make out the bushy form of Lionheart at the controls. His arm is extended from the window in a thumbs-up signal. *Don't give up, buddy. This isn't over.* This minimally comforting sight, and the sun hovering over the hills behind it, is immediately occluded by the menacing, and severely displeased form of Lucifia.

"So Swami," she says, administering a vicious kick to his ribs. "Are vee in pain? Vere dus it hurt?" She uncaps something slim and plastic in her right hand. A hypodermic needle glints. She squats over him. "Zis vill take away all zee pain. Now vich one of your balls vould you like zee injection in? Hmm?" She scrapes the needle up the skin of his thigh, edging towards the hem of his shorts.

"Lucifia! We need him. Remember?" It is Deela. "Get in the chopper and take the girl to where we discussed. Now."

"No! I don't vant to!"

"Lucifia!"

"OK!"

She snaps the cap back on the needle, then stomps her foot like a frustrated prom queen. The stomp, however, is slyly aimed at the side of Gilligan's head, where it lands with authority. That, combined with the blows to his solar plexus and ribs, causes him to lose consciousness. Set adrift amidst the hypnagogic frontiers of memory and self-knowledge, he is only very vaguely aware of the sounds of approaching sirens, and that of a quickly receding helicopter.

30. Gilligan's Mission

"We have got a problem."

Deela leans forward across Chloe's desk. Her pupils, like those of a night creature, are wide black pools. Her eyes are compelling and a little frightening, as if something behind them is gnawing at her brain with an unholy blend of eagerness and desperation. Gilligan looks at her hands spread on the desk. The Divine Bhagwan's personal secretary has been biting her formerly perfectly manicured nails, specifically the thumb and forefinger of her right hand, which are rounded nubs. The remaining eight remain impressively long, with a hard red gloss.

Maybe it takes a fresh major crisis for her to start a new finger.

Chloe is present, skulking near the wall behind her desk. She leans back in her wheeled office chair, legs straight, ankles crossed, arms folded, her brow furrowed beneath her sheepskin curls. Only forty minutes or so have passed since Seatrice was abducted. Gilligan's head and gut have recovered. Only his ribs retain an ache from where Lucifia kicked him. He is beginning to thoroughly hate that bitch. *And not just her. All of them. To hate with gusto. Like Keats did. That's where it's at.*

"The problem," Deela says, "is that the outside world will not leave us in peace. They hate our freedom. They're frightened by the fact that we are creating a new man here, a new type of human being who is not afraid to give up the senseless race for material objects. Men and women who will dare to live beyond their society's conditioning." Deela gets up and begins pacing the confines of Chloe's trailer like a

298

caged tigress. "But they are strong. They have a tank." Her fists are balled tightly, her arms stiff as bowling pins. "So *we* must be strong. We must fight. We must be clever. We must be proactive!"

She wheels on Gilligan, and in a voice flirting with being an outright shriek demands, "Whose side are you on, Swami?"

"Side? Well, I'm on the Divine Bhagwan's side! And the side of getting Seatrice back. Where did you take her?"

"Yes, of course. Of course." She softens her tone but continues pacing. "Our Master is being threatened. Threatened! Clearly! Presently! Those half-wit rednecks across the river want to smash everything we've built. They have weapons that will destroy us if we don't stop them first!" She fists those manicured fingernails (and the two chewed ones) down onto the desk. The rims of Gilligan's nostrils feel their breezy wake. Her nose, which has a very delicate hook at its tip, is thrust to within inches of his own. "And yet they, as bad as they are, are not the least of our concerns. You've heard of Fryberger, Swami? Attorney General Fryberger? Of course you have. I have hard intelligence that he has a search warrant for the Master's house, and a second warrant for his arrest on immigration fraud charges. They are planning, tomorrow afternoon, when many reporters and cameramen from around the world will be here, to move in and arrest our Master. The bastard just wants the publicity! We have two sets of enemies, possibly working together, invading our commune on Master's Day, the beginning of our Second Annual Universal Celebration!"

"It's my sannyas birthday, too!" interjects Chloe. "I want me party."

Deela glances back at Chloe, then rolls her eyes briefly at the ceiling.

"Do you agree Swami, that they must be stopped?"

"Well, s—"

"At all costs!?"

"At all...? I—"

"Shut up!"

Deela pauses, half glances back towards Chloe, who is smirking. She turns her wide brown orbs to look straight into Gilligan's eyes. She scrapes the backs of two fingernails lightly through the hair at his temple, grazing the cartilage of his ear.

"Too bad about your girlfriend."

The words feel as if those nails, the sharp ones, were pincers into his throat, threatening to rip out his larynx.

"Where is she?" *Bitch,* he adds, barely avoiding saying it out loud.

"Don't worry. Your little 'Fraulein' is safe."

"She's not German. She's Dutch."

"Whatever. She's officially suspected of having AIDS. You know, that new disease?"

"Officially suspected? What kind of crap is—?"

"Don't worry. You're clear. And so is she, though she *could* be exposed any minute now." Deela makes a show of looking at her Lady Rolex, a stylish white gold model, gifted to her by the Master. She smiles beatifically, squeezes his shoulder, circles behind him. "You know Swami, (she leans in, her mouth close to his ear) once you come back, I've got a feeling she'll be declared well enough to be released."

"Come back?"

"Yes. Come back. We have a little mission for you on the further shore. Something that will definitely slow our enemy down for a day or two while we get our legal department in gear and even more of the mass media here. We need to stop their invasion before it starts."

"Talk to them. Negotiate with them," says Gilligan. "Bring the media in on it. Dillard just wants to feel important."

"We don't negotiate with terrorists!" Deela screams in his ear. "We are proactive! We stop them before they get started! Now, are you willing to do this little job for us or do I tell Lucifia to give your precious blonde an injection?"

Gilligan, his chest and belly stony hard with apprehension, stares straight ahead. Tight lipped, he nods very slightly.

"Excellent!"

She slaps him between the shoulder blades. He is dangerously close to vomiting.

"What do you want me to do? Sink the barge that the tank is on?"

"No. No. Nothing so overt. That could be considered an Act of War. We have something more subtle in mind and you're the right person for the job. You've been over to the Persephone complex; you know the layout; you've met some of the people. And," here she again smiles sweetly, "we know we can count on you."

"When?"

"Tomorrow. Fryberger is supposed to be meeting with them around lunch time to 'calm the waters' I suppose. He probably wants to talk them out of the invasion so he can come in and have all the glory. "

Something in Gilligan's belly turns, an angry spouting that resists the impulse to meekly acquiesce and hope for the best.

"I need to talk to Seatrice."

"You can talk to her all you want when the job is done."

"Now. I need to talk to her now, please."

His words and tone are so firm and polite that Deela sighs and apparently gives in. Gilligan has learned something about how to get what he wants from people from his encounter with Alvin Dark.

"Very well. Chloe, make it so."

"Rawt boss."

She turns to Gilligan, wrinkles her nose in a snarl.

"Troublemaker!"

The beeps of the touch-tone phone are heard as Chloe dials.

"Gilligan. That's a funny name, isn't it Chloe?"

"Rawt, funny." She whispers into the phone. "*Hello Lucifia. We need you to do something for us....*"

Deela stands very close to Gilligan. Her face looms in front of his. Its fine brown skin is unblemished, save for a small beauty mark on the topmost curve of the cheek below her right eye. Gilligan again marvels at the size of her dilated pupils. *Is she on drugs?* There's a warm flush in her cheeks and throat. He feels the heat of her. Her hand again reaches out to caress his ear, grazing the lobe this time. She closes her thumb and fingers so the nails dig into the sensitive skin and cartilage of the back of the ear. She squeezes and pulls hard, so Gilligan, jerked out of his chair, falls to his knees in pain. Were the nails not the bitten ones, but of the more lethal length, his ear would be completely skewered, so vicious is the attack.

"Let go! Let go, you fucking bitch. Ow! Ow! OW!"

"I don't like being manipulated, Swami Gilligan." She hisses these words into his other ear, brushing against it with her lips as she does.

Gilligan clutches at her hand then instinctively flings an elbow up into her ribs, as hard as he can. Winded, Deela grimaces and crumples to her knees. As Gilligan pries her hand away from his ear, she tumbles forward, causing them both to lose their balance and sprawl awkwardly onto the gleaming linoleum floor of the trailer. Gasping, her weight on top of his prone form, Deela has hooked her forearm around his throat and is squeezing hard. He pulls himself to hands and knees, lifting her with him, and then rolls, smacking her body into the office chair which careens across the tiles into the back wall, causing the huge Bhagwan Comes to America poster to flutter upwards into a rolled-up position with enough violence to dislodge it from its bracket. Chloe, still on the phone, manages to snag it with her free hand before it can fall to the floor completely.

Enraged and aroused, Gilligan twists Deela's arm away from his neck and flops her to the floor, surprising himself with his own strength. He straddles her and folds her wrists down onto her chest, pinning her. He hears a growling noise. It's coming from his own mouth. He mashes her hands down into her breasts. He wants to penetrate her, beat her, fuck her.

A blow to the side of his head sends him toppling, dazed, onto his back. The brief sight of the acoustic ceiling tiles is quickly blocked by the stocky figure of Chloe. She is holding the push buttoned body of the telephone in one hand, and the receiver, which she has just decked him with, in the other. It is this that she extends down to him.

"Here," she says. "It's for you."

He puts the receiver, which feels like an anvil in his hand, to his ear, wincing as it contacts the earlobe Deela injured.

"Hey you."

This is what they always said.

"Hey you," he whispers.

Woozy and cracking down the middle, he cannot speak further for a few long moments. He hears her sweet breathing and the keening of hawks in the background.

"You OK?"

"They've got me in a nice room. They say the drugs will make me better."

"Drugs? What drugs?"

"OK. OK. Enough pillow talk!" Chloe easily wrestles the receiver from his numb fingers. "Don't worry sweetheart. You can talk all you want in a couple of days. G'bye."

Gilligan slumps back down on the linoleum. He notices Deela is gone. When did she leave? The security door behind the fallen picture hisses open.

"Oh Gilligan!"

Deela re-appears with a cheery smile. Their tussle seems to have invigorated her. She is holding a plastic vial the size of a pill bottle in each of her hands. They are each half full of an oily yellowish liquid. "We kept them in the fridge just for you." She shakes them up and holds them in front of him.

The bubbled contents creep down the translucent walls. "They're a special dressing. Lucifia's recipe. We just want you to sprinkle some on the salad of the bad guys at lunch tomorrow. Then they won't feel so good about attacking us. Fryberger should be there, supposedly to convince them to let the due process of law take its course. Make sure he gets some too."

Deela's black hair is disheveled. She hasn't adjusted her tunic after their tussle and she is showing generous cleavage. The swells of her bosom are still red where he pressed down on them so fiercely. Gilligan suppresses a giggle.

"What's so funny?"

Gilligan senses from her tone that she is measuring his balls for a quick, vicious kick.

"Nothing. It's just that the salad dress—" He doubles over, nearly overcome with the urge to laugh, "these guys are hunters, farmers, soldiers. They're carnivores, man. They aren't going to be eating any fucking salad."

"That's your problem. You will do this and you will do it before noon tomorrow. Just sprinkle some in their food. Any food. You'll have saved the ranch. You'll be a hero. And you'll be back together with what's her name again."

"Seatrice. What if someone dies, or something?"

"No one is going to die. They'll just feel sick for a while. I mean running for the outhouses sick. No one died in Heiferville, did they?"

She smiles coyly at Gilligan, letting him in on a great secret. Her pupils are so dilated she looks a Koala bear. A drugged Koala bear.

"We'd bought up so many residences and had moved so many sannyasins into that one horse town that we probably would have won the mayor's race anyway. It was too bad though that so many of the so called 'natives' happened to get sick on election day, including the former mayor and her entire town council."

"Yeah," says Chloe. "A real shayme. Maybe it was something they ate—like the ketchup at the greasy spoon where they all had breakfast! Har har har! Har har har har har!"

Chloe's laugh is roughly equivalent to the sounds Gilligan imagines a rutting bull kangaroo would make.

"Ketchup. Perfect. Put it in their ketchup." Deela presses the vials into Gilligan's hands. "Don't even think of opening them until the time comes."

"But how do I—?"

"I've already told Slowma you've been reassigned. Whatever you need, the commune will provide. Just tell them it is for me. Tell them to call me on channel D, if they have any doubts. And I don't care how, Swami. Just get it done. Right?"

There's a pause. Gilligan tumbles the vials in his warm, slippery hands.

"Right?"

He looks up at Deela and nods.

She brings her hands together in a namaste. Her face has a mocking look on it. "Good choice, swami." An inviting luster appears briefly in her eyes, then is swallowed by the dark pools of her pupils. "Now get out of here."

After Gilligan has left, Deela tenderly and deliberately indulges in a self-hug and strokes her upper arms and shoulders. Trailed by Chloe, she wanders back into the Hemlock Grove living room and again stands before the vista afforded by the huge picture window. It is the early stage of a prolonged July sunset. The stainless steel spool on the far side of the Van Gogh Bridge is a flaming orange mandala, a golden crown above the graceful lines of Enlightenment Hall. Above and beyond that, the waters of the ceremonial Yahoo! Waterfall tumbling into the pond fronting the Master's house plash and glitter in the light.

"Chloe," murmurs Deela. "Sometimes one can only contemplate one's own brilliance with reverence and awe. I feel such love for me that words fail and all there is is pure gratitude for the fact that I am here." Her fingers continue to stroke and squeeze the backs of her arms as she speaks.

"Can I ask you something, Boss?"

"Anything, Chloe dear. You know that."

"Don't we *want* those rednecks to invade? Weren't we going to use the chaos to get away with the money? If that bloke succeeds in giving them the salmonella then—"

"Chloe. Chloe. Chloe. Oh ye of little faith. The first little detail is that chances are excellent he will not succeed. Our Canuck friend is a nice guy with *some* potential, but no more than that. He's hardly commando material. And when they catch him with the poison, what will happen?"

"They'll kill him, I reckon. And be madder than hell at us! They'll figure they have every reason to come in here with guns blazing. Dayla, you're a genius!"

"Correct. But there's more. The best part is that on the off chance he does succeed, that isn't salmonella in those vials. It's steroids: testosterone, Anadrol, and a few others. Lucifia says they're the wonder drug for the eighties. Ingesting them should make those boys feel like supermen. Angry supermen. So you see Gilligan's mission, win or lose, is a win-win! Now, why don't you get Patipaticake and we'll lower those bags into our spot in the tunnel. Tomorrow looks like it is going to be an awfully busy day."

31. Gilligan's Enlightenment

Gilligan steps from Chloe's trailer at Hemlock Grove. The air is warm and dry, exquisitely comfortable. He and Seatrice had been sleeping al fresco the last few nights, enjoying the stars and each other in a cozy niche in one of the hillsides adjacent to his A-frame. His ear throbs; the whole side of his head and face aches from the smack Chloe gave him with the telephone, which complemented Lucifia's earlier stomp. He is consumed with anxiety for the well being of his lover, his friend, his everything. He remembers Kildaraj putting on the respirator, the ends of Flamhir's moustaches curling from behind the surgical mask as they drove him down the sketchy dirt road behind the recycling centre.

Back there, near those two hills where the hawks circled and cried out, there must be some kind of sequestered medical compound. That's where she is. Rattlesnake country.

He is ready to head over there. Attempt a rescue. Get her, and get the hell out. *Fuck everything else.* But Lucifia and Tootie would almost certainly be there. And the poison is heavy in his pockets. *Plus Deela has given me authority. Whatever I need, she said.*

The Middle Way, the main street of the town, is full of sannyasins newly arrived for the festival— walking, greeting, laughing, hugging old friends and lovers not seen in many months. The patio of the Zorro the Meditator Restaurant, fully repaired after the unfortunate shit truck episode, is jammed. The pounding beat of the disco, punctuated by whoops of joy, indicates the meet market is firing on all cylinders. Gilligan, his hands in his pockets, each fisting a plastic vial sloshing with poison, walks through it all like a hippie down Bay St., his mind on a completely different wavelength. At the crossroads, the bus to Macarena is waiting. It will take him away from the pink flush of the western sky. Away from the Recycling Depot, Hippocrises and the hills where the hawks circle and cry. Away from his beloved. But only for now. He has to think.

The rosy grandeur on the western horizon has receded to a ribbon's glow as he clambers to the top of the hill. The moon, the Guru Purnima (Master's Day) moon, a white whisker shy of full, is ascending the eastern sky. It illuminates the pebbled hump of the hill's summit. Gilligan's shadow precedes him as he arrives, puffing from exertion. He can see the tiny canyon where he and his workmates drank beer around the campfire last summer, on the full moon night they forged all those beer tokens and hatched the infamous shit truck escapade. He discovered this spot then and had recognized it as his own particular 'place of power'. To the west, well off in the distance, is the swooping form of Enlightenment Hall, and the graceful silhouette of the Van Gogh Bridge, complete with the fluted wheel and dangling mops. Rising proudly to the right are the twin mounds between which nestles the master's house. Between those hills and the horizon, reflecting here and there in the curves of Little Snake Creek, the lights from the Middle Way shine brightly. The beat of the disco thuds faintly, like a far-off heart.

He settles in cross-legged on the peak, facing west, to the left of Enlightenment Hall- the direction where he is sure Seatrice is being held. He folds his jacket and scrunches it under the base of his spine for lift. He takes the vials of poison, stirs their bases into the gravel. He contemplates their mild Easter Island tilt, the miniature moonshadows they cast. He inhales deeply and exhales over a last panoramic survey of the moon-washed valley, the winding road and creek, the pink blush on the horizon. He closes his eyes.

I can't just sit here when they've got Seatrice. No, wait. It's because I don't know what the fuck to do. Meditation, well medita-

308

tion and the chicks brought me here, OK chicks and meditation, let's be honest. But meditation had better help me now. Didn't Buddha say something about 'right action'? That's what I need. Right action. To make the right choice. And my 'monkey mind' isn't going to figure that out. What? I'm supposed to be a fucking hero and poison people, including lawmen, to save the Ranch? Is this a desperate times, desperate measures thing? There's probably a fence around that compound, maybe a security checkpoint. What if that Tootie is there? I'd need a tranquilizer gun set for rhino. If I could just get to Seatrice, we could outrun her. That's for damn sure. God I feel her. She's OK now. I heard her on the phone. Breathe. Watch the breath. That's it. Breathe. Oh Baby. What am I gonna do? Poison those buggers? Serve them right. Jesus Christ, why aren't those clueless fuck-ups off lynching niggers or bashing gays? Why us? Well, Dee-la did hurt Dillard. And she's got Seatrice. Fuck what a bitch. Why do women get that way? Because they're not getting properly fucked? Daddy issues? Shit the whole world has Daddy issues. And let's not even start on Mommy.

OK. Gilligan. Johnny. John Price Jr.. Whoever the fuck you are behind all the names. This is getting you nowhere, instead of now-here. Breathe, you asshole. Breathe. Watch the breath. Quit fucking thinking. Quit criticizing yourself. You got more than enough of that from Dad. Yeah and way too much praise from Mom. No wonder you're such a fuck-up. Quit criticizing! OK! I forgot. Leave me alone. We have to learn to be alone, not lonely, alone in the here and now, that's what DB says. Breathe. Settle into the body. The body is wise. The mind is fucked up. Arrgh. My body hurts. These ribs are throbbing, I'd like to take a chainsaw to that fucking Lucifia. Yow. That's dark. And my head! Why am I always getting hit in the fucking head? 'Cause I'm an Aries. A ram's always butting into things. Existence is trying to knock myself out of my head. Seatrice is an Aquarius. Air and fire. The perfect mix. God she's beautiful. Fuck my ear hurts. I can feel every heartbeat throbbing in it. Well then feel it. Feel it. But shut up about it. Feel your body. Feel your pain. It is out of emotional pain stored in the body that the thoughts come. Feel the pain and let the thoughts dissolve like clouds.

Swami Satyam Gilligan, remembering the teachings from hundreds of hours spent listening to the Divine Bhagwan's taped discourses, begins to follow his breath. He feels it enter at the nostrils, the nose hairs bending upstream then downstream, like seaweed pushed by waves. He feels his spine straighten a little, as if pulled upwards from the top of the head. His ribs expand on the in-breath, the pain on his left side a continuous reminder to watch.

Ow! God that hurts. That's my heart, hurting. Hurting. Is that all it does? Hurt? And my solar plexus feels like I've swallowed those vials whole and the plastic's burning in the stomach acid. Breathe. Quit whining. Watch the breath. You are not your feelings, not your thoughts. You are the watcher. Feel the ground. Hear the crickets. Listen to the silence behind the sounds. Watch this moment. Be this moment. Let the moment decide.

There's a rhythmic sloshing in his ears. It envelops his eardrums, caresses them, in a background thrum, as insistent as a rising tide. His nostrils tingle and dilate. Tears form under his eyelids.

There are keys here. Things I'm missing. What am I missing? Power. I'm missing power. No balls. Ball-less wimp sissy. Always in the background. Oh that's brilliant. Beat yourself up. Typical. Shut up. Shut up. The breath. Go deep. Oh yeah. Deep breath. Oh baby. I like to kiss you.

The crickets are loud. He feels the cool glow of the moon on his eyelids. He sighs, turns his mind from frustration, anxiety, and desire to the crickets, the silence behind the crickets and the moon.

Where's the power? Here and now, where is the power?

Another sigh. The crickets. The moon. A tickle in his lower belly. The moon is bright enough that the dark hoods of his eyelids are tinged with red. He remembers closing his eyes and looking at the sun as a kid.

Shapes like enlarged corpuscles. It's the blood in the lids that's red. Who told me that? Miss Roberts, she of the luscious lips, in grade two.

The cell-like phantasms floating on the rusty screen before his eyes fascinate him. They join and separate in a globular dance in rhythm with the throbbing in his ear and the chirps of the crickets.

Mitosis! That's what it's called. I'm witnessing cells doing mitosis! Wait! Don't get caught up. Don't get carried away by the mind. Stay present. Breathe.

The thrumming sound is louder, a discernable thudding in tune with crickets' chants. It is his heartbeat, pulsing softly in his eyelids, faintly intertwined with the subtle tickling sensation in his lower belly.

Breathe. Watch. It is in the subtleties of feeling that the key lies. We do so much crap- smoking, drugs, drinking, sex, games to distract the mind and just enjoy being human- at least for a while. But we miss the subtleties, the nuances of being that are our greatest delight. Shit. That's brilliant. I should write it down. Now I'm congratulating myself instead of criticizing. It is the same thing flipped over. Mind! Mind! Mind! Just be! Be! Be!

He sighs and begins to let go, feels small muscles letting go in his jaw, around his eyeballs, up and down his spine.

This clamp around my jaw is a vise of unspoken words. Vise. Vice. Those words may be more closely related than I thought. I? Boom, the ego's back. 'I' is just a word in my mind. There's no 'I', just what is.

He feels the weight of his body settling through his bones into his folded jacket, which is also chirping like crickets. He sinks into the moment: the play of pink on his eyelids; the air molecules snaking down his nostrils; his spine alive to the mass of the hill beneath it. He begins to see his mind as chunks of thought and emotion that intertwine and drift, clot and flow, like platelets, corpuscles, and white blood cells. His resentment towards his forever distant father, always on some other fairway, is like a cancerous growth snagging cheery red cells with malignant tentacles.

Don't give it any energy. Forgive. Accept. Widen the view. The crickets, the hill, the moon are here with me. Dad has his own choices.

An ache in his solar plexus is the leaden weight of his mother, the crickets click like knitting needles and he is dragged down a funnel into murky river water where water-logged babies bump each other and drift away. He is sitting in their den in Denlord Estates. He is twenty-two years old and just back from a lonely month of 'finding himself' in Europe. He leans forward on the fold-out couch, the one with the rubber 'harp strings' under the cushion. Blue shag carpet under his feet. No magazine. No TV. No Mom. Just himself and his father. His fingers are sweaty as he lights a cigarette, his first-ever in front of the old man. He is told the facts: about her imaginary Carribbean lover, how she held onto the knife in the kitchen and wouldn't stop talking, how she went catatonic and burnt her leg with her low-tar cigarette, how she had shock treatments, how she's still in the hospital. *"I understand that she was talking to you a lot before you left, sometimes late at night. What did she say? What did you tell her? No, Dr. Schindler doesn't think it's a good idea for you to see her right now."*

Ah. My fault. I talked her into going nuts. You were always jealous of me, you prick, because I got way more of her love, such as it was, than you ever did.

Gilligan seethes there on the hill for many minutes, with hurt, guilt and outrage writhing in his chest like a nest of acidic snakes. A tear or two tumbles from his cheek and spatters on the plastic caps of the poison. They make a hollow sound, a tiny drumbeat that jerks him back into the present.

Seatrice!

This thought surges through him like a cleansing flood.

What the fuck am I going to do? Shit. There's that 'I' again. Just be. Breathe. The silence behind the sounds. Feel the presence of space.

He's better now, more centered. His watches his thoughts, his mind. He begins to see his mind as thought clusters floating in the rivers of his bloodstream. He sees his sleepiness as a blockage, an aneurysm whispering seductively of other times and places to the merry corpuscles in their red frocks, some of which are foolish enough to be enveloped. He sees his nastiness as vigilant white knight cells, their barbed armor dripping with the poison of righteousness. And his idealism is the plasma, carrying everything else along on a river buoyant with the elixir of hope.

The snakes writhing in his chest calm themselves and elongate along the bones of his limbs. He feels an opening in his thighs and forearms, the awakening of a spacious bodily intelligence where the crickets also chirp. His body feels hollow and huge, like a vast watery space within which swims the entirety of the outside world. Some part of him realizes that he has stopped talking to himself. The urge to congratulate himself on doing so floats by like a chunk of ice on a dark river. He waits, eagerly and exultantly, for the *Kundalini* energy to awaken, for an explosion of fiery heat in his sacrum, that will kindle each ascending vertebrae in his spine like a dry tumbleweed, igniting chakras, ravaging its way upwards like a demented fire-god, filling the meridians of his supernal body with bliss and overflowing through the crown of his head, the *Sahasrara* chakra, the thousand petaled lotus. Then his Universal Mind would awaken. He would see all. Know all. Be all.

Fear of the future. Hope for the future. It is all mind stuff. Right. It's like the Master is here with me. He knows all the pitfalls.

Another deep breath and a sighing exhale. He begins to listen with his skin, his toes and feet. The crickets, the hill, on whose massiveness his form is but a small pimple, the soft tang of sage in the air; the stars, the great white pulse of the moon; what do they have to tell him? Thoroughly intrigued, he forgets himself and listens. He is aware of lightness, of light. The moonlight, the sounds of the crickets, the very air moving in and out of his body are all light, light comingling in an electric dance. *We are made of the same stuff as the stars. How could it be otherwise?* These words of the Master are the last thing he remembers before he disappears into an abyss of bliss.

The curtains of his eyelids rise to reveal an entirely new theatre of being. He has returned, but was never away. He is here, but also there. The moon remains high; the shadows cast by the vials of poison have lengthened only slightly. Threads of pink, like mohair filaments, continue to blush the western horizon. He casts his mind in that direction and cavorts amongst the filaments, climbing them and riding their sway like a pole vaulter in the Olympics or a young lad clinging to a bowed sapling that he has shimmied up. He blows himself up into a giant luminous being, bestriding the glimmering pink freeway that is the horizon, surveying the entire ranch as if it were a miniature village in a train set. He knows that this is imagination, that he in 'reality' still sits on the hilltop hearing the crickets. He thinks of something Ezra Pound (*that fascist*) said, that *"only the imagination is real."*

This freedom, this unbounded mind is the true reality, the natural reality. And the world, as we perceive it, is really a kind of imagining in the mind of God, of All That Is. That's it, the deeper meaning. Only the imagination is real. And I understand it. I've **experienced** *it. I must be fucking enlightened! But wait wait wait. It happened, but now you're thinking it, so just let the happening be. 'Let the happening be!' I should write that down too.*

Swami Satyam Gilligan stretches out his legs, the right one is an unresponsive clump of pins and needles. He picks up the vials of poison, runs his right thumbnail across the ridges of a cap. *Clackety clack. Like the baseball cards we used to clothespin against our bicycle spokes, making them into motorcycles.*

Gilligan stands up, thrusts the vials deep into his pockets, and shakes out that right leg. He may still be a screwed-up (albeit possibly Enlightened) Canadian, but something inside him is rumbling like a Harley at a small town intersection. He knows what he needs to do. He must go and speak to the Master on a direct Enlightened Being to Enlightened Being basis. He must go now and in secret. And he knows exactly how it can be done.

32. The Heart of Lightness

During his 'Enlightenment Experience', when he bestrode the horizon like a diaphanous colossus, when he was gifted with the power of insight (much like owning the X-ray spectacles advertised in the back of his boyhood comics), Gilligan saw clearly in his mind's eye Newfyamo's tunnel and the place where he had hit his head on the motion sensor. He knew the tunnel forking to the left must lead to the Master's house and it is here that the unfolding moments that are Enlightenment have brought him. The joints he steps over between culvert segments are clean and perfectly fitted. The motion-sensing lights strung overhead come on as before, illumining a ceiling that is a shade or two whiter than the tunnel to Hemlock Grove left behind him. This is the way. He smells it in the dank concrete tang emanating from the walls around him. As he walks, his right hand repeatedly snakes into his jacket pocket and palms the two vials of poison, tumbling them over the top of each other, cycling them in time with the lights that float overhead, one after the other.

The sounds of his footsteps echo telescopically ahead and behind him. He jogs on silent supple toes, forcing his breath to trail silently to and from his nostrils as he listens intently for clues as to what might lie ahead. After several minutes, Gilligan stops. A new sound, other than the clicking of the lights and the thud and scrape of his footfalls, has impinged on his consciousness. There is a sea-like roar coming from some distance ahead. There is a fresher hint of moisture in the air as well, like the fragrance that foreshadows rain. He resumes his gait, with renewed alertness. The roar grows

315

louder. There is a variance in the tunnel ahead, a dark open-ing in the curve of the right hand wall.

Heart pounding, Gilligan approaches, stooping till he is bent almost in two. The roar, as it increases in volume, be-comes the distinct sound of water splashing into water. A trickle runs into the seam at the base of the 'Y' where the two tunnels converge. He carefully peeks around the corner to the right; his eyes near the level of his knees.

He sees a short tunnel, maybe ten feet long, and a few concrete steps at the top of which is a narrow doorway cur-tained by a roaring sheet of water several feet in front of it. The door, fully swung inwards is finished on the outside with flat rocks. Walls of similar rocks, faintly visible in the dark-ness beyond the doorway, frame the dark goggle of the water-fall. These are the stones chosen by Gilligan and Lionheart in Hoodoo Canyon a year earlier. A lever, impishly made out of a baseball bat, and positioned like a railing beside the steps, is clearly the mechanism that opens and closes the secret door which can only be behind the ceremonial Yahoo! Waterfall that feeds the pond in front of the Master's house. The goal is very near. The secret door, so carelessly left open, adds more caution to Gilligan's step. *Perhaps someone is planning a quick exit.* As the roar of the waterfall is completely left behind, a new sound assails his ears. It begins as a distant wave crash-ing the length of some murky coastline, but soon echoes in the tunnel like a herd of berserk bulls.

Ahead of him a rounded turn to the left is illumined by a glow that stains its curves a ghastly pink. The sound fades to silence, then builds again, as if a phalanx of surfers were lobbing clusters of exploding munitions onto a rocky shore. It originates around the corner, from near the source of the bloody glow. The furrows of consternation in Gilligan's face dissolve to the crinkles of a mild smile as he realizes what the sound is.

Someone is snoring. Big time.

Again he lowers himself, this time to hands and knees, to peer around the corner. He is confronted by the cold porcelain gloss of a toilet mounted on a platform built some eight inches above the curved floor of the tunnel. The platform is tiled in creamy marble infused with pink and red striations. There is more than a whiff of urine. Glowing overhead is a lone, wire-caged red bulb. Beyond the toilet is a kitchen cabinet and sink, evidently scavenged from one of the Ranch's trailers. On the counter is a compact fridge, topped by a toaster oven whose door droops open. The middle rack protrudes like a tongue and supports an empty bottle of Guiness. On the floor below the oven, is a Mandala Pizza box, from the ranch's own take-out and delivery service. On the right side of the extra-wide tunnel is a counter dominated by a large reel to reel tape machine. Its spools are a good twelve inches across. They turn slowly with a faint creak at the nadir of every revolution, like the plaintive chirp of a small bird dashed against a window by the wind.

Reclining almost horizontally in a wheeled office chair between the counters, like a rickety, delicately balanced human bridge, is none other than Lurchamo. The X of his feet rests just in front of the reels; the unkempt curls at the back of his head are just above the pizza box. It is from him that the monstrous, cannonading tones of the snoring emanate. Beyond Lurchamo is a door. Ranch issue steel, a horizontal ridge in its knob indicates that it locks from this side. Over Lurchamo's eyes, adapted to block out the light, are the thick domes of his headphones, their padded bridge cleverly twisted to support his neck. Between snores, along with the reel-chirps, Gilligan hears, possibly from the headphones, the faint sounds of children playing. Lurchamo's listening perch is highly precarious; the two front wheels of the chair are a good four inches above the gloss of the marble floor. His heels, clad in classic high-boot Perspehones dyed a soft mauve, are dangerously close to slipping from the edge of the counter they rest on.

Gilligan must get beyond the barrier that Lurchamo's body forms across the width of the tunnel. The diving forward roll, a simple gymnastics technique taught by Britishfield Public School's curly haired, chunky legged, whistle blowing, Miss Ronson back in grade three, should be just the ticket. But the landing area between Lurchamo and the door — which presumably leads directly into the Master's house — is worrisomely truncated. He must keep his roll quiet, and tight, without too much forward momentum. The polished surface of the marble is sure as to be far less yielding than the buttoned grey floor mats back in Britishfield's gym.

He stands up slowly and centers himself opposite the sag of Lurchamo's abdomen. The bodily barrier is definitely too high to attempt a simple straddle step. He breathes deeply, letting his arms swing as he rocks his weight back and forth. He will have to time his dive so he lands in mid-snore. So resounding, so cacophonous, is the din emanating from Lurchamo's open mouth and nostrils, it would surely mask any scuffling thumps and bumps Gilligan might make. He shakes out his fingers, expels a deep breath, crouches, and springs.

He sails over Lurchamo in fine form. His body knifes through the spittle-laden sonic cloud of a particularly egregious snore. He lands on flexed hands and arms, immediately tucking his head so he can roll on the curvature of his spine. Perhaps the initial spring is too powerful, too leonine, for a situation where the tidier pounce of a housecat would suffice. An excess of momentum brings his heels over his head in a discombobulated blur. His feet plant themselves on the floor at the very base of the metal door. He stands up swiftly — too swiftly. Like a heavy walnut twirled at the end of a string, his head's motion brings his face smacking into the unyielding metal surface. The even less-yielding metal of the doorknob gouges deeply into his lower belly at a point halfway between his navel and his manhood, causing a Heimlich-like gag response. Winded, eyes bulging, tongue protruding like some glam-rock megastar's, he feels a trickle of blood beginning to creep from his left nostril as pigeon-toed, and unable to gasp for breath, he slides down the face of the door like a flattened cartoon character. For a moment he begins toppling backwards like a felled tree. He musters enough presence of mind to twist his torso away from the wall and wrench himself into a semi-crouch so that his plummeting form barely misses Lurchamo who remains bridged and somnolently unaware. Gilligan thumps onto the marble with a loud groan, protecting his face from further indignity by tucking his forearms and clenched fists in close to his chest. Lurchamo's snore ends, leaving only the sound of plastic skittering on marble.

Gilligan follows the sound with his eyes, turning his head one-hundred and eighty degrees. His nose splatters a pattern worthy of Jackson Pollock onto the abstract swirls of marble. As pain wings its way through his skull and down into his gut, it occurs to him that his Enlightenment, scarcely an hour old, may not have been quite complete. *We may have to downgrade it to a satori..* Wedged under one of the office chair wheels that supports Lurchamo is a vial of Gilligan's poison.

His nose throbs, continues to bleed a slow trickle. By happy coincidence, a crumpled paper towel, muddied by pizza sauce, lies between the wheels of the chair. Gilligan unballs a fist and claws it to his face. He shoves a torn streamer up the secreting nostril while mopping up the inadvertent artwork beneath his head. He gathers himself into a squat and, spreading his arms wide, is able to place the fingertips of one hand on the wayward vial and those of the other on the doorknob. He gently tests the locking flange, turns it all the way to the left. He snatches the vial, feels the chair's wheel move, twists the doorknob and slips through the doorway as quickly as a tongue burnt by soup retreats behind teeth. As the closely fitted door snuffs shut behind him, he hears the clatter of the office chair collapsing onto marble, the thud of

Lurchamo's body and a muffled imprecation: "Oh bloody cri-key!"

He waits for many seconds with his back against the door, both hands clutching the knob which has locked behind him. His heart pounds with apprehension that he will feel it turn under his hands, that he may have to deal with Lurchamo trying to force his way in. A bead of sweat trickles from an armpit. A tendril of the paper towel stuffed up his nose flutters as he breathes. He hears nothing, feels no touch against the knob.

Maybe this isn't the first time Lurchamo has experienced a rude awakening at his listening post. Maybe he's just cracking open another Guinness.

As his fear subsides and his eyes adjust, Gilligan sees that he is in the deepest recess of a narrow storage room. It is very dark. There is a faint smell of chlorine. The outlines of wooden shelves hover to either side. Ahead is the ghostly perimeter of another door, in which floats a small rectangular window. Its glass is darkened, and incorporates a grid of safety wire. It casts a pale, elongated rectangle of grey light which undulates on the ceiling with subtle wavy lines. From beyond the door he hears sporadic splashing and some faint, but very beguiling, feminine giggling. He is in the storeroom of the Master's private swimming pool.

He tucks the paper towel further up his nose, wipes the back of his hand, still sweaty from exertion and fright, across his top lip and over the undersides of his nostrils. He glides noiselessly between the shelves and peers through the window into paradise.

Though seen through a darkened glass, the richness of the scene is dazzling. Beautifully fitted marble tiles, like the ones in Lurchamo's hideout, comprise the flooring of the entire pool area and of the pool itself, which has no edges. It is an egg-shaped hollow, perhaps four feet deep in its midsection, which runs for about 35 feet. The effect is much like that of a cultured marble sink-top on a grand scale. The ceiling, a series of cedar beams defining a gently sloping grid of sky-lights, starts low and vaults high over the pool. Streams of light from the moon, bright enough to reflect off the wavelets, cast dancing patterns onto the walls and the foliage of the many trees, flowering plants and bushes that are pleasingly arranged in pots and planters throughout the pool enclosure. It is said that many species of gorgeous exotic butterflies have been imported and make their homes here. If any such flit about in the moonlight, they are unnoticed by Gilligan. His eyes are enslaved by the two gorgeous, exotic, and thoroughly naked women frolicking in the Master's pool.

One is Angelica, the Little Annie Fanny look-alike who had somehow, at least temporarily, convinced Dillard to em-brace sannyas and is now Newfyamo's main squeeze. Angeli-ca, up to her thighs in moonlit water, bends at the waist to embrace a giant rubber duckie which floats, along a with life-sized white plastic swan, in the shallow end of the pool clos-est to Gilligan's vantage point. The sight of her breasts bunch-ing against the plastic curve of the duckie's neck causes his fingers to delve into his pocket to adjust his swiftly hardening dick. Instead, they encounter the plastic vials of poison. He remembers his mission and Seatrice's plight.

What's happening to her? Have they drugged her? Who's guarding her? What if she falls for her guard, her kidnappers, like Patricia Hearst did? I must focus on my mission and nothing else. This is no time to be a fucking wanker.

He tears his eyes away from Angelica's superb form, only to have them be captivated by a second vision of femi-nine loveliness at the far end of the pool. This woman is older, but no less beautiful. He long red hair is soaked straight back from her face, which features large green eyes and fine pink lips. Her figure is bountiful, yet delicate. She is stooping gracefully over the water, extending her hands and arms to catch and guide a body that floats towards her with the most leisurely backstroke imaginable.

The Master's presence suspends time, telescopes simple moments into an unfolding kaleidoscope whose hues are tinged by eternity. His gliding form is as still as a log in a slow moving river. Then an arm sprouts from the surface and arcs in a as unhurriedly as one of Ptolemy's spheres across the firmament, only to settle back into the water, pore by flooded pore, until the serene log reappears.

The woman cradles the Divine Bhagwan's head as he reaches her and very gently turns the floating form so it is heading back in Angelica's direction. She giggles as she does so. The Master is murmuring something amusing. The hypnotic sequence of log, arcing arm, log, arcing arm begins again. The Master's backstroke is completely silent.

Gilligan is utterly unsure how to proceed. Surely there are plenty of Samurai and Peace Officers just outside the pool doors. If he is captured and sent to Deela he, Seatrice and likely the Ranch itself will be lost. If those paranoid paramilitary rednecks overrun the commune, the Master's life will definitely in danger, unless he is first arrested by Attorney General Fryberger. And then, the Master is so delicate that being in jail would probably kill him within a day or two. However entrancing the scene, Gilligan cannot remain an observer behind a small dark safety window.

He turns the knob and slips into the pool area. He takes a couple of steps and swiftly kneels in the moonlit rectangle cast by one of the skylights. Though amidst some huge pots of hibiscuses, he is clearly visible from the pool. He will sit quietly, trust, and wait to see what happens. He kneels on the hard marble, slides the soggy paper towel out of his nostril and places it in a nearby hibiscus pot. His nose has mercifully stopped bleeding. He closes his eyes, striving with every molecule to look peaceful and non-threatening. It will surely be the older naked ma who sees him first. He tries to cast a loving, reassuring vibe in her direction, through a heart clanging like a blacksmith's hammer on the anvil of his breastbone. He settles in and begins to breathe, monitoring the scene through

322

the veil of his slightly parted eyelashes. His trepidation swiftly gives way to feelings of rapture and bliss.

The Master's arm, dappled by reflected light waves, wheels upwards in a dripping arc, then settles seamlessly back into the water. The older ma reaches out her hands to cushion the shoulders of the oncoming Master and again turns the floating log of his being in the opposite direction. Her arms, extended like a dancer's, are languid and soft. Her hair, wet between her shoulder blades, is the color of fresh rust. Her skin is lustrous, a pearly antique white, highlighted by pink undertones.

Gilligan, with a sharp intake of breath, finally recognizes Nivea, the beautiful English rose who for years has been the Divine Bhagwan's constant caretaker and companion. It was the overhead view of her splendid breasts that had caused him to lose his balance the day he fell from the Master's house. Nivea is surrendered to the Divine Bhagwan. She has opened her heart, her being, and her mind to him for many years. His divine presence has permeated her witnessing consciousness so completely, that she now, even has she turns him, turns *as* him, sees her beautiful self looking down, and the moonlit skylights above her head. Thus, it is as much through her Master's eyes as her own, that she glances up and looks directly at Gilligan.

The curtain of his eyelashes trembles open under her gaze. Her eyes are the green of the forest's first leaves in spring. Fragrances of cedar, sandalwood, and cinnamon enfold him. He's in a kitchen in the woods, a safe haven from which endless adventures beckon. He's at home. Tears begin to run down his cheeks. He didn't know it could be like this. So simple. So good.

To sound the alarm does not occur to Nivea. Besides, the nearest help would be Kildaraj in the other part of the house. The Divine Bhagwan has requested that no guards be within Shangri Ohlala. Gilligan's physical beauty, his peaceful aspect, engross her. *He's the fellow that fell from the roof.* She unconsciously rubs the scar in the pad at the base of her thumb. His normally faun-like eyes are nearly glaring with urgency. He signals to her with a simple pantomime that he wishes to speak to the Master.

Gilligan is feeling the spiky, chain-mailed fist of panic thrusting into his solar plexus. Nivea brings her fingers to her forehead, pulls them tight along her scalp to wring out her hair. Her devotional peace is shattered. She has to make a decision, not merely cater to needs, and someone other than her beloved Master is involved. She holds that pose, squeezing her hair thoughtfully. Gilligan, holding her gaze, sees, as well as feels her distress. He gestures for her to be calm, makes what he hopes is a reassuring face.

It come across as rather goofy and elicits the hint of a smile from Nivea.

"Nivea."

Faintly, from somewhere many dimensions removed from the connection between Nivea and Gilligan, a voice comes again, louder.

"Nivea!"

The Master's head crashes into Nivea's haunch with all he force of a styrofoam battering ram. She shrieks, mortified that she could have been so distracted from her duty of cushioning the Divine Bhagwan's turn. Angelica, seeing Gilligan for the first time, also shrieks. The giant rubber duckie squirts from her grasp and scuds briefly across the pool, nuzzling soundlessly into the plastic swan. Gilligan does not move. He closes his eyes completely, waits for the footfalls of the guards.

They do not come. He hears Angelica swimming to the Master's side, then some quiet conversation, at the end of which he hears the Master say:

"Let's do the brushes first."

A wave of relief and gratitude washes over Gilligan. *He is going to talk to me.*

All goes quiet, quieter than before. Just the occasional lapping and dripping of water. There is no chlorine smell here, just the earthy odor of the pots and the musky mix of fragrances from the many blooms around the pool. They seem to permeate Gilligan's body, slyly slipping intoxicants into his bloodstream. He feels good. Very good. He feels his heart, still thumping strongly, but slowing down, calming itself and being healed in the blissful presence of the Master. He knows Seatrice, the Ranch, all the Master's work are at dire risk, that his mission is one of utter urgency, but the thick pall of bliss suffocates his resolve, seduces him into the psychedelia of sensations, and imaginative splendor that comprise his present moment. The hard marble floor under his knees, the rubber heels of his Peresphones digging into his butt, the quiet of the desert night, the pale glow of moonlight on his eyelids, the presence of the two gorgeous women. He breathes a little more deeply. Can he smell them? The sandalwood and cinnamon of Nivea? *Yes. Yes. Oh yes, there it is.* And what of Angelica? Where is her scent? He breathes deeply again, almost overwhelmed with pleasure. Buttered popcorn. He swallows, enjoys the lumpy journey of the salivary nectar down his throat and esophagus which conjures the image of a gondola on a Venetian canal. A thin trickling tear slithers down the smooth curve of his cheek.

Rejoice, for you are the new man. Rejoice, the kingdom has come, now and forever.

"Excuse me."

Thy will be done, not mine.

"Swami."

Thy will, unknowable, immeasurable, unfolding, happening here and now in the dance of every electron-

Angelica's splash is practiced and wicked. Delivered by the cupped wing of her hand smacking a divot from the water's surface, it flings a watery comet straight into Gilligan's face. Gilligan, rudely yanked from another 'spiritual' experience, opens his eyes ready to tell whoever splashed him to fuck right off but his pique is plucked from his throat by the sight of the naked Angelica, the blonde hairs of her pussy beaded and dripping, with her hands on her splendidly curvaceous hips in an unmistakable posture of impatience.

"He's ready to talk to you," she says.

She turns and swims to the far end of the pool, where Nivea is brushing the Master's hair. Angelica's buttocks seem as round and white and tight as a pair of volleyballs.

"What do you wish to speak to me about?"

The Master's voice is languid, with an undercurrent of implied laughter. It has been surprisingly natural for Gilligan to take off his clothes and wade into the water which, it is said, is imported from a glacial spring that burbles beneath a monastery in Tibet. Its temperature is regulated to within one tenth of one degree of optimum by a network of radiant subcutaneous pipes.

He kneels in the shallows, on the warm smoothness of the swimming pool's marble floor, just a few feet from the Master. His shoulder blades are nuzzled occasionally by the pliant, bulleted foam of Angelica's breasts as she brushes his loosened ponytail. Nivea, positioned similarly behind the Divine Bhagwan, brushes the fringe of his hair (the upper dome is completely bald) and the luxuriant white mass of his beard. The pink mother of pearl in the brush's head glistens as it travels down the moonlit fibers. Precious stones sparkle in the knob of its handle. Angelica presses a knee into Gilligan's sacrum as her brush tangles in a recalcitrant area. The Master's brush never tangles, hitches, or wobbles. It flows with immanent smoothness, like a seagull banking low over whitecapped waves. Nivea adheres to the Master, while rarely touching him. Her lovely face, eyes downcast to the beard, hovers over his head like a halo. Gilligan, the sexual antenna between his legs tuned into numerous multi-pleasured signals on extra-exquisite frequencies emanating from Angelica's sumptuous form, vaguely hears the Master's question. He grapples for a way to answer it before he's swept completely downstream by indulgence's distracting currents.

"Bwah bwah bwah," he says.

He feels his lips moving, but his tongue is like a wet, knotted rope. His hair releases its grip on Angelica's brush. She pitches forward slightly, grazing her nipples down his shoulder blades.

"Sorry," she whispers, her warm mouth inches from his earlobe.

"Bwah bwah bwah," he says again, as if to accentuate an important point.

"Is this swami perhaps German?" asks Bhagwan.

"He's Canadian I think," murmurs Nivea.

"Do they not speak English?"

The occlusion stuffing Gilligan's mouth bursts like a water balloon hitting hot pavement. The Master's gaze holds his heart's attention like a tender newborn. The feeling that they share a joke intensifies. Gilligan wants to shout, laugh, sing.

"We have to get you away from here," he hears himself say. "You are in danger and terrible things are being plotted by some of your own sannyasins."

"What kinds of things?"

Gilligan slips past Angelica; the wayward periscope of his dick hooks briefly in the crook of her arm; she, glancing sideways, briefly turns up the corner of her mouth in a hint of amusement. He sidestrokes to the edge of the pool and retrieves the vials of poison which he thoughtfully left atop his recently shed clothing. In blissful slow motion, he returns and settles before the Master.

"I am in love with someone," he says.

The poison. I wanted to talk about the poison.

"I'm so afraid that she'll be hurt. They're holding her with the ones who have AIDS. She loves me too, Bhagwan."

She does! She does!

Gilligan's world, in these moments, is becoming stunningly simple and clear.

"Love is good," says the Master.

The enormous brown eyes roll down slightly to glance at the vials whose plastic-capped ends protrude like cannons from between Gilligan's hands which he has unconsciously folded into a namaste position in front of his heart.

"Poison," says Gilligan. "Salmonella I think. Deela's idea. I'm supposed to sprinkle it on the salad of our enemies. Dillard, that creepy guy with the knife who took sannyas, has got a bunch of paramilitary rednecks together across the river. They've got at least one tank, and who knows what else. They plan to move in tomorrow afternoon. The immigration authorities are coming too, headed by Attorney General Fryberger. They have a warrant to search your house and to arrest you."

The Master does not speak for many moments. He remains still, nodding his head slightly as if processing the information. He makes a gentle gesture for Nivea and Angelica to continue their brushings. Appalled by what they were hearing, they had paused in mid stroke.

The Master stops the nearly imperceptible nodding of his head. Gilligan feels Angelica re-bind his hair. Nothing is said. The Master has closed his eyes and appears to be meditating as Nivea continues combing his beard. Gilligan does not want to be rude. He clears his throat. He clears his throat again, loudly.

"Ahem!"

The master's eyes droop upwards.

"Yes?"

"Well?"

"Well what?"

"What should I do?"

"It is your life. Do what you feel is right. Now I must meditate."

If love were a blast furnace, Gilligan is standing in its open doorway as the Master says this. His heart lights up like a roman candle which sends glittering sprinkles of joy throughout his body. Thoroughly discombobulated by gratitude, he can only namaste and bow his head. The Master again closes his eyes. Gilligan's audience is ended.

Buoyed in spirit by the clustering pulsars of bliss the Master has funneled into his body, Gilligan's thinking mind is on temporary hiatus. Ushered without comment from the pool area by Nivea, he is alone in the Master's house. No security guards, just a spacious, empty central corridor. On the front side is the Master's personal living area. To the rear are work and living spaces which are the domiciles of his support staff. Gilligan follows a thrumming sound into a cheerful studio festooned with the Master's robes, hats, sandals and socks in various stages of readiness. A middle-aged woman, long fingered, with a bulldog-like lower lip, sits behind a sewing machine.

He taps lightly on her open door. "Burning the midnight oil eh?"

The woman looks up and smiles briefly as she continues to work.

"How come there are two of each?" Gilligan asks.

Indeed, hanging beside every one of the Master's beautifully sewn, brocaded, and, in some cases, spangled robes, is its duplicate.

"Oh. Well, at first they are back-ups, just in case. But then these festival robes are given to rich sannyasins who make large donations. I mean *very* large donations. Double the robes means double the money for the commune. See that jar there?"

She jerks her lip in the direction of a very tall and wide mason's jar which appears to have a white horse's tail suspended from the underside of its lid.

"Those are strands of his beard. We collect 'em from his clothes, his brushes, when he gets a trim. You get a full one, in its own crystalline acrylic casing, for any donation to the Foundation of over twenty thousand dollars U.S.."

"Wow. What a gift. You're Shenilla aren't you?"

He is inwardly pleased he managed to remember the name of Lionheart's wife, the Divine Bhagwan's milliner and seamstress. His enlightenment experience on the hill and the encounter with the Master has blasted much of the extraneous crap and chatter out of his head, leaving necessary details more accessible.

"Could you tell Lionheart I need to talk to him. Urgently."

"You're Gilligan, the Swami from Hoodoo Canyon, aren't you? I've heard Alchemendra says you are the man of the moment."

"Well," sighs Gilligan, "shit's happening, that's for sure."

"Moment to moment, beyond time," she closes her eyes as she incants, "you are the first and last man." They are brimful of dreaminess when she opens them.

"I feel like I'm in a fucking movie," Gilligan mutters inwardly.

Shenilla, suddenly bright, normal, and sewing says, "I'll tell him. He's staying here with me tonight. You'll find Kildaraj one door down to your left."

The question is barely beginning to formulate in his mind when it is answered. He knows the good doctor has sleeping quarters in the Master's house and that enlisting his help will be crucial.

The polite knock interrupts Kildaraj's meditation. Gilligan had half expected to find him in bed with two or three beautiful mas. He reflects for a moment, with his newfound clarity, that perhaps he tends to sexualize things too much in his mind, that maybe his adolescence has been ongoing.

The room is modest, with just a bed and a large work desk. One wall is devoted to shelves containing medical files and literature. Kildaraj, seated on a large cushion on the carpeted floor, expresses a little surprise.

"Well, if it isn't Swami Snakebite! What brings you here, sir?"

Gilligan holds the vials of poison in front of him.

"These. Whoa. You look like shit."

It is true. The Doctor's normally serene countenance is drawn-looking, his complexion pallid. Kildaraj motions Gilligan to pull up a floor cushion. Gilligan, preternaturally aware as never before, puts his fingers to his lips before Kildaraj starts talking. He mouths the word 'Deela' and pantomimes the act of eavesdropping. As best they can, they sweep Kildarj's room for bugs. One, of the same species as the device which Lurchamo plucked from his attaché case after he interrupted Gilligan's extremely pleasant encounter with Basmati almost a year earlier, is found under the twisted-off mouthpiece of Kildaraj's phone.

"Wow, just like in the movies," Gilligan says as they, after some minutes of fingers to the lips excitement, watch the device swirl clockwise down Kildaraj's toilet, launched on an acquatic journey to the Pope Paul Sewage Lagoon.

When they are settled on the cushions of the living area, Kildaraj says, "I was closing up shop. Hippocrises is closed except for dire emergencies until after Satsang with DB tomorrow morning. I thought I was alone, doing a final check of the drug stocks in the lock-up, when I felt something prick me in the rear end, like a bee sting. It was only when I began passing out that I realized I'd been stuck by some sort of hypodermic, a tranquilizer, possibly morphine, at a dosage easily large enough to kill me. I came to less than an hour ago and found my way here."

"But why —?" Gilligan's interjection is cut off as Kildarj says "Am I not dead? Because of this." The doctor extends a small leather wallet at arm's length. "See the liquid in behind the plastic? I don't know if the hypo was flung like a dart, or through some sort of blowgun, but I was saved by my wallet.

My skin was barely punctured, but it still caused me to pass out. I'm bloody lucky to be here, old boy, I can tell you that."

Gilligan is speechless. The enormity of it, that someone could be evil enough to try to kill a beautiful being like Dr. Kildarj washes over him in a sickening wave.

"I was just considering what I must do about it," Kildaraj continues. "Call the Peace Force, or the police..."

"Speaking of poison..." Gilligan holds up the vials. He must tell this now. He feels like he is on autopilot, propelled by some greater, invisible force. "There's a situation I need your help with. I'm hoping, since you knew enough to meet him in Hoodoo Canyon you'll know how to contact Alchemendra, and through him, Alvin Dark. It's said that you two are poker buddies."

Kildaraj grins radiantly, despite his wanness. "Yes, we go way back, to before either of us found the Divine Bhagwan. Alchmendra's helping Mr. Dark with corporate morale, and with accessing contacts in the Far East. Last I heard, they visited a Zen master on Mount Baldy and were heading to Las Vegas on their way here."

Phone calls crackle from the doctor's private line as efforts are made to contact Alchemendra and Alvin Dark. Going to the authorities with the attempted murder of Kildaraj is considered and discarded for the moment. He has carefully preserved the hypodermic needle extracted from his wallet, but that is the only evidence. Also, the Peace Force is the local law enforcement body and Deela happens to be their chief. She would be in charge of any investigation and that could only end badly.

"I'm remembering something clearly now," says Gilligan, "something I heard Deela say when I was under that map table at Hemlock Grove and they were all coked up. I think I kind of blocked it out of my mind because I wanted to believe everything here was beautiful. See, she put Angelica with Dillard because she knew he'd fall for her, get dumped, and be super pissed about it. She said she wanted to turn up the heat on the rednecks, provoke the Million Friends of God's Country. Bringing in the street people and threatening to take over the county with their votes was part of it too. When everything was in chaos, she said they'd 'skedaddle' with over a hundred million of the commune's money."

"I believe you're right about that, old boy," says Kildaraj. "I've quietly been conducting an internal investigation on behalf of the Foundation. Huge amounts are unaccounted for. But our first priority is to preserve the Divine Bhagwan's life. I can tell you, as his physician, that his health would not stand up to any time in a jail cell whatsoever. His allergies would run amuck!" Kildaraj raises a finger in with passionate emphasis.

"Dillard may be a nitwit", says Gilligan, "but I think he will kill the Divine Bhagwan if given the chance. He's already tried once and since he got back from prison he looks meaner. Down by the river, the way he held that knife up, it was like he was delivering some kind of curse."

"But if Deela wants the 'rednecks', as you call them, to cause trouble, why would she send you to poison them unless...", Kildaraj rubs his chin thoughtfully for a few moments, "she's sure that you'll be caught! That will provoke them even more!" The Divine Bhagwan's physician rises from his cushion and claps his hands. "She's going to betray you, old boy! Tip them off that you're coming! That's bloody brilliant!"

Kildaraj, due to the lingering effects of the narcotic combined with standing up so quickly, experiences a dizzy spell and quickly sits down again, his face once again pale. Both men close their eyes and move deeply into meditation, an effortless and natural occurrence here in the heart of the Buddhafield. Two doors down and across the hall, the Master is receiving his 'nighty-night' relaxing massage.

Gilligan, in the moment as never before, watches with wonder as his mind patches together his Ranch experiences into a vision of how events could unfold in a way that saves

Seatrice, protects the Divine Bhagwan and prevents Deela from making off with the commune's money. It unfolds before him like a tapestry, scene by scene. He surveys these imaginative enactments of future events as if from a throne, studying them with awestruck rapture, like a medieval architect poring over his plans for a cathedral.

When he opens his eyes and begins to speak, he is dazzled by his own insight and eloquence as he expounds the plan to Kildaraj. He is pleasantly surprised to the verge of being stunned, when the older man, whose color has returned, again rubs his noble doctor's chin and says, with a gleam of admiration in his eye, "You know Swami Snakebite, I think you may well be onto something."

When they are joined by Lionheart, Shenilla and Nivea, the subject of whether or not to approach the Master with the details of Gilligan's plan is broached.

"Not possible," says Nivea. "He will be in silent meditation until the Satsang tomorrow morning. And besides, I believe our young friend here has already told him more than enough."

"As his personal physician," says Kildaraj, "I have a duty to safeguard his health. Why don't we simply take him now? Hustle him down to the Learjet and go? Lionheart, you're our pilot. Let's seize the moment right now. If the Divine Bhagwan doesn't want to cooperate, I shall bloody well drag him along for his own good."

"You bloody well had better not go against his wishes!" Nivea's eyes are flashing and her voice is almost shrill as she leans over and pokes Kildaraj in the chest for emphasis. "I suggested immediate departure to him after our young friend here accosted him in the pool. He won't abandon his people on Master's day. He said he wishes to speak to them at tomorrow morning's Satsang and to do his drive-by. We will not resort to your bullyboy tactics, Kildaraj, howsoever you might enjoy them." Nivea's tone turns teasing, angry and drily contemptuous all at once.

Kildaraj opens his mouth to assay a riposte but thinks the better of it.

Gilligan gleans that these two have a history. Up close these exalted people, who've spent so many years with the Master, are far more human than he'd imagined them to be.

"The Learjet's not ready anyway," says Lionheart. "She needs fueling, a systems check, maintenance tune-up and hypoallergenic detoxification before I'd risk taking the DB up in her. I can have her good to go for tomorrow though. In the meantime I think we can give those invaders more than they can handle." He struts across the room like the gamest of roosters. "We've got plenty of Uzi's and side arms and I've got an idea or two about how we might battle that tank, though we're fresh out of armor piercing munitions. We've got the hills; we've got guerilla warfare. We'll beat them the same way the gooks beat us."

"No one is going to beat anybody, at least until the Master is safe," says Kildaraj. "Our plan depends on Gilligan here somehow convincing Dillard to confront the Master without inflicting violence on the commune. I suggest you concentrate on making sure the Learjet is ready by tomorrow afternoon. We may well have to 'skedaddle' ourselves. Meanwhile we have a great deal of work to do."

"Right," says Gilligan. "Pitter patter. Let's get at her." The others, with the exception of Lionheart, look at him oddly.

"That's construction talk. Pitter patter- never mind."

After a spontaneous group hug, they disperse to their separate tasks. All are deeply aware that none may falter or stumble if Gilligan's plan to save the Master is to succeed.

33. The Fridge of Darkness

It is very early in the morning, well before the dawning of Master's Day and the grand beginning of the Second Annual Universal Celebration. Gilligan tugs open the refrigerator door as gently as possible. The glare that issues from the side by side Amana is as alarming as a Stalag searchlight; the sound of the compressor kicking on might as well be an air-raid siren. He strives to calm himself. Deela's fridge is full of goodies. A large bowl of chocolate icing is prominent on the top shelf.

Didn't Chloe say that her birthday was today? Easy boy, we're here to avoid poisoning people, though it would serve them fucking right.

Gilligan smiles and removes the vials of poison from his pocket. When his work is done, he closes the refrigerator door and tiptoes back to the dislodged photo table and tunnel entrance. Lying prone on Deela's carpet, he takes a sausage-sized tube of Crazy Glue from his pocket. Its procurement involved a late night trip with Lionheart into the massive parking garage built into the hillside behind the Divine Bhagwan's house. This structure, known to only a few, is where the scores of the Master's Rolls Royces and other luxury vehicles are stored and serviced. It is home to, and manned by, none other than the venerable Cheerstha, the man who, with his tow truck, was the first on the scene on the occasion of the Divine Bhagwan's Enlightenment some thirty two years earlier.

The Master's first disciple and lifelong mechanic, whose Airstream trailer home blends seamlessly into the jumble of workbenches, tools and spare parts that is the service area of the garage, is something of a legend because he does not leave the garage, not even for the most auspicious of Satsang or Darshan occasions. Lionheart seems to know everyone and the Master's first disciple is no exception. Cheerstha greeted him warmly and offered them both tea, despite the fact they had clearly awakened him from a deep sleep. They took their tea from a workbench a few yards away from the same pool-bottom blue bulletproof Rolls (said to have been owned by Idi Amin) that had been the Master's Day vehicle one year earlier. Cheerstha had it in readiness for this year's event. While Lionheart and Cheerstha were talking in low voices, Gilligan sauntered over and ran a finger over the area where Dillard's knife had gouged into the base of the driver's side window. It was as smooth and pristine as the skin of a baby.

"Here we go, Swami," said Lionheart, holding up the tube of Crazy Glue. "He had it right here waiting for us."

Their tea finished, Cheerstha ushered them cheerfully from the garage, wishing them the best of luck with their 'adventure'. There was something simian about the way he moved, as if his legs had bowed and his arms were lengthened and strengthened from reaching into and tightening the metal guts of so many engines for so many years. He namasteed to them, bringing fingers permanently darkened by grease to his chin, as they left.

"I will see you tomorrow, then."

"What?" said Lionheart. "We're not coming back."

"No," said Cheerstha. "I am coming out. Akshat (Cheerstha is one of very few who would ever refer to the Master by his given name) wishes me to do something for him. I do not know what, but I can feel it coming."

"Right," said Lionheart, clapping him on the shoulder. "You're turning into a squirrelly bugger in your old age, aren't you? We'll see you when we see you then."

"You'll see me tomorrow," repeated Cheerstha. "Good night."

Gilligan remembers this curious prediction by the old mechanic as he unscrews the top of the Crazy Glue, releasing acetone-tinged fumes. Hanging down through the carpeted trap door of Hemlock Grove's trailer, he can barely reach the concrete circumference of the manhole opening below. He squirts a generous bead all around the ledge onto which will fit the steel City of Portland manhole cover. Working quickly and concisely, he repositions the huge map table into its ringed indentation in the carpet and lowers himself onto the rebar ladder rungs embedded in the manhole's side.

"What the hell," he mutters to himself. "Might as well be thorough." So saying, he applies the Crazy Glue to the wooden perimeter of the trap door as well. He remembers the commercial where one drop of the glue on the top of a helmet supports the entire weight of a guy hanging from the ceiling.

If Deela tries to escape this way she's going to be seriously displeased. His smile of pleasure and satisfaction is truncated as his thoughts turn, as they want to almost every moment, to Seatrice and whether she is safe. *Trust Swami. She's safe for now. I can feel it.*

He pulls the heavy weight of the manhole lid onto the concrete rim, feeling a mild slippage as it squishes onto the bead of glue. *Will it bond instantly? Maybe I should wait a minute or two and then test it? Yeah, wait Gills, then test it. Now I'm calling myself Gills. Something's fishy about that. God I'm funny.*

He knows that within six hours Master's Day morning Satsang will begin. This day, or rather the previous day — Canada Day 1983 — which began with the wrapping up of the Truck Farm job, saw the ranch threatened with invasion, Seatrice abducted before his eyes, and himself involved in tooth and nail battles (all of which he lost) with virtually every one of the ranch's ruling bitches. Not to mention his subsequent 'enlightenment' on the hill behind Macarena and his journey to and acceptance within the very heart of the Buddhafield.

But now the buzz of Enlightenment and the flame of Presence that the Master had kindled in his heart are overwhelmed by an earthen wall of exhaustion. He needs to sleep. But first he must wait a few minutes before testing whether the glue around the manhole cover will truly hold.

The string of lights that illuminate the way back to the airport exit click on as he descends the rebar ladder. He slumps to the floor at the base of the shaft, in a semi-sitting position against its wall, in the same spot where he sleepily refused to recognize the drug-fueled evil in Deela's machinations one year earlier. He sighs and stretches out his legs. He dares not close his eyes for fear sleep will overwhelm him instantly. His gaze, wandering idly, alights on the first of the rebar rungs beside him. Curiously, it is only a few inches above the curved surface of the tunnel floor, and of no possible use as a step. Yet there it is, embedded in the wall of the shaft like the more utilitarian one some twelve inches above. Or is it? There are clean dark rings, spaces around the circumferences of the rebar where it enters the concrete at either end. They look something like pistons going into cylinders. On an impulse, Gilligan grips the rebar and tugs it towards him. One end easily pulls clear of the wall by a good six inches. It is the handle to some kind of mechanism, like the baseball bat was to the secret door behind the waterfall. He cranks it upwards, pulling the free end into a vertical position. There is a click and the wall he leans against nudges outwards into his shoulder blades. It is a hatchway, cleverly fitted into the seams of the concrete. As Gilligan swings it open, a black canvas hockey bag, with the word Bauer stenciled on it in white flops to the floor. Behind this bag, which is approximately the size of a small walrus, three more have been stuffed into the secret closet. Gilligan, now very awake, unzips the one in front of him.

It contains nothing but money, money wrapped into the tight packets that Chloe had learned to create as part of her late father's smuggling business. These are the proceeds from Bhagwan Communes International that she managed to skim, swindle or otherwise appropriate from the commune's devotees. It was amazing how the profits from a few hundred worshippers each paying a hundred dollars a day in cash for the privilege of doing the Master's work from 7 A.M. to 7 P.M. add up. Another satchel contains the fruits of Lucifia's duplicity at Hippocrises— money that she and Tootie had been able to snare when Kildaraj was otherwise engaged. The main haul, another two hockey bags worth, is the product of outright larceny. One night earlier, Chloe, Tootie and Deela robbed the Mahaclaptrap office of Bhagwan Foundation International, the repository for the large note donations and diamond encrusted Rolexes given to the Master over the years. Swami Clint Eastwood, the excitable Polish welder, was reassigned to kitchen duty in Macarena for the Second Annual Universal World Celebration so some of his equipment could be commandeered. Tootie, with some help from Deela and Chloe, toppled a mammoth safe, and, thanks to the skills Chloe had learned helping her father weld in and torch out contraband from his aircraft, a massively valuable haul was extricated from a hole cut in its bottom. Then she discreetly spot-welded the door closed from the inside and they cleverly returned the safe to its original position. Anybody trying to open it would assume the door was jammed or wouldn't unlock. It wouldn't be until well after the July 4 long weekend that anyone from the safe company in Portland could possibly come to take a look. By then Deela's and her conniving coterie expected to be long gone.

Gilligan ponders what to do for a number of minutes. Finally, he drags the bags free of the hatchway and closes the door, guiding the rebar handle back to its original position. He clambers back up the rungs and pushes upwards on the manhole cover, gently at first and ultimately as hard as he can with both hands. It does not budge. With a grunt of satisfaction he heads down and slings the Bauer satchels over his shoulders. He carries them as far as the fork in the tunnel that leads to Shangri Ohlala. There, under the floor of the now quiet open air disco, beneath the motion sensor that he hit his head on a year earlier, he leaves two of them in the middle of the walkway. They will be a marker and a gift for those to follow if his plan unfolds as it should. They other two he takes with him. If the plan falters, these at least will not fall into the wrong hands. He sings softly to himself as, burdened with the two bags, he trudges down the long tunnel to the airport exit.

34. The Master's Voice

Master's Day morning Satsang is the major kick-off event of the Second Annual Universal Celebration. Close to twenty thousand red-clad sannyasins from all over the world, all sniffed and secured, fill the linoleum acreage of Enlightenment Hall to near capacity. This is their chance to sit silently in the presence of the Master, to commune with him on a heart to heart level. It is also their chance, before he arrives, to fill the hall with the excited drone of the latest gossip. News of the impending invasion has somehow percolated through the entire commune. Versions of who and how and when range from a full division of elite U.S. Army paratroops dropping in to declare martial law to a band of renegade sannyasins, lead by Alchemendra, plotting to hijack the Master's vehicle sometime during his ceremonial drive-by. All versions, especially those that verge on being correct are summarily laughed off as just another Ranch rumor, or possibly a 'device' instituted by the Master himself to raise everyone's consciousness.

Some of the more evolved sannyasins prefer the silence of Satsang over the evening Darshan (where the Master typically gives a discourse) because the silent core of the master/disciple connection is more profound when words are not there to get in the way. During Satsang after forty minutes or so of meditation in the Master's presence, soft music is played which gradually grows in tempo and volume until the Master himself is standing and leading the crowd in dancing and celebration.

This Satsang, however, is different. At the end of the meditation, the Divine Bhagwan remains seated—his chair is

a top-of-the-line Lazy Boy, specially upholstered to complement his robe of the day—and gestures for a microphone. To
the astonishment of all, he begins to speak:

"Beloved Sannyasins. It has come to my attention that
this commune may come under attack later in the afternoon.
It is not a joke." Some nervous laughter in the hall immediately silences. "Let us welcome them with flowers, with songs,
with dancing. There will be no shooting by my sannyasins.
No one will even hold a gun. I am tired of seeing the guns.
Nivea." Here the Master gestures towards Nivea, who is
standing on the platform that accesses the 'mopsters' clothesline. She in turn waves to a vehicle that is idling on the Van
Gogh Bridge some two hundred yards away. It is a black Lincoln Continental convertible from 1961, said to be a replica
and former backup to the one JFK rode to his death on that
fateful day in Dallas. The top is down. As it approaches Gilligan sees that the driver is none other than the venerable
Cheerstha. He has, at the behest of his Master, emerged from
his garage at last. The Lincoln cruises to the Northeast corner
of Enlightenment Hall, beside the clothesline platform that
Nivea stands on. Cheerstha drives onto the linoleum, parking
the Lincoln beside the low stage where the music group band
awaits its cue. "I have asked Cheerstha—he is my oldest sannyasin—to help with getting rid of the guns. Is Deela here?"

This question causes laughter to roll through the auditorium in a wave that gains and sustains a substantial volume
for many seconds. For Deela is very much there, standing
guard at the edge of his podium as she always does, wearing
her mirrored Highway Patrol sunglass with her customized
Uzi and silver bullets slung around her waist. As the laughter
goes on and on the Master remains sweetly and serenely
deadpan. As the brown sheen of her skin flushes to close
proximity to the crimson of her clothing, it is impossible to tell
whether or not he is joking. Finally she steps directly in front
of him and raises her arm like a schoolgirl, provoking a fresh
onslaught of hilarity.

"Ah, here you are," says the Divine Bhagwan. "Deela, please see to this. Every gun and every bullet is to be placed into Cheerstha's car. When the invaders come, we will welcome them with flowers, with meditation, with singing and dancing. If they come for me, then I will give myself to them. My life is fulfilled. If it is to end in a crucifixion, then that is good too. I ask the reporters, the television people who are here, to pay attention. Let the world see that we are not a violent people. It is America who chooses to violate us. Let the world see that we celebrate everything, even the destruction of this commune. Even the destruction of me."

There is a profound silence in the hall as the Master ends this speech. Deela stands quaking before him for many moments, then brings her hands together in a Namaste. She turns and faces the red-clad multitudes that carpet the linoleum acreage of Enlightenment Hall to its outermost fringes. To Gilligan, who arrived tardily and is seated hundreds of feet away, she appears to have lost her aura of power and in this instant is nothing more than a chastened little girl. But the instant passes, as all instants do, and a great cheer arises from the throng as her fingers drop to her gun belt and unclasp it. She is willing to sacrifice to get what she wants and she understands that the Master's initiative may well play directly into her hands. She raises the gun belt high over her head and manages to make something of a triumphal procession out of marching across the front of the hall. There is another cheer as she drops her most precious possession into the back seat of Cheerstha's convertible. She motions for the guards that ring the perimeter of the hall to do the same. They comply, as will all sannyasin guards, samurai and Peace Force officers throughout the Ranch. All are eager to fulfill the Master's wishes and to be part of what feels like the unfolding of a pivotal moment in history. That their actions may lead to the Master's death is unthinkable.

"Good Deela." There is a chuckle in the Master's voice as he says this. "Once all the guns are collected, Cheerstha will feed them to a dragon I have heard of called the Rock Crusher. We are a peaceful commune; I have been teaching inner peace, I have *been* inner peace for more than thirty years. Nothing is more important than showing an insane world what this means. I thank all of you, my sannyasins, for helping me to do this today. Now, let us celebrate."

So saying, the Master puts aside his microphone and gestures for the musicians to play, and for his people to begin dancing. After some brief, consternated chatter, led by the gentle gyrations of the Divine Bhagwan, the crowd gets to its feet and begins to dance. Once begun, they let themselves be lifted higher and higher by their Master's exhortations and the bliss generated by his presence, until the final ecstatic Yahoo! when he disappears behind the podium's wall.

35. Commander Dillard

After the Satsang, using the authority given him by Deela, Gilligan acquires Narzesh's old crew vehicle, the brown Ford Ranger which he and Morris used on their now legendary cruise. He crosses Toasto's fully re-built bridge and heads for the pier that fronts the now former shoe factory. The day is warm, but wet, an aberration for July in the high desert. Drizzle falls off and on. A low cloud ceiling shrouds the surrounding hilltops in mist. On his drive from Enlightenment Hall Gilligan passes through more than one stretch of dense fog amongst the hills. But the sketchy roadways of the Truck Farm and the one leading to the pier, baked firm by the summer sun, are still perfectly navigable. He cuts his engine and watches the activity across the river for a few minutes.

The Sherman tank still rests on the barge, its thirty tons of weight almost submerging the pontoons of the simple craft. A row of empty Northwest Passage beer bottles sit on the flat top of the tank's turret. Evidently the invasion preparations by the Million Friends of God's Country militia have involved imbibing a good deal of liquid courage. A few military type jeeps are parked near the Persephone complex. One, ominously, has what looks like a tripod-mounted machine gun in the back. It is now late morning, with the promised invasion just over two hours away. Yet the overall scene at the pier on the opposite shore and the complex beyond is one of a moist lassitude which mirrors the weather conditions perfectly. No men swarm over the cast steel hull of the tank nor tighten the bolts of the sprockets which drive its massive treads. No soldiers are in sight anywhere. Just the beer bottles, the jeeps, and half a dozen pick-up trucks clustered in the parking lot of the complex indicate that anything is happening at all.

"Well, pitter patter." Gilligan mutters to himself. He jumps from the pick-up and pulls the truce flag that he, whilst driving through the fog near his old tent habitat at Fareezuryingyang, realized would be necessary. Finding a white flag in a commune where all the denizens wear shades of red might be a problem, but Yingyang's bath and shower trailer provided everything needed. The unscrewed handle from a damp-mop made a fine pole. He then cut, using a Stanley knife from the truck's toolbox, a flag's length of white fabric from the trailer's eco- and hygiene friendly endless-towel dispenser. He stands at the end of the pier and waves his makeshift creation back and forth in a way he hopes says *don't shoot me, I just want to talk.* Soon he is noticed. A rowboat is dispatched from the further shore. The rower, a bearded, stringy fellow wearing camouflage pants and vest, has a beer perched on the bench between his legs.

"Well?" he says, swinging the boat around so he is facing Gilligan.

Gilligan shrugs and tosses the flag in the direction of his truck. "Take me to your leader," he says, putting his hands in the air.

"You looked pretty lonely over there waving that white flag. You people surrendering?"

The questioner is Dillard. He is wearing a celery colored Persephone track suit that has been deliberately smudged with dirt and oil to provide makeshift camouflage. His hair, longer, greasier and snakier than ever, is combed straight back over the thinning area at the crown. He looks up from a blueprint-sized duplicate of the aerial photograph of the Ranch which is embedded in Deela's coffee table. It is spread on a crude plywood table. Each corner is held down by an empty beer bottle. Less empty versions are within the fists of most of the militia men, many of whom are loudly gathered around a card game in the rearmost portion of the barn which is serving as invasion headquarters.

"Well, yeah," answers Gilligan. "I guess we are surrendering. All our guns have been destroyed and the Master has offered to meet with you after his drive-by. He's willing to put his life in your hands."

"Your guns have been destroyed! Are you people nuts? You don't destroy guns! Boys, this pinko says their guns have all been destroyed!"

The noise in the barn suddenly hushes as the import of Dillard's announcement sinks in. Jarvis, the fellow who rowed Gilligan across the river, approaches the table. He wears a new Seattle Mariners baseball cap. His prominent Adam's apple shoots up and down his throat like a county fair's bell-ringer as he speaks.

"God help us, you people are surely depraved. What did you do? Burn them? Some of them may still be all right if you only burned them."

"We fed them through the rock crusher. Trust me, they're toast."

A collective empathetic groan emanates from the militiamen. Most of them have owned firearms since their preteen years, pieces given to them by their fathers. Weapons passed down and lovingly cared for through generations. The thought of those steely straight, superbly machined barrels being mutilated is abhorrent to them.

"How are you people going to defend yourselves?" shouts Jarvis. "You know we're going in there in less than an hour!"

"We're not," says Gilligan. "We're going to welcome you with open arms."

"That's the most disgusting thing I've ever heard," spits Jarvis. "Don't you people got no self respect?"

"The point is," interjects Dillard, "that we are going to have a free hand over there. We can liberate any American hostages and me and my friend here can send the devil back to hell!" Dillard unsheathes the knife from his leg and stabs it for emphasis into the map of the Ranch. Two of the beer bottles topple, roll, then clink into each other while bookending the knife which rises like a dark tower over downtown Bhagwanville. "And where and when does the devil plan on putting his life in my hands?"

"At his house, after his drive-by. Near his front door, opposite the big waterfall fountain that you can see from Enlightenment Hall. I wouldn't do anything then if I were you. There'll be loads of media there."

"National media?"

"Oh yeah. Rumor has it that *Sixty Minutes* arrived this morning. They're doing a follow up piece on us."

"'Thou shalt have no other gods before me'. That's the first commandment, pinko, and I have been called upon to enforce it. I shall do so and I shall be famous for it, way more famous than my daddy ever was!"

"You don't need to invade the Ranch," says Gilligan. "Attorney General Fryberger is coming to arrest the Divine Bhagwan after drive-by this very afternoon. He'll be put in jail. You'll get what you want."

"Hell," says Dillard. "I don't want him arrested. I want him dead! See, my Daddy's book says winners finish what they start, and that's exactly what I intend to do." There is laughter from some of the men within earshot. "Besides," he continues, "I'm not so sure Mr. Fryberger is going to make it. See, he was fixin' to come here first and tell us all to be good, law abidin' citizens while he and his deputies went and did their jobs. But, you know it's a long ways from Salem most, of it on a long and winding back roads. Person could get a flat tire or two or three or four on the way. And if they did— Jarvis, where's the nearest tire repair place? About twenty miles from here?"

"That'd be my place," answers Jarvis with a smirk. "Cept its closed cause I'm here!"

More laughter.

"Listen, Dillard," says Gilligan. "I know for a fact the Divine Bhagwan is ready to surrender to you. Don't harm his people and he'll accept whatever comes."

"You mean what's comin' to him!"

"Whatever. Just give him some dignity. Let him finish his drive-by all the way to his house. He needs to see his people one last time."

Dillard looks at Gilligan for a few moments. He rubs his jaw.

"How about that bitch, Deela? Is she going to surrender to me too?" Here Dillard un-sticks the knife from the table and brandishes it under Gilligan's nose. "Because if I get a hold of her I'm gonna stick this up her ass and give it a good twist. You ever had something stuck up your ass, pinko?"

Gilligan considers sharing his grim experience with Lucifia, but prudently decides to change the subject.

"I know your daddy, Dillard. I talked to him for a long time up in his office. He really cares about you, but he doesn't know how to handle you."

Dillard lets the knife point drop and regards Gilligan with bug-eyed astonishment. He turns his face upwards and lets out a primal scream which echoes amongst the rafters of the barn. "Aharrrg! Get this guy out of here! Throw him in the river and let him swim back, if he can! Come on boys. It's time to get this show on the road!"

"Commander." A boy of about sixteen, the younger brother of one of the militiamen strides into the barn. "We've just received a communication from the other side. She said she was an American patriot and she wanted you to know that this Gilligan guy had been sent over here to poison us."

There is a collective outburst of anger at this revelation. The burly twosome who are leading Gilligan from the barn slam him up against the doorjamb. One of them wears a Rambo style headband and undershirt.

"It was the bitches!" shouts Gilligan. "They wanted me to but I'm working against them. I brought no poison. Ask Jarvis!"

Jarvis removes his Mariners cap and runs his fingers through his hair.

"I searched him before he got in the rowboat," he says finally. "He was clean."

Gilligan glares at the boy. "The person who called? Did she have an accent?"

"Yeah, she sounded funny. English, maybe."

"Chloe. They set me up."

Dillard thrusts his knife point into the soft tissue under Gilligan's chin. He turns it like a corkscrew, drawing blood.

"On second thought," he says, "we'll just keep you handy. If you've been lying about the guns, or any of my men so much as coughs or has a tummy ache…" He jabs and twists a little deeper. "I think you get my point. Tie him up boys, and gag him. He's had his say."

Dillard returns to the plywood table. "Sampson, I believe its time to take your detail to the ford. The crossing point is here." He indicates on the map a point some five miles up the river. "Once you cross, you can pick up this road here and liberate these buildings on your way into town."

Gilligan, who is being bound to a nearby post, peers at the map. Dillard is indicating Hippocrises, Mydad and Sariputput. Precariously close to where Kildaraj confirmed Seatrice is being held.

"Once you hit this road, send about six guys to secure the entrance to the airport, which is up over here."

"OK, OK, Dillard. I know the mission. You don't have to go over it a hundred times!"

"What is it?"

"What's what?"

"The mission."

"The mission is," intones Sampson, who is a large, square-headed fellow with a deep voice, "is to liberate any brainwashed Americans. Don't fire unless fired upon. Blow up any buildings that look like they contain weapons... like all of them." Jarvis smirks as, amidst more laughter, he and a group of over a dozen men hop into two jeeps and a formidable looking armored vehicle. They roar off on the road that leads up river.

"As for you—" Dillard turns and faces Gilligan, who is having a Persephone logoed sock stuffed into his mouth, "you'll be riding with us."

36. The Invasion of the Ranch

Dillard's expeditionary force gains the further shore on Persephone's shoe factory land. First off the barge is the Sherman tank. An M4A1, with a sleek cast steel hull and a muzzled 76 mm cannon, it was rescued from the scrap heap of the Korean War by Jarvis's father and kept in a Quonset building behind their service station where it was, over a period of years, restored to working order. With a crew of five (only two of whom know what they are doing) and a complement of twelve armor-piercing shells, twelve explosive shells and twenty-four bottles of Northwest Passage beer, it is a formidable fighting machine. Following after the tank, in stages, are two military style jeeps and four pickup trucks. The men, aside from the tripod machine gun on one of the jeeps, are armed with a combination of hunting rifles, shotguns, and at least two handguns each. Their staging area is on the far side of Toasto's bridge.

The first site to be liberated is the vegetable washing area. Its worshippers have returned from lunch and from greeting the Divine Bhagwan as he heads out on drive-by. The tank, vehicles, and armed men milling about by the barge can be easily seen, so the sannyasins are prepared, as per the Master's instructions, to welcome the invaders who eventually cross the bridge in a column, led by Dillard, carrying a bullhorn in the lead jeep. A very fine rain falls, and lowering clouds continue to oppress the hilltops.

"We do not intend to harm anyone," Dillard announces over the bullhorn.

The invasion force, despite the tank, looks more ragtag than fearsome. But the men in the jeeps and pickups are fingering their rifles nervously, while keeping them pointed at the sky. Gilligan, his hands tied in front of him with the strongest Persephone shoelaces, is in the seat behind Dillard. The dozen or so Truck Farm worshippers form a group facing the invaders and begin singing variations on the 'Hallelujah' chorus from music group. Some carry balsa wood baskets of vegetables to offer to the invaders.

Narzesh, wearing a simple red T-shirt in lieu of his Peace Force uniform, is at the front of the group. He briefly catches Gilligan's eye and registers some concern over his bound and gagged condition. The sannyasins move forward as a group. One very pretty ma begins putting flowers into the soldiers' gun barrels.

"We offer asylum to any Americans brainwashed by this cult," announces Dillard.

The piercing blast from the bullhorn causes the pretty ma to jerk back a proffered daisy. Her eyes widen as they alight on Gilligan. Narzesh approaches the jeep with a basket of pickles.

"What kind of asylum?" The question is shouted by an older gentleman. He wears red coveralls, but no mala. His cheekbones are dense with ingrained dirt. He was among the first bus load of street people brought in the previous night.

"We offer you food and drink and safe passage back to civilization," broadcasts Dillard.

"You got any Jack Daniels?" shouts the man.

This dispels some tension as both sides chuckle. The ma with the flowers is now on the running board of one of the pickups, her elbows on the window ledge, talking to the young farmer driving it.

"You boys want some vegetables?" says Narzesh. "We've got plenty.

You can let our man go now. This is going to be all over the news. Sixty Minutes is on its way."

Dillard's hand moves past the automatic pistol at his hip and fingers the butt of the big knife strapped to his leg.

Gilligan thrusts his bound hands closer. *Cut me free, asshole, or they'll nail you for kidnapping.* His mental exhortation has no effect as a new threat, an approaching helicopter, appears on the horizon.

"Sweet Jesus, here they come." Dillard, deep in the snake pit of his brain, has apparently been expecting treachery. He draws his pistol from its holster. He points at Gilligan's face.

"You people come closer!" he shouts at the sannyasins. "They won't try anything if we are all in a group. Fire if fired upon, men!"

Back-dropped by the hilltop mists, the bright red dragonfly of the Ranch's helicopter heads directly for them. Some of the militia men train their rifles on it. The sannyasins obediently crowd around Dillard's jeep. A final, on-life-support 'Hallelujah' has its plug pulled and dies on someone's lips.

"Jarvis!" Dillard screams. "Where's that surface to air missile?"

"Sampson's got it!" Jarvis' head and elongated neck emerging from the deck hatch of the tank resemble a jack-in-the-box.

"Damn! Well maybe when they see I'm ready to blow your head off they won't try anything." Dillard waves the gun in Gilligan's direction while keeping his eyes on the approaching aircraft. For Gilligan, there is no fear, just a preternatural alertness. He feels like he is performing in some hyper-real movie. He need only be ready for his cue.

The helicopter swoops in on a non-threatening elliptical path. The side door is open. Framed within it is the beautiful Angelica, wearing much the same sexy mini T and shorts outfit as when Gilligan first saw her in Hemlock Grove. She is embracing a large mesh laundry bag bulging with something pink. She upturns the bag and begins pouring the contents on the gathering below.

"You!" mutters Dillard, dropping the pistol to his side. "You!"

"Here it comes! Take cover!" screams Jarvis, bringing a machine gun to bear on the helicopter. Some of the sannyasins are waving their hands crosswise over their heads in welcome. With the suddenness of a striking rattlesnake, Dillard's pistol arm whips skyward and he fires twice. Jarvis doesn't even release the safety catch of the machine gun. He sees that what is emerging from Angelica's overturned bag is a stream of bright pink rose petals. They cascade above invaders and sannyasins alike, fluttering briefly only to quickly plummet as they are burdened with droplets of misty rain.

It is Dillard's first bullet that kills Angelica. It hits her between the eyes, in the *Ajna* chakra, the mystic portal for insight, then tumbles through her brain, lodging itself in the bony wall at the back of her skull. Her spirit, which for the most part dwelt and frolicked in the fountains of the *Anahata*, or heart chakra, is released. Her body, formerly so beautiful and perfect in Gilligan's eyes, folds inwards on itself and tumbles from the swerving helicopter. It swerves because Dillard's second bullet shatters the window to the right of the pilot, who is, of course, Lionheart. He instinctively jerks the joystick to pull the aircraft away from the line of fire. Angelica's body, freefalling through a curving contrail of rose petals, does a slow somersault and lands flat on its back on the rain slicked roof of the vegetable washing facility. It slides head first down the incline at a funereal pace.

"Shit!" Lionheart, swinging the copter around and looking down through his shattered cockpit window, sees there's nothing that can be done for Angelica. He knows that an hour earlier the Ranch's phone lines were cut, doubtless as a prequel to the invasion. He, and the people who are waiting for him off the Ranch, may be the only hope for a situation that is obviously spinning out of control. Welcoming the invaders with the rose petals from Master's Day drive-by had been Deela's idea. He'd agreed readily because it made absconding with the copter so much easier. But he'd been a fool to go in so low. And now Angelica, whose connection to Dillard Lionheart was only vaguely aware of, is dead. He pulls the machine high out of firing range, guns the engine and turns across the Big Snake River, towards the south. He has very little time.

Rose petals flutter down. Some stick on the wet black bough of the Sherman tank's cannon. Others cling to the wet black snakes of Dillard's hair. Gilligan's attention, along with that of everyone else, has been riveted by the spectacle of Angelica's fall from the helicopter. The invaders and sannyasins grouped around Dillard's jeep cannot see her form sliding down the sheet metal incline until her head, preceded by bloody droplets, appears dangling over the eave.

"There she is!" shouts Dillard. "Don't let her fall!"

He, Narzesh, and the street person with the sooty cheeks gather in the fall zone as slowly, slowly gravity claims the remains of the beautiful young woman. It is at the moment the weight of her head causes the rest of her body to follow and fall that Gilligan, his hands still bound, leaps over the back of Dillard's jeep and runs. No one seems to notice nor care. Narzesh, tall and long-armed is able to reach up and capture Angelica's head and shoulders and ease her descent. They lay her on the grate above one of the huge fiberglass vegetable washing tubs. Dillard, stone faced, is heard to mutter, "Well that's it then. There's no going back now."

When he returns to the jeep, he is shaking. His face is pale. The black of his beard stubble is stark against it. He picks up the bullhorn and proclaims. "Behold the fate of the sinner! One who was turned to sin by the Devil's hand! We remain steadfast in our mission. Those who wish to be liberated remain here. We shall return!" With that, Dillards expeditionary force regroups and heads through the misty rain and fog towards the next site to be liberated: Macarena cafeteria.

Gilligan, meanwhile, taking full strides that haven't let up, is clomping across Toasto's bridge. He knows Angelica is dead; he saw the cherry colored pit appear between her eyes like a ghoulish caste mark. The cinematic detachment he felt earlier in Dillard's jeep is gone, replaced by a gagging dread. His suburban sensibilities are not wired to process horror. The beautiful Angelica, who surely never hurt anyone, is gone. His beautiful Seatrice could well be next. He races to his pickup parked near the pier. The Stanley knife is still on the front seat. Clenching it between his knees, he is quickly able to sever the shoelaces which bind his wrists. In the distance, on the road above the vegetable washing area, Dillard's convoy is disappearing into the mists which continue to crowd the hills.

When he wheels past the vegetable washing facility, Narzesh is in the middle of the road, waving his arms widely. Angelica's body, laid in state on the tub, is shrouded by a crimson rain poncho, over which the remaining flowers and heaps of rose petals have been placed. The Motorola on the seat beside Gilligan crackles to life. Narzesh jumps in beside it.

Attention all crew leaders. Attention all sannyasins. This is Deela speaking. Our ranch is being invaded. All sannyasins are to come to Enlightenment Hall. Those with clearance must come to the Divine Bhagwan's house. We want everyone to be there to support our Master when we return from drive-by. Come now. Attention all crew leaders. Attention all sannyasins. This is Deela speaking. Our ranch is being invaded...

As the message repeats itself, Gilligan turns the volume to a low murmur.

"Damn!" He smacks the unyielding rim of the steering wheel. "She's trying to provoke something. Make a scene so they can get away."

"She can't resist being at the center of things, man. That's what's happening," says Narzesh. "We've got to get up there. Warn everyone to clear out. If all those guys start shooting it's going to be a bloodbath."

Gilligan steers the pickup up the road at a moderate pace. He does not want to overtake Dillard's convoy.

"Dillard's lost his mind," he says. "Those other guys didn't look too keen on shooting anyone though. I think they are more interested in getting drunk and playing the Great American Liberators."

"You may be right," says Narzesh. "A couple of them looked shook up over what happened to Angelica. And when they left one of them said they were going to 'liberate' the beer supply at Macarena."

"That's perfect," says Gilligan. "We can slip by them while they're at it. Believe it or not, there is a plan in place that just might save the situation. We've got to get Dillard face to face with the Divine Bhagwan without anyone else being killed."

Gilligan turns left at Koubiya, the ranch's dairy barn.

"Hey!" yells Narzesh. "Where the fuck are you going? The enemy is that way!"

"Part of the plan," says Gilligan. "Someone I've got to talk to. If you don't like it, you can get the fuck out!" He skids the pickup to a halt.

"Jesus Christ," says Narzesh. His hand is on the door handle. "You used to be so meek and mild. What the fuck happened?"

"Meditation happened. Love happened. I'll only be a minute. If you want to stand there getting wet till I come back it's up to you."

Narzesh runs his fingers over his moustache and goatee. He sees a sincerity, a new depth of self-assuredness in Gilligan's eyes. He grins.

"Fuck you," he says, resigned.

"No, fuck you." Gilligan pops the clutch and speeds up the Koubiya spur road as fast as he dares. It is less than a kilometer to the horse barn which he knows Swami Morris is tending it for the festival. Gilligan finds the big New Zealander filling water buckets in the stalls. The smell of horse hangs thick in the damp air. Through the wide rear door of the stable Gilligan sees Bear contentedly plucking at some moist grass tops.

"Hey Kiwi! What are you doing here? I thought you were a sheep guy."

"Sheep. Cows. Horses. I fuck 'em all, mate. They don't complain. Know what I mean? Nudgenudge. Winkwink."

"I need your help, buddy. Something of huge importance."

"Anything for you mate, you know that." Pause. "What's in it for me?"

"Dinner on me at Zorro the Meditator."

"Go on," says Morris. "I'm listening."

Gilligan takes a deep breath and begins to speak. He keeps the news of what happened to Angelica to himself.

Meanwhile, in the pickup, Narzesh is tuning the Motorola to the Bang Pas Zoo frequency.

"Lionheart come in. Lionheart, are you out there? Over."

"Slowma here. Lionheart has disappeared with the helicopter. No one seems to know where. Is that you Narzesh? What's happening at the truck farm?"

"Nothing good. We've had a casualty. Repeat. We've had a casualty. Slowma, we've got to keep our people away from the Hall and Shangri Ohlala."

"Not possible Narzesh. Everyone is here. I'm here. Deela has left the drive-by and is coming to talk to us. There's also a report that some other invaders are trying to ford the river up in the Hippocrises area. No word of any violence. The Divine Bhagwan will be here in less than half an hour. I don't know what we were thinking, letting him go on drive-by at a time like this. Over."

"Fuck," mutters Narzesh to himself. He hits a couple of sharp blasts on the truck's horn, urging Gilligan to come out of the horse barn. "Well, he is the Master," says Narzesh into the Motorola. "Listen, Slowma, we've got to at least stop their tank. If it gets anywhere near all our people…"

"Roger that." Narzesh, behind Slowma's voice, hears the crowd beginning to sing Bhagwan songs. "Lionheart and Swami Ted are working on something for that. I know because I had to authorize…"

At this point Slowma's voice is drowned out by a mixture of static and singsong as Gilligan jumps back into the driver's seat and slams his door shut. "OK buddy," he says. "Let's roll." They race down the spur road, turn left on the Pathless Path highway, and head for the heart of the Ranch.

When they emerge from the hills onto the small plain dominated by Enlightenment Hall, it is clear that Deela's call for a conflux of sannyasins has been stunningly effective. The building is more than half full of swarming, chattering, red clad figures, a churning sea of seekers uncertain about which way to turn. Hundreds more line the nearer bank of the creek, where they can best view the ceremonial Yahoo! Waterfall and pond. A significant trickle has suffused the bridge, evidently seeking to negotiate access to the Master's house through the Gated Gates.

Aside from the front entrance, little of the house, set back amongst the redwoods between the rounded hills that shelter it, can be seen. It is the waterfall, some twelve feet high, pouring into the stone-rimmed pond on the front lawn that is the focal point for those who would know where the Master resides. A steady drizzle is falling now and the tips of the redwoods kiss the undersides of the lowering clouds. Parked on the stone-faced slope of the waterfall bridge, is Deela's white Bronco. Perched at its apex is Deela herself. She is talking through a powerful bullhorn, exhorting the sannyasins to get as close to the house as possible.

Gilligan sees that it would take many minutes to wheedle their vehicle through the throngs clogging access to the bridge. He skids to a halt at the creek bank's edge.

"Want your truck back?" he says to Narzesh.

"Yeah, man. I'm going to work on stopping that tank. Good luck." With a quick, mutual nod of manly appreciation,

Gilligan slams the door as Narzesh picks up the Motorola and slides into the driver's seat. Gilligan runs along the base of the creek bank towards the bridge, splashing through the shallow waters where necessary. He must be at the house when the Master arrives from drive-by.

"Hey swami, it's wet enough!"

Sannyasins crowding the bank protest as he splashes them. He runs past a van painted with the CBS eye and *Sixty Minutes* logo. At least some of the world's media is here to document whatever history will be made. He ducks under the bridge and clambers onto its superstructure on the Enlightenment Hall side. The pressure-treated beams, plated and bolted together to make a graceful sidewall are easy to climb, and he is soon well above the heads of the crowd on the bridge's deck. Testing a theory his overactive mind had mulled during his time working on the Master's roof, he leaps into space and grabs the lowest sling of the clothesline hung across the creek for the Enlightenment Hall mops. There are none dangling now, due to the wet weather. The taut line, made of top grade stainless steel twined within space age nylon, is easily strong enough to support his weight. Thanks to Enlightenment Hall being situated on an elevated portion of the plain, gravity causes him to spool effortlessly downwards towards the Master's side of the creek. The tubular steel wheel sings like a chorus of owls or a windswept grove of bamboo flutes. It flings water beads from its rim like starry spokes from a galaxy's core. Gilligan's butt barely misses the top of the deer fence as he is forced to let go and tumbles into an inglorious heap near the far end of the bridge. He is quickly surrounded by samurais.

"Let him come up," commands an amplified voice. "Send him directly to me." Deela, somewhat surprised to see him, wants a report on his mission. She is waving her bullhorn-free arm in an unmistakable expression of impatience.

"Well?" says Deela, as Gilligan, huffing and puffing from the climb, approaches her perch above the pond. The bridge's stone facing is topped by a low wrought-iron railing cleverly shaped to repeat the OM symbol. Below it the water-fall, some ten feet wide and twelve feet high, plunges to the pond's surface in a broad semi-translucent sheet. Out of breath, knees wobbly, Gilligan has a moment of uncertainty. Lying seems like an excellent option.

"Mission accomplished," he gasps. "I just came from the Truck Farm. They managed to cross the river but haven't shown any signs of getting sick."

"You don't say. There's a rumor there's been violence. Someone killed?" Deela has difficulty keeping a hopeful note out of her voice.

"It's true. Angelica. Dillard shot her out of the helicop-ter."

"Oh dear. Such a lovely girl." Deela's tone is wistful. She actually cares about Angelica in a way that borders on be-ing non-Machiavellian. A big part of her though is secretly pumping a fist in triumph. *The steroids must be working.*

Gilligan indicates the Motorola on her hip. "I've done what you asked. Now tell them to let Seatrice go."

"Not quite yet, pretty-boy," sneers Deela. She lifts the bullhorn to her lips. "Fellow sannyasins, the invaders are kill-ing our people. They are going to kill our Master unless you are prepared to make the ultimate sacrifice. Lay down your bodies in front of their tanks! Anyone giving their life for the Master will surely die enlightened!"

"You lead the way Deela. We'll be right behind you!" The voice belongs to Toasto. The brawny American has climbed to the upper beams of the Van Gogh Bridge's super-structure. He takes a wide stance at the apex of the rain-slicked beams. With his hands cupped to his mouth, he is easily heard by those on both sides of Little Snake Creek.

Shaggyvan, who is also climbing within the truss of the bridge shouts, "A case of champagne to the first one that joins her lying down in front to the tanks! Deela! Deela! Deela!" He begins a chant which Toasto is quick to join in on. It was often

heard back in her good old days when the Master was in silence and her words were his. The chant, begun as a mockery,
spreads to the sannyasins on the bridge and then out to the
earnest masses sheltered in Enlightenment Hall.

"Here they come!" This shout from Toasto easily su-
persedes the chanting, which quickly dies out.

Emerging from the hills and fanning out in a ragged
line across the plain is Dillard's invasion force. The 'liberation'
of Macarena cafeteria has gone smoothly. The sannyasins
worshipping there had already left, summoned to Enlightenment Hall by Deela's all points appeal. So the members of the
Million Friends of God's Country Militia have liberated all of
yesterday's left over Hemlock Grove chocolate cake and a
goodly portion of the beer on tap. Their ravages were witnessed by only one person, a rotund swami named Morris
who, accompanied by two horses, arrived there on business of
his own just as the invaders were leaving.

Within the Sherman tank, Jarvis, his thoroughly lubri-
cated Adam's apple bobbing like a turbo-charged piston, is
about to realize a lifelong dream.

"Men, let's fire that cannon. Seventy-six millimeters of
sound and fury. Let 'em know we're here!"

"Here he comes!" A second mighty shout comes from
Toasto, whose right arm and forefinger are extended like a
sailor's from the crow's nest of an old whaler. To the south of
them, on the furthest edge of the plain, is the speeding form of
an aquamarine Rolls Royce. It is trailed by a Peace Force Jimmy. The Master is returning.

"Fire!" shouts Jarvis.

The mighty cannon of the tank belches smoke and
flame. A shell screams through the damp air. There is an explosion at the furthest edge of Enlightenment Hall where fortunately no sannyasins are clustered. It is at this point that
many of the ten thousand or so gathered there abandon Enlightenment Hall (and the chance to greet the Master) and lit-

erally run screaming for the hills. The remainder crowd into the area of the hall furthest from the explosion.

Gilligan, from his vantage point on the bridge above the waterfall, has as fine a view of the battlefield as any general could hope for. But his attention is claimed by Deela who suddenly shoves the bullhorn into his belly.

"Take this," she says. "I've got places to go right now. Keep telling everyone to get in their way, slow them down any way they can."

Gilligan squares up to her and stares her down. "No fucking way. That's not the plan."

"Do it swami!" Deela whips the Motorola from its holster.

"Or I tell Lucifia to put your precious little blondie to sleep right now."

"NOOOOO!" Gilligan blasts the bullhorn directly into Deela's left ear. She drops the Motorola and clasps her hands to the sides of her head. He pounces on the device and quickly lobs it over the railing into the pond. Deela staggers to the Bronco, drags and pummels the massive figure of Swami Lamborghini out of the driver's seat where he has been waiting with his usual patience. The huge, gentle swami, though curious about the explosions, is also frightened by them and reluctant to leave what he imagines to be the security of the white Bronco. But Deela's will prevails and he is left standing on the driveway as she jumps aboard and, leaning on the horn, follows the circular drive past the entrance to the house and back down the hillside to the Van Gogh Bridge. The explosions have cleared the way almost completely. Even Toasto and Shaggyvan have deserted their perches high on the trestle. The Bronco speeds past the hall and fishtails around the corner to the right, heading for Hemlock Grove.

"Hey, Lamborghini! What's with the sword?" Strapped to the big Italian's back, its handle behind his cranium, is his sheathed samurai sword.

"She make-a me wear it Little Buddy," he says to Gilligan. "Hurts-a my back when I drive."

Smoke and flame thunder from the tank's muzzle again. The shell explodes well behind Deela's retreating vehicle.

"It won't be much good against that," says Gilligan, indicating the tank.

"You'd-a be surprised, Little Buddy. This is-a Japanese steel. Cuts-a through everything like-a butter."

"Holy shit. Would you look at that?"

From behind the far end of Enlightenment Hall, one by one, a phalanx of bright orange bulldozers and front end loaders appears. Marshaled the night before, they are part of Lionheart's contingency plan. They come in a line across the plain, blades and buckets raised high as shields against the firepower of the tank. At their center, flanked by D5's which look like dinky toys in comparison, is the Ranch's massive Caterpillar D10. At 87 tons it is almost three times the weight and boasts close to twice the horsepower of the Sherman tank.

Jarvis and his comrades in the tank, drunk and thrilling to the prospect of combat, are more than willing to take on the mechanized might of the commune.

"Let's take out the big one, boys!" shouts Jarvis. "Then we can mop up the pipsqueaks! Fire!"

The tank's cannon roars and scores a direct hit on the D10's upraised blade. The massive bulldozer's operator is Swami Ted, the Vietnam veteran dying of lung cancer. The shell pierces the blade, leaves a charred hole the size of a melon, and then whistles harmlessly past Ted's booth without touching the rest of the dozer.

"Bad choice, buddy," mutters Ted. He jams the throttle to the floor. Jarvis fired an armor piercing shell, one designed to inflict damage by slicing cleanly through the skin of an enemy tank and then to pinball around in its confined space, gouging and splattering the flesh of the crew in the process. The result is only cosmetic damage to the D10's nineteen foot blade. An explosive shell, on the other hand, would likely have been fatal.

At this moment, whizzing between the line of invaders and the Ranch's 'cavalry' is the Master's Rolls Royce. He makes it safely to the Van Gogh Bridge. His escort vehicle, some fifty yards behind, does not. Its rear end is clipped by the tank, causing it to go into a long, skidding spin that crashes it into the blade of a front end loader. The remaining Ranch vehicles, driven by Bang Pas Zoo stalwarts such as Narzesh, Qavi Ralph and Shanosserpan have formed themselves into a reverse V, with the D10 at its nadir. Jarvis realizes too late that his tank is being funneled directly into the blade of the far larger machine. Dillard's jeep and the other invading vehicles go wide around the arms of the V and follow the Master's Rolls towards the Van Gogh Bridge. Tracking down the 'devil' is evidently their first priority. The tank's machine gun fires a few ineffectual bursts just before the collision with the dozer. There is a grinding clash of metal on metal as the D 10's giant blade bends the tank's cannon backwards as if it were made of rubber instead of steel. Then the tank itself is pushed sideways. Its treads turn uselessly and it gouges a furrow in the field as it is pushed inexorably towards the bank of Little Snake Creek. This it tumbles down, landing capsized, the muzzle of its bent cannon dipping into the burbling waters like a thirsty elephant's trunk. The thousands of brave sannyasins remaining in Enlightenment Hall, after Namasteing to their Master speeding by (who is, of course, sufficiently in the moment to give them a quick backhanded wave of benediction) break into a hearty cheer on seeing the tank vanquished. Dillard's jeep crosses the bridge and stops at the Gated Gates, whose security arm blocks the way after the Rolls containing the Master and Nivea has trundled on towards the ceremonial Yahoo! waterfall and bridge.

There is a contingent of some twenty of the bravest sannyasins manning the gate. They are Peace Force officers, samurai (three of which carry swords in the same manner as

Lamborghini), Shaggyvan, Toasto, Smoothsill, Anugruffa, and some members of the Master's household such as Lionheart's wife Shenilla. Gilligan notices with a twinge of joy that Slipsma, his former girlfriend and 'friend in high places' is amongst them. She did not leave with, nor attempt to follow Deela. None have firearms since the Ranch's arsenal, as per the Master's instructions, now lies in a twisted metallic bundle atop an aggregate hill out at the rock crusher. They stand, arms folded, feet spread, three deep behind the painted red and white slashes of the security arm.

"Get out of the way!" shouts Dillard from his jeep. "We've come to give you your freedom!"

"You mean like you gave Angelica her freedom?" It is the normally soft spoken and quiet Smoothsill who steps forward and confronts the invaders. The news of Angelica's death had spread through the sannyasin population in a matter of minutes. "Is that how all you men want to be remembered, as murderers?" The tall, moon-faced swami strides up and down the line of vehicles as he speaks. "The media is here. The world is watching. There's the *Sixty Minutes* van. Their cameras are recording everything." Indeed, a cameraman, clad in a hooded rain poncho, has mounted a tripod and cellophane-draped video camera on the van's roof. Some of Dillard's soldiers look guiltily around, their eyes shifting from Dillard to Smoothsill to the camera on the far side of the creek. Others though, including the wild-eyed and over-muscled young man wearing a Rambo style bandana and undershirt who mans the machine gun mounted in back of the second Jeep, seem eager and twitchy, pointing their weapons at a different sannyasin target every few seconds. Dillard draws his own pistol and points it directly at Smoothsill.

"Only those impeding our efforts to eliminate the devil's dictator will be harmed! Starting with you, Big Mouth." Dillard clicks back the pistol's trigger for emphasis. Meanwhile, the Ranch's massive construction vehicles, leaving Jarvis and the rest of his crew to extricate themselves from the overturned tank, are chugging towards the Van Gogh bridge with the intention of completely blocking the invaders' only avenue of escape.

"Hold your fire! The Master wishes to speak to the invaders! Let them come through." It is Gilligan shouting through the bullhorn. The Master, whose aquamarine Rolls is idling at the foot of the Yahoo! Bridge Gilligan bestrides, has expressed no such wish, but the bullhorn combined with the Master's proximity, give the young Canadian the requisite authority. "Raise the gate. The Master wishes to speak with Dillard personally." He repeats this with some gusto, as after a great deal of wobbling, it now appears as if his plan to save the Master has a chance of succeeding.

Soon after the Yahoo! Waterfall was turned on (it is fed by powerful pumps housed beside Little Snake Creek) the Master had made it his custom to end his drive-by by walking the ceremonial Yahoo! Path. Lovingly paved in polished pink quartz, it curves down a gentle slope below the Yahoo! Bridge and runs behind the translucent sheet of the waterfall. After several steps, it emerges from behind the watery wall on an equally gentle slope, which the master walks to a point opposite the front door of the house. The walkway is regularly strewn with fresh cedar granules and rose petals, the blended scents of which, enhanced by the rain, waft up the face of the waterfall to Gilligan's nostrils as he watches the arm of the Gated Gates rise. It is said that the master takes particular delight in the sound of running water since he nearly drowned in the Ganges at the age of four, an incident which brought him substantially closer to his subsequent enlightenment at twenty three. The path-walking tradition has proved to be delightful as well for the sannyasins fortunate enough to be in the vicinity to welcome him home after drive-by, as he would namaste to all before disappearing behind the waterfall which, of course, provoked a Yahoo! and Fallachami meditation, with the further reward of a second namaste when he emerged.

"Lamborghini!" The huge Italian is squatting on his haunches at the edge of the ceremonial path. He is talking in a low voice to a peacock which has chosen this moment to strut from the sheltered area behind the waterfall and display his magnificent span of tail feathers.

"Yes-a little buddy?"

"I want you to cut them off at the circle turn. Send them straight to the front door of the house. Tell Dillard and his buddies, the Divine Bhagwan will speak to them after the ceremonial walk. Tell them it's his last request."

Lamborghini smiles and nods like a child who's been given permission to buy a Popsicle. To Gilligan's surprise and momentary consternation, as the giant swami strides towards the crossroads just a hundred or so feet away, he extracts the gently curving length of his samurai sword from behind his head and begins sweeping it as a pointer in the direction of the house. There is brief palaver at the crossroads, during which Dillard shoots Gilligan a piercing glare which he returns with a conciliatory shrug. Dillard rolls his eyes and leads his caravan of half a dozen vehicles up the incline of the driveway towards the front door. He has come this far. He can wait a few minutes more for his moment of glory.

Now the question is, will the Master make the ceremonial Yahoo! walk, or does he consider it to be too wet? All is quiet. The rain falls. The windshield wipers swish. Droplets ping against the bell of the bullhorn which dangles from Gilligan's right hand. The Master speaks to Nivea. She nods her head, and, with a glance (mixed with apprehension and relief) at Gilligan, she gets out of the vehicle and pulls an umbrella from the back seat. Unfurled, it is uncommonly commodious, and brilliantly white. She shelters the Master from the rain as she opens the door for him. He namastes to Gilligan, to Dillard and his gunmen waiting at the front door, and to the TV truck and throngs of sannyasins across the creek and in Enlightenment Hall. Gilligan notices that a second CBS cameraman has taken up a position at the far end of the pond. *Was*

370

that what the Master was waiting for? A line from Jesus Christ Superstar flashes through his mind: *"If you'd lived now you could have reached the whole nation; Israel in 4 BC had no mass communication."*

The Divine Bhagwan motions Gilligan to come to him. "Let me speak through that please."

Gilligan turns on and holds up the bullhorn for the Divine Bhagwan to speak through.

"My sannyasins," he says. "I see we have guests. Please continue to welcome them, no matter what happens. Even if I am crucified, that is OK. The world is watching. How an enlightened man dies is the greatest lesson possible. Let it happen as it should."

With two fingers, he gently nudges the bullhorn's mouthpiece to indicate completion. Gilligan lowers it and turns to watch as, under the umbrella's sheltering bowl, the Divine Bhagwan and Nivea carefully tread the fragrant footpath down behind the waterfall. The fact that Dillard and his armed henchmen are waiting for him on the porch does nothing to detract from the joy the Master takes, as with Nivea on his arm, he disappears behind the shimmering, burbling waterfall.

The Yahoo! by the scores of sannyasins close to the scene is echoed by the thousands across the creek, who have gathered in deep lines along its bank and the northern side of Enlightenment Hall.

This is Gilligan's moment. His efforts to persuade Dillard to allow the Master this ceremonial gesture have paid off. He jumps into the still idling Rolls. Adjusting the seat backwards as he goes, he drives as quickly and carefully as he can over the Yahoo! Bridge and along the driveway whose edge is strewn with the prone, soggy forms of Fallachami-ing sannyasins. He smiles to himself as he glides by Dillard, giving him a reassuring thumbs up. He crosses the Van Gogh Bridge just as the D10, D 5's and front end loaders arrive.

Gilligan speeds in front of and through them, beeping his horn at Swami Ted, Narzesh and the other operators. He's not going to waste a moment on explanations. He's done what he can for the Master and the commune. Getting to Seatrice is now his only priority. He guns the Rolls past the bordering lines of the now standing and very surprised looking sannyasins who are seeing for the first time one of their own driving the Master's vehicle. He feels G forces pull the weight of his body into the plush Corinthian leather of the seatback as he clears Enlightenment Hall and smoothly accelerates in the direction of the Recycling Depot and the compound where Seatrice is being held.

37. The Sound of Thunder

A distant thunder sounds as the Divine Bhagwan and Nivea move behind the Yahoo! Waterfall. Cued by the sound, the rain makes a quantum switch in gears and begins pummeling down ferociously. The waters of the pond froth into a mohair of tiny geysers; the CBS cameraman hunched at the far edge turtles deeply into his poncho. Through the shroud of the rain and the semi-opaque surface of the waterfall, Dillard can make out the vague shape of the white umbrella, but little else. The deluge lasts less than a minute, though the thunder to the southeast continues. The sky brightens. A few overlarge drops continue to fall, scattershot, like random droppings from an immense flock of birds.

"Why in the hell don't they come out?" Dillard mutters.

The thought flashes through his mind that he has been had, that there may be an escape route behind that waterfall. He takes a half step forward, only to be stopped by the sight of the umbrella, a segment of its ribs bent under the weight of the waterfall, as it forces its way between the walls of rock and water. The Divine Bhagwan and Nivea emerge and, after the requisite namastes, soon stand before Dillard on the driveway. The would-be assassin is somewhat above them on the veranda's decking; he is framed by the portico which shelters the front door.

"You'd best step back little girl," says Dillard. "This is between me and him."

"The Divine Bhagwan will listen to you," says Nivea loudly. She steps back towards the waterfall pathway, folding the umbrella as she does.

Sporadic, oversized raindrops continue to fall, but the scene has brightened considerably, as if the balance of the day's rain was expelled in one great, final splutter. But the sound of thunder, in the distance somewhere behind the huge hill to their left, continues to grow ominously. The Master, alone in the middle of the driveway, clad in his magnificent robe and hat, looks punier to Dillard, without the presence he once had.

"You aren't so high and mighty now, are you?" Dillard shouts. "The first commandment is, Thou shalt have no other gods before me! You call yourself a god, brainwashing innocent people, deceiving them? Making them give you all those cars?"

Dillard pulls his knife from its sheath and advances towards the Master. He is trembling with righteous anger, but his movements are jerky, uncertain. Something is not right. Female screams are heard from nearby sannyasins, and from across the creek. Nivea has disappeared.

"If I prick you, God," he screams. "Will you not bleed?" The knife trembles in front of him as Dillard approaches the Divine Bhagwan.

The Divine Bhagwan steps back nimbly, avoiding Dillard's approach.

"Stand still sinner! Meet your Maker like a man!"

"Fuck you, asshole!" says the Divine Bhagwan. So saying, he turns and, hiking up his robe to reveal a well-worn pair of work boots, scrambles atop the deck of the jeep with the tripod mounted machine gun. The young Rambo look-a-like, smoking a cigarette and absorbed in the Dillard/Master drama, is too astonished to react as Newfyamo (for it is indeed he, garbed in the backup robe and hat and disguised by Shenilla with the recovered strands of the Master's hair and beard which Gilligan had noticed hanging like a horsetail in the oversized jar) lands a vicious punch to his nose, knocking him sprawling to the driveway. The young swami swiftly commandeers the machine gun. Swinging it this way and that he screams, "Drop your weapons now!"

Some of the invaders comply immediately. Others, including Dillard, only stand in place in stunned silence, their weapons still at their sides. There is a roar from the crowd on the far bank and from those still in Enlightenment Hall. Hundreds of fingers and arms point to the southeast, along with the CBS camera perched on the van on the far side of the creek. The thunder, which has steadily been increasing in volume, now resolves itself into the sound of helicopters, three of which swing from behind the hill. Two are military Sikorskys, each with a complement of National Guardsmen. The third is the ranch helicopter, piloted by Lionheart. He lands it on the driveway on the far side of the Yahoo! Pond while the larger machines touch down on the plain across the creek.

"Drop them!" screams Newfyamo again. "Your party is over!"

Dillard's henchmen, most of whom are just good old boys out to protect their idea of America, know they are beat. Those who have not already done so lay down their weapons and put their hands behind their heads as Attorney General Dave Fryberger and three armed deputies emerge from Lionheart's helicopter. Lionheart, though he would dearly love to be part of the action at Shangri Ohlala, knows that he has more piloting duties ahead of him. Having deposited his passengers, he immediately lifts off and flies in the direction of the Ranch's airport.

Meanwhile, emerging from one of the military helicopters, along with several geared up and helmeted National Guardsmen, are two more familiar figures: Alchemendra, dressed in his familiar gleaming white, and Alvin Dark.

"Not for me, it isn't." Dillard, red-faced, trembling with rage, has stood transfixed in the middle of the cobblestoned driveway over the many seconds in which all this has transpired. He does not want to face his father. He does not want to go back to prison. He sheathes his knife and draws his automatic pistol. He fires first at Newfyamo, who drops like a stone off the far side of the Jeep. As a desultory sprinkling of sannysins on the far creek bank reflexively shout Yahoo!, Dillard jumps back onto the vantage point of the decking under the portico of Shangri Ohlala's front door and opens fire on anyone and everyone wearing red.

38. The Rescue

The road to Hippocrises, like most of the roads at the ranch, is closely flanked by large hills. As Gilligan pilots the Master's bulletproof, glittering aquamarine Rolls (when it belonged to Idi Amin it was presumably a more subdued hue, though Africans, generally speaking, do enjoy bright colors) around the corner before the left turn into the recycling depot, he sees the two jeeps and the armored personnel carrier of Sampson's force heading towards him. These worthies, having encountered some difficulties in fording the Big Snake River, have only just emerged from the hills and found the Hippocrises Road. Flooring the gas pedal, he cuts in front of the invaders and rounds the corner into the Recycling Depot entrance in a wild skid, missing the lead jeep by several yards. The Rolls careens sideways on the wet gravel and slams into a pile of lumber. The vehicular testament to British engineering scatters two by twos like toothpicks, and speeds past the deserted depot and onto the trail the unfortunate Flamhir had been taken down months earlier. In less than three minutes he comes upon the AIDS complex surrounded, as Kildaraj said it would be, by the same high deer fencing as protects master's house. The gates are closed.

No problem. Another dent or two won't hurt. Gilligan hunches his shoulders and again squeezes the accelerator pedal downwards. The Rolls shoulders the gates aside like a vengeful cowboy flinging open saloon doors.

The complex, much like Hemlock Grove, consists of large trailers in an L shape. A small Datsun pick-up is parked in front. Heading towards it, carrying a large box, is the tall, unmistakable form of Lucifia. Gilligan heads straight for her at high speed. Lucifia, on this particularly stressful day, is self-medicated beyond the pale, and stands dumbfounded at the sight of the Master's vehicle heading directly towards her. Only at the last second does she jump sideways, spilling the box's contents — large foil-wrapped packets, and vials and bottles of all manner of drugs — over the gravel surface. Gilligan, enraged at the sight of her and the thought of what she might have done to Seatrice, ploughs into the Datsun, rolling it onto its side as it catches the porch steps of the trailer. He jumps out and immediately assaults the still prone Lucifia, falling onto her with his knees, cuffing her about the head and rubbing gravel into her face.

"Where is she?" he screams in her ear. "The blonde. Where is she?"

"In zere." She gestures towards the nearest trailer. "Zee first room. Just a sedatif I give her..."

"Get off her! Get off her!" A new voice, high and piping, sounds behind Gilligan. A beefy hand grips his ponytail and drags him off of Lucifia. It is Tootie, who has emerged from the trailer with another box of contraband. She lifts Gilligan bodily, by his ponytail and the seat of his pants and flings him against the metal siding of the trailer. As he crumples to the ground, she raises a huge red-booted foot, the knobbed sole of which frighteningly fills his field of vision as she brings it down towards his staring eyes. He jerks his head aside just in time. The boot, instead of mashing his face, sticks for a moment in the mud and weeds at the trailer's base. There is a staccato burst of machine gun fire. Bullets ping off the Rolls and thwack into the siding of the trailer. Sampson's trigger happy contingent is approaching the busted gates of the complex.

"Tootie! Vee go!" Lucifia has shoved the boxes into the back seat of the Rolls. She jumps into the driver's seat.

"Wait for me. Wait for me!" Tootie lumbers over and jumps into the Rolls with surprising alacrity.

Perhaps inspired by Gilligan's Wild West entrance, and certainly intimidated by the armored personnel carrier which continues to spray machine gun fire, Lucifia turns the Rolls towards the northern wall of the steel mesh fence and attempts to ram through it. But there are no gates to fling open and the mesh, though it tears free of the posts, clings to the front of the vehicle and wings out to either side, biting and tangling with sagebrushes and shrubs, slowing their forward momentum to a fast crawl. Lucifia begins honking the horn furiously, as if that might somehow blast them clear of the confining web.

Gilligan, unhurt, regains his feet. He is gratified to see Sampson's entire force move in pursuit of the Rolls. "Cease fire, men!" Sampson shouts. "Let's take him alive!" Evidently they think the Master himself may be inside the Rolls. Gilligan immediately climbs the steps into the trailer, which is a replica of that at Mydad, where he spent his own convalescence after the snakebite incident. He finds Seatrice, fully clothed, head and shoulders propped up by pillows on a hospital bed. Her eyes are closed. There is a thin glaze of moisture on her cheeks and forehead. They are rosy with warmth. Her face is framed by blond curls. He kisses her eyebrows, her lips, and her lips again. She struggles to open her eyes.

"Hey you," she murmurs.

"Hey you." His heart unconscionably gladdened, he slides his arms beneath her and picks her up like a baby. She wraps her arms around his neck.

He kisses her again. "You come with me?"

She grins, nods and clings to him more tightly. Whatever Lucifia gave her induces effects that are far from unpleasant. *Thank God the bitch was telling the truth.*

As he steps around the smashed Datsun, he sees, well beyond the stripped fence line, the Rolls, still encumbered by the dragging wings of mesh (which in turn are encumbered by a considerable amount of entwined vegetation) is being surrounded by Sampson's swiftly moving vehicles in the manner of Indians around a settler's marooned wagon. His heart singing within him, and tenderly carrying a burden which seems somehow to be carrying him, he slips through the gate and heads to his right, into the hills and away from the Ranch.

39. Deela Gets Wet

Nivea, thoroughly out of breath, manages to catch up to the Divine Bhagwan, Kildaraj, and Shenilla at the fork in the tunnel that leads to Hemlock Grove. It had been easy to slip back behind the waterfall and into the tunnel while New-fyamo, disguised as the Master, dealt so admirably with Dillard. The Divine Bhagwan, having wandered some distance down the tunnel in the direction of the airport, is poking one of the dangling overhead lights with his finger, observing the play of light on the sides of the tunnel as the bulbs up and down the string waggle. Shenilla and Kildaraj, who accessed the tunnels via Lurchamo's deserted listening post, are hunched over and wondering at the two hockey bags full of cash that Gilligan left the night before.

"It's the commune's money," says Kildaraj. "No doubt about that. But why in the blazes would she leave it the middle of the tunnel?"

"For a quick getaway?" says Shenilla. None of them are aware of the part Gilligan played in depositing the bags.

Sounds of banging and scraping come from the Hemlock Grove tunnel spur. Kildaraj jogs to investigate. From below the manhole cover, at the base of the rebar ladder, he hears sounds of clawing at the hard surface and Chloe's distinctive accents:

"I don't now why it won't fucking open, but it won't!"

Kildaraj smiles. He can't resist climbing up the ladder and placing his mouth close to the lower surface of the thoroughly glued manhole cover."Hello Deela!" he singsongs. "We have the money you stole, Deela. You're never going to see it again Deela. They're coming for you Deela. Good-byeeeee."

"Right people," he says on returning and shouldering the bag of cash. "We'd best be off quickly."

They move on down the tunnel towards the airport, hindered only by the Master's graceful, but very stately gait. If all goes well, at the runway's edge, not far from the gurgling expanse of Little Snake Creek that Newfyamo and Gilligan crossed one year earlier, Lionheart and the Learjet will be waiting.

"Ahhaarrrgh!" screams Deela. Her fists are balled; her head is thrown back as she directs her rage at the acoustic tiles above Hemlock Grove's living room. She's heard Kildarj's taunts, faint echoes from the shaft that resound in her belly like the whisperings of a devil. Her father, from time to time, would whisper over his desk to a burly man with a hard face, a man whose name she didn't know. Whisper things that even she, his secretary and daughter, could not hear. Things that finally brought the police who killed him, the blood from his head a crimson pond on the empty expanse of his burl-grained desktop. The demigod doctor has a way of pushing her buttons. "I hate that son of a bitch!" This last is directed at Patipaticake, who is standing by in the kitchen with a cooler full of provisions meant for their now seriously delayed journey.

Damn the Master! Deela thinks. *My gun, my precious, my silver bullets, all gone! Why didn't I have backup weapons? A secret cache? That's what Daddy would have done.* The rain pounding overhead suddenly stops, as if a faucet was turned off. She gives her head a shake, strides to the droplet-streaked picture window. In the distance, three helicopters swing from behind the hill to the southeast of the Master's house. One is the Ranch's, the other two are military.

"Oh dear," she mutters to herself. "Chloe! Lurchamo!" she shouts down the trapdoor, which Lurchamo managed to pry open, despite Gilligan's glue. But the manhole cover has proved to be unassailable. "Never mind, we'll never get it open! Patipaticake! All of you! Into the Bronco! Our only chance is to head off Kildaraj and whoever the hell is with him at the airport. Let's move!"

The drive to the airport from downtown Bhagwanville, even at full speed on deserted roads, is a good five minutes. It is somewhere in minute two that Lionheart, airborne in the helicopter for the same destination, clatters through the space above the white Bronco. A quick descent and a moment's recon confirm what he already knows: the vehicle contains Deela and her henchmen.

"Lionheart to Arrowhead. Lionheart to Arrowhead."

"Arrowhead here."

"Arrowhead, we've got local hostiles, currently wanted for attempted murder of our doctor, heading for the airport. Recommend you send one of your choppers and secure the airport ASAP."

"Roger that, Lionheart. We've got live fire, repeat live fire here at initial landing. Will secure airport ASAP. Over."

The young commander of the National Guard helicopter squadron sounds thoroughly stressed to Lionheart's experienced ears. Something's going down that means the airport is going to wait, at least for the time being. The Bronco enters the smallish, flat valley containing the landing strip, airport and motor pool buildings which are well ahead to his left. Racing parallel to the creek, which runs broad, shallow and straight for a kilometer or so, Deela will soon reach Robya, and the airport itself. Halfway along this stretch, near the secret tunnel's entrance, somewhat concealed by the limbs of the junipers lining the creek, is the Learjet, fueled up and sanitized by Lionheart himself in the wee hours of the morning.

"Well buddy," he says. "You're supposed to be a great pilot. Let's show 'em a little something." He takes a deep breath and, pushing the joystick forward, swoops down behind the Bronco, so the skis of the copter (which, in the early days of the Ranch, he had Swami Clint Eastwood reinforce so the copter could be used as an aerial forklift) are just a few feet off the road's surface. "Anyone care for shish-kabob?" he shouts. He deftly maneuvers the curved end of the pilot side ski, so it smashes through the rear window and penetrates deeply into the interior of the Bronco. Gunning the engine, his free hand flies over the controls compensating furiously for the extra, lopsided weight. He lifts the Bronco some twenty feet off the ground. He dares not go higher, but he doesn't need to. It is only two or three minutes flying time above the surface of the creek until he reaches the dam that forms the mile-long stretch of Lake Krishnamirthless. Here he must gain altitude, and he does, some thirty more feet that allows the helicopter and its burden to clear the dam. But the strain of rising is too much. The ski gives way its precarious hold and the Bronco falls as Deela, Chloe, Patipaticake and Lurchamo scream. There is a huge splash; windows roll down. Deela, agile as a cat, climbs onto the roof of the Bronco, which bobs temporarily afloat. She shakes her fist and screams at Lion-heart. As the copter banks and heads back towards the air-port, a handful or two of rose petals, remnants of Angelica's fall, flutter from the open side door of and rain down upon Deela, the Bronco, and the widening circles of ripples around it.

40. Dillard Loses his Head

Overwhelmed by frustration and rage, Dillard fires wildly, pumping shot after shot into the line of sannyasins at the edge of the driveway near the Yahoo! pond. There are shrieks and screaming as all but one turn and run down the driveway in the direction of the Van Gogh Bridge. Two mas, one of whom is buxom Abreatha from Macarena are wounded, though not grievously. They are helped down the slope by their fellows.

"Stop!" A single voice roars out, seemingly from everywhere, as if every molecule in the moist summer air, the wet hills, and the lowering sky have simultaneously shouted the word. Like a stunning overhead thunderclap it freezes everyone in the scene, including the runners who condense in a huddled knot on the driveway behind the CBS cameraman, who, the hood of his rain poncho now thrown back, is frozen behind the whir of his video camera. It will later be said that even the Yahoo! Ceremonial Waterfall stopped in mid plunge at this moment.

It is Alchemendra, summoning all his presence, all the energetic 'suchness' and consciousness which makes him part of the scene and the scene part of him, who shouts, who contrary to the sacred precepts of the whitest of magics, imposes his spiritual will on another- in this case Dillard- and makes him cease, at least for a few moments, what he has chosen to do. But the effort drains him of all strength, all vitality. The dazzling figure in the immaculate white suit slumps sideways, would fall to the ground were he not caught and steadied by Alvin Dark.

"For God's sake," says the magician. "Shoot him."

Captain Arrowhead, just off the radio to Lionheart (who at this moment soars above the tail of Deela's white Bronco) is astride the doorway of the military helicopter.

"Can't do it sir," he says. "The big guy is in the way."

Indeed, the only sannyasin to maintain his position at the edge of the cobblestone driveway, directly across from Dillard's slightly elevated position on the entryway decking, is Swami Lamborghini. Even Dillard's henchmen, their weapons abandoned, have taken cover on the far sides of their vehicles. There is only Dillard, momentarily frozen with his gun upraised, and Swami Lamborghini, his samurai sword still dangling at his side, facing each other in showdown position across the Parisian cobblestones of Shangri Ohlala's driveway. The rain is stopped completely. There is the occasional pattering of drips from the nearby redwoods, then a crash and tinkling of glass. A low-set skylight over the Master's pool, pierced by one of Dillard's wild shots, has given away.

The sound seems to awaken Dillard, to bring him back from wherever Alchemendra's *voice* has sent him. The passion, like dust snapped from a rag, has gone out of him. He feels only the methodical reptilian coldness of the deranged killer. *How many can I take down before they get me?*

Lamborghini is not where he is out of any sense of heroism, nor any thought that he could take down the gunman with his sword. The gunshots have terrified him so much that he cannot move. The gigantic, black-bearded Italian remains trembling twenty feet from where the shots were fired. There was a tragedy when he was a small boy. He and his late older brother were playing, had found their father's hunting rifle... A therapist back in Spoona recommended he join the Samurais to help him overcome his fear. She said protecting others as he could not protect his brother would be good for him. A very sad part of Lamborghini wants to tell Dillard to go ahead and shoot. Tell him he deserves it. But there are no words, just a choking knot of fear. Dillard raises his half closed eyelids and looks at Lamborghini. Lamborghini pees his pants. Dillard laughs, a nasty hateful laugh, and shoots. The laughter snaps Lamborghini from fear to rage. A bullet tears through his left arm, another into his side, as he raises his sword high and, roaring like a bull, charges the gunman. Dillard, now deadly calm, takes careful aim at the Italian's broad forehead and fires. The hammer clicks on an empty chamber.

"Jesus Christ," says Dillard an instant before Lamorghini's sword, swung in a mighty arc, severs his head from his body as cleanly and easily as ripe fruit is plucked from a twig. The head plummets down the front of Dillard's body which remains hideously standing for a moment or two after the cleavage before slumping backwards under the portico. Dillard's noggin clunks off the edge of the decking above the cobblestones and is impelled horizontally. It skitters between Lamborghini's legs. Spewing bloody spirals, it barrel rolls across the cobblestones and bounces amidst the cedar granules and rose petals strewn on the hard quartz surface of the Yahoo! Ceremonial Walkway. There it kicks well to the right and bobbles down the grassy slope to the pond. It hits the flat, sacred stones from Hoodoo Canyon that form the pond's rim, and, with an ungainly hop, plops into the still waters in front of the Cyclopean eye of the CBS camera. There it bobs face up, eyes staring, floating for a few seconds with the snakes of Dillard's hair writhing around it in a gruesome halo. Finally, mercifully, it sinks, with the tips of the hair disappearing last.

"Mama mia!" says Lamborghini. His sword clangs to the cobblestones. He sinks to his knees with blood streaming from his side.

Alvin Dark, still supporting the taller, heavier Alchemendra, feels something rip down the middle of his chest. His vision tunnels so he sees only the head of his son bobbing on the surface of the pond. With an anguished cry, all strength leaves him so the tycoon and the magician he supports fall together in an inelegant tangle into the soggy, muddy trough left by the D-10's manhandling of the Sherman tank.

Lamborghini is quickly surrounded by Attorney General Fryberger's deputies, their guns drawn.

"Get a medic over here!" shouts Fryberger. "Secure the area!"

Armed troops rush across the Van Gogh Bridge and over to Enlightenment Hall. The two military helicopters take off, one to secure the airport and the other to reconnaissance for any other militia activity.

Newfyamo, still be-robed but with a goodly section of his ersatz beard missing, is pulled from behind the jeep by one of the deputies. Dillard's bullet only grazed him, plowing a furrow just above his left ear through the thickly knitted, beautifully brocaded fez style cap he wears to match the Master's attire.

"Are you Akshat Chandreshekar, a.k.a. the Divine Bhagwan?"

"No. I'm Swami Anand Newfyamo."

"Well, Mr. Newfyamo, I suggest you tell me where the real Bhagwan is right now, or I shall place you under arrest for aiding and abetting a fugitive."

"My best guess…" Here Newfyamo pauses as a new sound, the streaky roar of a jet aircraft is heard approaching from the north, above the clatter of the receding helicopters. "There," says Newfyamo, his finger following the white Learjet racing across the sky above them. "He's right up there."

The jet, snow-white against dark clouds that are lifting to reveal the occasional patch of blue, makes a long, leisurely circle overhead, as if viewing the Ranch for one last time. Lionheart (for after depositing Deela and company in the drink, he arrived at the airport in perfect synchronicity with the Master's party) waggles the wings in farewell, then banks the jet containing the Divine Bhagwan, Shenilla, Kildaraj and Nivea in the direction of Cuba, the nearest place they feel certain to receive refuge.

An appeal to the thousands of sannyasins who remained in Enlightenment Hall throughout the drama produces thirty-two doctors of whom thirty-one are psychotherapists. Thus there is counseling aplenty for the wounded while they wait for the physician and medic to treat Swami Lamborghini, whose wounds, while serious, will not be fatal. He will survive, give up being a sannyasin, and become a farrier, tending to the hooves of horses in the farmlands of northern Italy. Alvin Dark has suffered a moderately severe heart attack and must be airlifted to a Portland hospital. He will stay positive, recover, thrive and eventually create the Dillard Dark Youth Foundation for disadvantaged young men. Alchemendra will give up his white attire from this day forward, eventually favoring blue jeans, sneakers, and baseball caps worn backwards. While remaining a friend and consultant to Alvin Dark and Persephone Enterprises, he will become a guru to many wealthy young entrepreneurs of the Internet generation.

For the fifteen thousand resident, visitor, and summer worker sannyasins on hand for the Second Universal World Celebration, the Master's departure can only mean one thing: the Ranch is over and a new exodus followed by a new pilgrimage to wherever he resettles has begun.

41. Lunch with Morris

For Gilligan, it is a twenty minute walk to where Swami Morris, his chunky kiwi sidekick, will be meeting them behind the first hill. Still carrying the half asleep form of Seatrice, totally forgotten by Sampson and his crew who are chasing down Lucifia and Tootie, he is just underway when he sees and hears the Learjet circling in the sky to the east of them. His heart soars with the plane when the wings waggle. Lionheart has succeeded. The Master will be safe. They will have found the commune's money. He will get them the rest, which he is confident is safe, when he can.

He finds Morris in a sheltered spot under a rock slab. He is eating from a tightly packed bunch of pearl-like grapes.

"Howdy amigo. These are surprisingly good, believe it or not. I grabbed loads from our winery. You wouldn't believe what happened up at his house. The Master's gone. Everybody is leaving. And did you believe that rain, mate?"

"Yeah, she really came down, didn't she? Do you want some grapes, baby?"

Seatrice opens her eyes three quarters of the way. "Too sleepy."

He kisses her and sets her down in a comfortable niche.

"What else you got to eat?"

"Fresh boiled eggs, a couple loafs of bread, more grapes, a huge hunk of cheddar, a shitload of trail mix, and about a dozen apples."

"Is that it?"

"Big container of potato salad and a jar of vegetarian bacon bits. Got everything else too, mate. Water, tent, blankets, matches, tea. All in Bear's saddlebags."

In a grassy patch nearby, their reins dangling, are Bear and Scar, the same horse Lionheart had ridden. Gilligan and Morris share a small vat of potato salad sprinkled again and again with dime-sized bacon bits, which morph from crunchy to chewy and succulent in the salad's moisture. Morris fills Gilligan in on the events at Shangri Ohlala. He'd heard them from Narzesh when they had crossed paths on the Pathless Path highway just a few minutes earlier. Narzesh, in his old pickup truck, had offered Morris a ride to Portland if he wanted one. Seatrice dozes. The sky brightens. The horses graze. A heat bug drones an insistent song. The potato salad, pilfered from Macarena's fridge, is cool and delicious. They scrape its last vestiges from the sides of the container. The sun becomes occasionally visible as the dark clouds give way to patches of blue sky. For a time they hear a helicopter circling and then descending on the far side of the hill. The air temperature warms appreciably. Morris burps contently, sighs, and stands up.

"Best be off then, mate. Got stalls to muck out. Can't just leave the horses. I'll stay here with them as long as it takes."

Gilligan stands up, hugs him warmly.

"Thanks buddy. Appreciate it."

Morris mounts Scar. "Best hold Bear. He'll want to come with us."

"Right. We'll do that dinner soon. Even better than this one."

"Cheers, mate. Take care of Bear. And the girl too."

Morris wheels Scar and trots off down the trail. Gilligan turns and snuggles back down beside Seatrice. He'll wait until she is awake enough to eat something before they hit the trail to Hoodoo Canyon.

42. Report

*I'm Harry Seasoner, reporting from the Bhagwanville com-
mune in the high desert of northeastern Oregon. A quantity of poison, reportedly disguised as salad dressing, has been found in the ice
box in Ma Anand Deela's kitchen. With me again is Dave Fryberger, Oregon's attorney general, and, we understand Mr. Fryberger, a
candidate for Governor?*

"We're still very early in that process, Harry. I don't want
to say too much now, lest my worthy opponents accuse me of taking
advantage of this very popular and esteemed national forum. I will
say that the people of Oregon are fed up with corruption and with
the massive sell-off of our best lands to Californians while the current Governor sits around twiddling his well manicured thumbs!"

"Admirable restraint, Mr. Attorney General. Admirable.
Now, what can you tell us about that poison?"

"Very little at this point, though we do suspect it may be the
same salmonella used against the citizens of Heifferville."

"What does the violence that occurred here mean for the future of this controversial commune?"

"It means it doesn't have one. The people here tell me that
with Mr. Bhagwan gone, no one will want to stay. They will go
where he goes."

"Do you expect him to be apprehended soon?"

"Yes we do. Their pilot filed a flight plan late last night for
the Bahamas. We expect to apprehend him on charges of immigration fraud if and when he lands there. The military has informed us
that they are not in the business of chasing after or shooting down
civilian aircraft."

"We understand that you have apprehended two individuals
believed to be involved in the poisonings, an assault on the commune's doctor and the alleged theft of the commune's money?"

392

"Indeed we have. Our recon helicopter located these individuals on the roof of a vehicle completely submerged in the middle of a lake just to the north of our current location. Fortunately for them the vehicle rested on the lake bottom as neither of them knows how to swim. We continue search for a Ms. Deela and Ms.Chloe, who did manage to swim to shore before we arrived on the scene. Charges of aggravated assault are also pending against a Ms. Lucifia and Ms. Tootie. Those females were allegedly detained for questioning by a half dozen members of the Million Friends of God's Country Militia and somehow managed to subdue all of them. The militia men were found to the west of here in a field near what appears to be a medical complex. Two had concussions, four had broken bones and all of them were drugged silly. We are offering a reward to anyone with information concerning the whereabouts of any of these four females."

"Can we expect arrests soon, Mr. Fryberger?"

"As far as we are concerned, these people are terrorists. They can run into the desert but they can't hide. We'll get them."

"Thank-you very much Mr. Fryberger. There you have it ladies and gentlemen. A so-called spiritual commune consisting of thousands of vegetarian meditators from all over the world, is dissolving. All around us people are crying, people are hugging, people are packing to leave. And why? Because the one reason they are here, the man they call the Divine Bhagwan, is gone, leaving behind a magnificent house and a garage filled with, at last report, close to one hundred Rolls Royces and other antique luxury vehicles. That's our news; that's our reality. This is Harry Seasoner, in Bhagwanville, Oregon. Now back to Bradley Michaels and a report on President Reagan's 'Star Wars' defense initiative."

43. The Future

The sky, now deep blue, is flanked by skerries of puffy cumulus cloud. Bear and his riders cast a long shadow, which molds itself over and around the rocks, junipers and sagebrush which shine and sparkle with residual moisture. Golden sunshine has warmed Gilligan, Bear, Seatrice and the saddlebags thoroughly, rendering their small horseback world completely comfortable. For Gilligan, were it teeming with rain, he would still be content. The lithe form clinging to him from behind is enough.

He has found the trail that he and Lionheart took to Hoodoo Canyon. He will go there with Seatrice, wait until the literal and figurative dust has settled at the Ranch. The shine of the rain combined with the evening sun are a refreshing dazzle for his mind. He feels like he is entering a fecund and exhilarating new era in his life. An era in which he will make his own decisions. He remembers the Master once saying that for a man the women he chooses are the signposts on the journey to the Self.

What's funny is that Seatrice is the first one I've really and truly chosen. I mean Slipsma chose me as her steppingstone to freedom, Bala chose me as her steppingstone to motherhood, Fleuritima-Fleuritima was what? Was I her steppingstone to healing, to getting over that separatist guy? Or was she my guide, my steppingstone to Seatrice? And I had no idea I was going to choose Seatrice until I found myself risking everything to be near her. Then the snakebite took her away and the Divine Bhagwan, in his own good time, sent her back to me. And my, how we've fallen for each other! So good choice happened. I, the part that is thinking this right now did not choose her. My mother didn't raise me to jump out of a moving jeep or risk shitting my pants in public. My heart chose her, in spite of the self my parents raised. Maybe that's it. Gilligan grins to himself and squeezes the hands wrapped around his middle.

"Hey you," he says. "You starting to wake up back there?"

"A little bit," says Seatrice. "I'm watching everything go by. It's beautiful."

"There's plenty of grapes and trail mix in the pouch to your right. Morris got us a little tent and enough food for a day or two." He takes a deep breath. "The Ranch is over. We have to decide what we want to do."

There are a few minutes of silence. They pass the spot where a year earlier Bear had spooked and run up the gravelly hillside.

"I have a flat in Amsterdam," says Seatrice. "I would like it if you came to stay with me there."

Gilligan's heart feels like it is going to explode with joy. In their springtime weeks of being lovers and workmates there had been no talk of a future together. It was silently and sadly accepted that when her tenure as a summer worker ended Seatrice would have to leave the Ranch and return when she could. Up ahead he can see the gorge that becomes the narrow high-walled entrance to Hoodoo Canyon.

"I don't think I can."

"What?" Seatrice is as surprised by his answer as he is.

"I've told you my mother's story, right? How she had a breakdown; my Dad's moved on to a younger woman. Well, she's alone in a big house. I think I've got to go back to Toronto and 'be there' for her. Help her get re-settled."

"Where does this come from? You haven't talked about this before." Seatrice's voice is not disappointed or angry. Just curious. They are in the high-walled gorge now. The rock walls converge swiftly so Gilligan's toes occasionally touch them on either side. The shadowy air around them becomes very cool. Gilligan wishes Seatrice would snuggle closer to him for her warmth and his own reassurance. But she does not.

Soon they emerge into the splendour of Hoodoo Canyon. There is a trickling stream of runoff babbling in its central channel. Mini waterfalls plunge down each of the shallow steps that rise to the Hoodoo ledge. Sunlight floods through the western opening. The Hoodoos are illuminated like misshapen cigars: the igneous caps at their peaks glow more brightly than the golden pillars of their bodies. Bear is thirstily gulping water from the stream when Gilligan answers her.

"I think- I think it was Angelica. When they laid her over one of the tubs we built, she wasn't sexy anymore, but she was still beautiful. All I could think was that she is someone's daughter; someone who is going to find out their daughter is dead. And Angelica will never be a mother. " Now Seatrice does snuggle closer, encircling him in a warm hug from behind as the horse continues to drink. Gilligan sighs. "Maybe I don't want to abandon my mother the way I feel my father has abandoned me."

They choose a camping spot below the ledge that supports the hoodoos and the altar-like 'meditation rock'. Seatrice tells him there were only four or five people in the aids complex. The only one who seemed truly sick was Flamhir. He had been sent to a hospital in Portland the day she arrived and had not come back.

Gilligan sets up their small orange and red tent in the sunlight, wedging the stakes into fissures or under large rocks. He and Seatrice make a campfire in a crude hearth others, perhaps over thousands of years, have used for the same purpose. She boils water for tea and begins peeling apples.

"Whatcha doing?"

"Making applesauce." Seatrice does not look up.

"Don't tell me you know how to cook."

"OK. I'll show you instead."

"You know if you just hung around looking good that would be enough."

"Enough for you, maybe. For now. But looks don't last. You need food until the end."

They eat as it falls dark. The applesauce is delicious. Gilligan is as tired as he has ever been in his life. He wants nothing more than to hold Seatrice close and fall into a deep sleep. She crawls into the double sleeping bag with him, lovely and naked.

"Hey you," he says as their bodies intertwine. Watched over by the hoodoos, they are walled in by the canyon and the sounds of crickets, the trickle of the stream and the occasional cry of a coyote. The bright light of the full moon penetrates the nylon roof of the tent and suffuses the interior with a silvery light. "You never answered my question. Would you come with me to Toronto?"

"You never actually asked," she says. "And yes, I will come with you. But we won't have a place, or money."

"No problem," he says brightly. "We can move in with my mother."

"Tell me you are joking." She is almost begging.

Instead of answering, Gilligan reaches across her and rummages in his clothing. "Ta dah!" he says. He holds up in the moonlight two thick packets of tightly wrapped one hundred dollar bills. "I figured the commune, under the circumstances, owed me some back wages. We'll find ourselves a nice place in Cabbagetown, or maybe the Beaches. It's beautiful in the summer."

She draws him to her, kisses him deeply. "O.K.," she says. "But promise me one thing."

"What?"

"That you'll come to Zunderdorp and meet my mother. She's going to love you."

"Running my life already, eh?" he sighs, and embarks on another very long kiss.

STOP!

☯ ;) ॐ

About the Author

J.R. MacLean is a late-blooming aspiring writer. He has been on the 'spiritual path' for many years, including a nineteen month stint at a commune in Oregon in the early 1980's. He has made a living running a one man company called Roots and Wings Home Improvements in Peterborough, Canada. His wife Marina is a well-known yoga teacher and yoga teacher trainer in the Peterborough area: Her website is www.marinamacleanyoga.com. They are the proud parents of two grown children, Jesse Dylan MacLean and Melody Elizabeth MacLean. J.R. can be reached via jrmaclean27@live.ca or through www.jrmaclean.blogspot.com.